P9-DMA-532

POKÉMON

BATTLE WITH THE ULTRA BEAST

2 GRAPHIC ADVENTURES

Adapted by
Simcha Whitehill

Scholastic Inc.

©2019 Pokémon. ©1997–2019 Nintendo, Creatures, GAME FREAK,
TV Tokyo, ShoPro, JR Kikaku. TM, ®Nintendo.

All rights reserved. Published by Scholastic Inc., *Publishers since 1920*.
SCHOLASTIC and associated logos are trademarks and/or registered
trademarks of Scholastic Inc.

The publisher does not have any control over and does not assume any
responsibility for author or third-party websites or their content.

No part of this publication may be reproduced, stored in a retrieval system,
or transmitted in any form or by any means, electronic, mechanical,
photocopying, recording, or otherwise, without written permission of the
publisher. For information regarding permission, write to Scholastic Inc.,
Attention: Permissions Department, 557 Broadway, New York, NY 10012.

This book is a work of fiction. Names, characters, places, and incidents
are either the product of the author's imagination or are used fictitiously,
and any resemblance to actual persons, living or dead, business
establishments, events, or locales is entirely coincidental.

CONTENTS

STORY 1: AN ULTRA-URGENT RESCUE

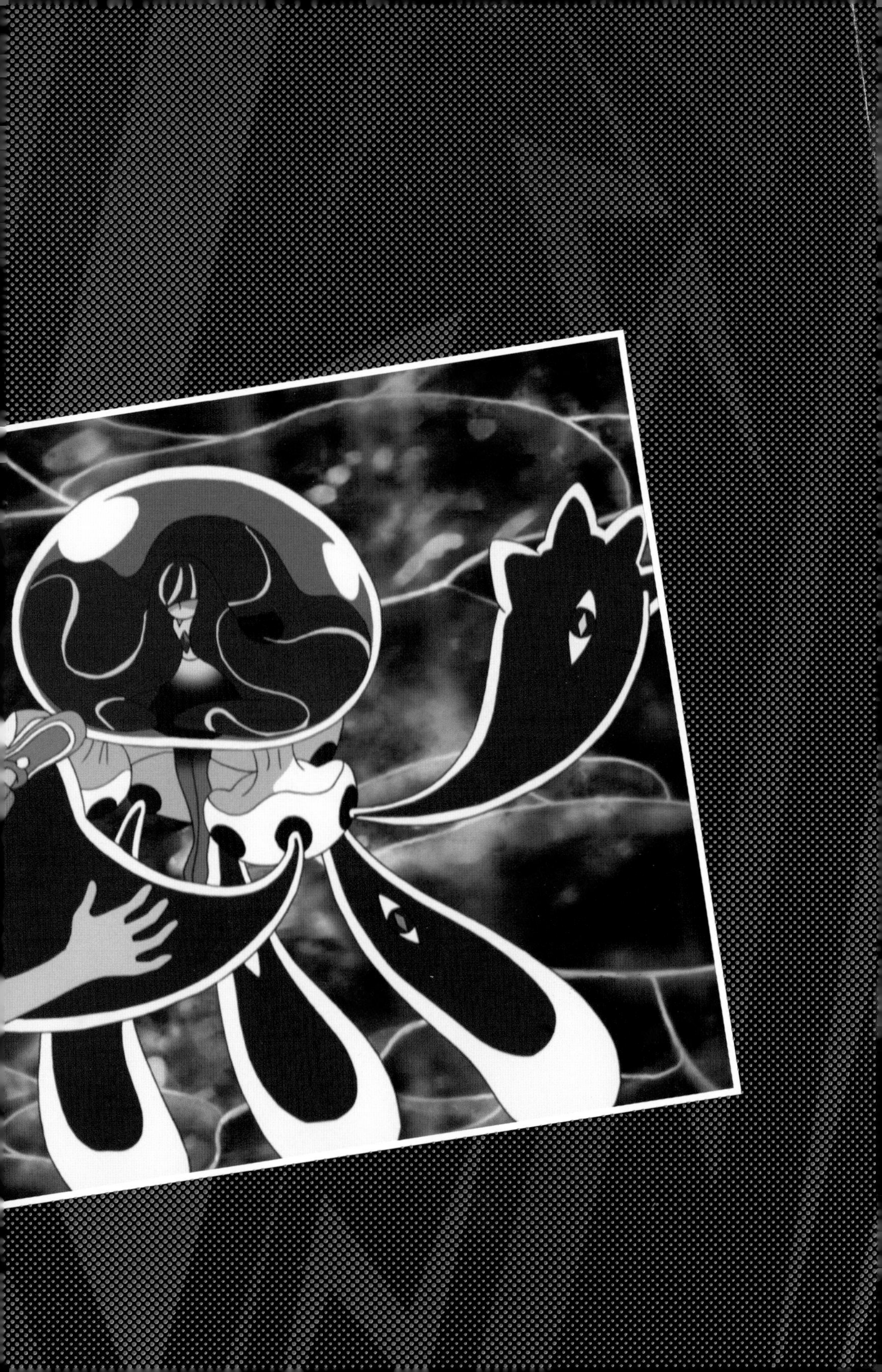

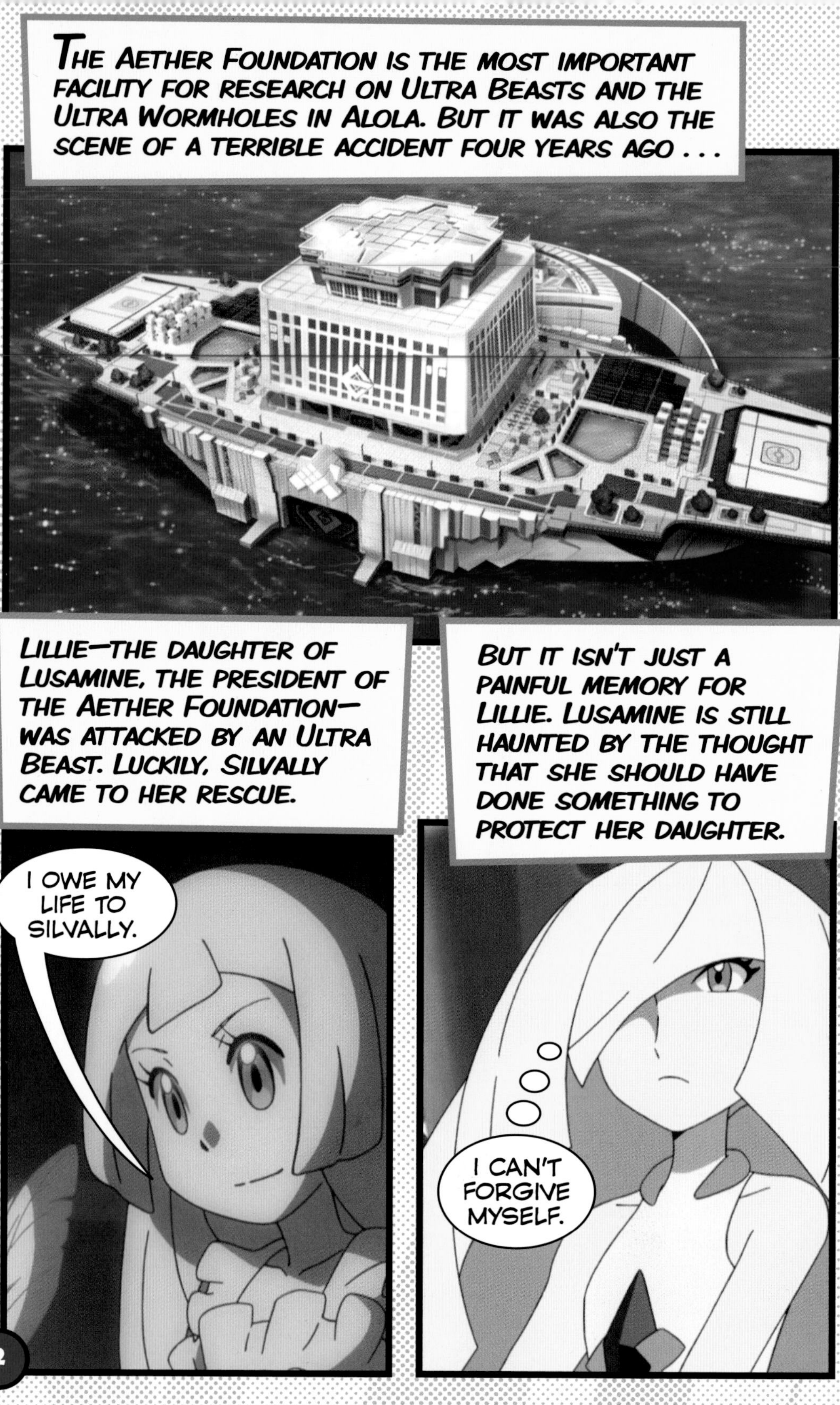
THE AETHER FOUNDATION IS THE MOST IMPORTANT FACILITY FOR RESEARCH ON ULTRA BEASTS AND THE ULTRA WORMHOLES IN ALOLA. BUT IT WAS ALSO THE SCENE OF A TERRIBLE ACCIDENT FOUR YEARS AGO . . .
LILLIE—THE DAUGHTER OF LUSAMINE, THE PRESIDENT OF THE AETHER FOUNDATION—WAS ATTACKED BY AN ULTRA BEAST. LUCKILY, SILVALLY CAME TO HER RESCUE.
BUT IT ISN'T JUST A PAINFUL MEMORY FOR LILLIE. LUSAMINE IS STILL HAUNTED BY THE THOUGHT THAT SHE SHOULD HAVE DONE SOMETHING TO PROTECT HER DAUGHTER.
I OWE MY LIFE TO SILVALLY.
I CAN'T FORGIVE MYSELF.

THE PERSON RESPONSIBLE FOR OPENING THE ULTRA WORMHOLE AND SUMMONING THE ULTRA BEAST WAS FABA, A COWARDLY SCIENTIST AT THE AETHER FOUNDATION.

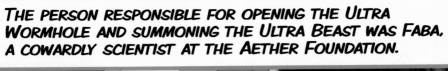

HE HAD KEPT IT A SECRET FOR YEARS. BUT WHEN THE TRUTH CAME OUT, HE WAS ASHAMED. HE BECAME DESPERATE.

THE ONLY WAY TO RECLAIM MY HONOR IS TO CAPTURE ONE OF THOSE ULTRA BEASTS THAT LUSAMINE ALWAYS DREAMS OF.

THEN THEY'LL SEE!

SO, HE HATCHED A PLAN THAT BEGAN WITH CAPTURING ASH'S FRIEND NEBBY.

CAN YOU SENSE MY EXCITEMENT, TOO, NEBBY?

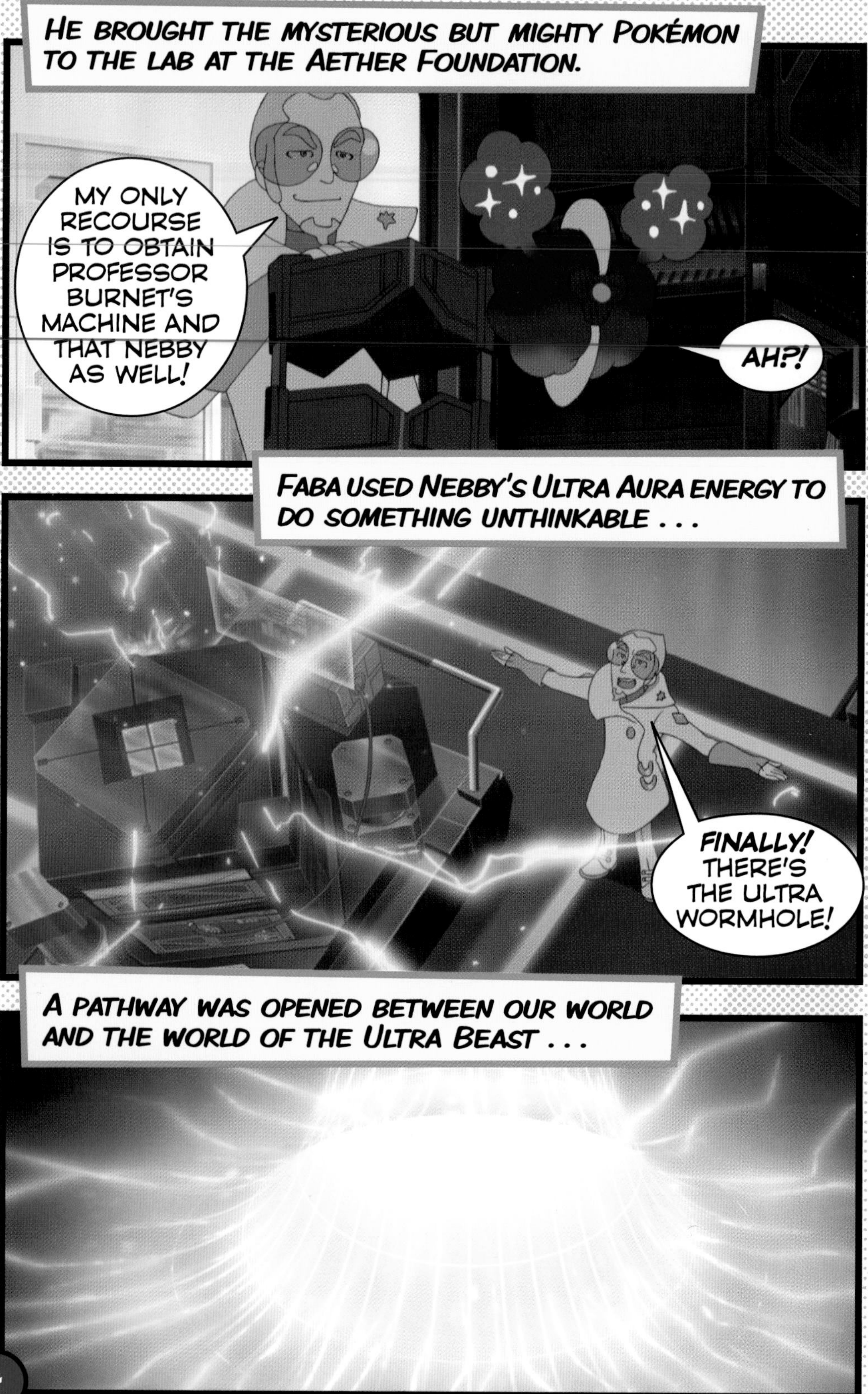
HE BROUGHT THE MYSTERIOUS BUT MIGHTY POKÉMON TO THE LAB AT THE AETHER FOUNDATION.
MY ONLY RECOURSE IS TO OBTAIN PROFESSOR BURNET'S MACHINE AND THAT NEBBY AS WELL!
AH?!
FABA USED NEBBY'S ULTRA AURA ENERGY TO DO SOMETHING UNTHINKABLE . . .
FINALLY! THERE'S THE ULTRA WORMHOLE!
A PATHWAY WAS OPENED BETWEEN OUR WORLD AND THE WORLD OF THE ULTRA BEAST . . .

LUCKILY, ASH AND HIS PALS ARRIVED JUST IN TIME TO CATCH FABA IN THE ACT!

GASP!

SOMETHING'S COMING OUT OF IT!

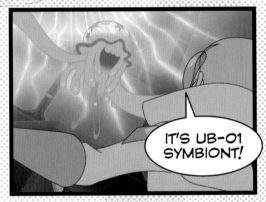

IT'S UB-01 SYMBIONT!

NO!

OH NO!

UH!

I'M THE ONE WHO HAS SUCCEEDED IN SUMMONING FORTH AN ULTRA BEAST!

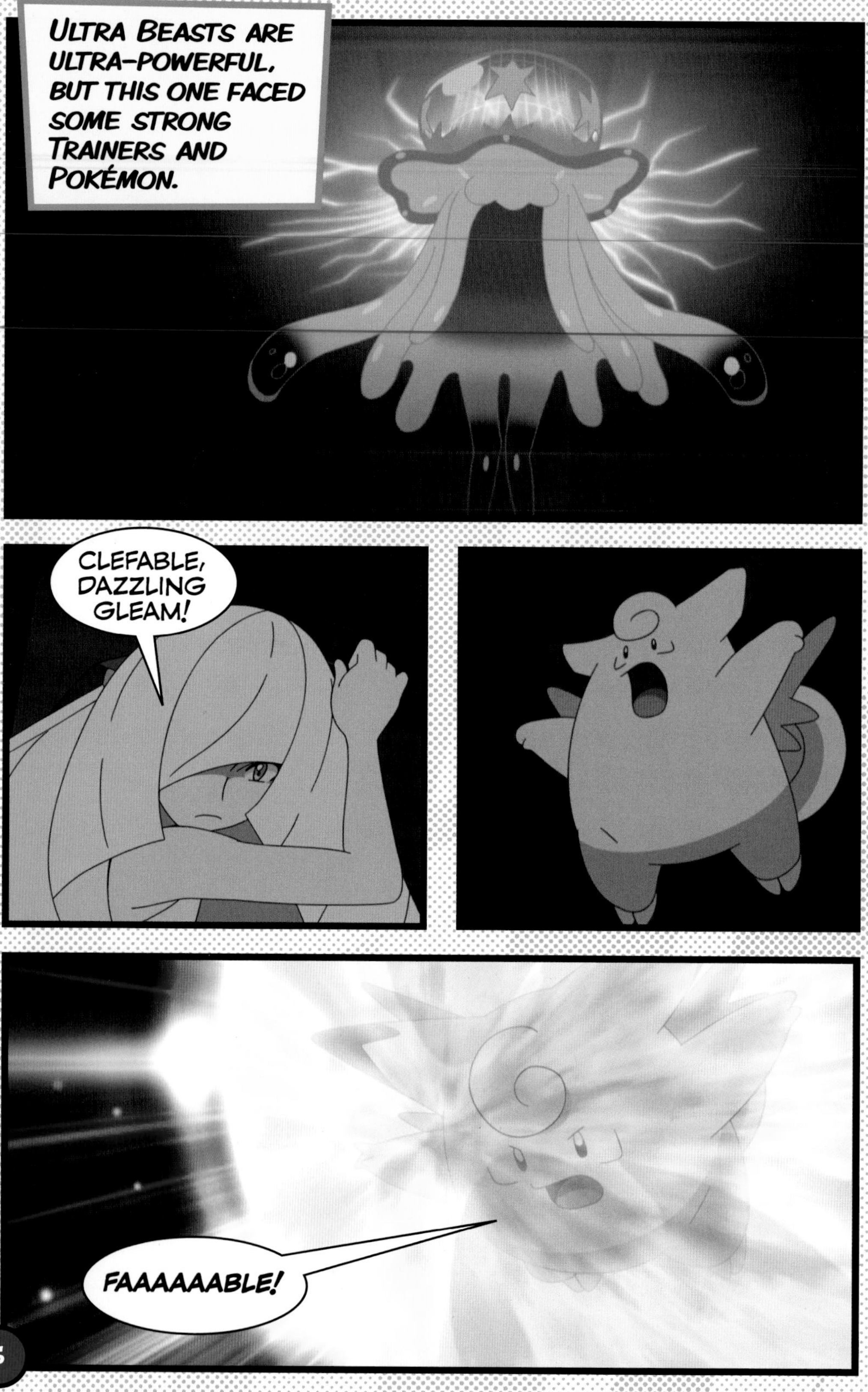
ULTRA BEASTS ARE ULTRA-POWERFUL, BUT THIS ONE FACED SOME STRONG TRAINERS AND POKÉMON.
CLEFABLE, DAZZLING GLEAM!
FAAAAAABLE!

ALL RIGHT, SILVALLY! USE AIR SLASH!

RRRRRRR!

QUICK, PIKACHU! THUNDERBOLT, LET'S GO!

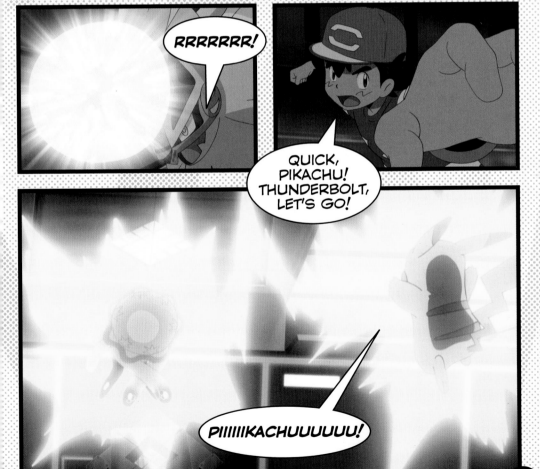

PIIIIIIKACHUUUUUUU!

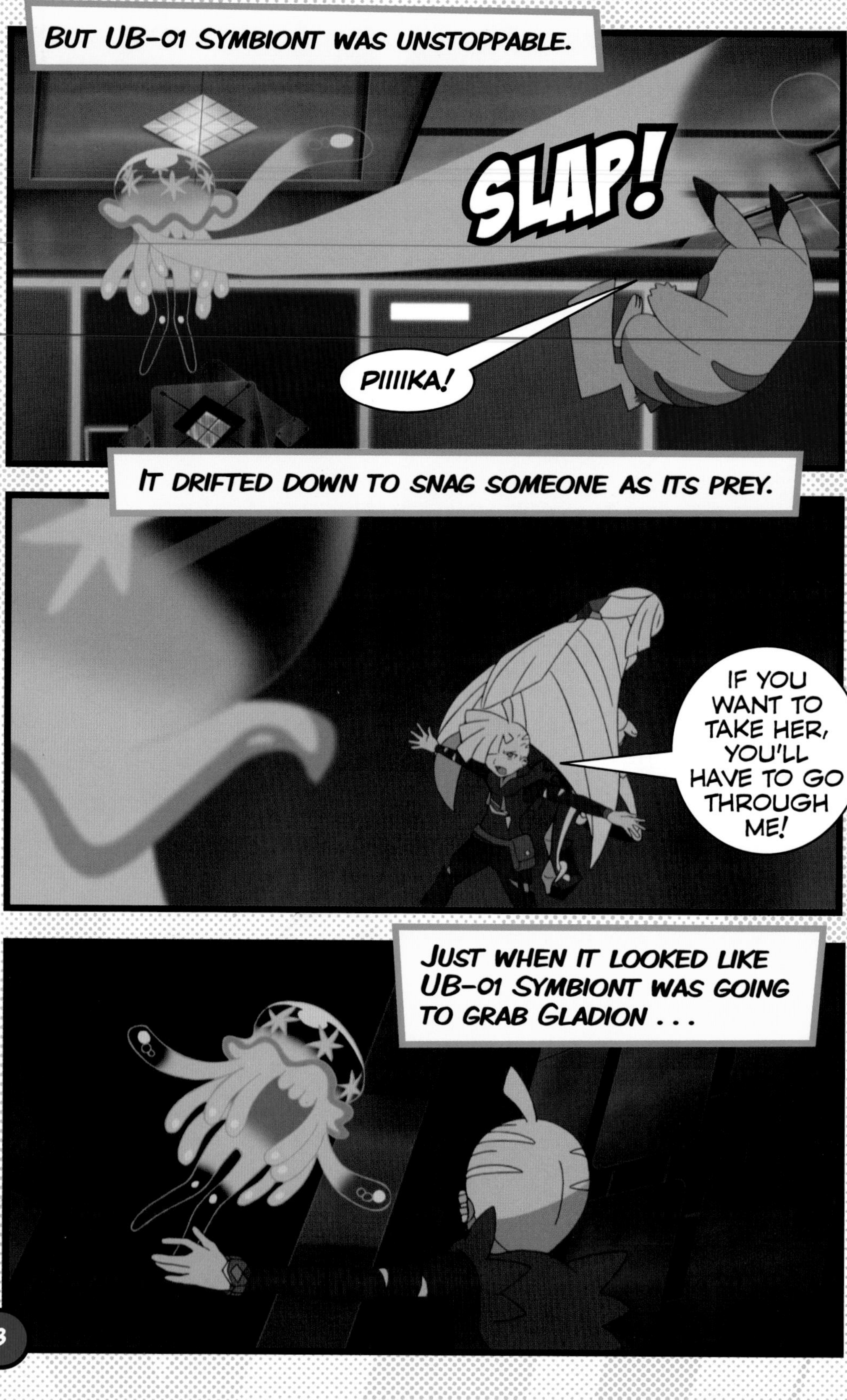
BUT UB-01 SYMBIONT WAS UNSTOPPABLE.
SLAP!
PIIIIKA!
IT DRIFTED DOWN TO SNAG SOMEONE AS ITS PREY.
IF YOU WANT TO TAKE HER, YOU'LL HAVE TO GO THROUGH ME!
JUST WHEN IT LOOKED LIKE UB-01 SYMBIONT WAS GOING TO GRAB GLADION . . .

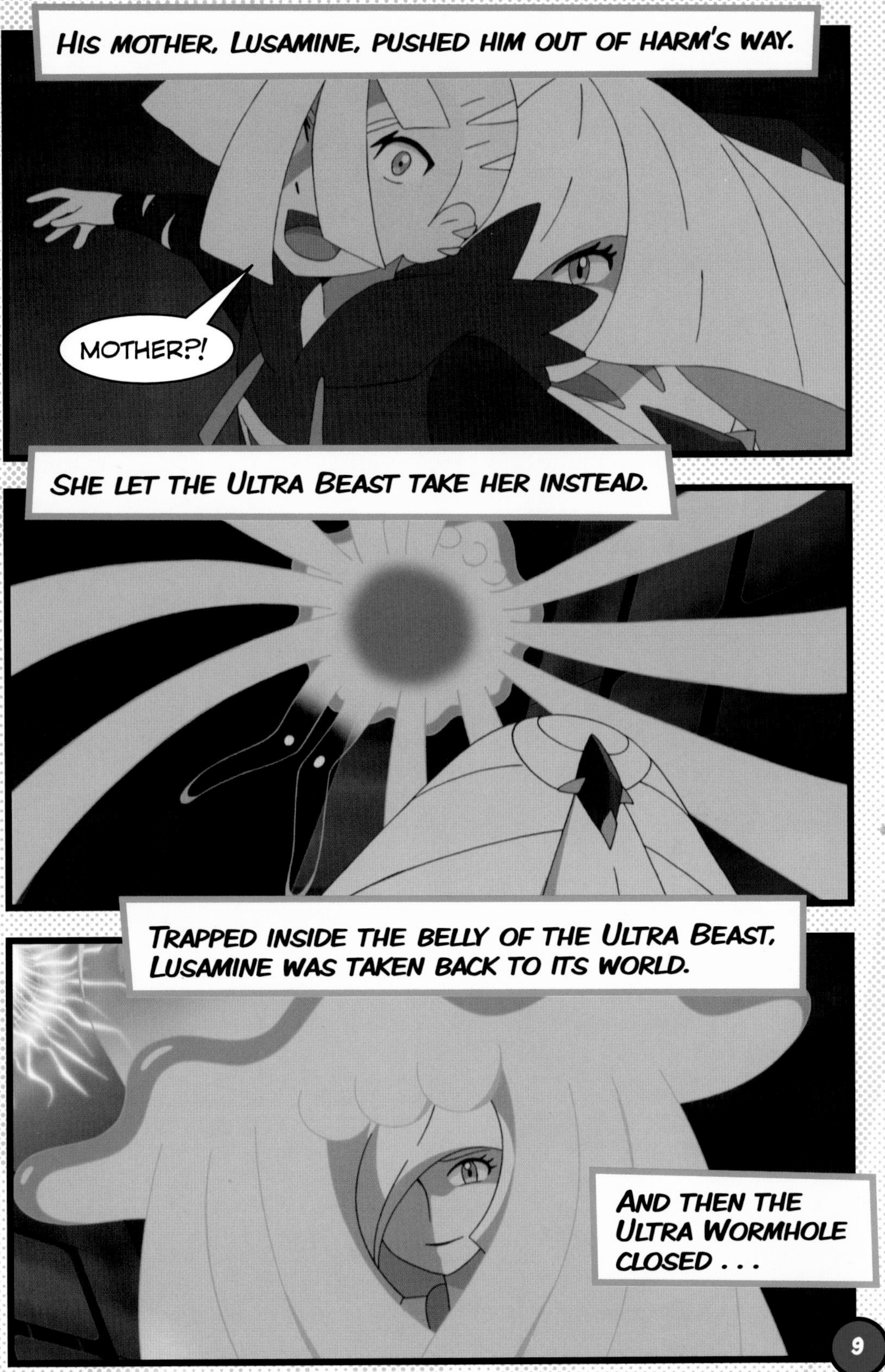

HIS MOTHER, LUSAMINE, PUSHED HIM OUT OF HARM'S WAY.
MOTHER?!
SHE LET THE ULTRA BEAST TAKE HER INSTEAD.
TRAPPED INSIDE THE BELLY OF THE ULTRA BEAST, LUSAMINE WAS TAKEN BACK TO ITS WORLD.
AND THEN THE ULTRA WORMHOLE CLOSED . . .

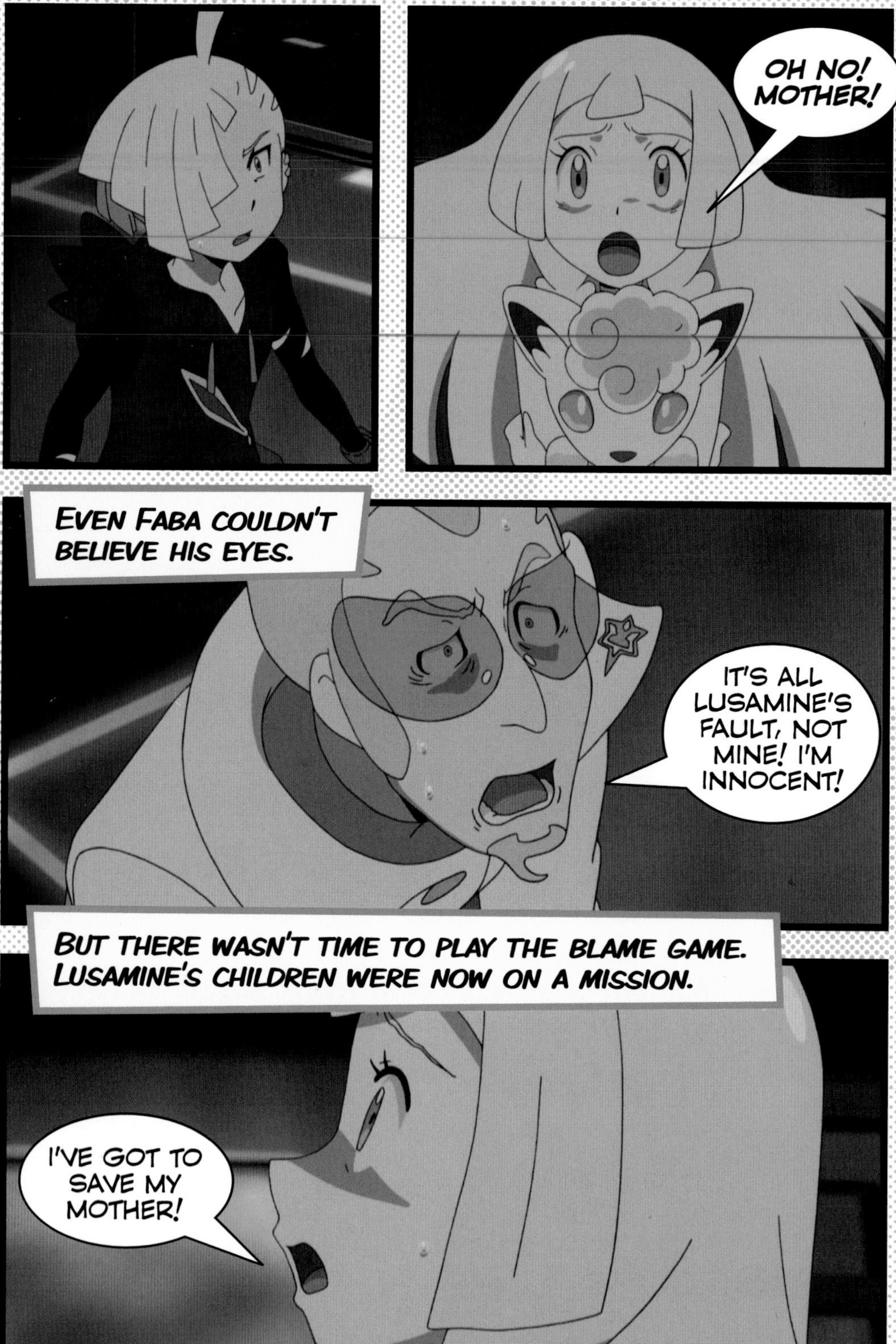

OH NO! MOTHER!
EVEN FABA COULDN'T BELIEVE HIS EYES.
IT'S ALL LUSAMINE'S FAULT, NOT MINE! I'M INNOCENT!
BUT THERE WASN'T TIME TO PLAY THE BLAME GAME. LUSAMINE'S CHILDREN WERE NOW ON A MISSION.
I'VE GOT TO SAVE MY MOTHER!

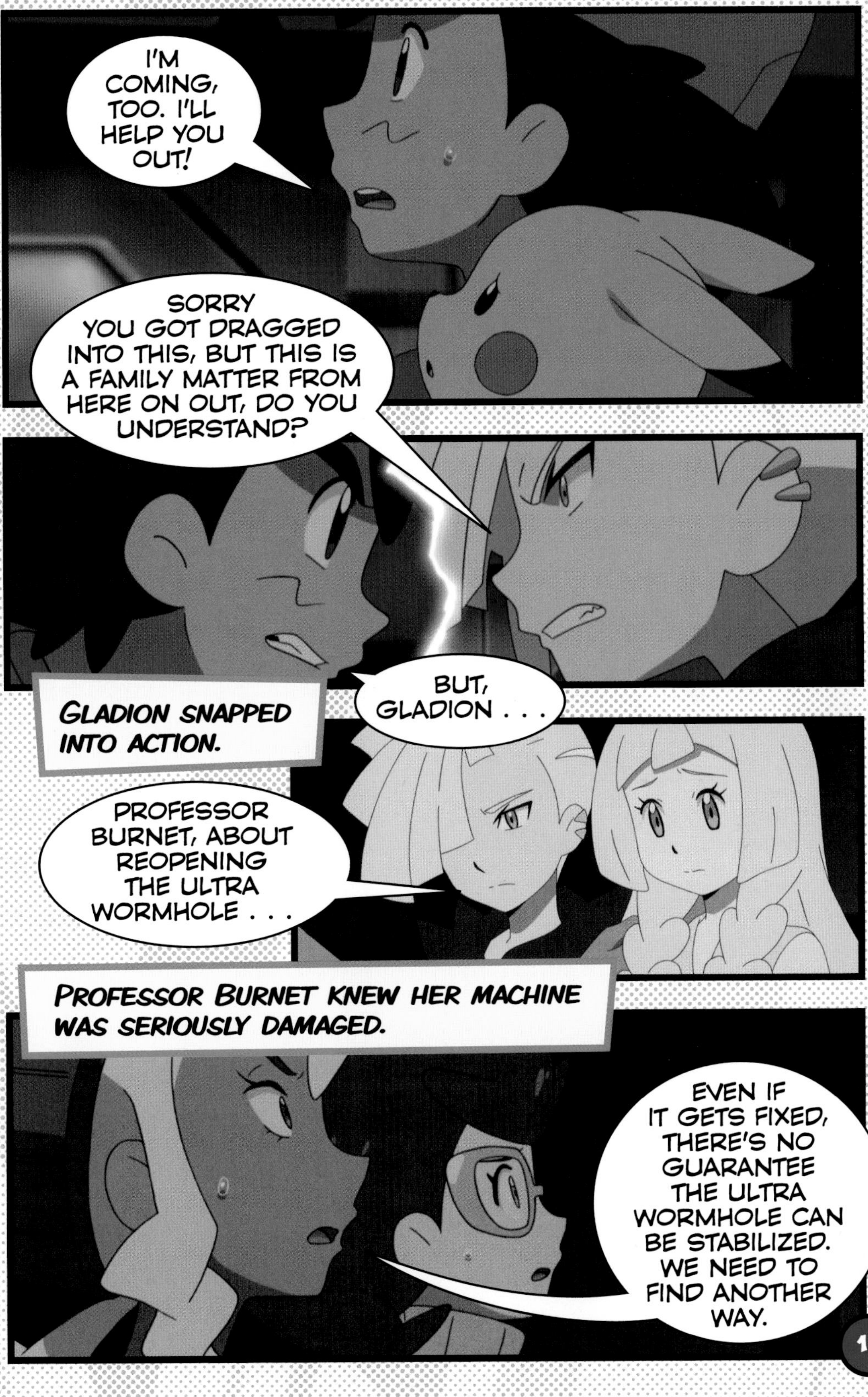
I'M COMING, TOO. I'LL HELP YOU OUT!
SORRY YOU GOT DRAGGED INTO THIS, BUT THIS IS A FAMILY MATTER FROM HERE ON OUT, DO YOU UNDERSTAND?
BUT, GLADION . . .
GLADION SNAPPED INTO ACTION.
PROFESSOR BURNET, ABOUT REOPENING THE ULTRA WORMHOLE . . .
PROFESSOR BURNET KNEW HER MACHINE WAS SERIOUSLY DAMAGED.
EVEN IF IT GETS FIXED, THERE'S NO GUARANTEE THE ULTRA WORMHOLE CAN BE STABILIZED. WE NEED TO FIND ANOTHER WAY.

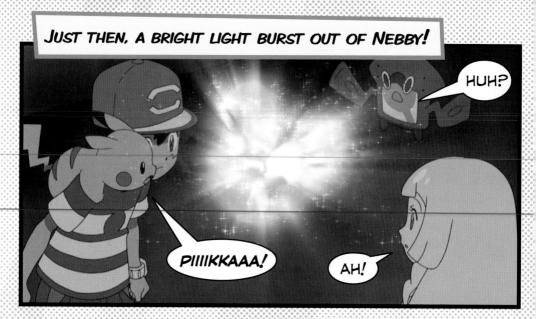

JUST THEN, A BRIGHT LIGHT BURST OUT OF NEBBY!
HUH?
PIIIIKKAAA!
AH!
ALL OF A SUDDEN, NEBBY GOT REALLY SMALL.
IT'S COMPLETELY IMMOBILIZED!

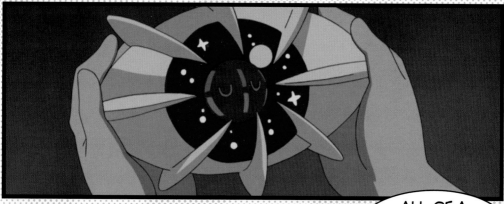

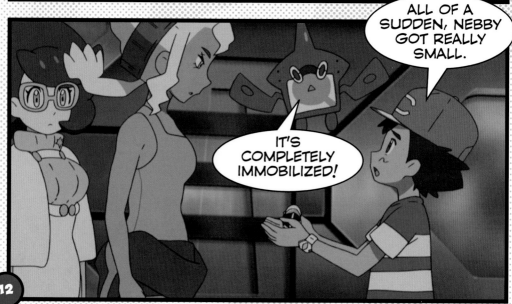

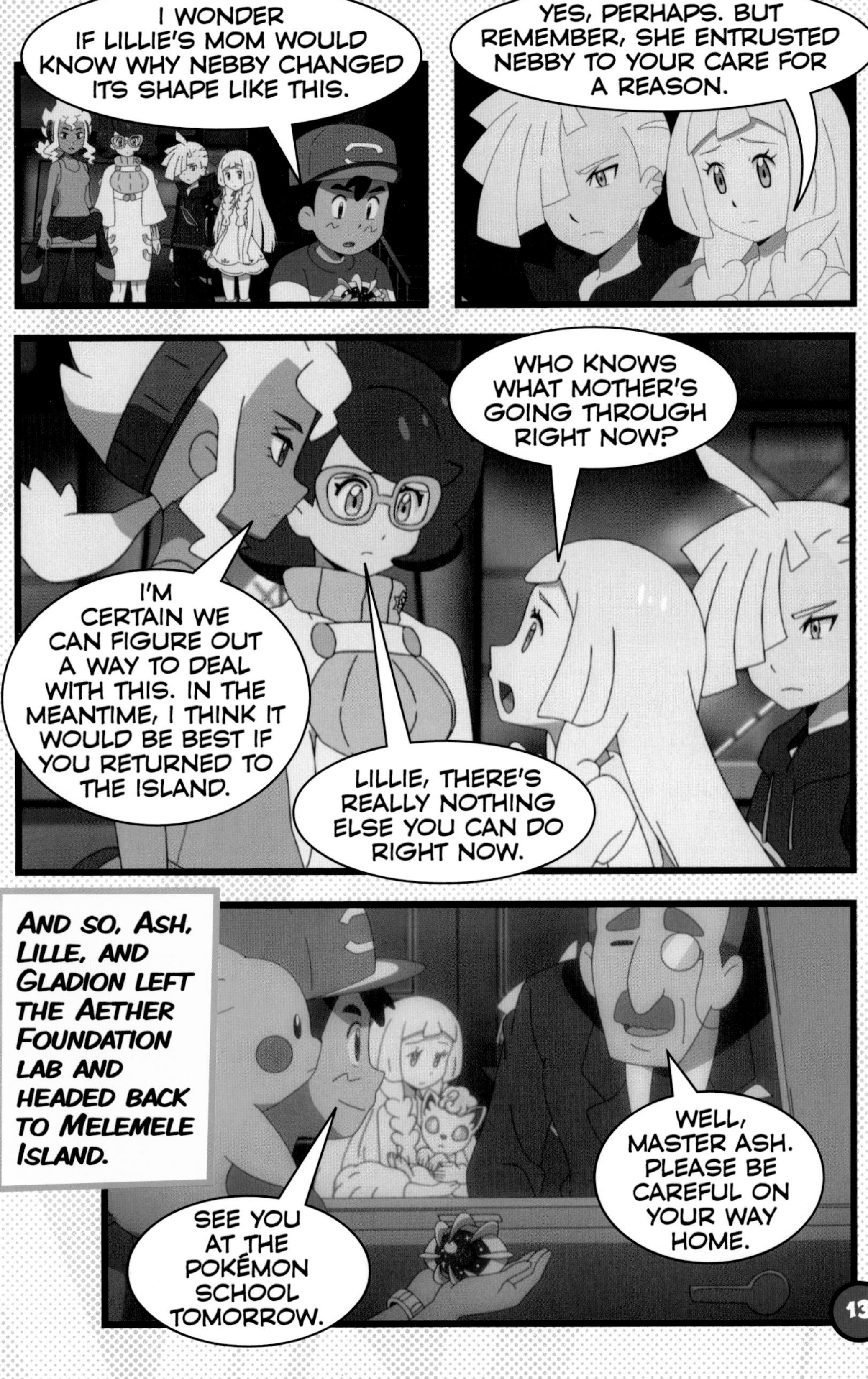

I WONDER IF LILLIE'S MOM WOULD KNOW WHY NEBBY CHANGED ITS SHAPE LIKE THIS.
YES, PERHAPS. BUT REMEMBER, SHE ENTRUSTED NEBBY TO YOUR CARE FOR A REASON.
WHO KNOWS WHAT MOTHER'S GOING THROUGH RIGHT NOW?
I'M CERTAIN WE CAN FIGURE OUT A WAY TO DEAL WITH THIS. IN THE MEANTIME, I THINK IT WOULD BE BEST IF YOU RETURNED TO THE ISLAND.
LILLIE, THERE'S REALLY NOTHING ELSE YOU CAN DO RIGHT NOW.
AND SO, ASH, LILLE, AND GLADION LEFT THE AETHER FOUNDATION LAB AND HEADED BACK TO MELEMELE ISLAND.
WELL, MASTER ASH. PLEASE BE CAREFUL ON YOUR WAY HOME.
SEE YOU AT THE POKÉMON SCHOOL TOMORROW.

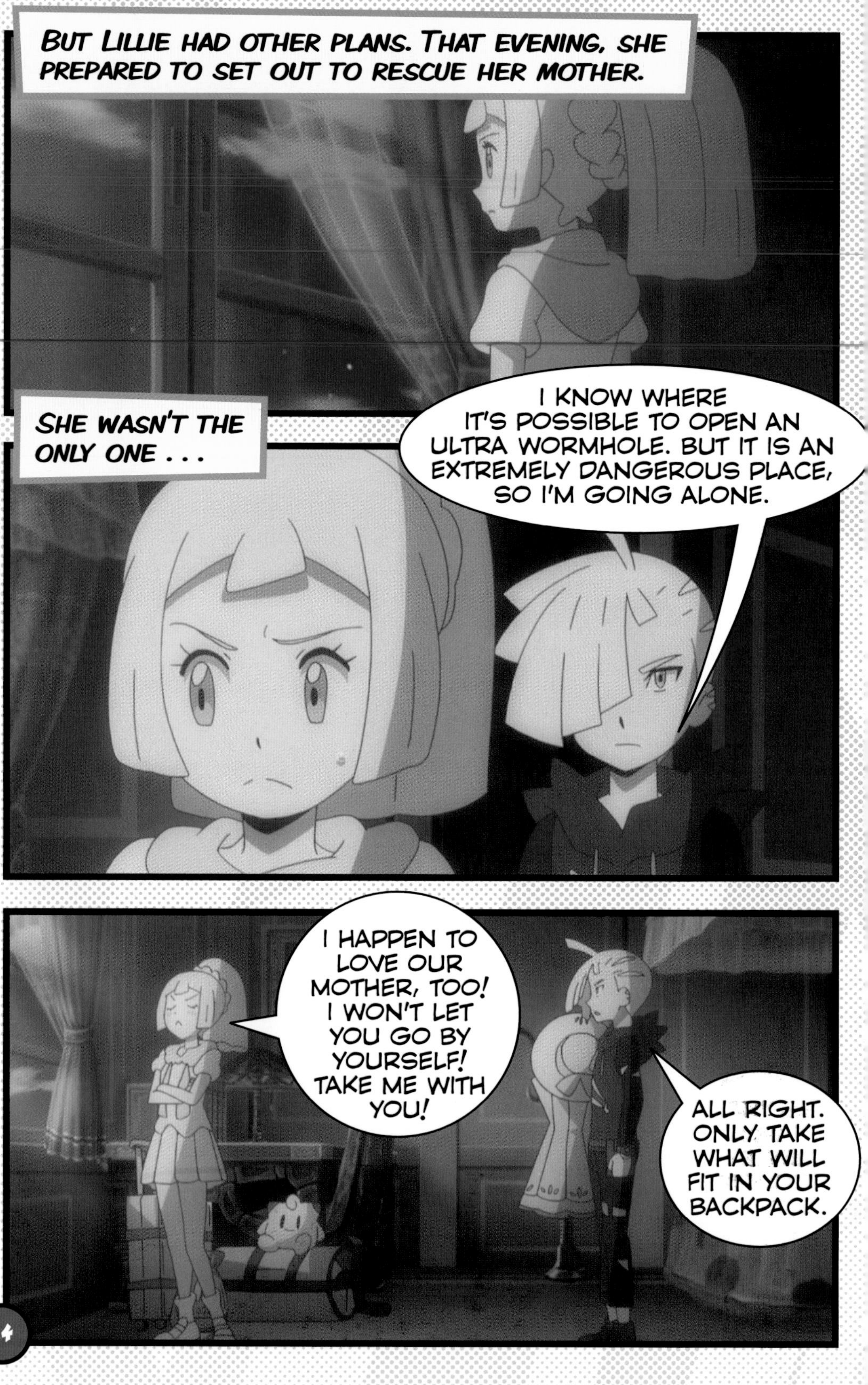
BUT LILLIE HAD OTHER PLANS. THAT EVENING, SHE PREPARED TO SET OUT TO RESCUE HER MOTHER.
SHE WASN'T THE ONLY ONE . . .
I KNOW WHERE IT'S POSSIBLE TO OPEN AN ULTRA WORMHOLE. BUT IT IS AN EXTREMELY DANGEROUS PLACE, SO I'M GOING ALONE.
I HAPPEN TO LOVE OUR MOTHER, TOO! I WON'T LET YOU GO BY YOURSELF! TAKE ME WITH YOU!
ALL RIGHT. ONLY TAKE WHAT WILL FIT IN YOUR BACKPACK.

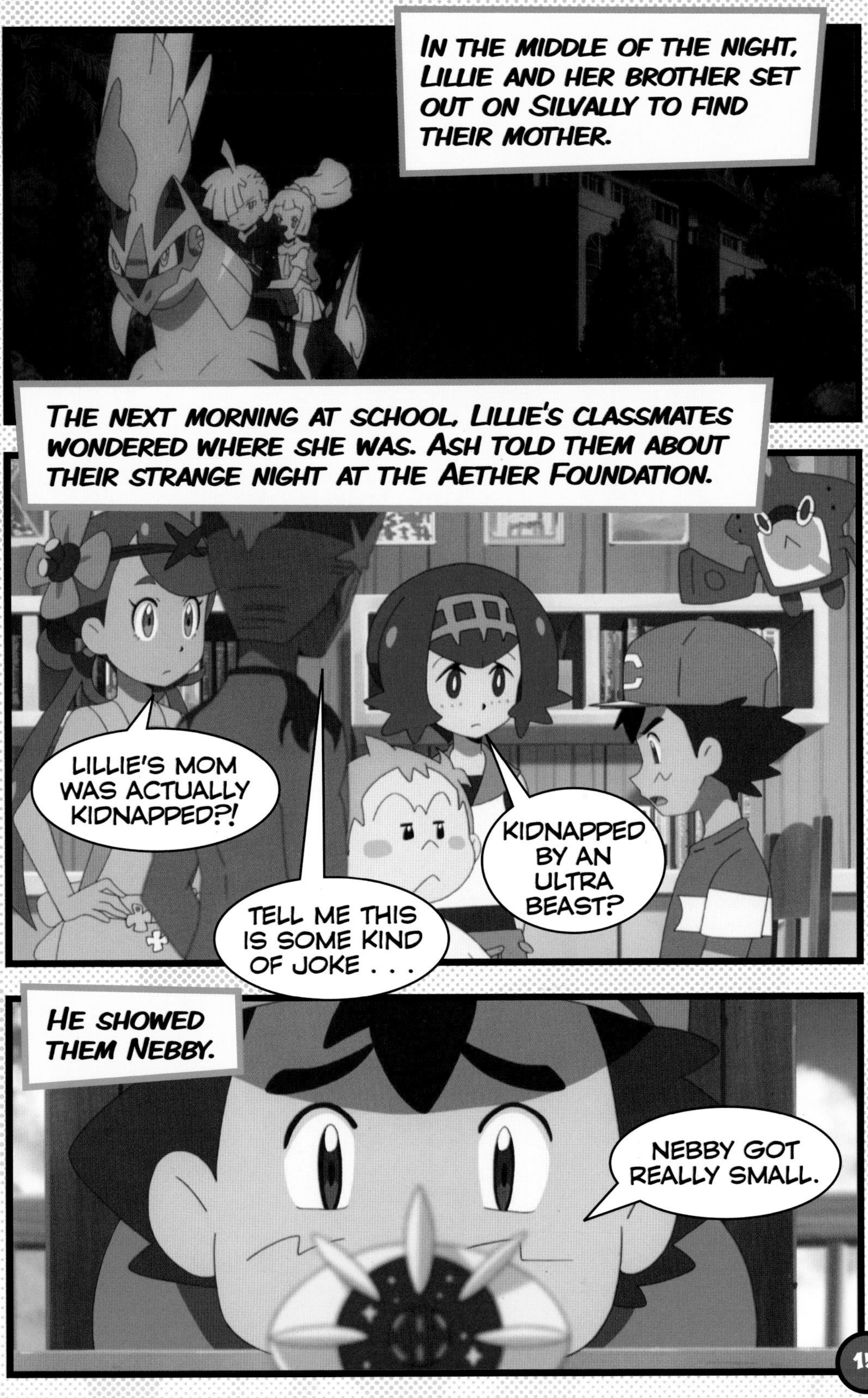

IN THE MIDDLE OF THE NIGHT, LILLIE AND HER BROTHER SET OUT ON SILVALLY TO FIND THEIR MOTHER.
THE NEXT MORNING AT SCHOOL, LILLIE'S CLASSMATES WONDERED WHERE SHE WAS. ASH TOLD THEM ABOUT THEIR STRANGE NIGHT AT THE AETHER FOUNDATION.
LILLIE'S MOM WAS ACTUALLY KIDNAPPED?!
TELL ME THIS IS SOME KIND OF JOKE . . .
KIDNAPPED BY AN ULTRA BEAST?
HE SHOWED THEM NEBBY.
NEBBY GOT REALLY SMALL.

PROFESSOR KUKUI AND LILLIE'S BUTLER, HOBBES, CAME INTO THE CLASSROOM.

SHE'S NOT HERE . . .

SIGH! IT SEEMS MISS LILLIE AND MASTER GLADION HAVE DISAPPEARED FROM THE MANOR HOUSE.

ASH SUSPECTED LILLIE AND GLADION LEFT TO FIND AN ULTRA WORMHOLE TO RESCUE THEIR MOTHER. HE DIDN'T KNOW WHERE EXACTLY THEY WENT, BUT THE KAHUNA OF MELEMELE ISLAND MIGHT . . .

LET'S GO SEE HALA RIGHT AWAY!

I'LL GO, TOO!

ME TOO!

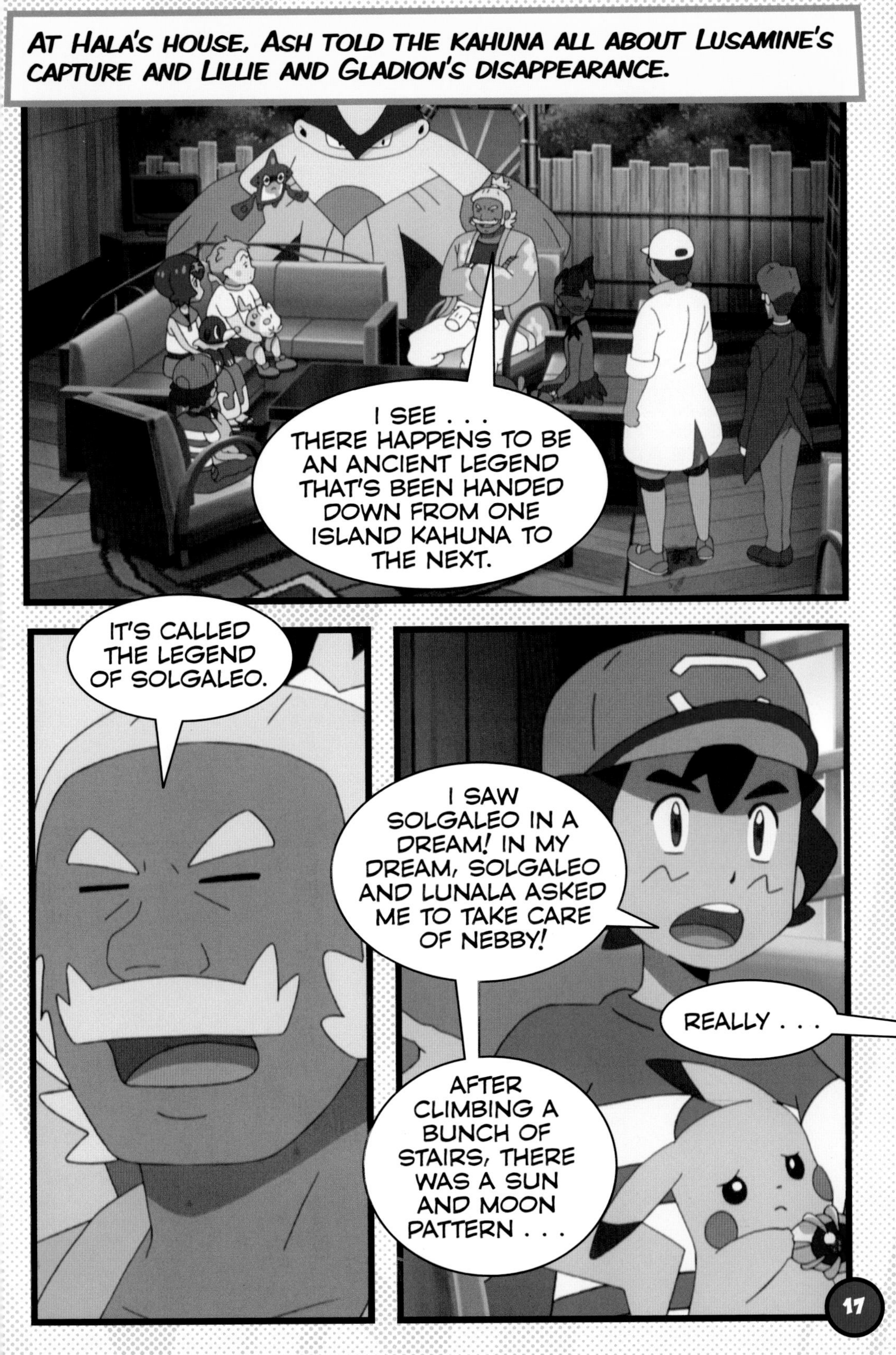
At Hala's house, Ash told the kahuna all about Lusamine's capture and Lillie and Gladion's disappearance.
I see . . . There happens to be an ancient legend that's been handed down from one island kahuna to the next.
It's called the Legend of Solgaleo.
I saw Solgaleo in a dream! In my dream, Solgaleo and Lunala asked me to take care of Nebby!
After climbing a bunch of stairs, there was a sun and moon pattern . . .
Really . . .

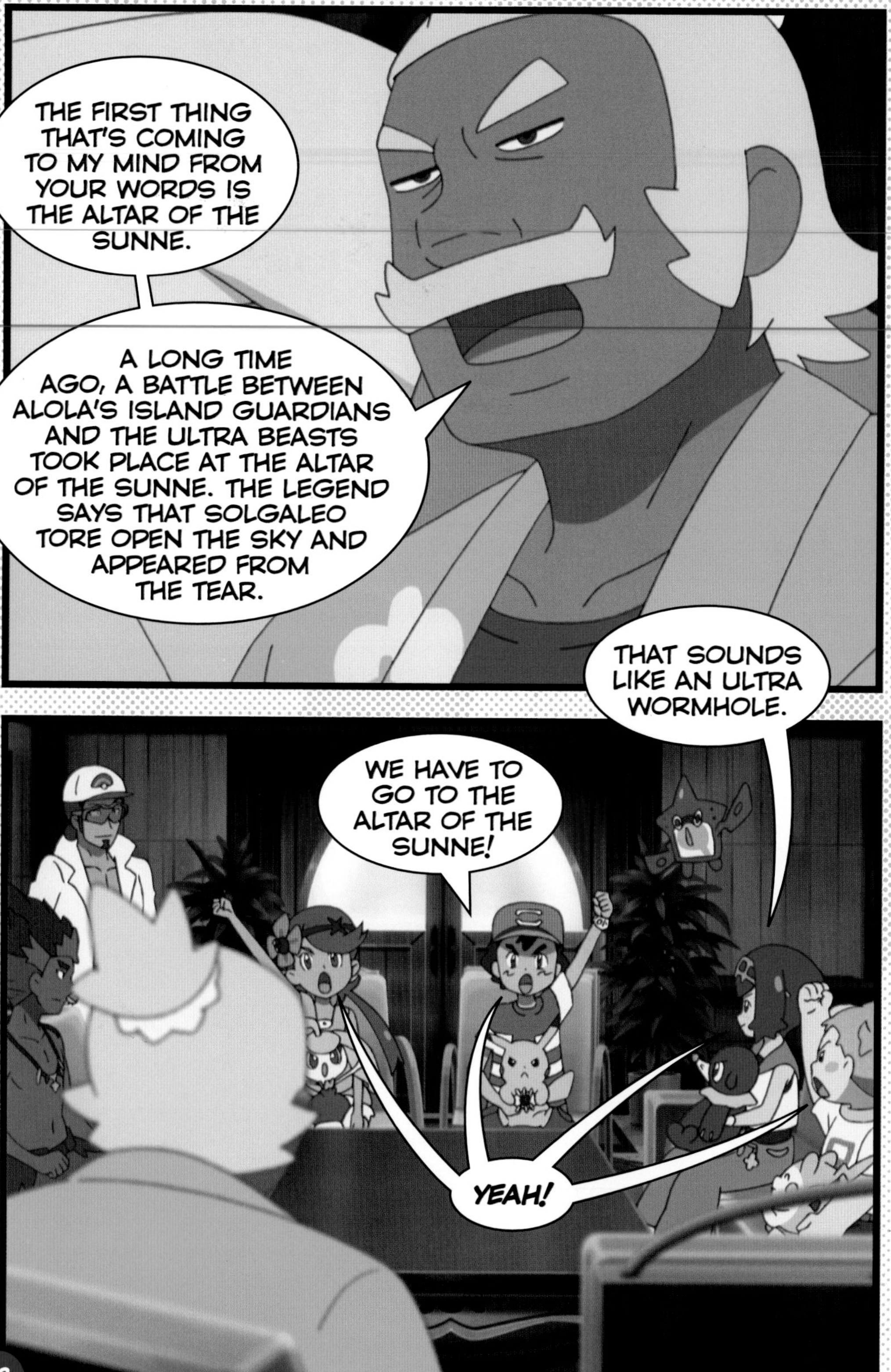
THE FIRST THING THAT'S COMING TO MY MIND FROM YOUR WORDS IS THE ALTAR OF THE SUNNE.
A LONG TIME AGO, A BATTLE BETWEEN ALOLA'S ISLAND GUARDIANS AND THE ULTRA BEASTS TOOK PLACE AT THE ALTAR OF THE SUNNE. THE LEGEND SAYS THAT SOLGALEO TORE OPEN THE SKY AND APPEARED FROM THE TEAR.
THAT SOUNDS LIKE AN ULTRA WORMHOLE.
WE HAVE TO GO TO THE ALTAR OF THE SUNNE!
YEAH!

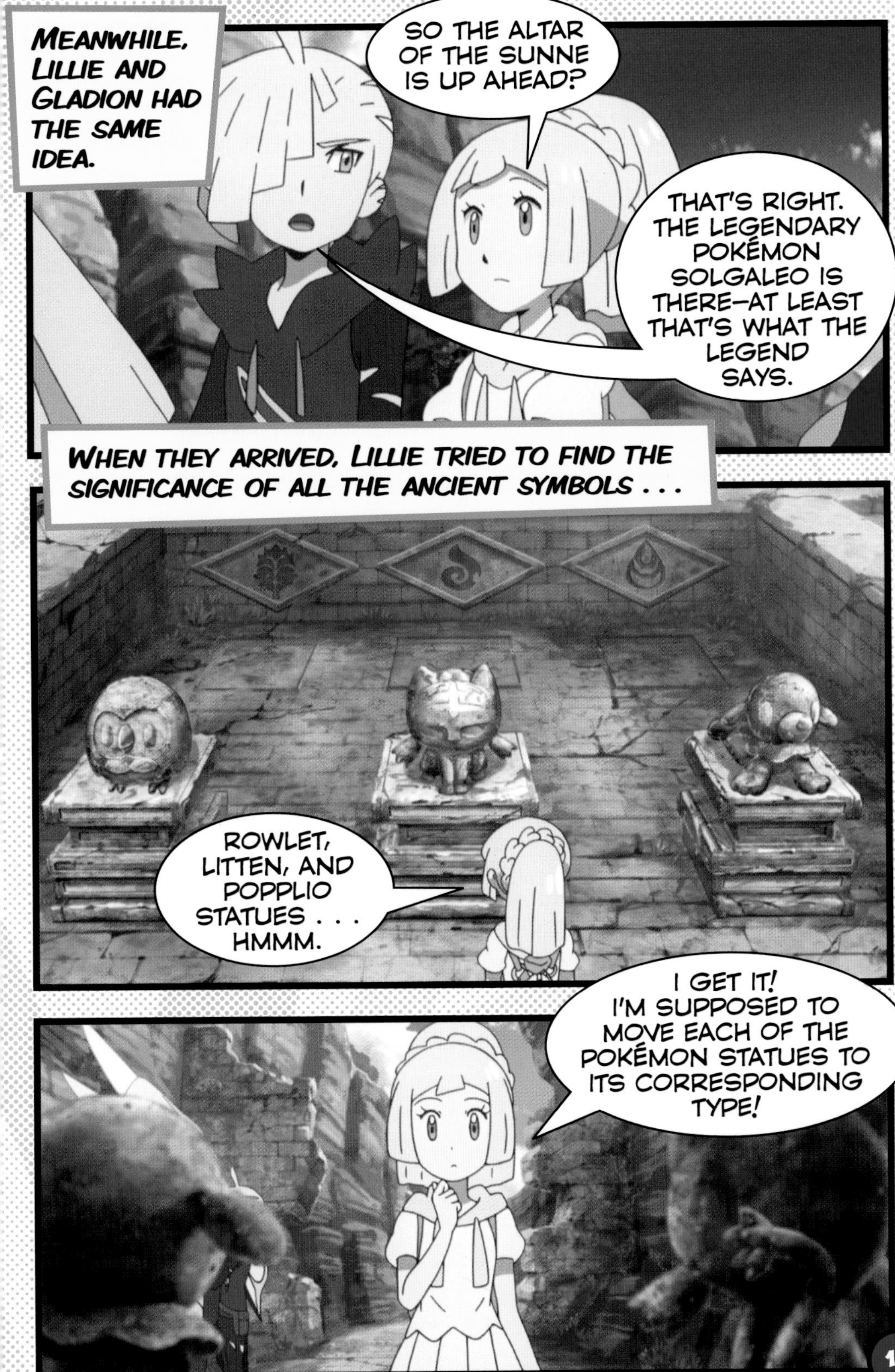
MEANWHILE, LILLIE AND GLADION HAD THE SAME IDEA.
SO THE ALTAR OF THE SUNNE IS UP AHEAD?
THAT'S RIGHT. THE LEGENDARY POKÉMON SOLGALEO IS THERE—AT LEAST THAT'S WHAT THE LEGEND SAYS.
WHEN THEY ARRIVED, LILLIE TRIED TO FIND THE SIGNIFICANCE OF ALL THE ANCIENT SYMBOLS . . .
ROWLET, LITTEN, AND POPPLIO STATUES . . . HMMM.
I GET IT! I'M SUPPOSED TO MOVE EACH OF THE POKÉMON STATUES TO ITS CORRESPONDING TYPE!

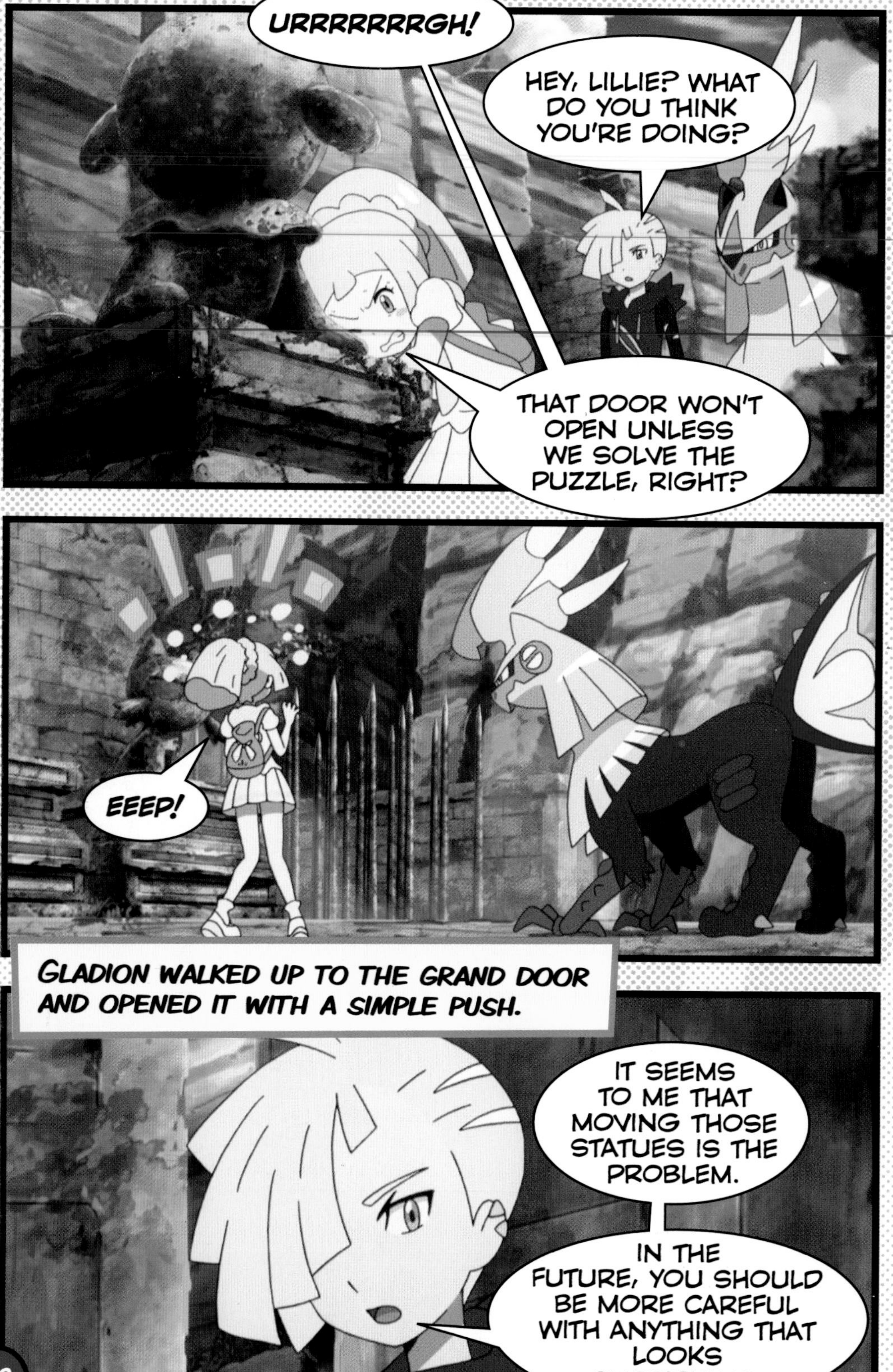
URRRRRRRGH!
HEY, LILLIE? WHAT DO YOU THINK YOU'RE DOING?
THAT DOOR WON'T OPEN UNLESS WE SOLVE THE PUZZLE, RIGHT?
EEEP!
GLADION WALKED UP TO THE GRAND DOOR AND OPENED IT WITH A SIMPLE PUSH.
IT SEEMS TO ME THAT MOVING THOSE STATUES IS THE PROBLEM.
IN THE FUTURE, YOU SHOULD BE MORE CAREFUL WITH ANYTHING THAT LOOKS SUSPICIOUS.

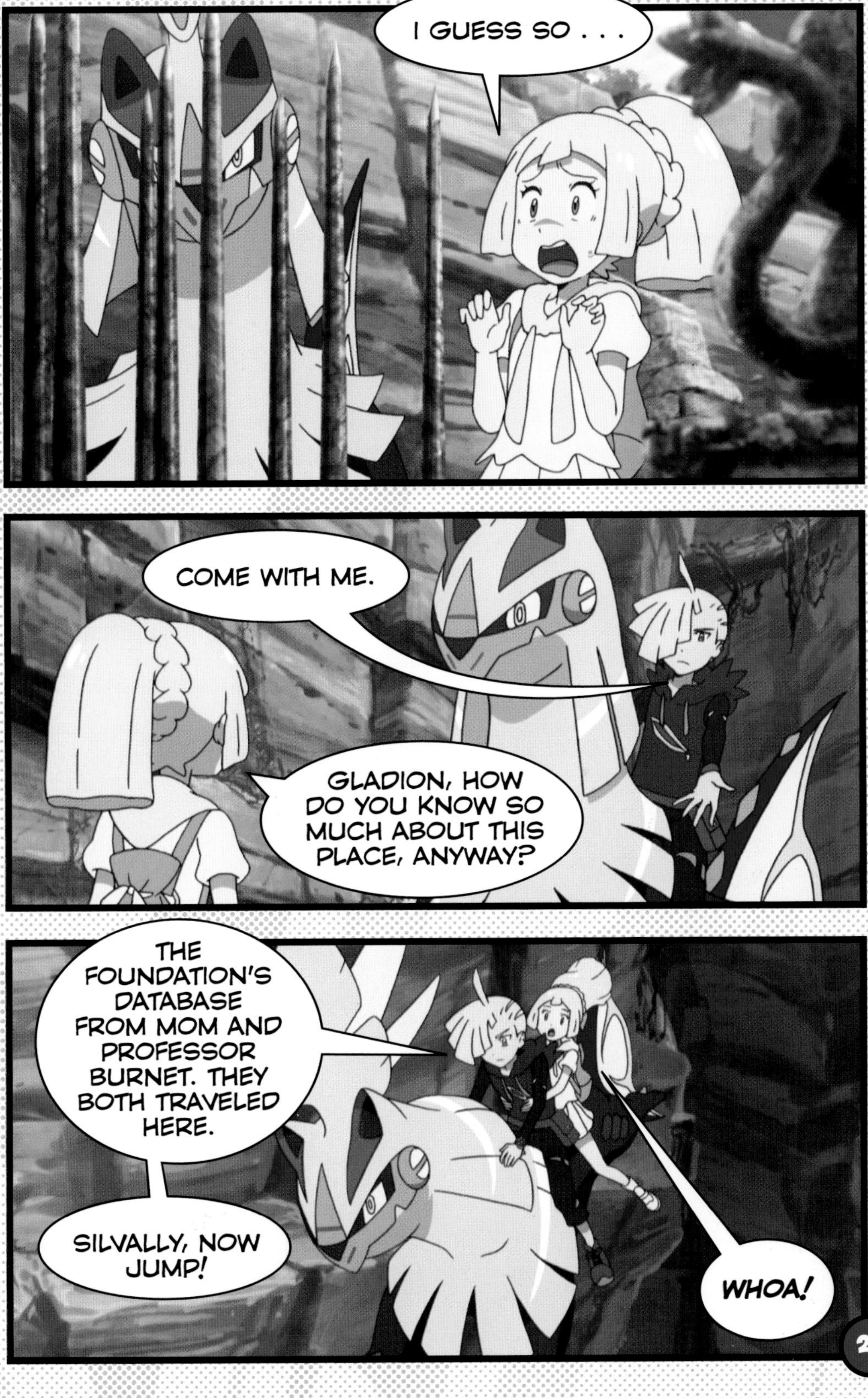
I GUESS SO . . .
COME WITH ME.
GLADION, HOW DO YOU KNOW SO MUCH ABOUT THIS PLACE, ANYWAY?
THE FOUNDATION'S DATABASE FROM MOM AND PROFESSOR BURNET. THEY BOTH TRAVELED HERE.
SILVALLY, NOW JUMP!
WHOA!

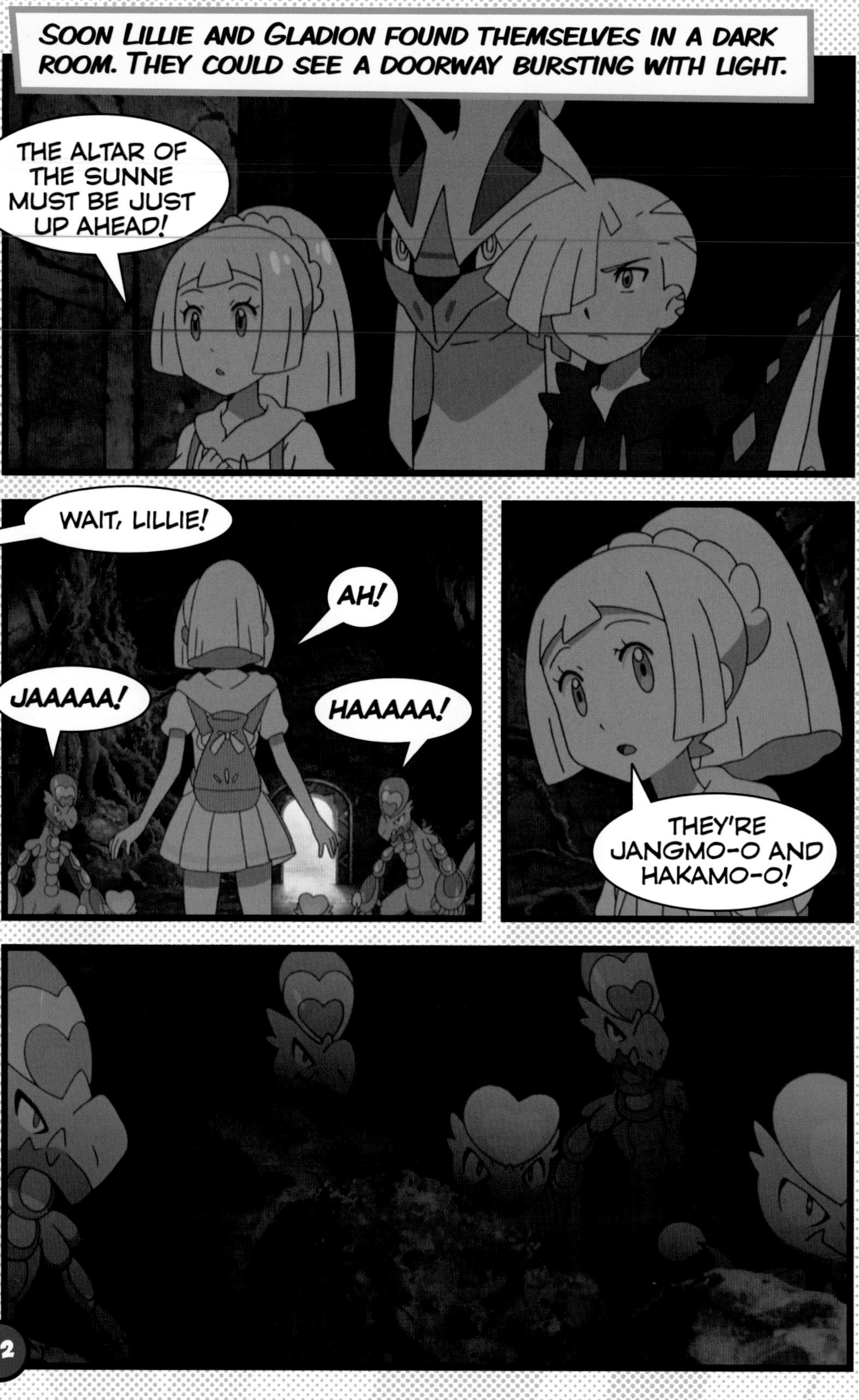
SOON LILLIE AND GLADION FOUND THEMSELVES IN A DARK ROOM. THEY COULD SEE A DOORWAY BURSTING WITH LIGHT.
THE ALTAR OF THE SUNNE MUST BE JUST UP AHEAD!
WAIT, LILLIE!
AH!
JAAAAA!
HAAAAA!
THEY'RE JANGMO-O AND HAKAMO-O!

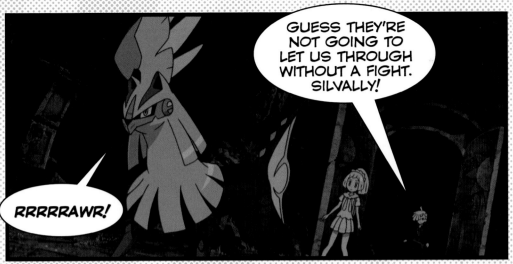

GUESS THEY'RE NOT GOING TO LET US THROUGH WITHOUT A FIGHT. SILVALLY!

RRRRRAWR!

LILLIE'S ALOLAN VULPIX POKÉMON PAL WAS READY TO BATTLE, TOO!

EEEEEE!

SNOWY, GO!

SUDDENLY, A GIANT POKÉMON APPEARED!

KOOOOO MOOOOO!

GASP!

23

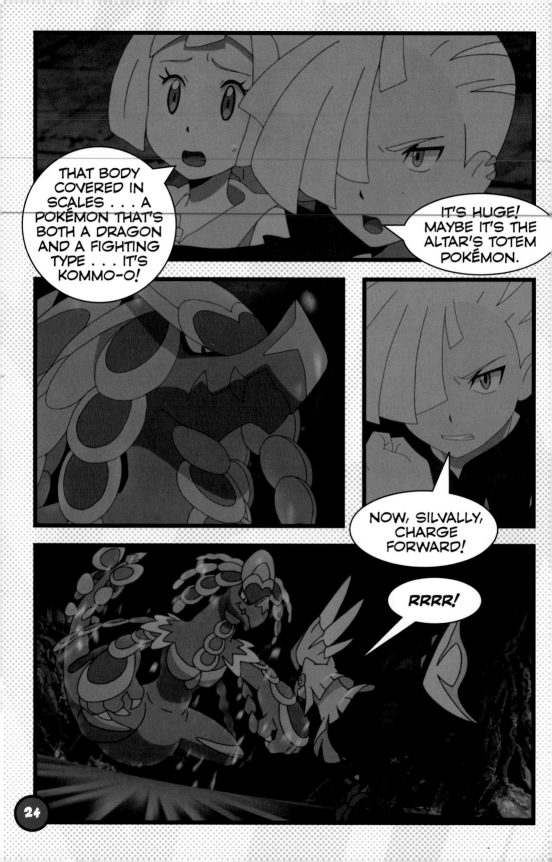

THAT BODY COVERED IN SCALES . . . A POKÉMON THAT'S BOTH A DRAGON AND A FIGHTING TYPE . . . IT'S KOMMO-O!

IT'S HUGE! MAYBE IT'S THE ALTAR'S TOTEM POKÉMON.

NOW, SILVALLY, CHARGE FORWARD!

RRRR!

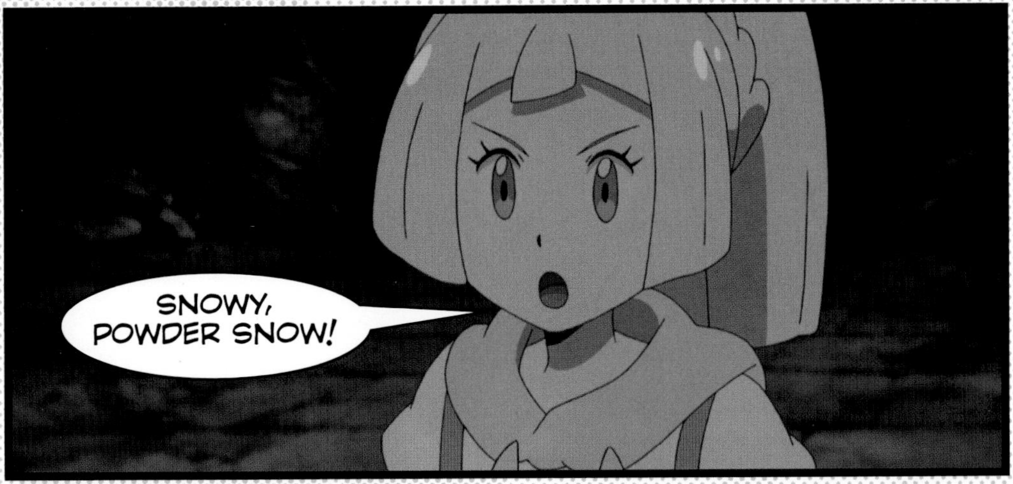
SNOWY,
POWDER SNOW!

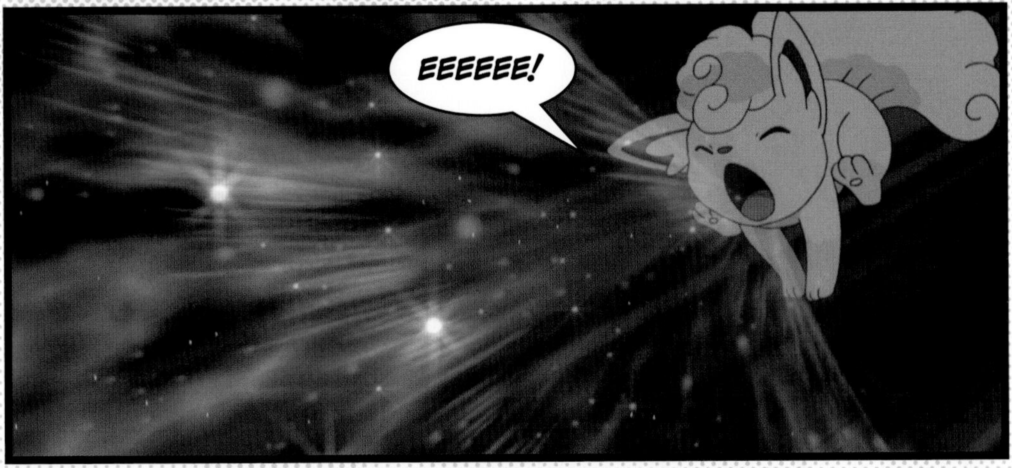
EEEEEE!

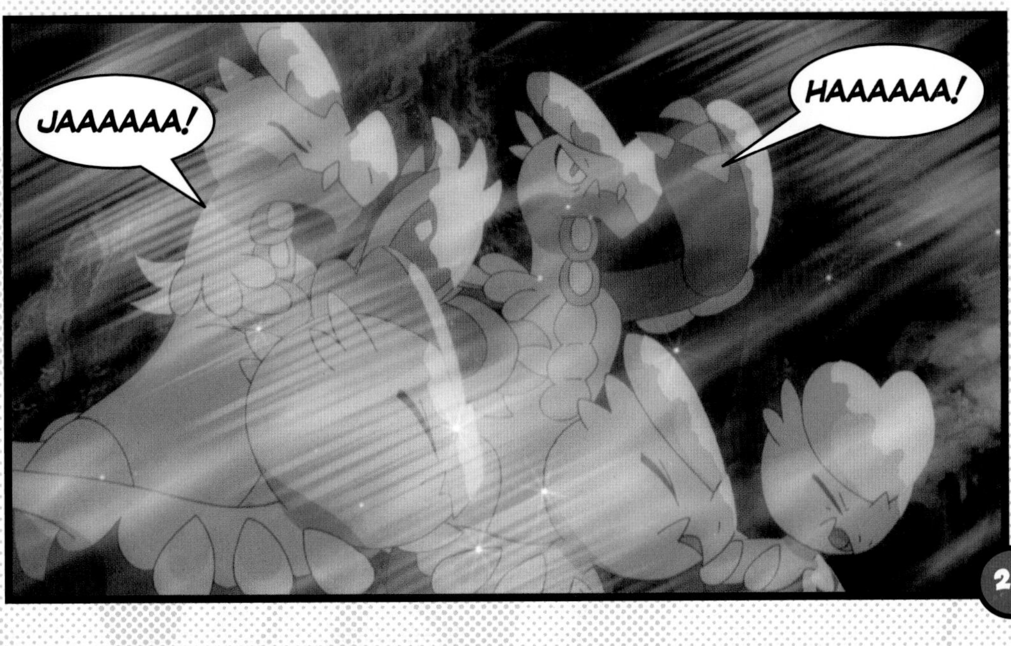
JAAAAAA!
HAAAAAA!

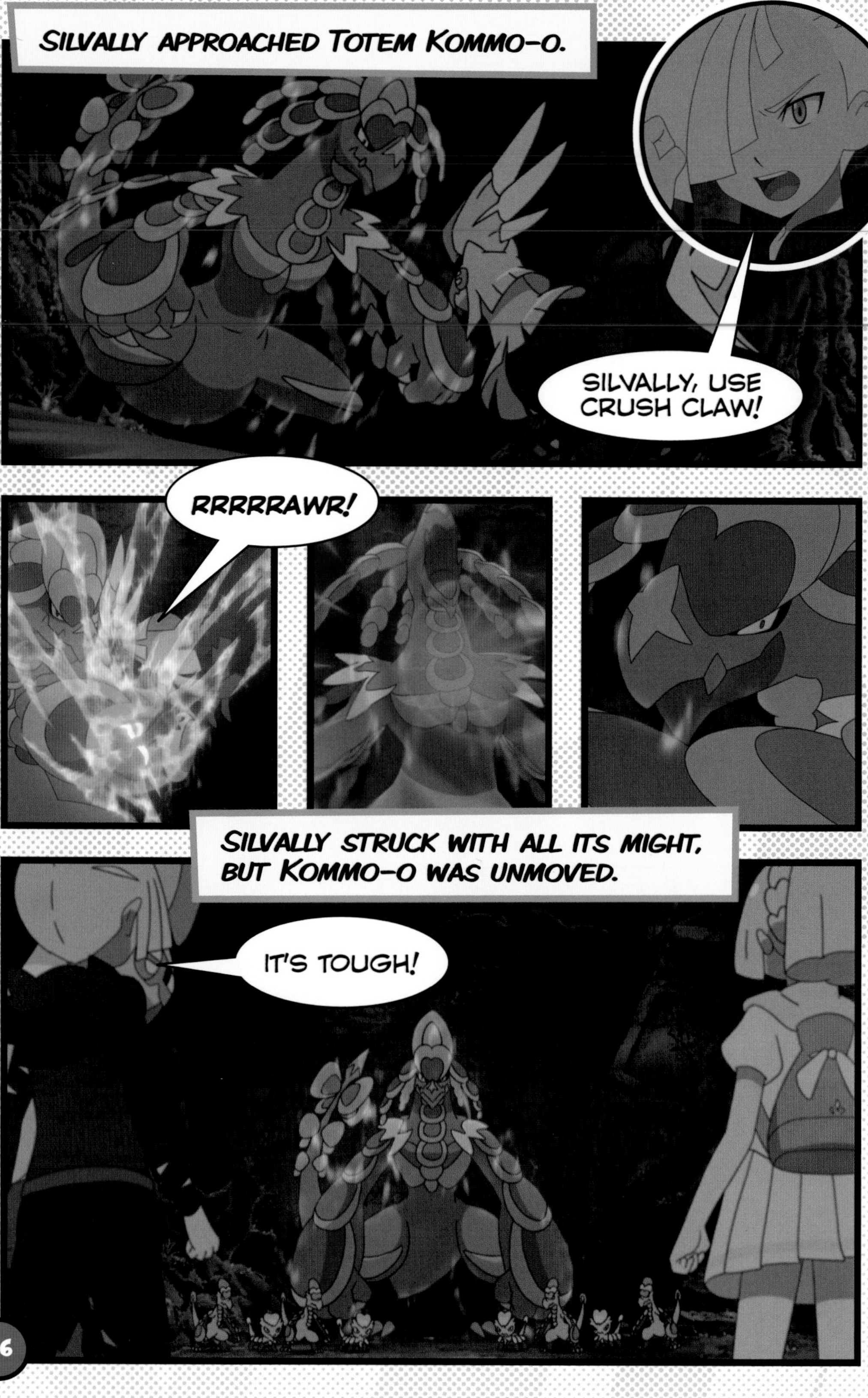
SILVALLY APPROACHED TOTEM KOMMO-O.
SILVALLY, USE CRUSH CLAW!
RRRRRAWR!
SILVALLY STRUCK WITH ALL ITS MIGHT, BUT KOMMO-O WAS UNMOVED.
IT'S TOUGH!

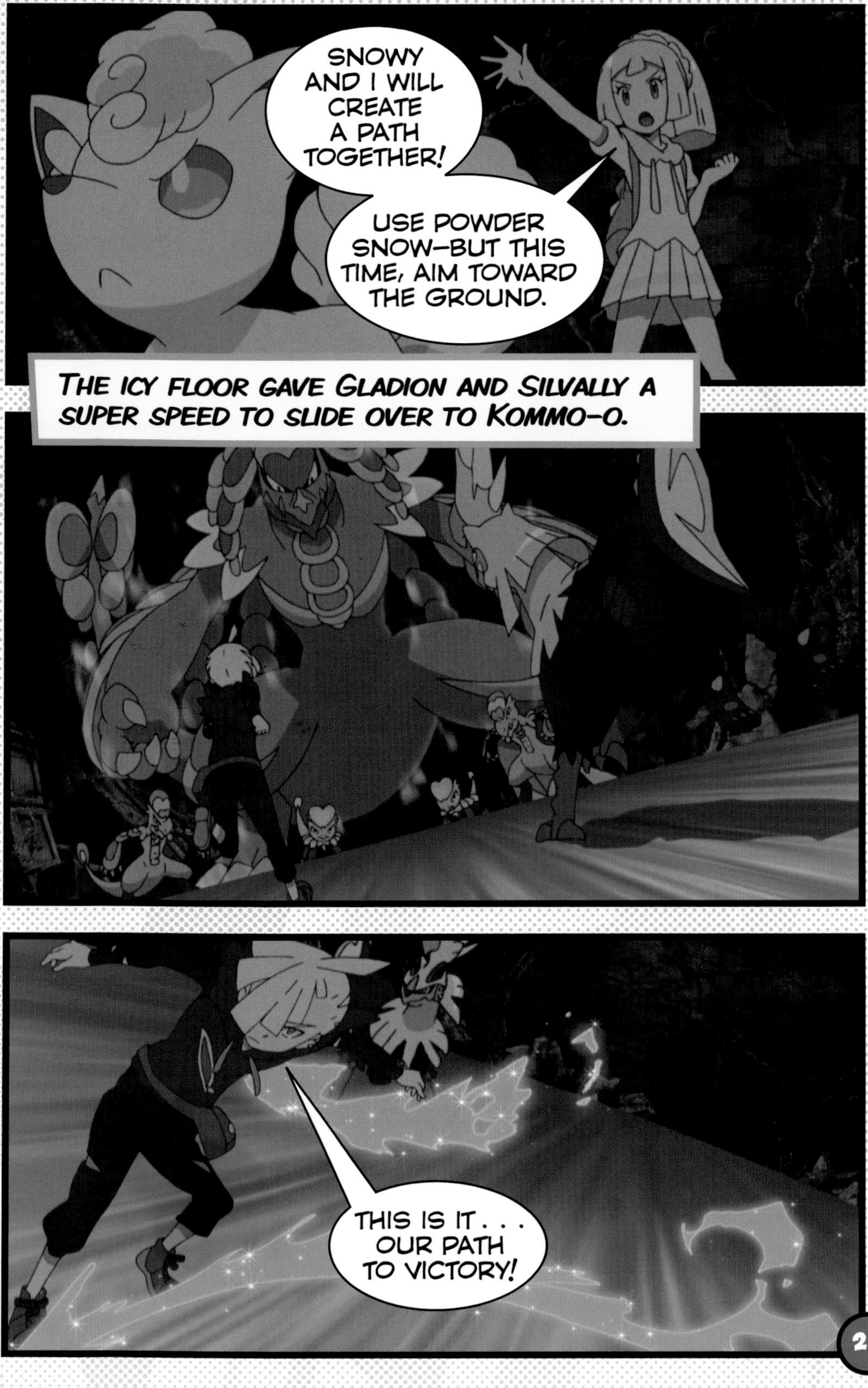
SNOWY AND I WILL CREATE A PATH TOGETHER!
USE POWDER SNOW—BUT THIS TIME, AIM TOWARD THE GROUND.
THE ICY FLOOR GAVE GLADION AND SILVALLY A SUPER SPEED TO SLIDE OVER TO KOMMO-O.
THIS IS IT . . . OUR PATH TO VICTORY!

DRAGON-TYPE CLAWS CAN'T PIERCE A FAIRY-TYPE'S ARMOR WHEN THE FAIRY-TYPE IS CLOAKED IN LIGHT!

BUT A FAIRY-TYPE'S ATTACK CAN SLASH THROUGH A DRAGON-TYPE'S SCALES! SILVALLY, MULTI-ATTACK! LET'S GO!

SILVALLY SURPRISED KOMMO-O WITH A DIRECT HIT!

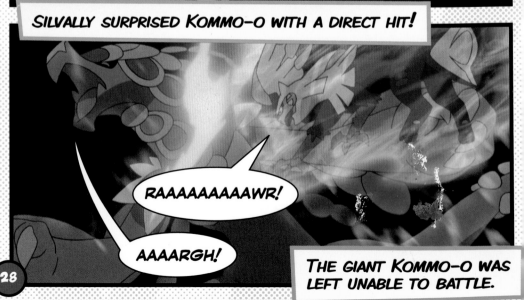

RAAAAAAAAAWR!

AAAARGH!

THE GIANT KOMMO-O WAS LEFT UNABLE TO BATTLE.

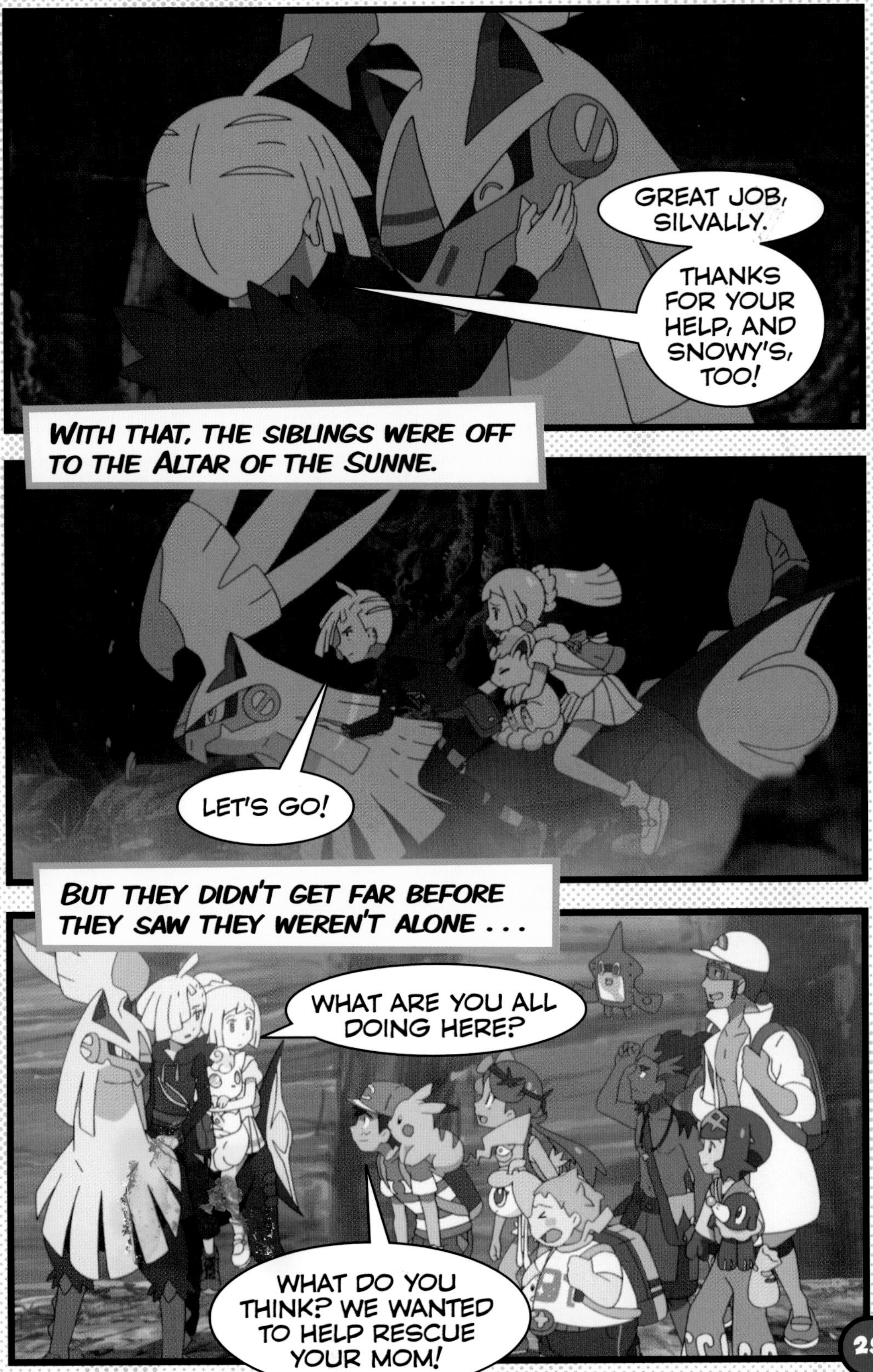
GREAT JOB, SILVALLY.
THANKS FOR YOUR HELP, AND SNOWY'S, TOO!
WITH THAT, THE SIBLINGS WERE OFF TO THE ALTAR OF THE SUNNE.
LET'S GO!
BUT THEY DIDN'T GET FAR BEFORE THEY SAW THEY WEREN'T ALONE . . .
WHAT ARE YOU ALL DOING HERE?
WHAT DO YOU THINK? WE WANTED TO HELP RESCUE YOUR MOM!

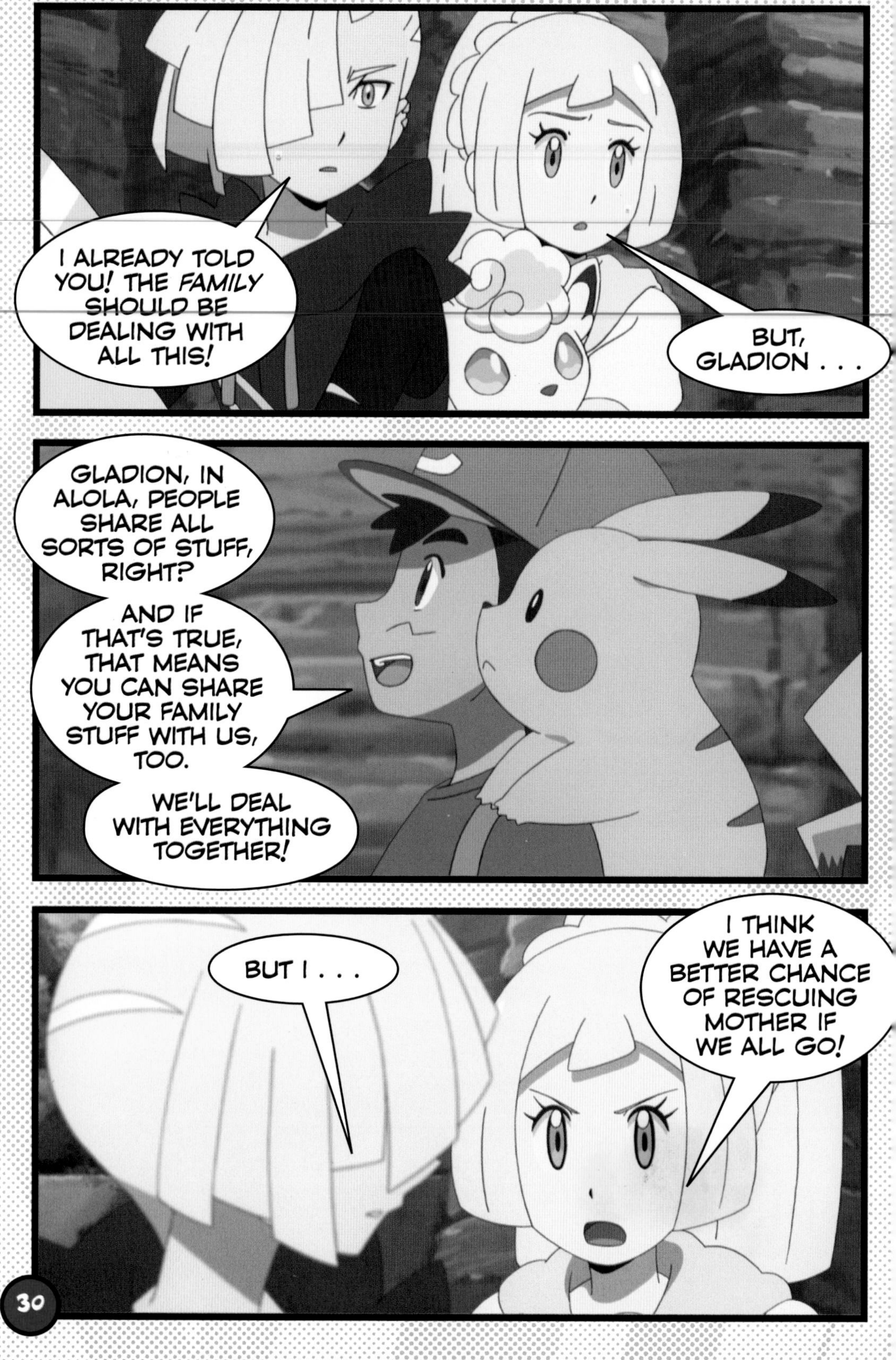
I ALREADY TOLD YOU! THE *FAMILY* SHOULD BE DEALING WITH ALL THIS!
BUT, GLADION . . .
GLADION, IN ALOLA, PEOPLE SHARE ALL SORTS OF STUFF, RIGHT?
AND IF THAT'S TRUE, THAT MEANS YOU CAN SHARE YOUR FAMILY STUFF WITH US, TOO.
WE'LL DEAL WITH EVERYTHING TOGETHER!
BUT I . . .
I THINK WE HAVE A BETTER CHANCE OF RESCUING MOTHER IF WE ALL GO!

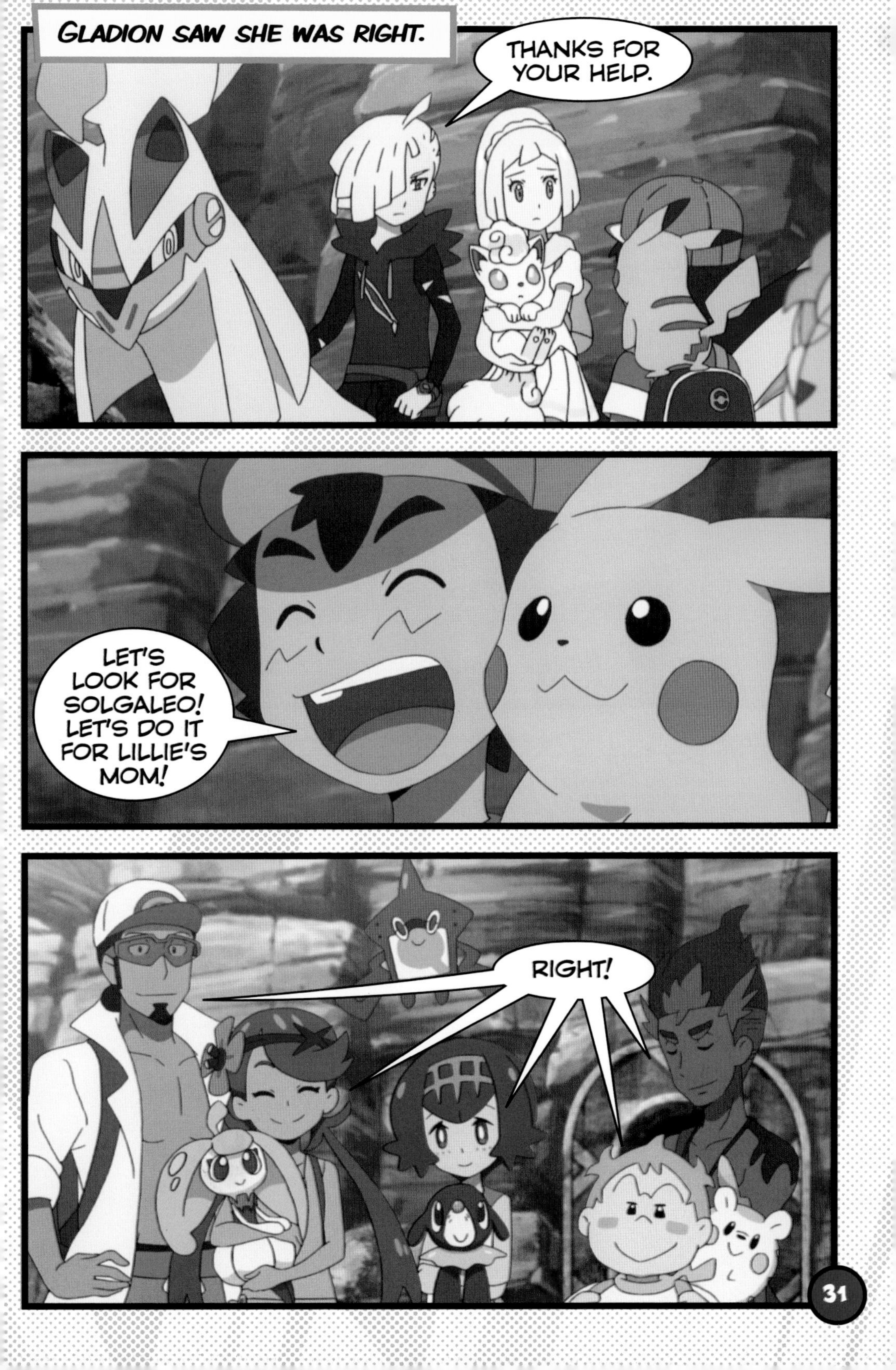
GLADION SAW SHE WAS RIGHT.
THANKS FOR YOUR HELP.
LET'S LOOK FOR SOLGALEO! LET'S DO IT FOR LILLIE'S MOM!
RIGHT!

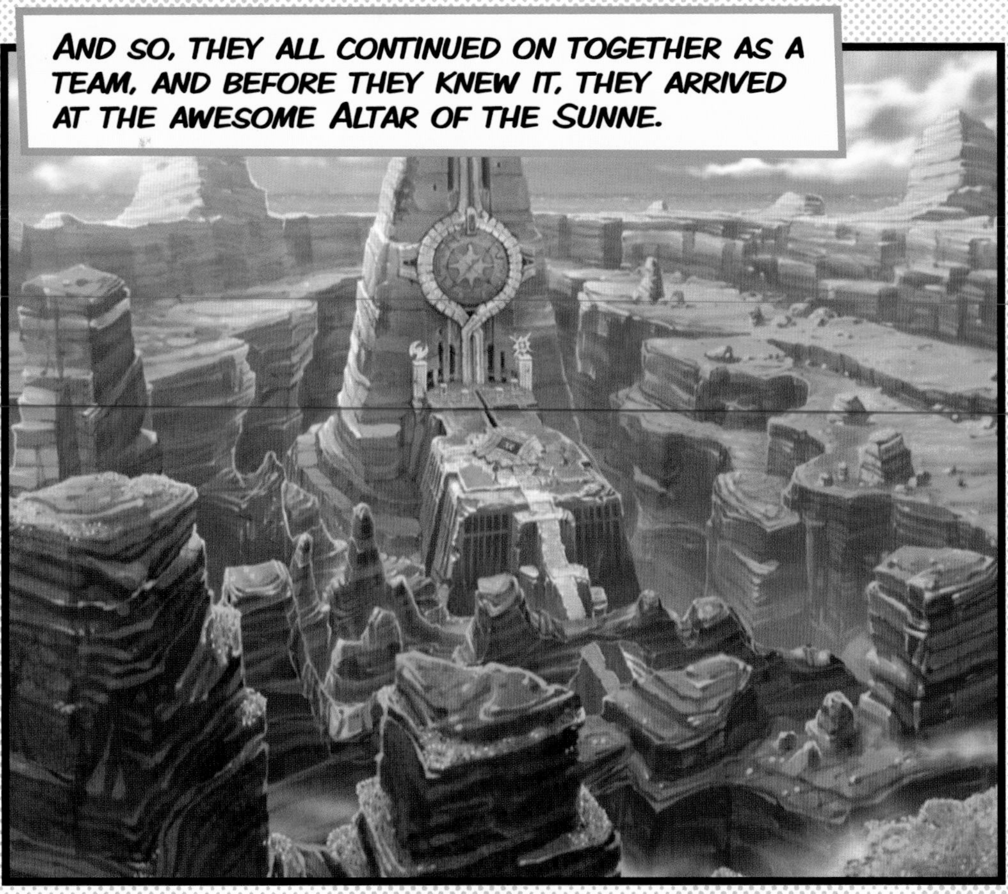
AND SO, THEY ALL CONTINUED ON TOGETHER AS A TEAM, AND BEFORE THEY KNEW IT, THEY ARRIVED AT THE AWESOME ALTAR OF THE SUNNE.

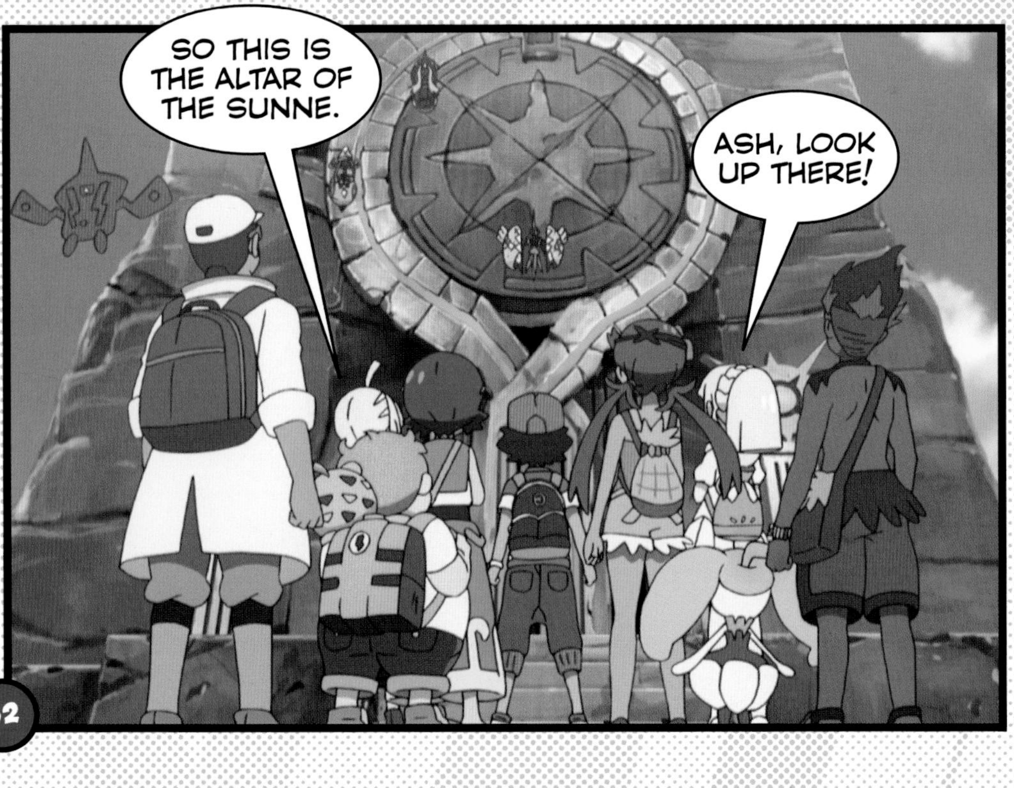
SO THIS IS THE ALTAR OF THE SUNNE.
ASH, LOOK UP THERE!

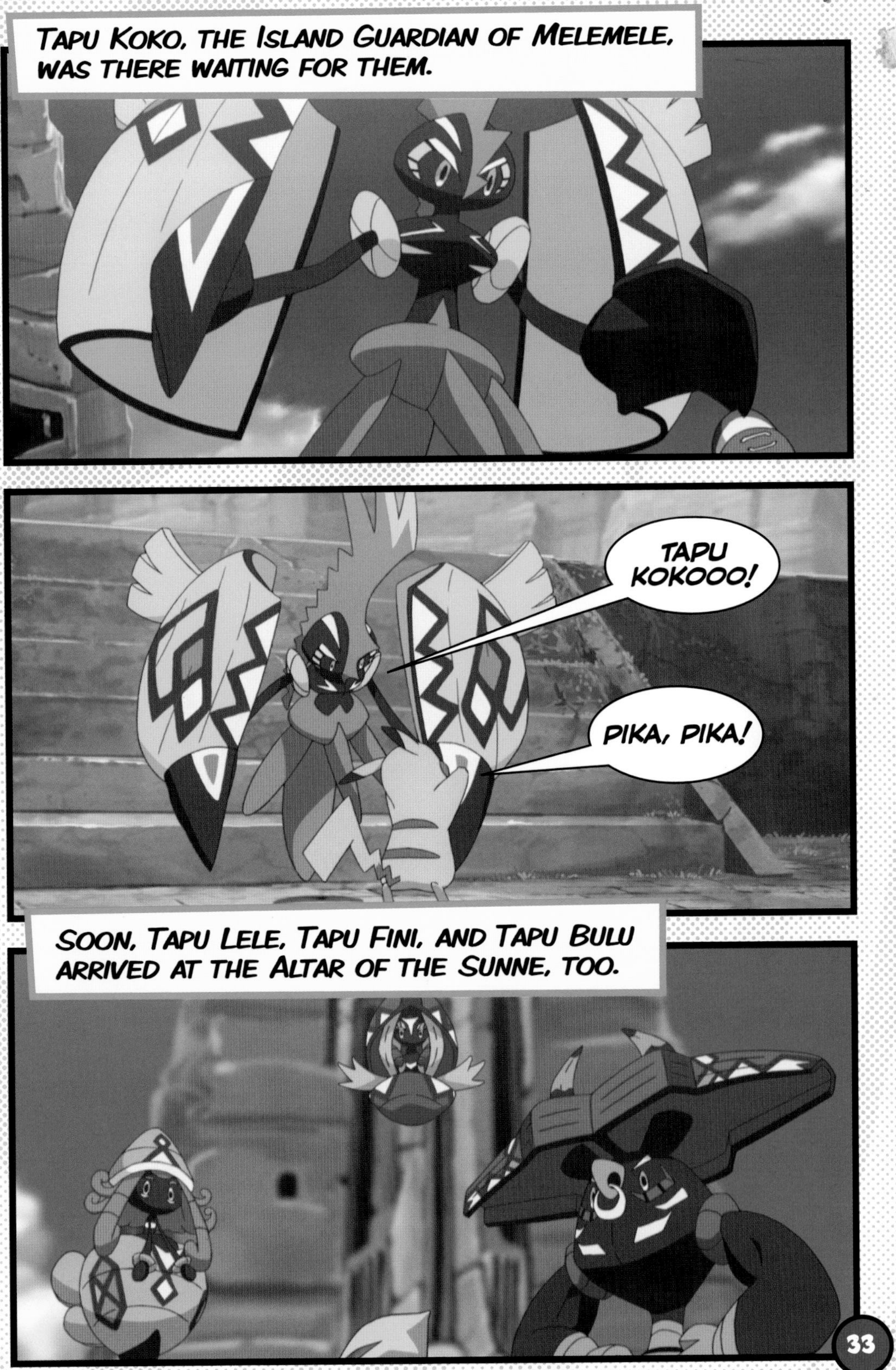
TAPU KOKO, THE ISLAND GUARDIAN OF MELEMELE, WAS THERE WAITING FOR THEM.
TAPU KOKOOO!
PIKA, PIKA!
SOON, TAPU LELE, TAPU FINI, AND TAPU BULU ARRIVED AT THE ALTAR OF THE SUNNE, TOO.

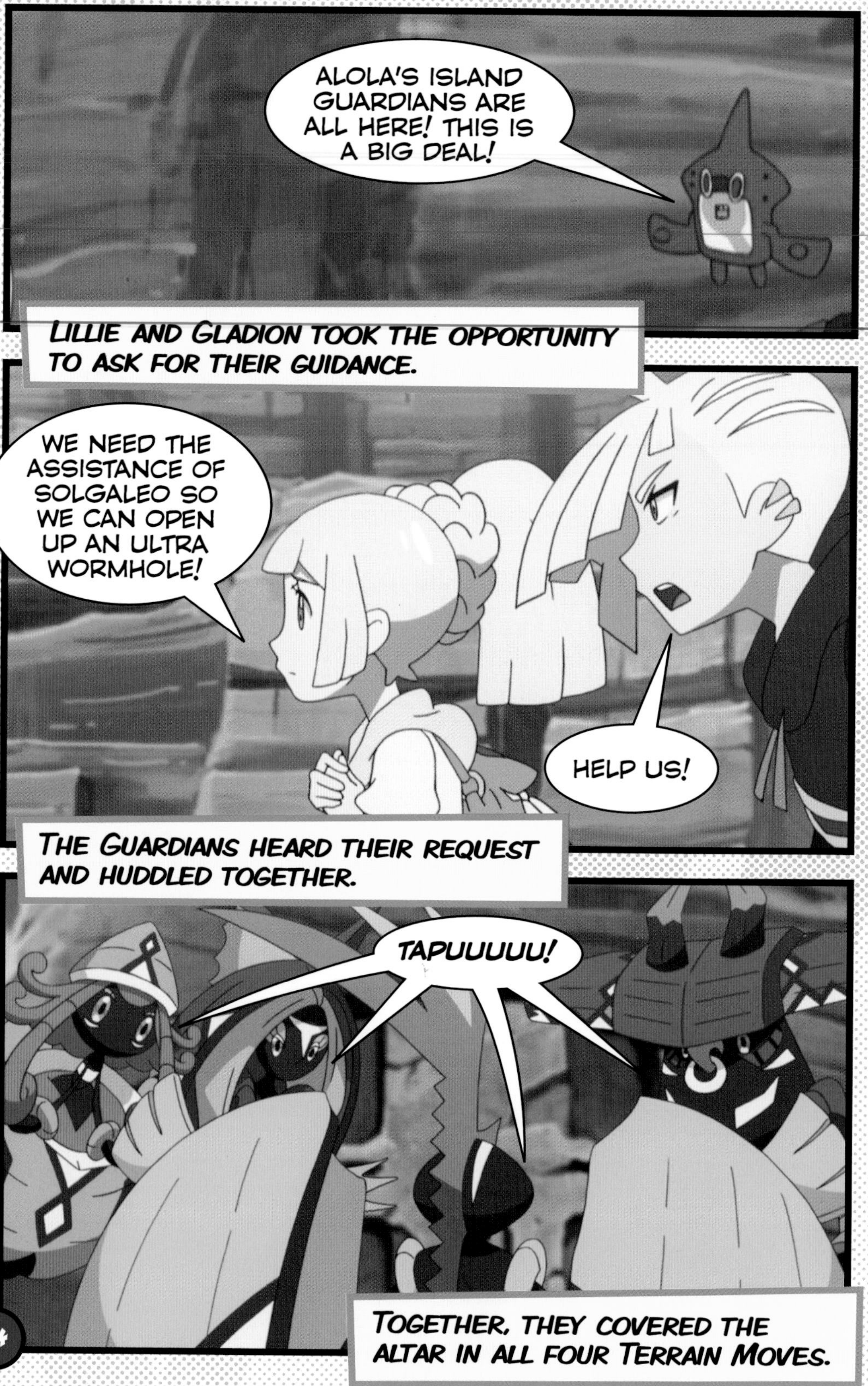
ALOLA'S ISLAND GUARDIANS ARE ALL HERE! THIS IS A BIG DEAL!
LILLIE AND GLADION TOOK THE OPPORTUNITY TO ASK FOR THEIR GUIDANCE.
WE NEED THE ASSISTANCE OF SOLGALEO SO WE CAN OPEN UP AN ULTRA WORMHOLE!
HELP US!
THE GUARDIANS HEARD THEIR REQUEST AND HUDDLED TOGETHER.
TAPUUUUU!
TOGETHER, THEY COVERED THE ALTAR IN ALL FOUR TERRAIN MOVES.

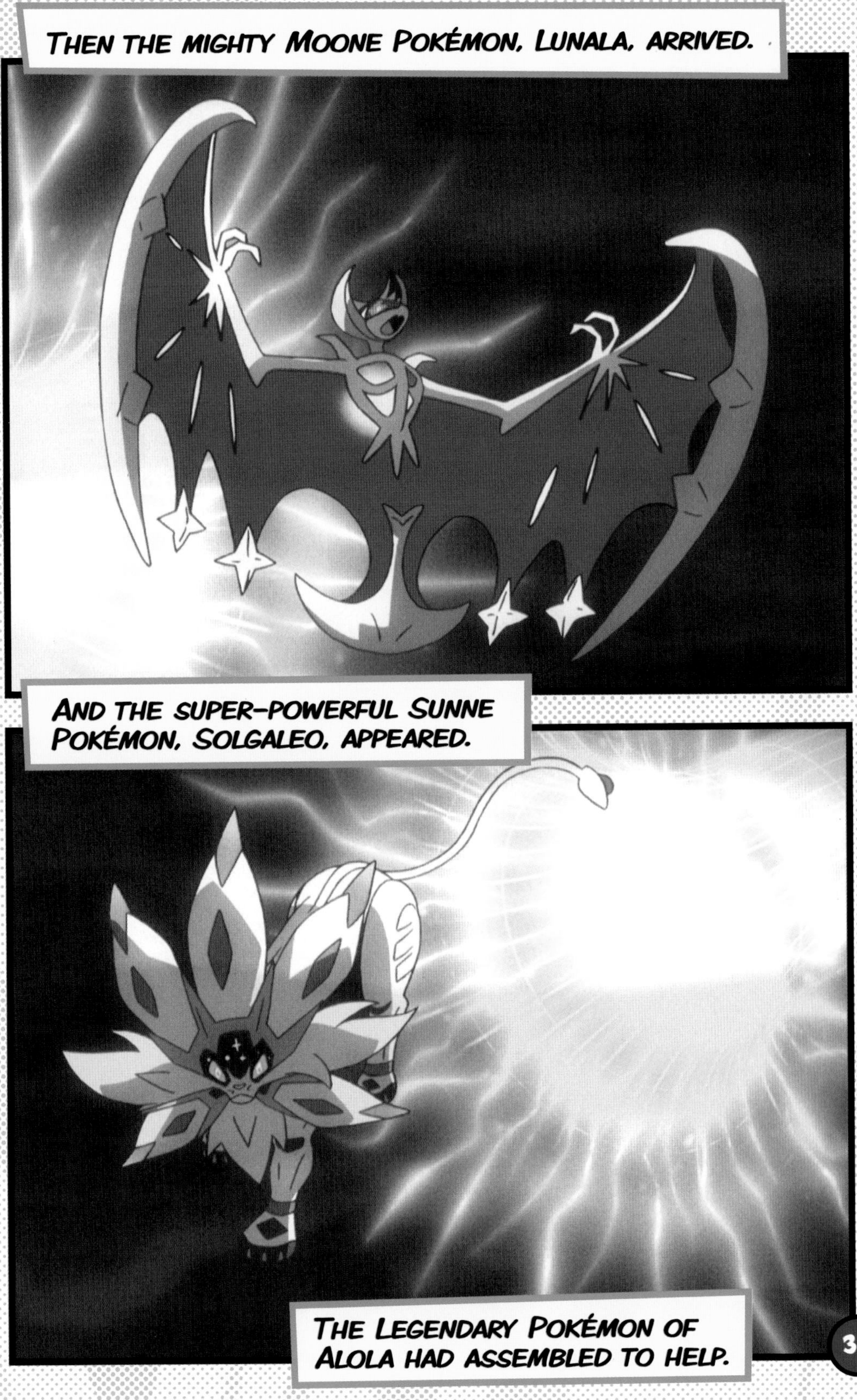
Then the mighty Moone Pokémon, Lunala, arrived.
And the super-powerful Sunne Pokémon, Solgaleo, appeared.
The Legendary Pokémon of Alola had assembled to help.

NEXT, NEBBY REAPPEARED! BUT IT WAS IN A FLASHBACK TO THE PAST THAT PLAYED LIKE A MOVIE. THE ISLAND GUARDIANS WANTED TO SHOW ASH THE REAL STORY OF HIS POKÉMON PAL.

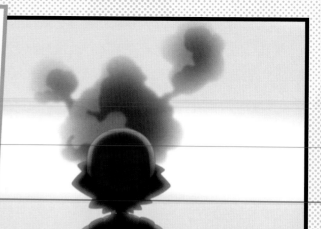

MANY MOONS AGO, SOLGALEO AND LUNALA MET WITH . . .

. . . THE FOUR ISLAND GUARDIANS. THEY GATHERED IN THIS VERY SPOT AT THE ALTAR OF THE SUNNE WITH NEBBY.

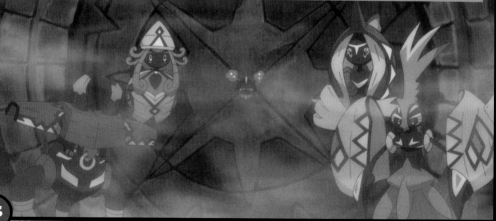

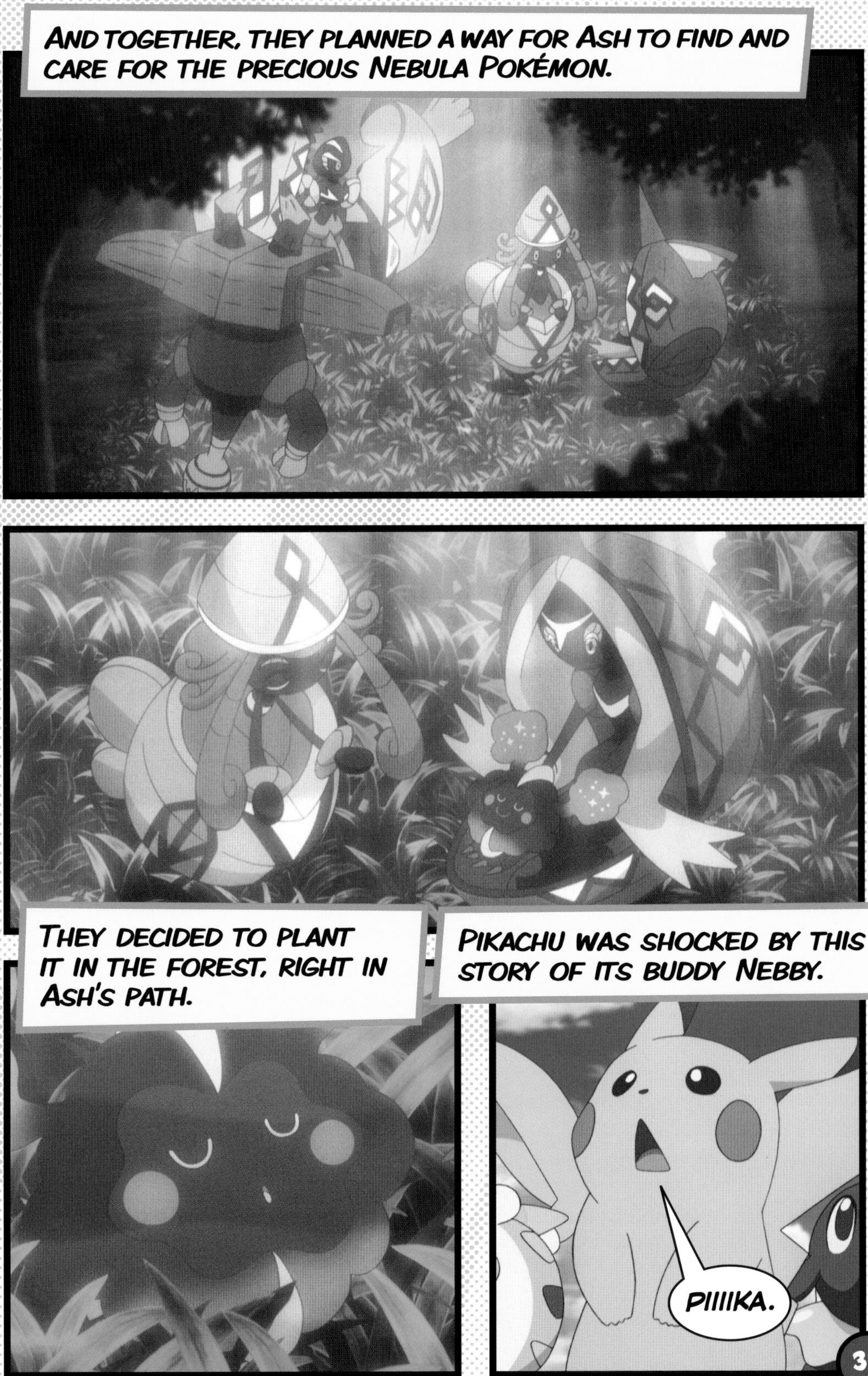
AND TOGETHER, THEY PLANNED A WAY FOR ASH TO FIND AND CARE FOR THE PRECIOUS NEBULA POKÉMON.
THEY DECIDED TO PLANT IT IN THE FOREST, RIGHT IN ASH'S PATH.
PIKACHU WAS SHOCKED BY THIS STORY OF ITS BUDDY NEBBY.
PIIIKA.

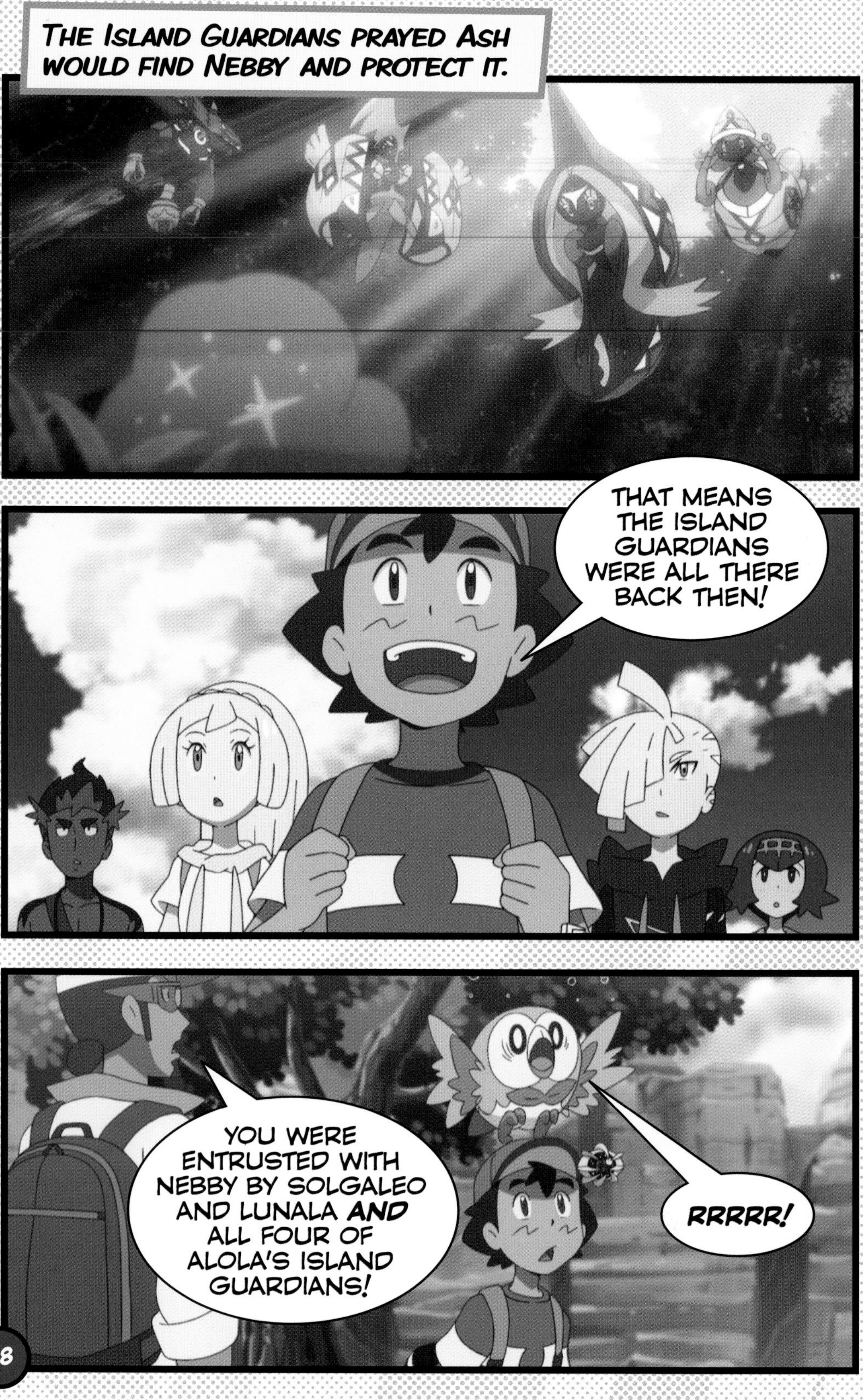
THE ISLAND GUARDIANS PRAYED ASH WOULD FIND NEBBY AND PROTECT IT.
THAT MEANS THE ISLAND GUARDIANS WERE ALL THERE BACK THEN!
YOU WERE ENTRUSTED WITH NEBBY BY SOLGALEO AND LUNALA AND ALL FOUR OF ALOLA'S ISLAND GUARDIANS!
RRRRR!

ASH KNEW JUST WHAT TO DO THEN.

HERE'S NEBBY. IT'S NOT MOVING OR ANYTHING. IT MAKES NO NOISE.

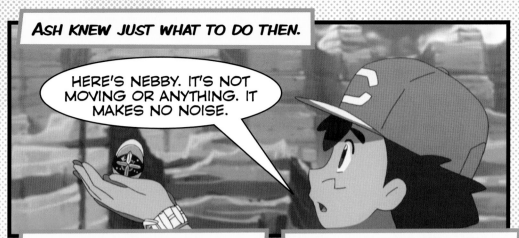

TAPU KOKO APPROACHED THE STILL NEBULA POKÉMON . . .

ALL IT DOES IS FLOAT AROUND.

IT FLOATED ALL THE WAY UP TO THE TOP OF THE ALTAR OF THE SUNNE . . .

UP TO TAPU FINI AND TAPU LELE.

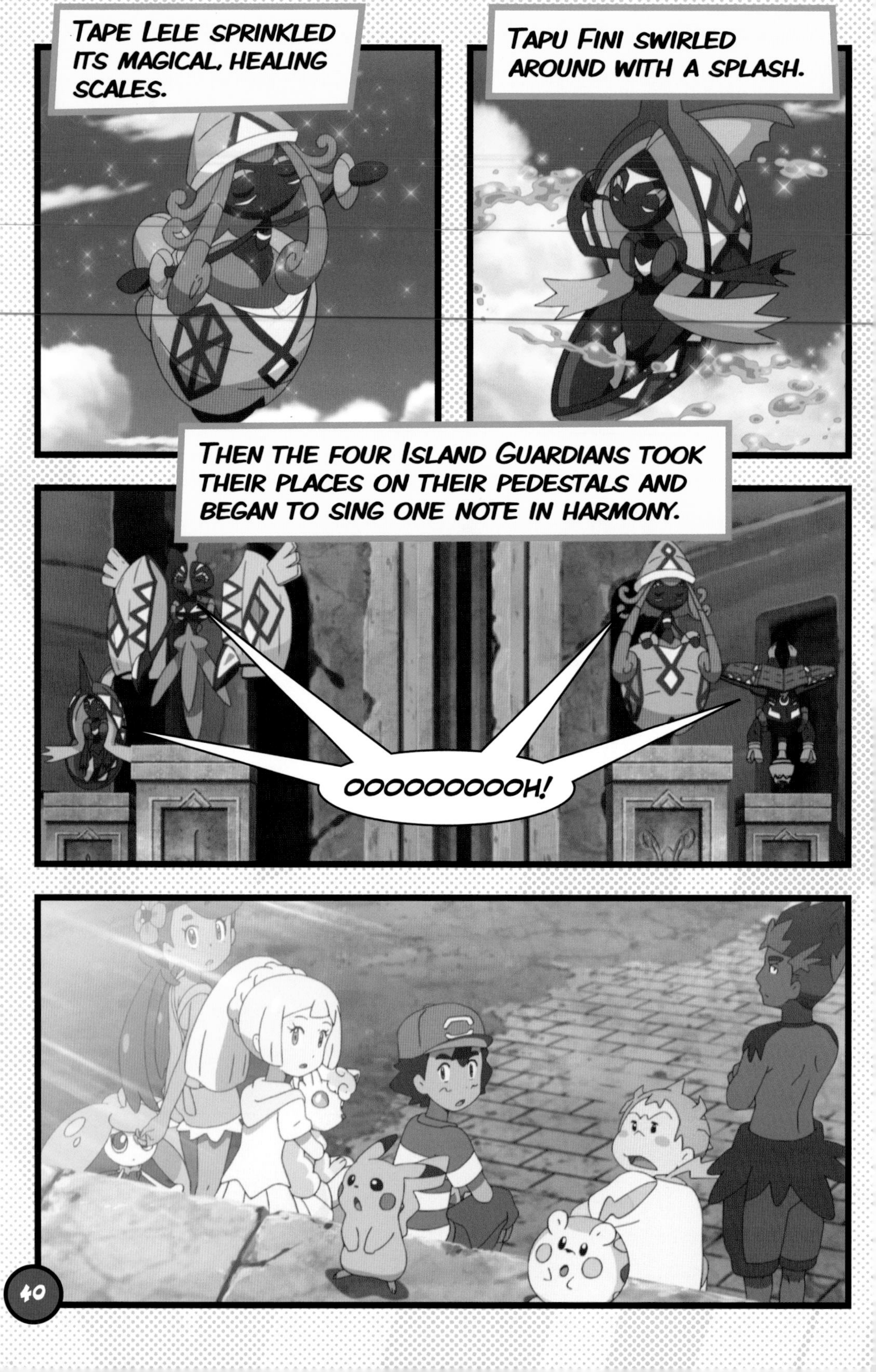
TAPE LELE SPRINKLED ITS MAGICAL, HEALING SCALES.
TAPU FINI SWIRLED AROUND WITH A SPLASH.
THEN THE FOUR ISLAND GUARDIANS TOOK THEIR PLACES ON THEIR PEDESTALS AND BEGAN TO SING ONE NOTE IN HARMONY.
OOOOOOOOOH!

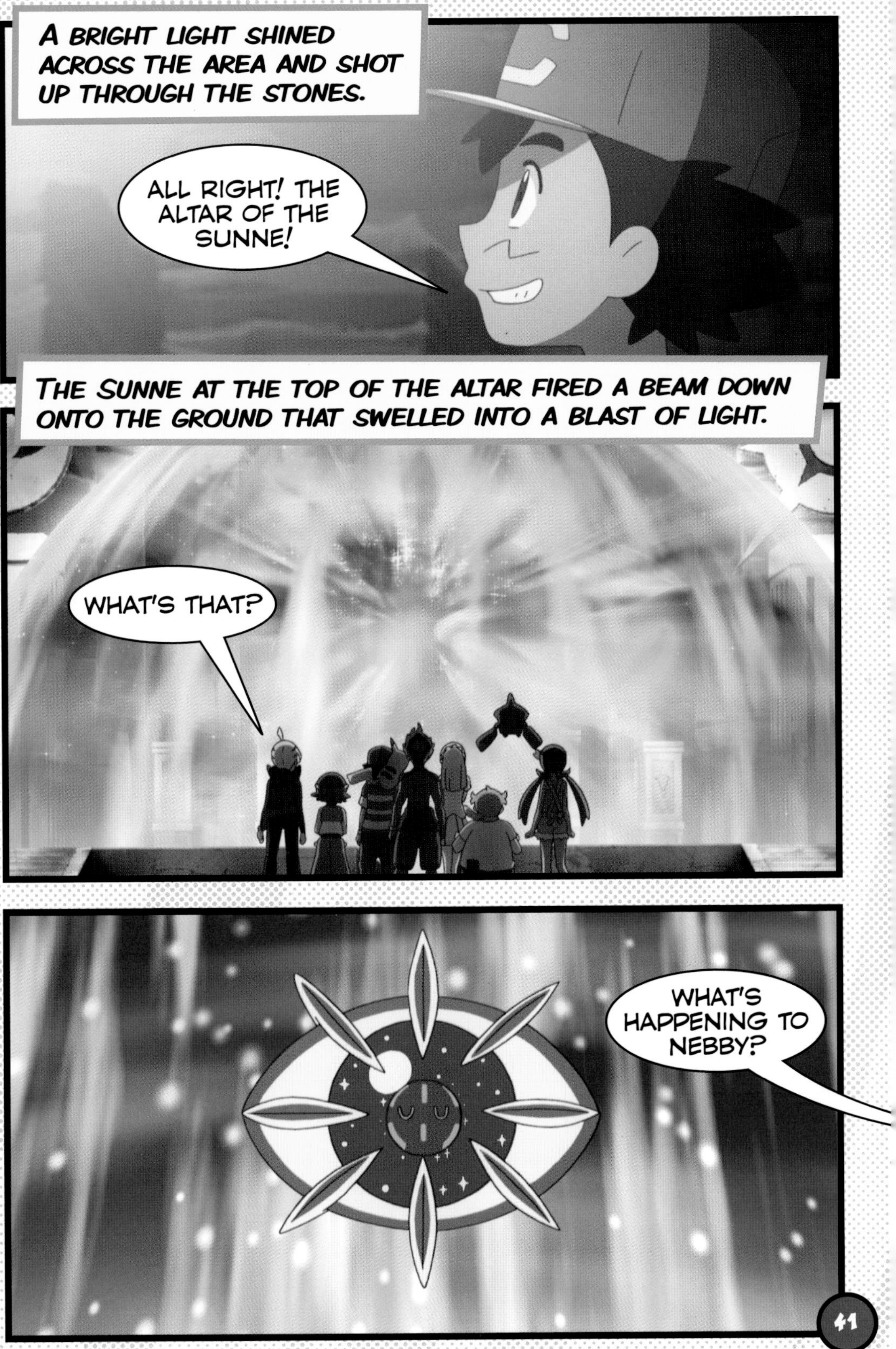
A BRIGHT LIGHT SHINED ACROSS THE AREA AND SHOT UP THROUGH THE STONES.
ALL RIGHT! THE ALTAR OF THE SUNNE!
THE SUNNE AT THE TOP OF THE ALTAR FIRED A BEAM DOWN ONTO THE GROUND THAT SWELLED INTO A BLAST OF LIGHT.
WHAT'S THAT?
WHAT'S HAPPENING TO NEBBY?

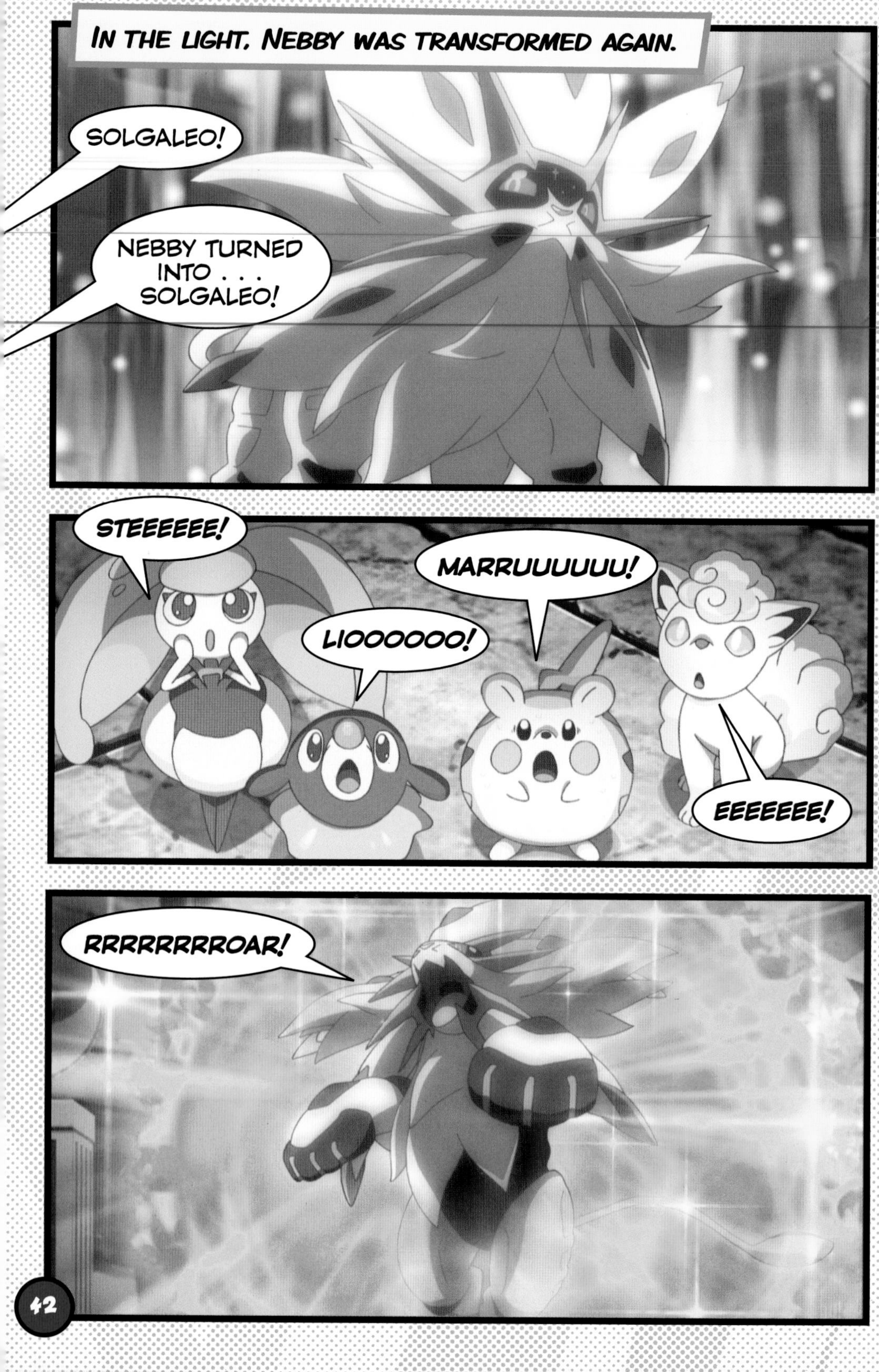
IN THE LIGHT, NEBBY WAS TRANSFORMED AGAIN.
SOLGALEO!
NEBBY TURNED INTO . . . SOLGALEO!
STEEEEEE!
LIOOOOOO!
MARRUUUUUU!
EEEEEEE!
RRRRRRRROAR!

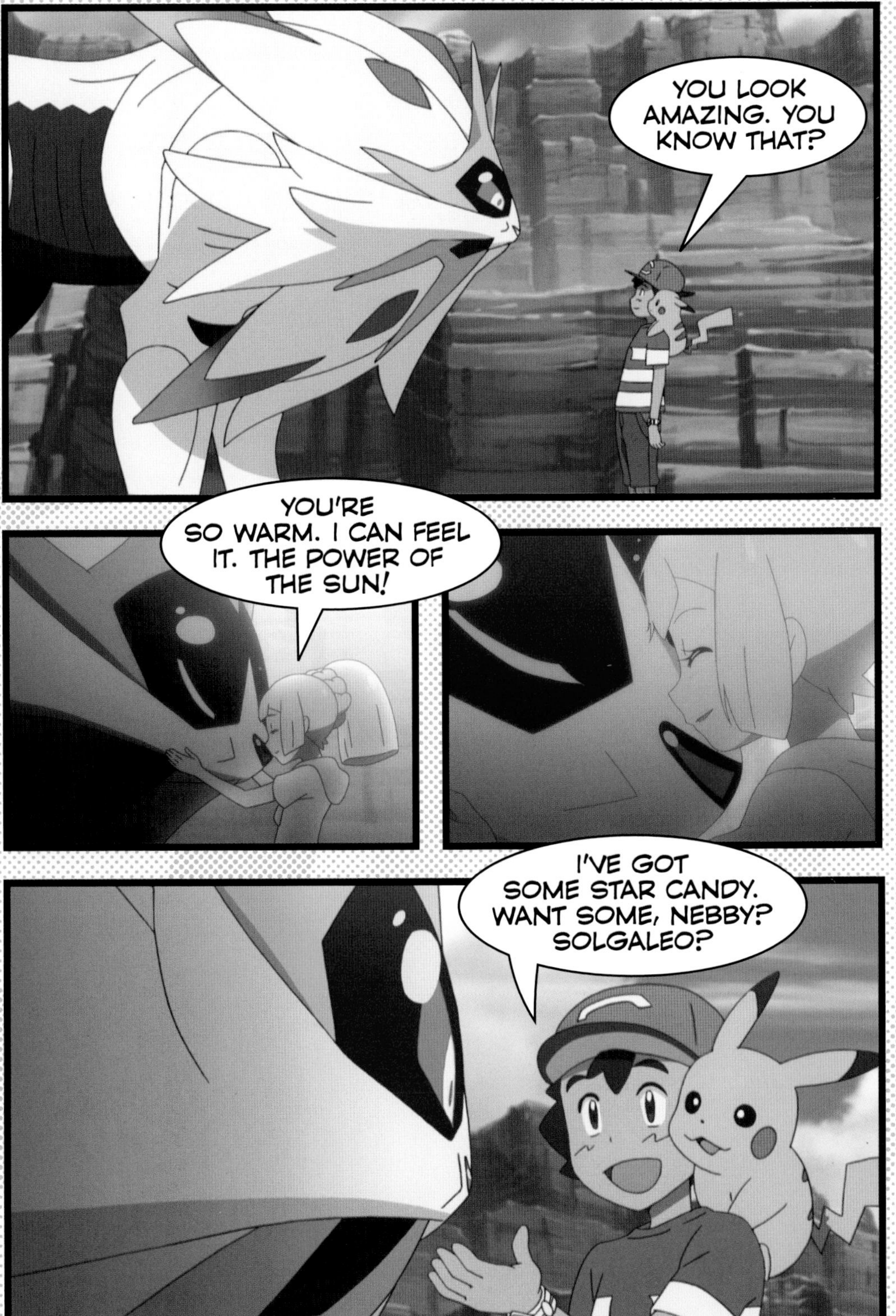
YOU LOOK AMAZING. YOU KNOW THAT?
YOU'RE SO WARM. I CAN FEEL IT. THE POWER OF THE SUN!
I'VE GOT SOME STAR CANDY. WANT SOME, NEBBY? SOLGALEO?

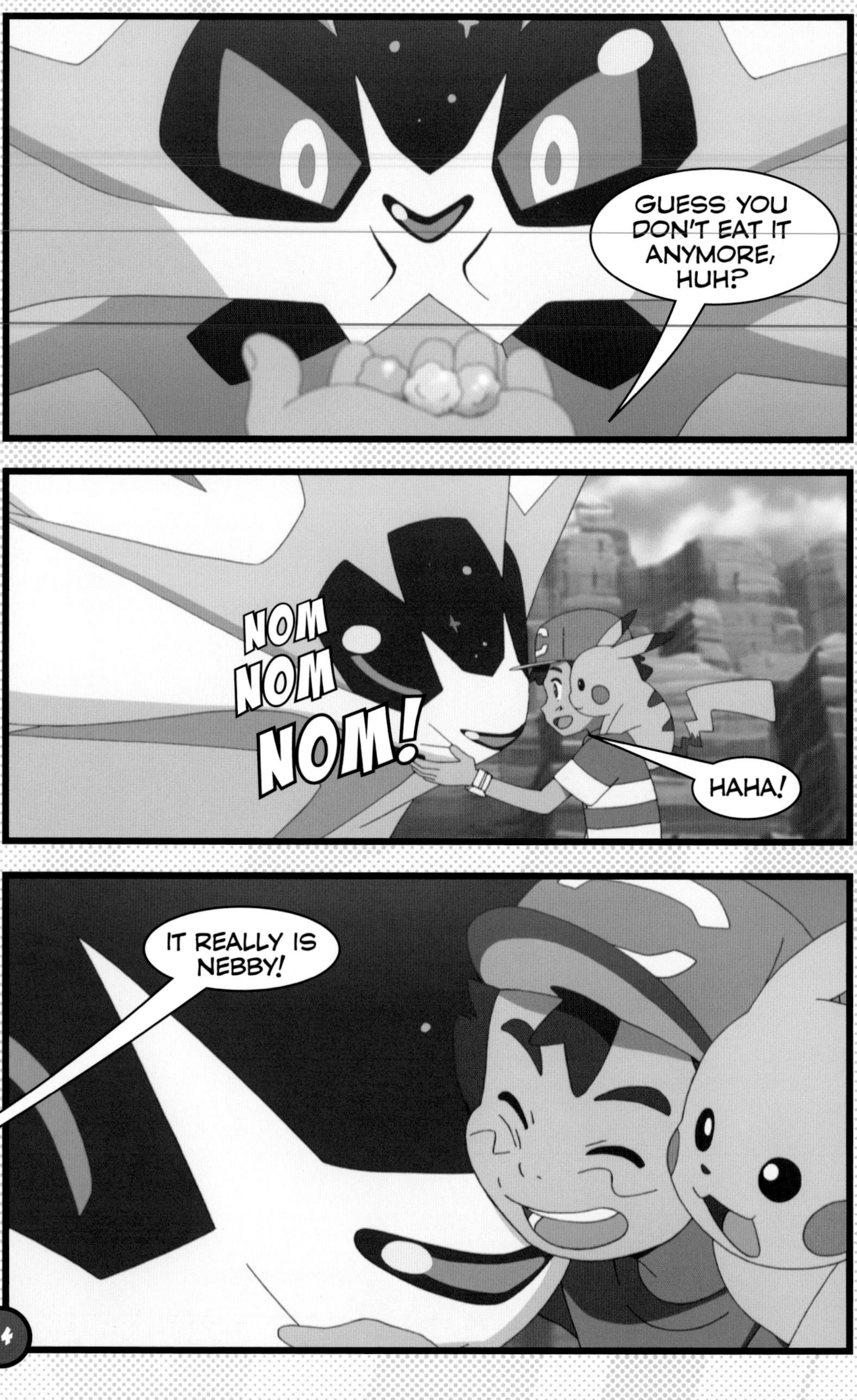
GUESS YOU DON'T EAT IT ANYMORE, HUH?
NOM NOM NOM!
HAHA!
IT REALLY IS NEBBY!

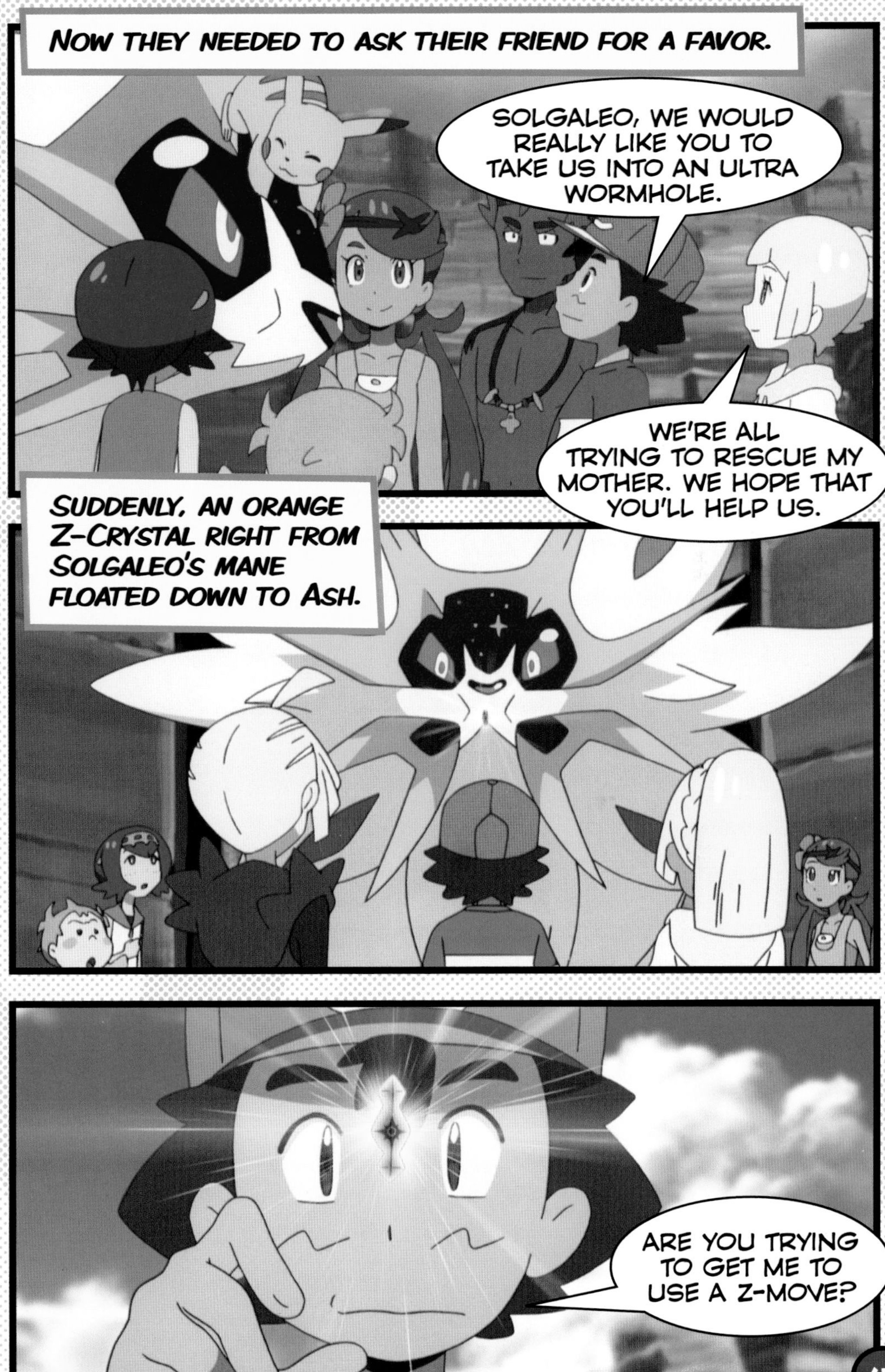
NOW THEY NEEDED TO ASK THEIR FRIEND FOR A FAVOR.
SOLGALEO, WE WOULD REALLY LIKE YOU TO TAKE US INTO AN ULTRA WORMHOLE.
WE'RE ALL TRYING TO RESCUE MY MOTHER. WE HOPE THAT YOU'LL HELP US.
SUDDENLY, AN ORANGE Z-CRYSTAL RIGHT FROM SOLGALEO'S MANE FLOATED DOWN TO ASH.
ARE YOU TRYING TO GET ME TO USE A Z-MOVE?

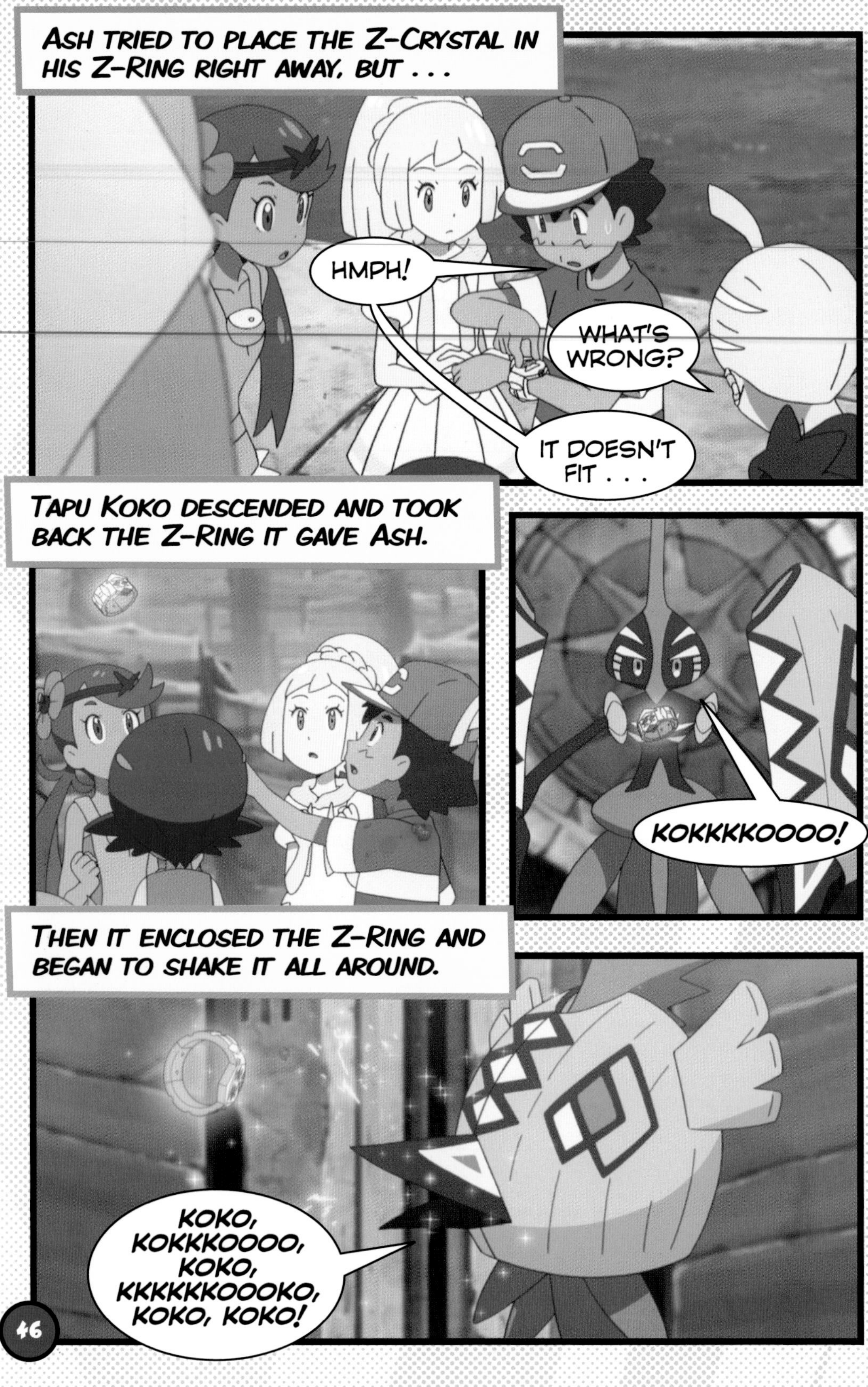
ASH TRIED TO PLACE THE Z-CRYSTAL IN HIS Z-RING RIGHT AWAY, BUT . . .
HMPH!
WHAT'S WRONG?
IT DOESN'T FIT . . .
TAPU KOKO DESCENDED AND TOOK BACK THE Z-RING IT GAVE ASH.
KOKKKKOOOO!
THEN IT ENCLOSED THE Z-RING AND BEGAN TO SHAKE IT ALL AROUND.
KOKO, KOKKKOOOO, KOKO, KKKKKKOOOKO, KOKO, KOKO!

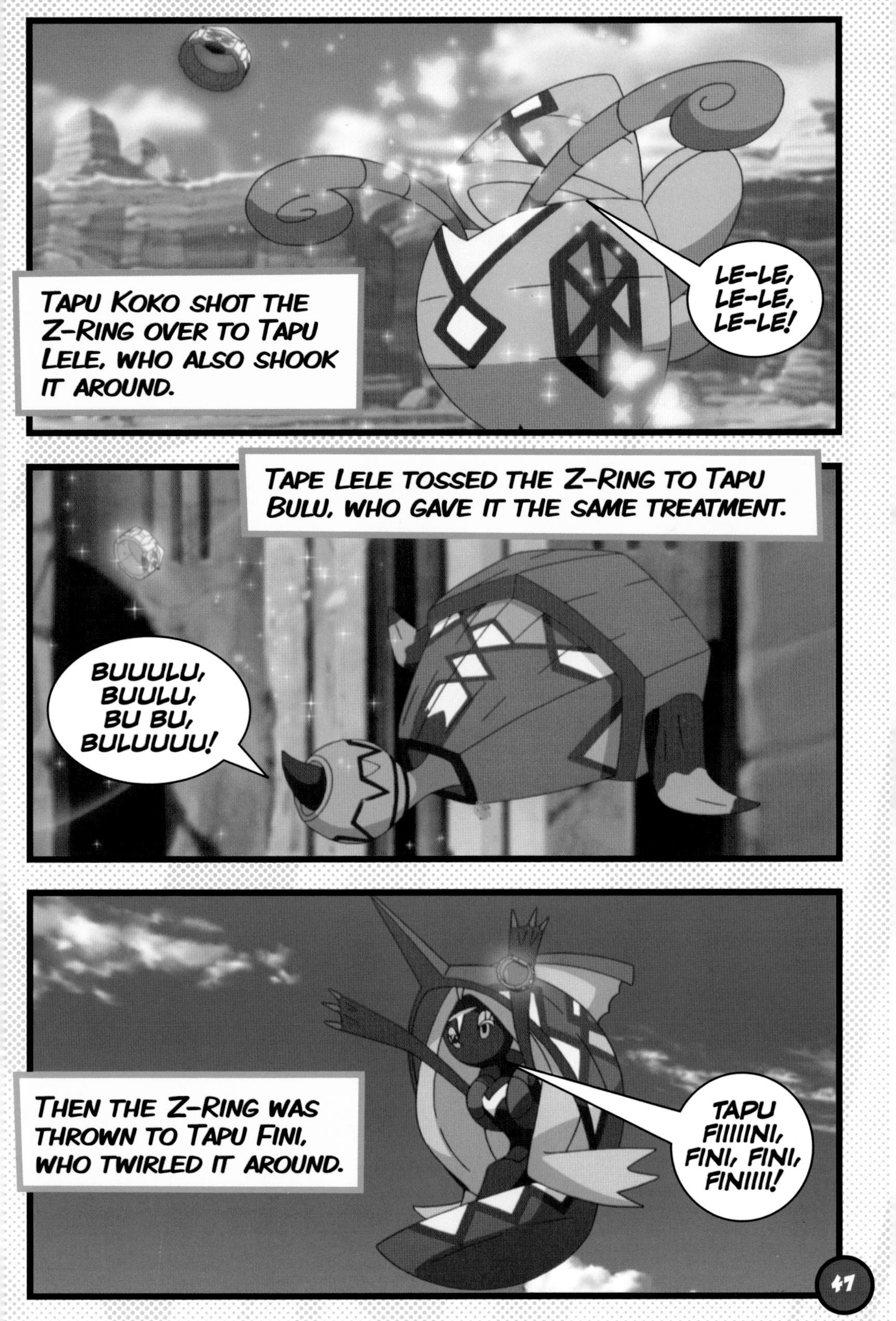
TAPU KOKO SHOT THE Z-RING OVER TO TAPU LELE, WHO ALSO SHOOK IT AROUND.
LE-LE, LE-LE, LE-LE!
TAPE LELE TOSSED THE Z-RING TO TAPU BULU, WHO GAVE IT THE SAME TREATMENT.
BUUULU, BUULU, BU BU, BULUUUU!
THEN THE Z-RING WAS THROWN TO TAPU FINI, WHO TWIRLED IT AROUND.
TAPU FIIIIINI, FINI, FINI, FINIIIII!

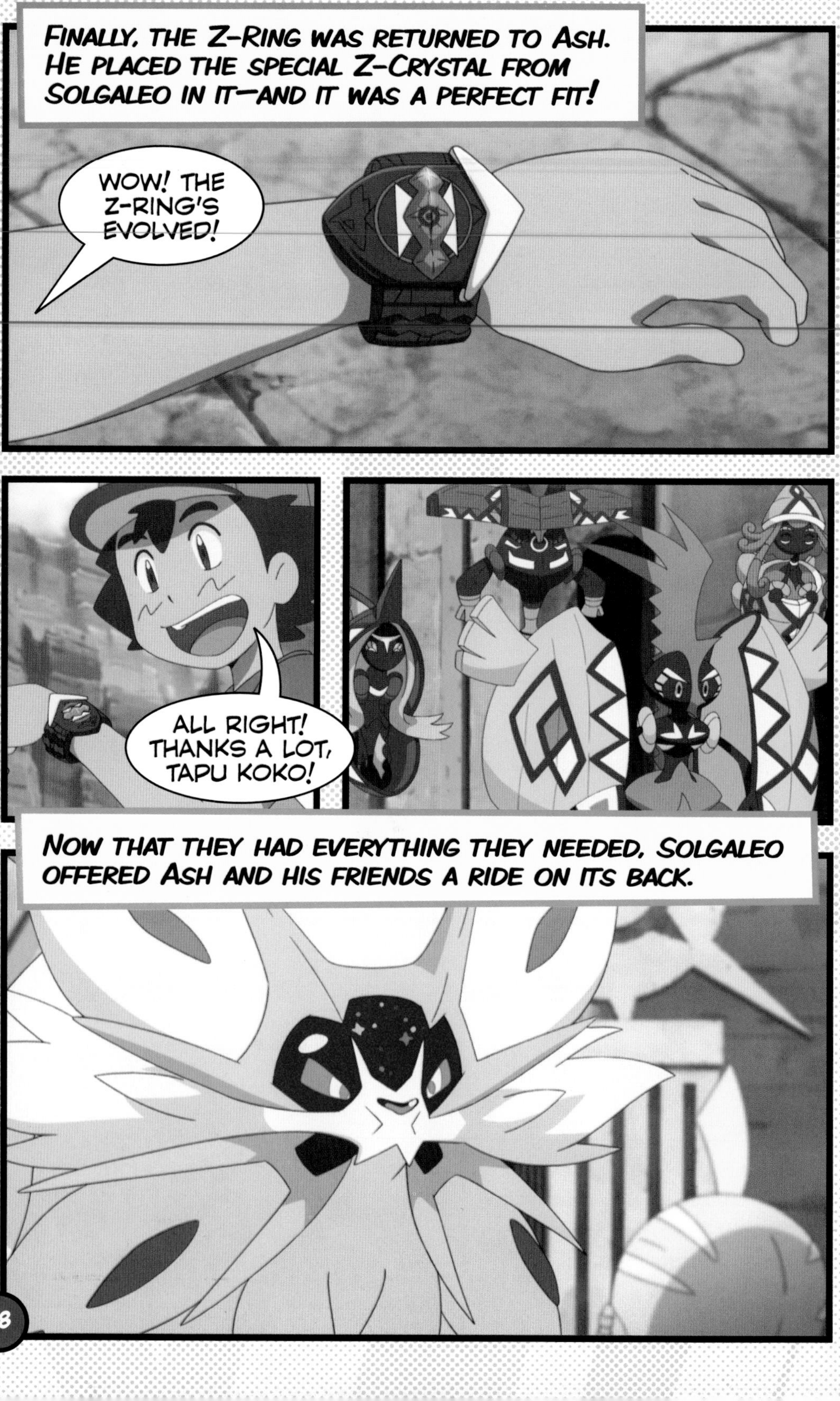

FINALLY, THE Z-RING WAS RETURNED TO ASH. HE PLACED THE SPECIAL Z-CRYSTAL FROM SOLGALEO IN IT—AND IT WAS A PERFECT FIT!
WOW! THE Z-RING'S EVOLVED!
ALL RIGHT! THANKS A LOT, TAPU KOKO!
NOW THAT THEY HAD EVERYTHING THEY NEEDED, SOLGALEO OFFERED ASH AND HIS FRIENDS A RIDE ON ITS BACK.

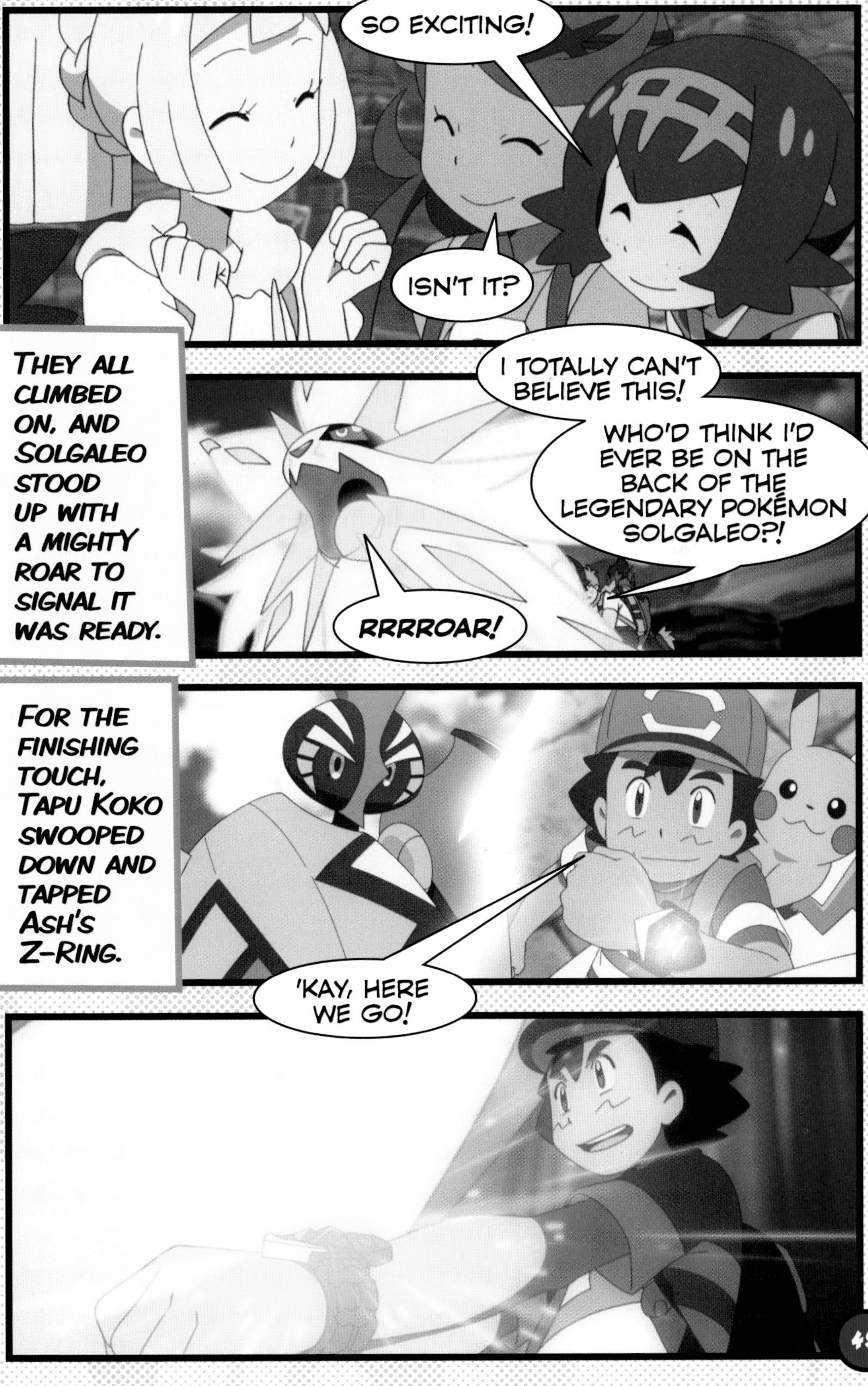
SO EXCITING!
ISN'T IT?
THEY ALL CLIMBED ON, AND SOLGALEO STOOD UP WITH A MIGHTY ROAR TO SIGNAL IT WAS READY.
I TOTALLY CAN'T BELIEVE THIS!
WHO'D THINK I'D EVER BE ON THE BACK OF THE LEGENDARY POKÉMON SOLGALEO?!
RRRROAR!
FOR THE FINISHING TOUCH, TAPU KOKO SWOOPED DOWN AND TAPPED ASH'S Z-RING.
'KAY, HERE WE GO!

THEN TAPU KOKO AND ASH BEGAN TO MOVE IN SYNC TO CREATE A Z-MOVE STRONG ENOUGH TO OPEN AN ULTRA WORMHOLE.

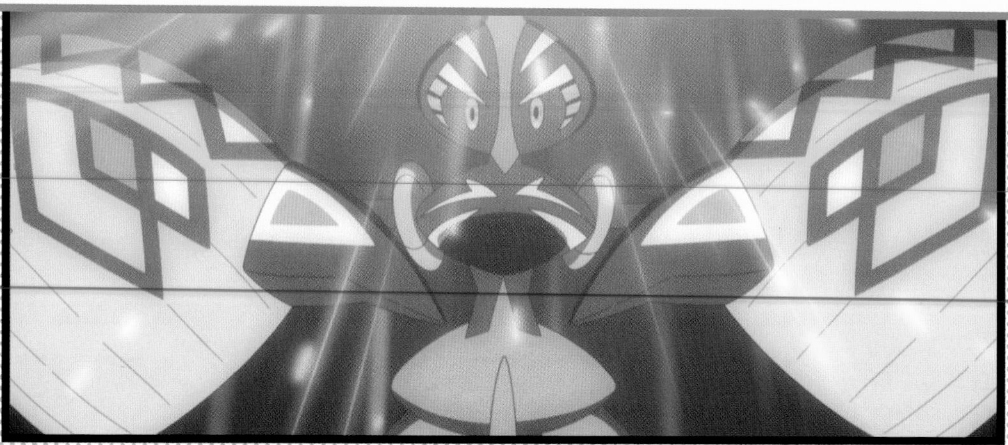

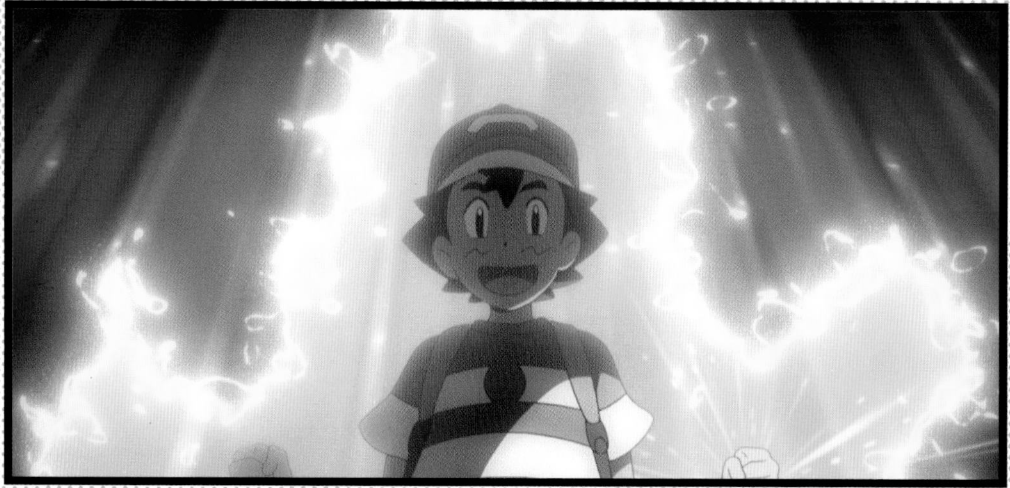

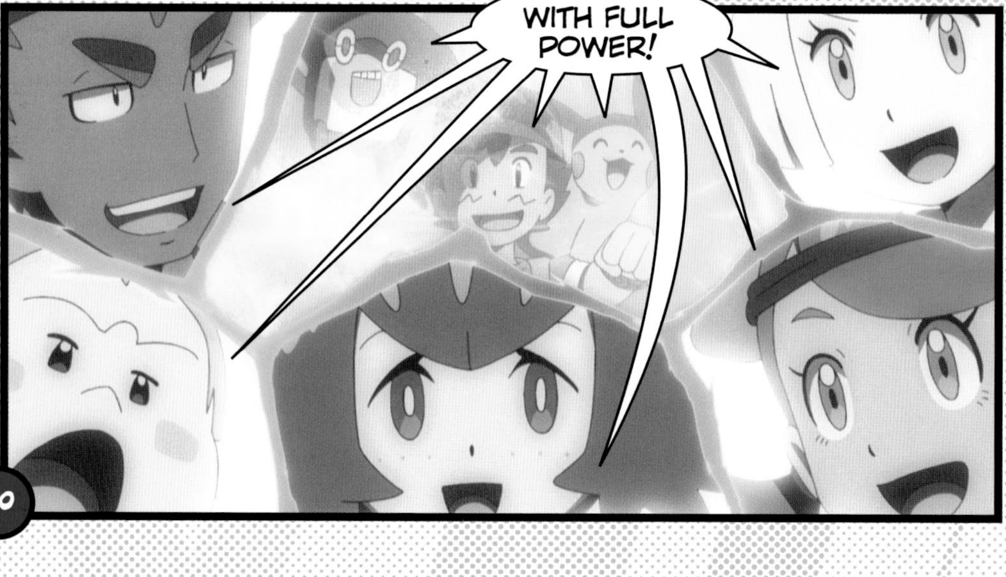
WITH FULL POWER!

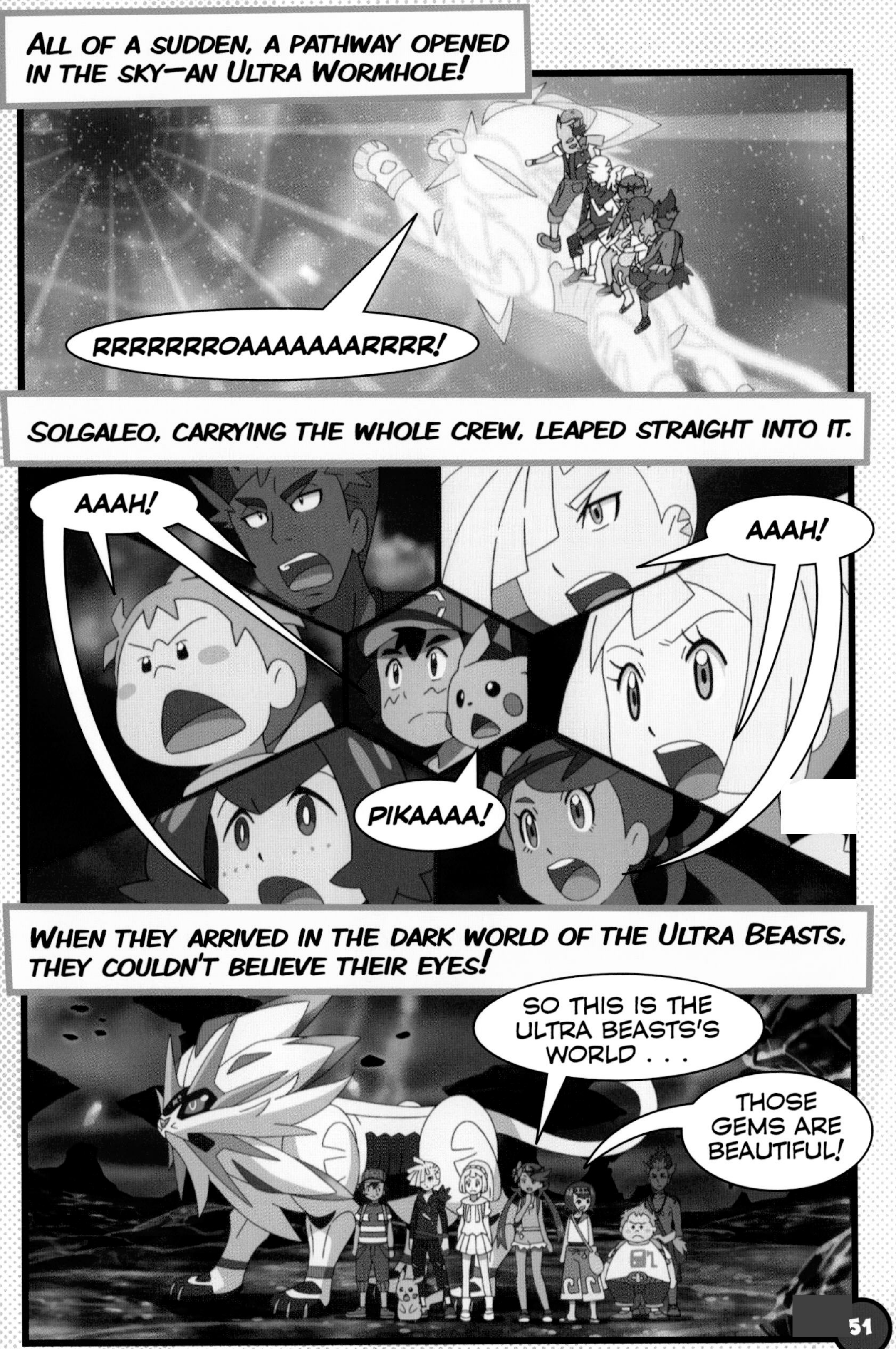

ALL OF A SUDDEN, A PATHWAY OPENED IN THE SKY—AN ULTRA WORMHOLE!
RRRRRRROAAAAAAARRRR!
SOLGALEO, CARRYING THE WHOLE CREW, LEAPED STRAIGHT INTO IT.
AAAH!
AAAH!
PIKAAAA!
WHEN THEY ARRIVED IN THE DARK WORLD OF THE ULTRA BEASTS, THEY COULDN'T BELIEVE THEIR EYES!
SO THIS IS THE ULTRA BEASTS'S WORLD . . .
THOSE GEMS ARE BEAUTIFUL!

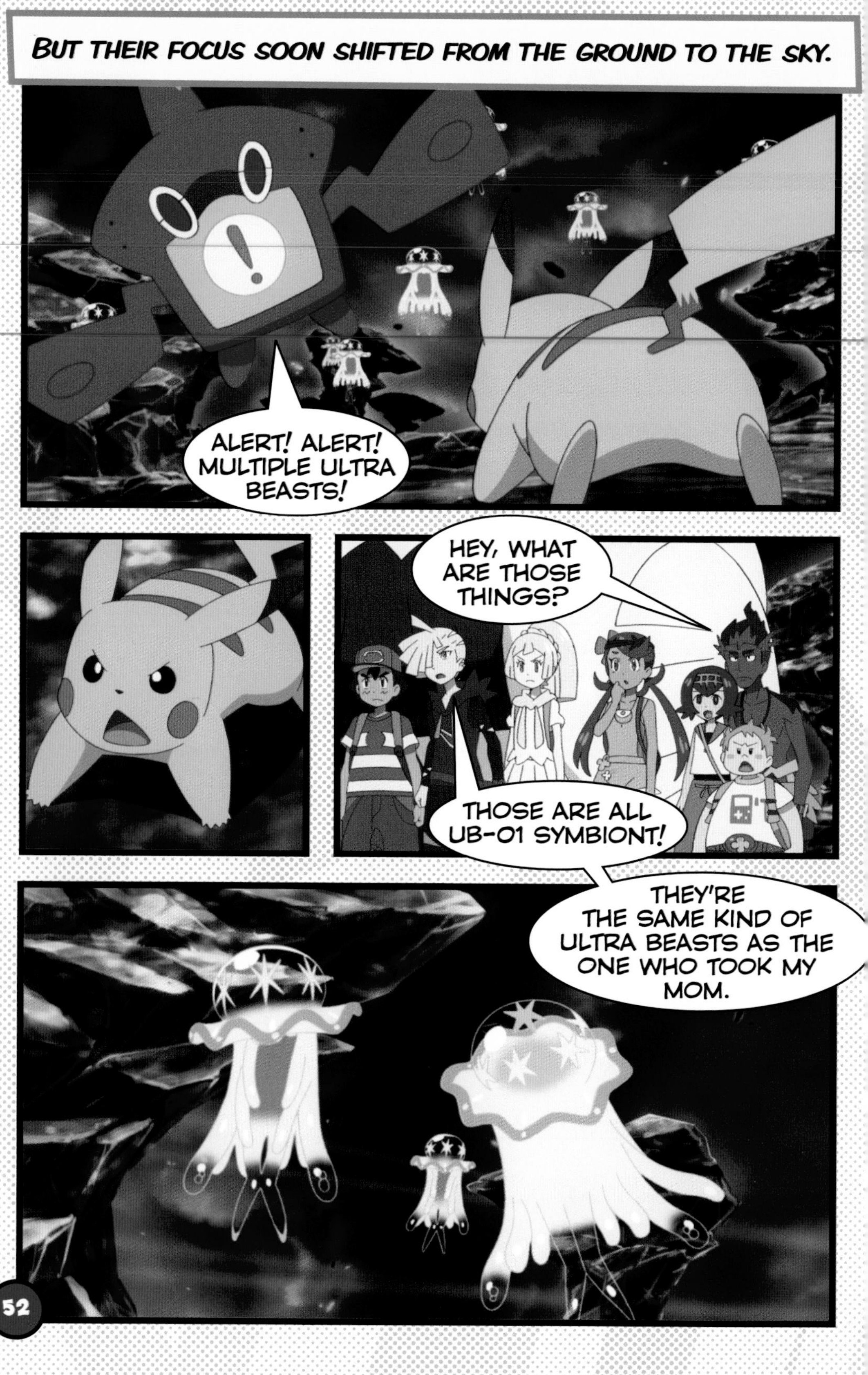

BUT THEIR FOCUS SOON SHIFTED FROM THE GROUND TO THE SKY.
ALERT! ALERT! MULTIPLE ULTRA BEASTS!
HEY, WHAT ARE THOSE THINGS?
THOSE ARE ALL UB-01 SYMBIONT!
THEY'RE THE SAME KIND OF ULTRA BEASTS AS THE ONE WHO TOOK MY MOM.

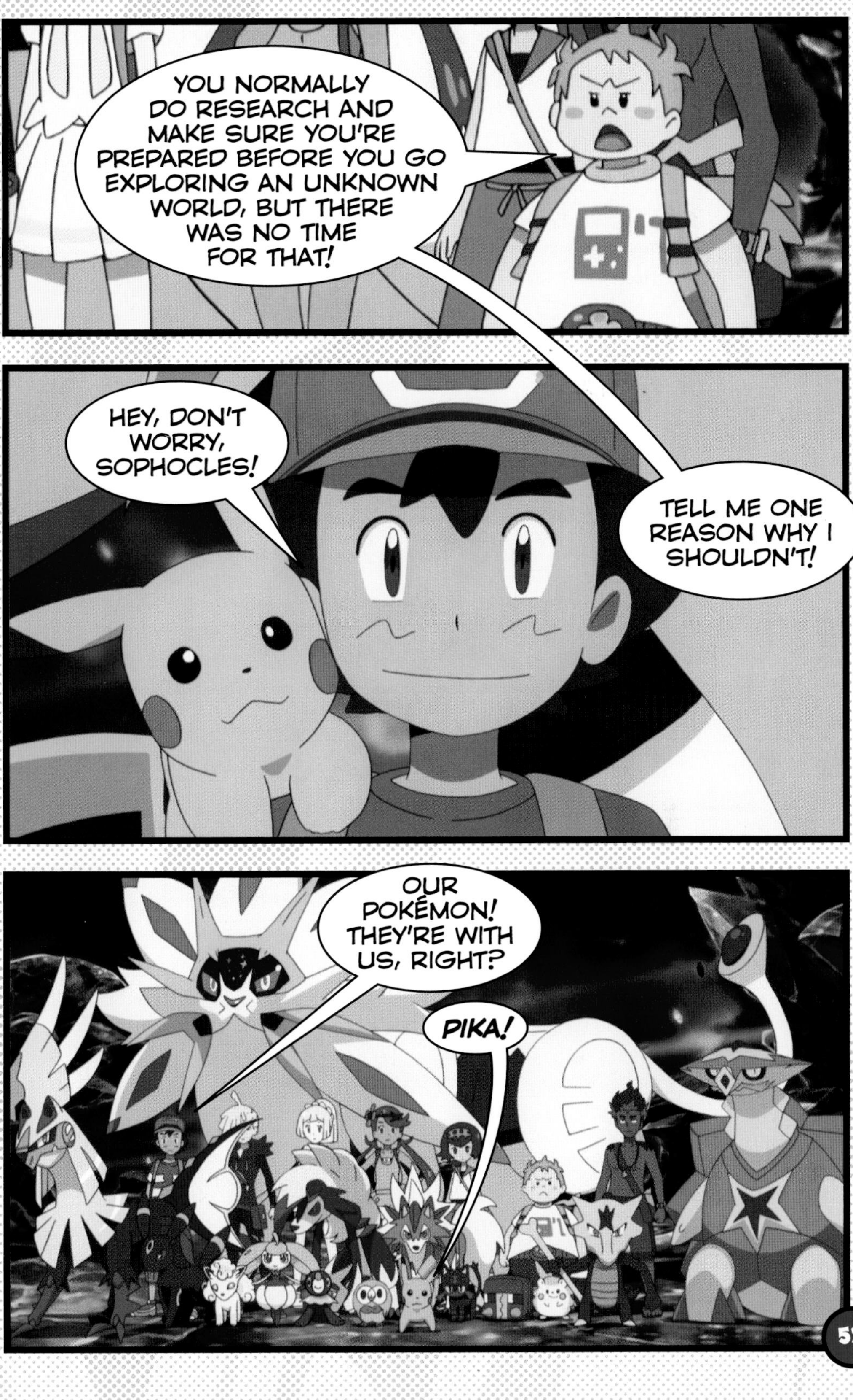
YOU NORMALLY DO RESEARCH AND MAKE SURE YOU'RE PREPARED BEFORE YOU GO EXPLORING AN UNKNOWN WORLD, BUT THERE WAS NO TIME FOR THAT!
HEY, DON'T WORRY, SOPHOCLES!
TELL ME ONE REASON WHY I SHOULDN'T!
OUR POKÉMON! THEY'RE WITH US, RIGHT?
PIKA!

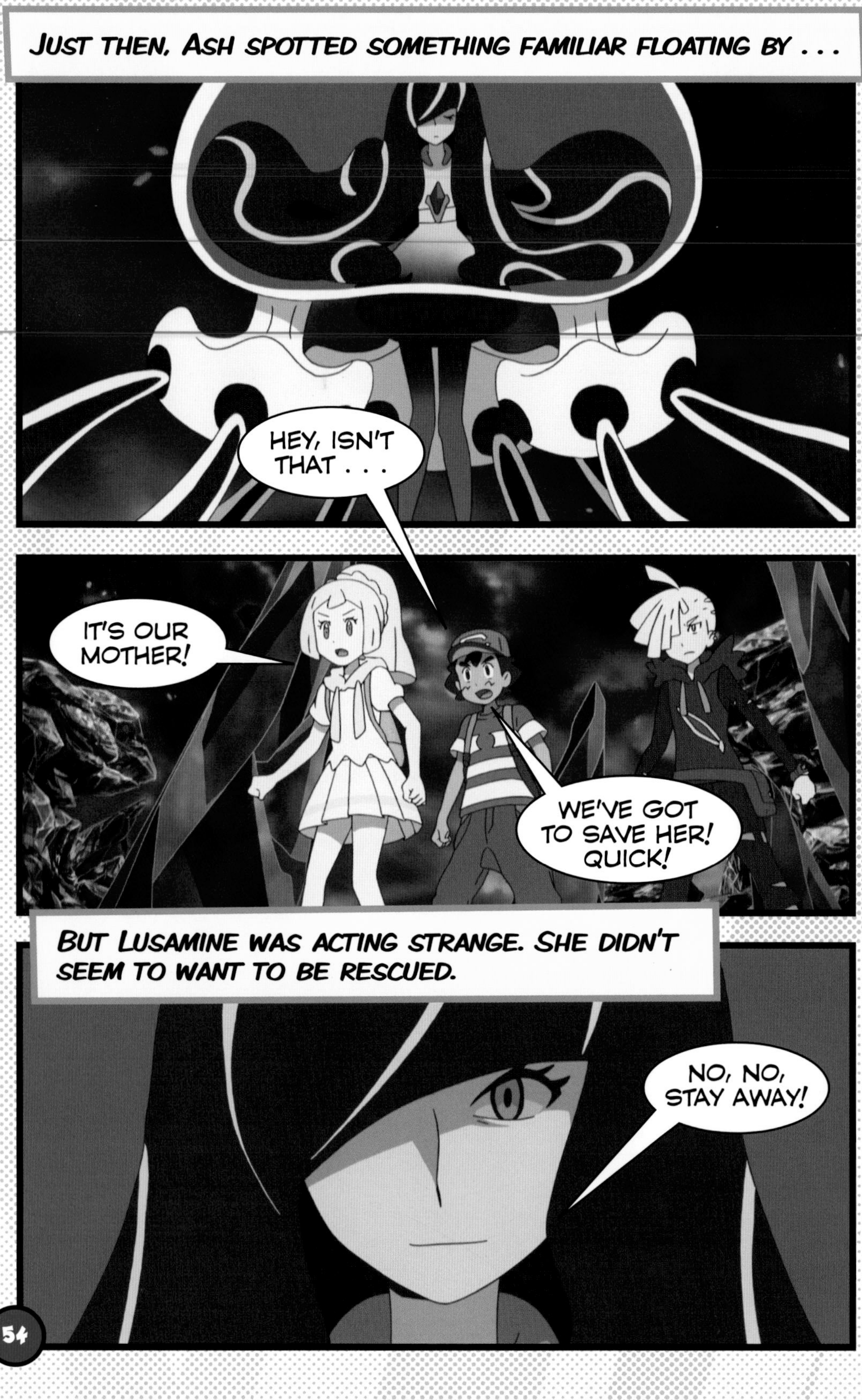
JUST THEN, ASH SPOTTED SOMETHING FAMILIAR FLOATING BY . . .
HEY, ISN'T THAT . . .
IT'S OUR MOTHER!
WE'VE GOT TO SAVE HER! QUICK!
BUT LUSAMINE WAS ACTING STRANGE. SHE DIDN'T SEEM TO WANT TO BE RESCUED.
NO, NO, STAY AWAY!

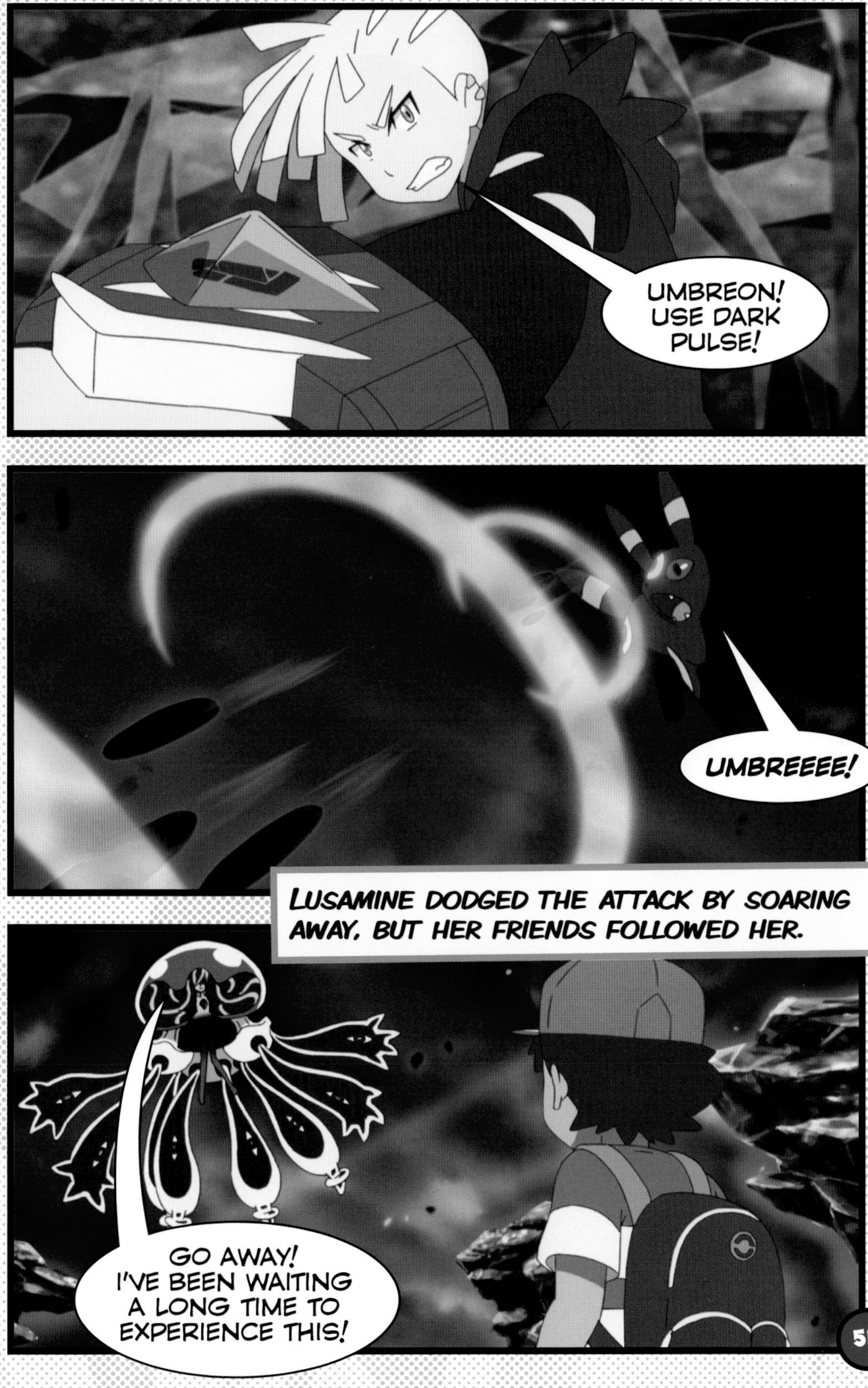
UMBREON! USE DARK PULSE!
UMBREEEE!
LUSAMINE DODGED THE ATTACK BY SOARING AWAY, BUT HER FRIENDS FOLLOWED HER.
GO AWAY! I'VE BEEN WAITING A LONG TIME TO EXPERIENCE THIS!

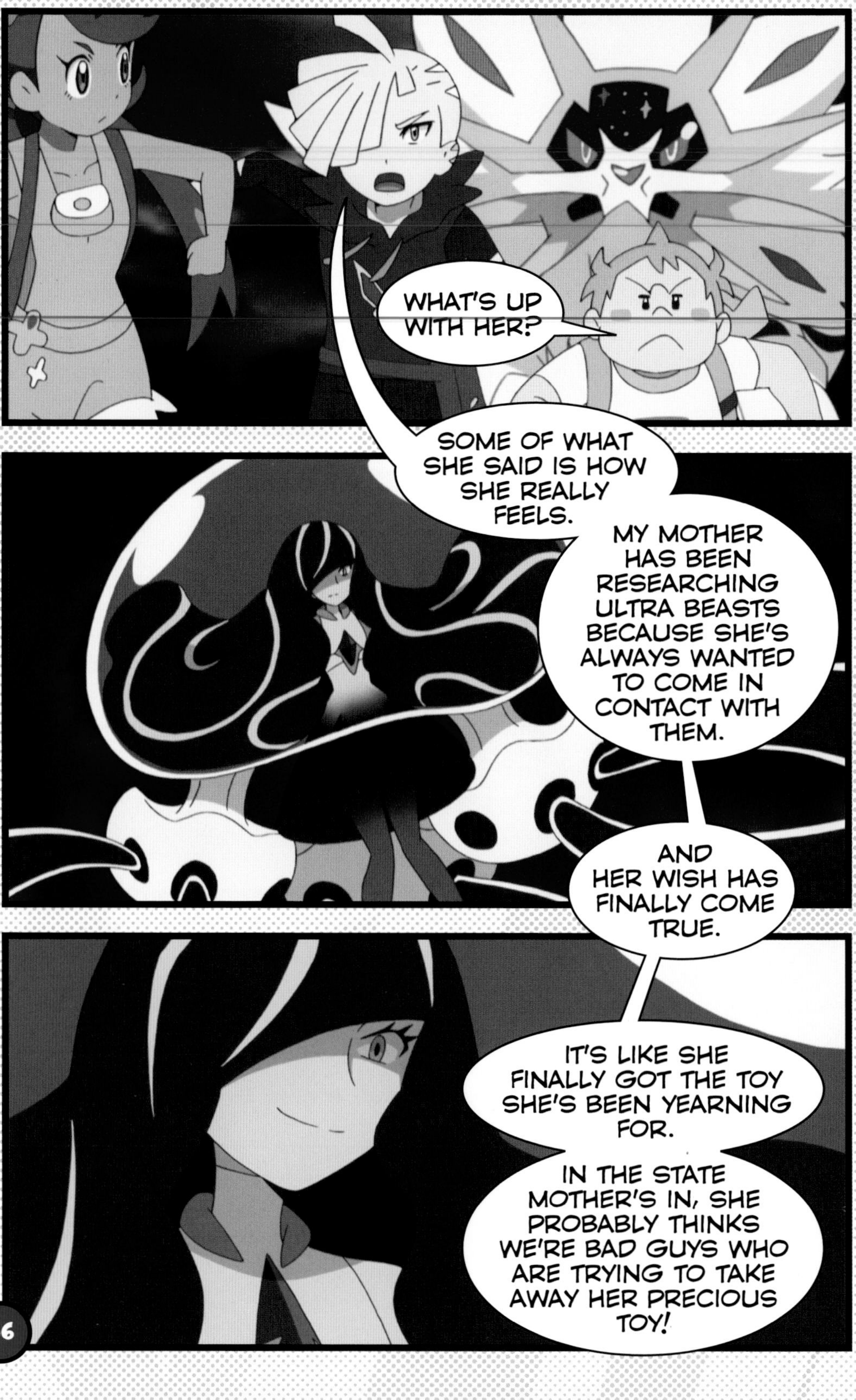
WHAT'S UP WITH HER?
SOME OF WHAT SHE SAID IS HOW SHE REALLY FEELS.
MY MOTHER HAS BEEN RESEARCHING ULTRA BEASTS BECAUSE SHE'S ALWAYS WANTED TO COME IN CONTACT WITH THEM.
AND HER WISH HAS FINALLY COME TRUE.
IT'S LIKE SHE FINALLY GOT THE TOY SHE'S BEEN YEARNING FOR.
IN THE STATE MOTHER'S IN, SHE PROBABLY THINKS WE'RE BAD GUYS WHO ARE TRYING TO TAKE AWAY HER PRECIOUS TOY!

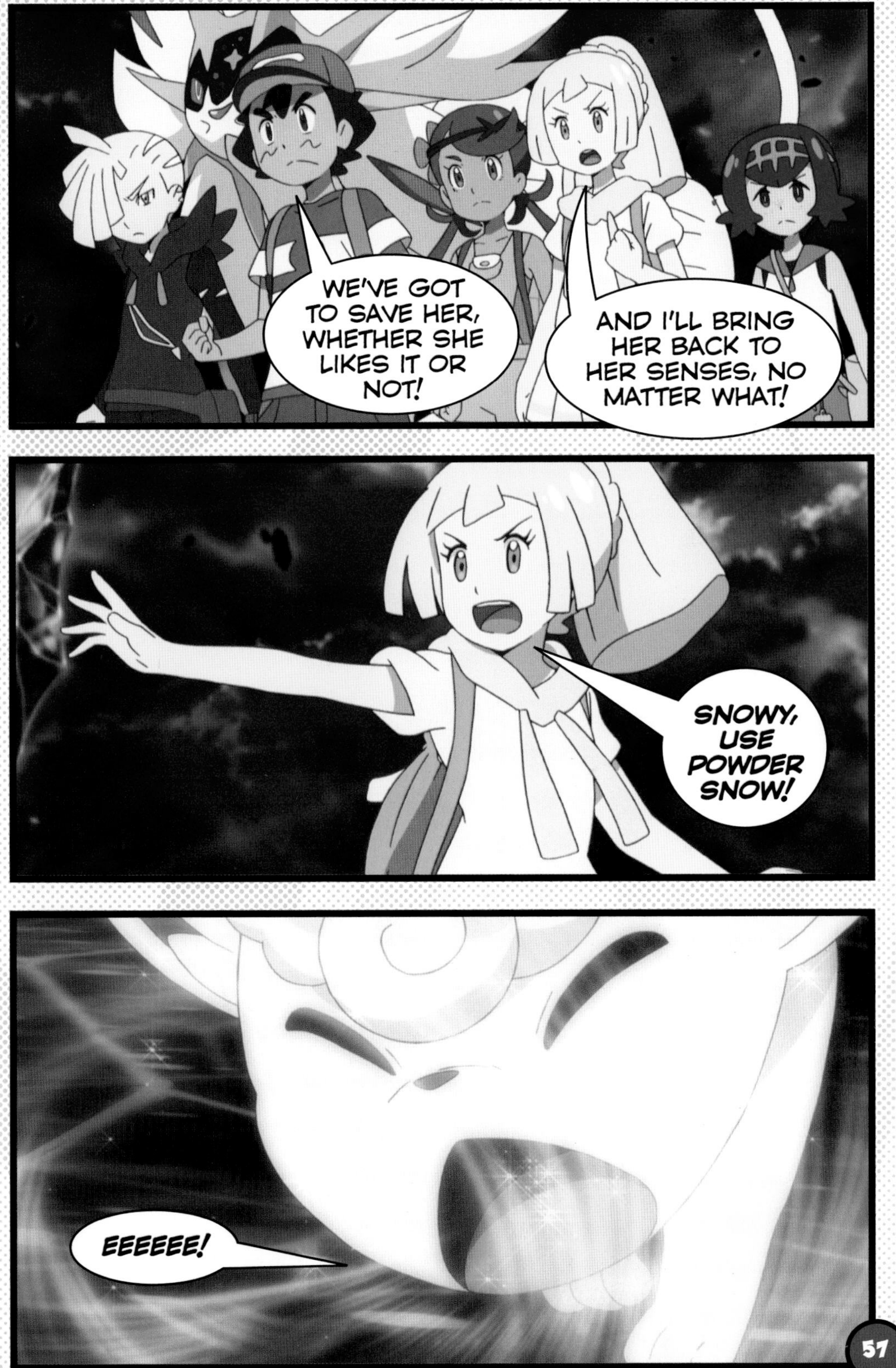
WE'VE GOT TO SAVE HER, WHETHER SHE LIKES IT OR NOT!
AND I'LL BRING HER BACK TO HER SENSES, NO MATTER WHAT!
SNOWY, USE POWDER SNOW!
EEEEEE!

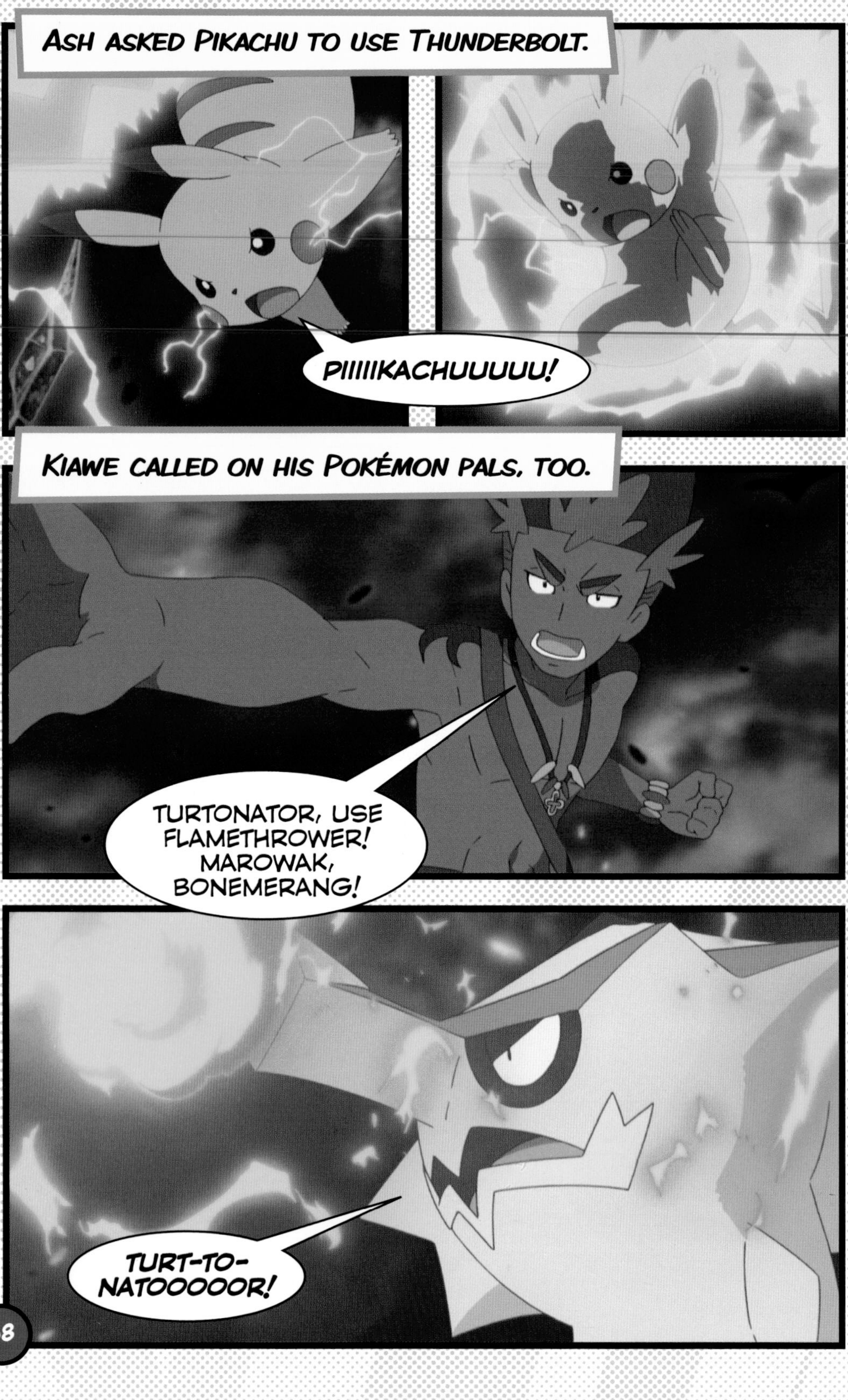

Ash asked Pikachu to use Thunderbolt.
PIIIIKACHUUUUU!
Kiawe called on his Pokémon pals, too.
TURTONATOR, USE FLAMETHROWER! MAROWAK, BONEMERANG!
TURT-TO-NATOOOOOR!

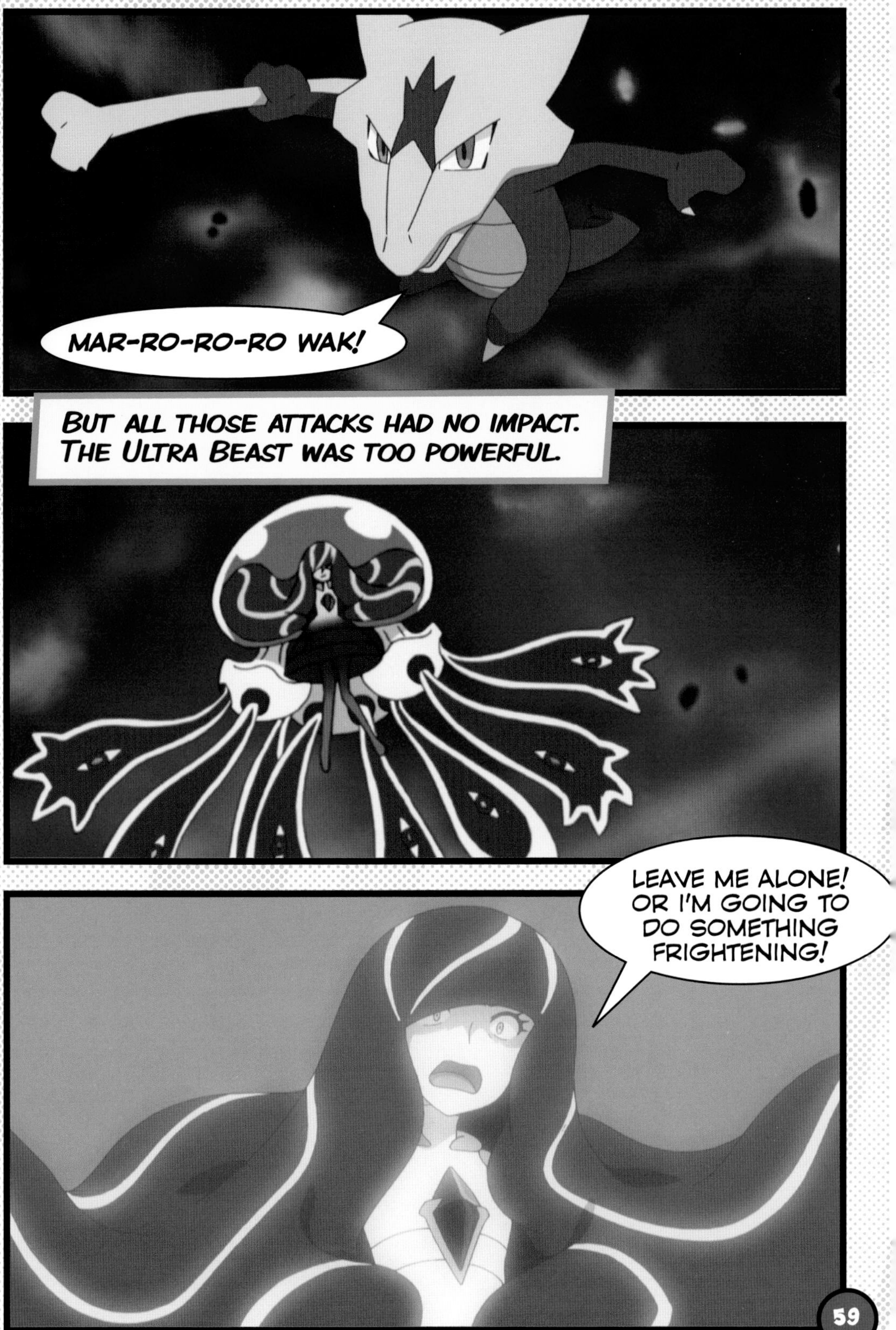
MAR-RO-RO-RO WAK!
BUT ALL THOSE ATTACKS HAD NO IMPACT. THE ULTRA BEAST WAS TOO POWERFUL.
LEAVE ME ALONE! OR I'M GOING TO DO SOMETHING FRIGHTENING!

LILLIE, GLADION, AND THEIR FRIENDS WERE NOT GOING TO GIVE UP. AND NEITHER WAS SOLGALEO.

ROOOOOOAR!

BUT LUSAMINE DID NOT MAKE AN EMPTY THREAT. SHE TOSSED A POKÉ BALL, AND OUT CAME . . .

SALAZZLE. THE TOXIC LIZARD POKÉMON.

TURTONATOR TRIED FLAMETHROWER TO FEND OFF THE POISON-FIRE-TYPE, BUT POWERFUL SALAZZLE WAS ABLE TO MATCH ITS INTENSITY.

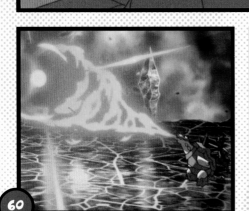

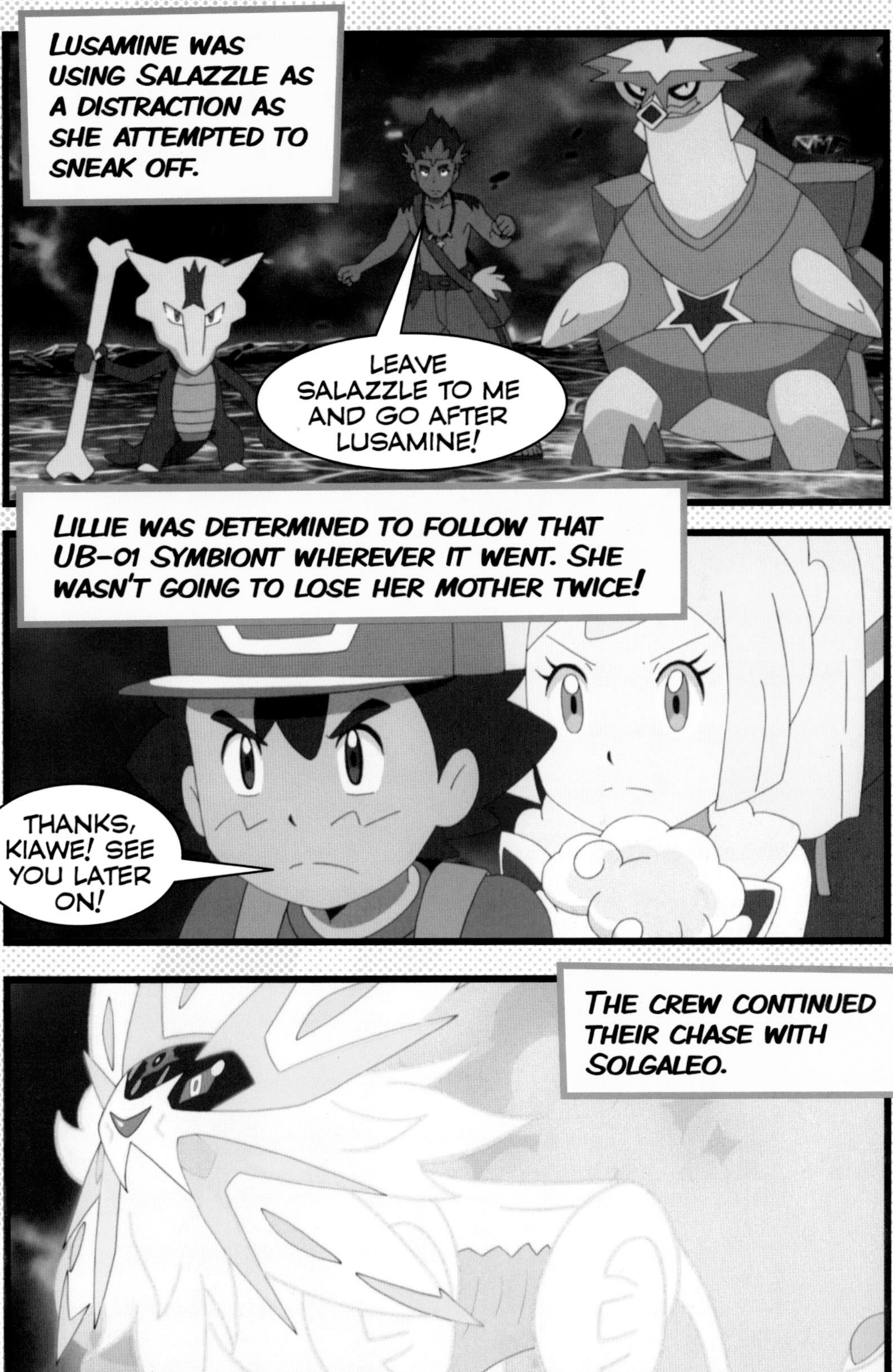
LUSAMINE WAS USING SALAZZLE AS A DISTRACTION AS SHE ATTEMPTED TO SNEAK OFF.
LEAVE SALAZZLE TO ME AND GO AFTER LUSAMINE!
LILLIE WAS DETERMINED TO FOLLOW THAT UB-01 SYMBIONT WHEREVER IT WENT. SHE WASN'T GOING TO LOSE HER MOTHER TWICE!
THANKS, KIAWE! SEE YOU LATER ON!
THE CREW CONTINUED THEIR CHASE WITH SOLGALEO.

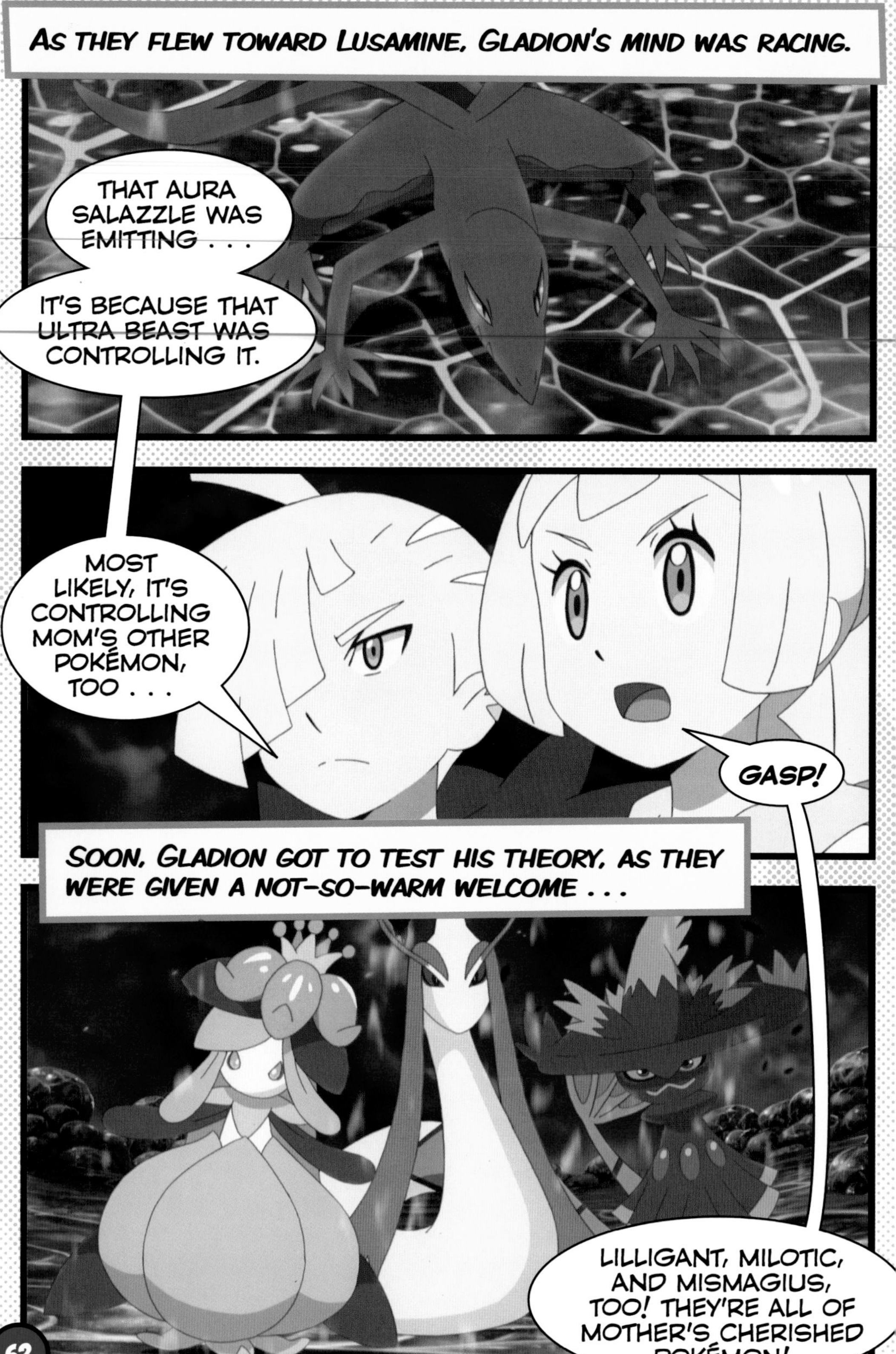
AS THEY FLEW TOWARD LUSAMINE, GLADION'S MIND WAS RACING.
THAT AURA SALAZZLE WAS EMITTING . . .
IT'S BECAUSE THAT ULTRA BEAST WAS CONTROLLING IT.
MOST LIKELY, IT'S CONTROLLING MOM'S OTHER POKÉMON, TOO . . .
GASP!
SOON, GLADION GOT TO TEST HIS THEORY, AS THEY WERE GIVEN A NOT-SO-WARM WELCOME . . .
LILLIGANT, MILOTIC, AND MISMAGIUS, TOO! THEY'RE ALL OF MOTHER'S CHERISHED POKÉMON!

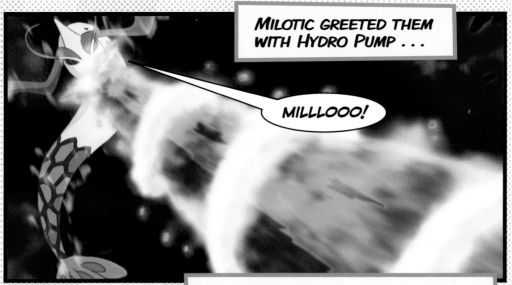

MILOTIC GREETED THEM WITH HYDRO PUMP . . .

MILLLOOO!

MISMAGIUS, WITH A THUNDERBOLT . . .

MAAAAAG!

POPPLIO, USE BUBBLE BEAM!

NOW, STEENEE, USE MAGICAL LEAF!

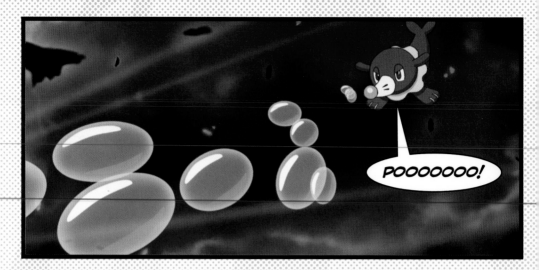

POOOOOOO!

STEEEEEENEEEEE!

As the battle ensued, Lusamine slipped away again.

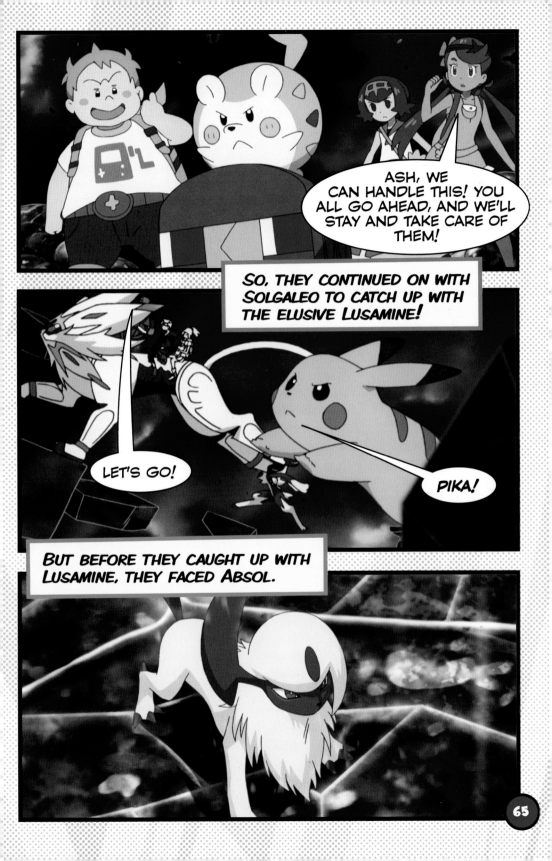

ASH, WE CAN HANDLE THIS! YOU ALL GO AHEAD, AND WE'LL STAY AND TAKE CARE OF THEM!

SO, THEY CONTINUED ON WITH SOLGALEO TO CATCH UP WITH THE ELUSIVE LUSAMINE!

LET'S GO!

PIKA!

BUT BEFORE THEY CAUGHT UP WITH LUSAMINE, THEY FACED ABSOL.

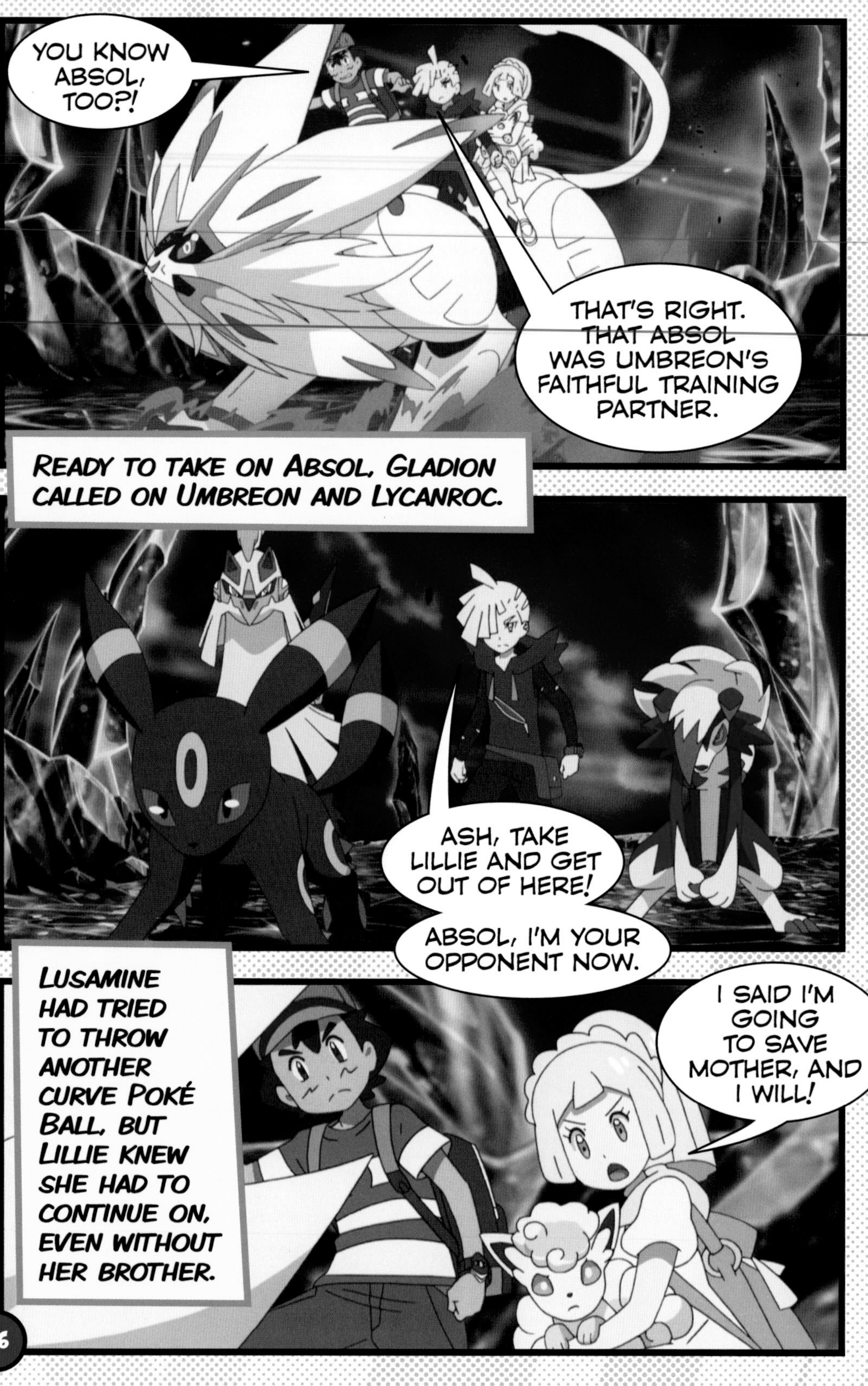
YOU KNOW ABSOL, TOO?!
THAT'S RIGHT. THAT ABSOL WAS UMBREON'S FAITHFUL TRAINING PARTNER.
READY TO TAKE ON ABSOL, GLADION CALLED ON UMBREON AND LYCANROC.
ASH, TAKE LILLIE AND GET OUT OF HERE!
ABSOL, I'M YOUR OPPONENT NOW.
LUSAMINE HAD TRIED TO THROW ANOTHER CURVE POKÉ BALL, BUT LILLIE KNEW SHE HAD TO CONTINUE ON, EVEN WITHOUT HER BROTHER.
I SAID I'M GOING TO SAVE MOTHER, AND I WILL!

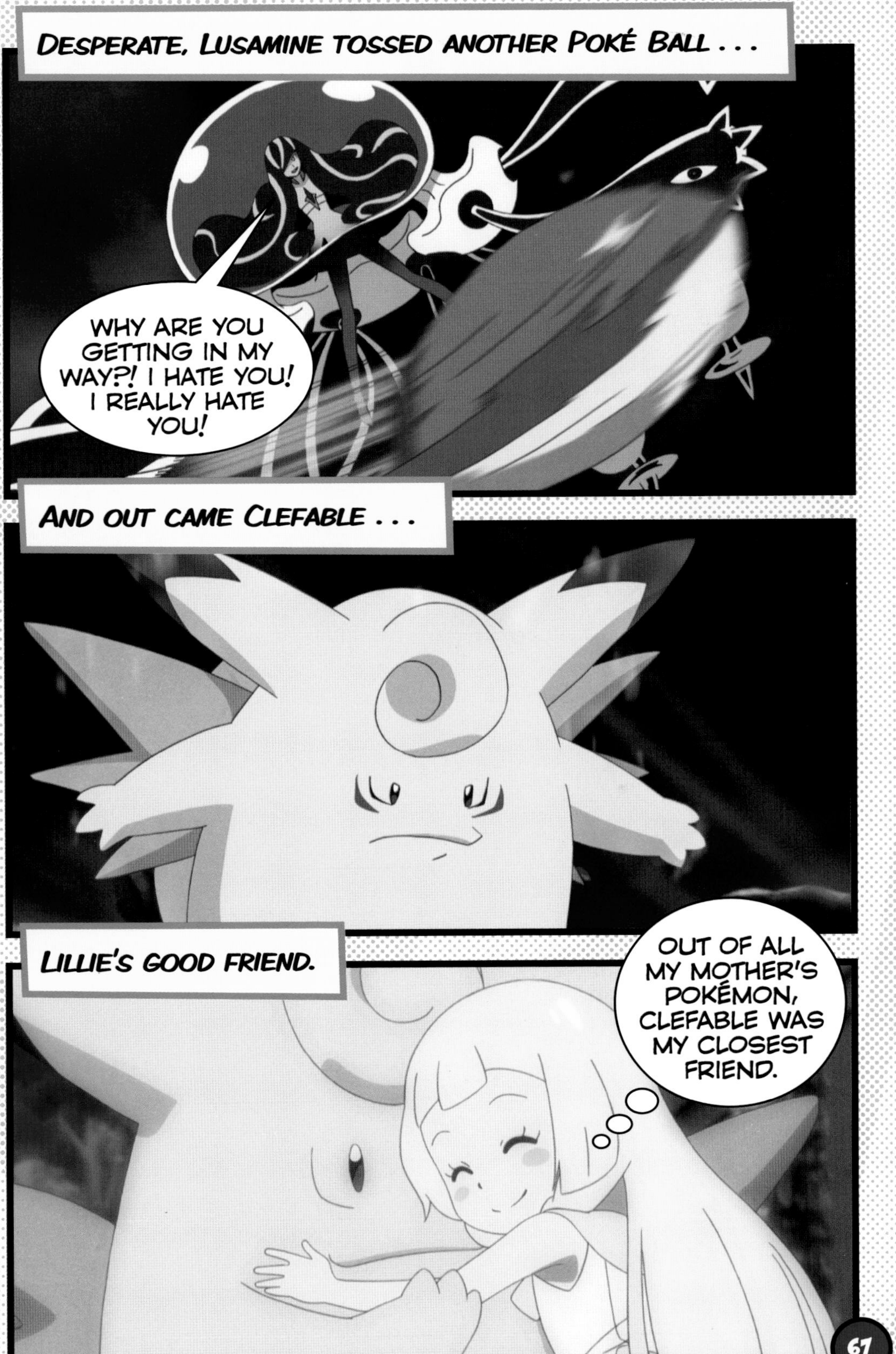
DESPERATE, LUSAMINE TOSSED ANOTHER POKÉ BALL . . .
WHY ARE YOU GETTING IN MY WAY?! I HATE YOU! I REALLY HATE YOU!
AND OUT CAME CLEFABLE . . .
LILLIE'S GOOD FRIEND.
OUT OF ALL MY MOTHER'S POKÉMON, CLEFABLE WAS MY CLOSEST FRIEND.

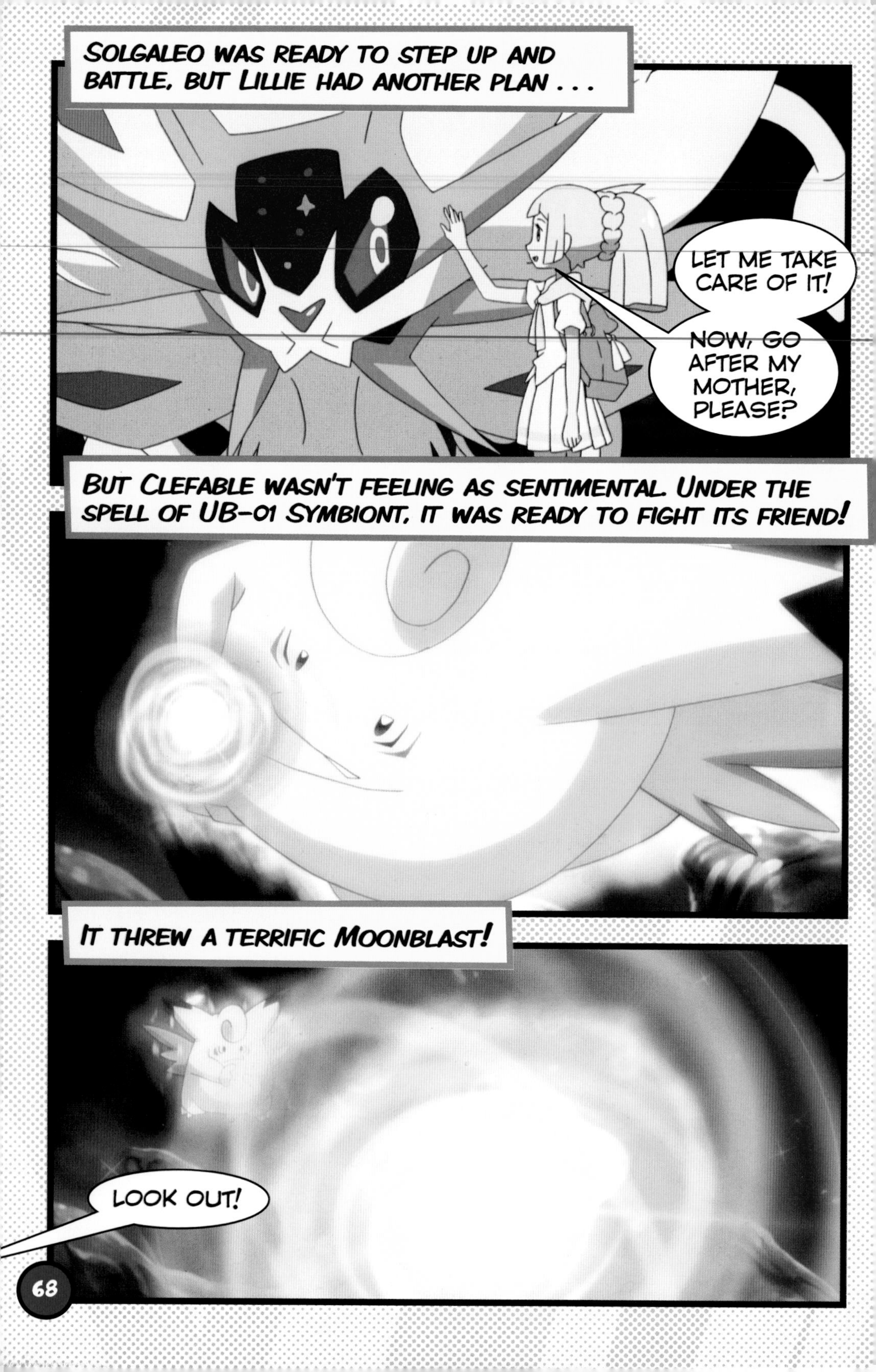
SOLGALEO WAS READY TO STEP UP AND BATTLE, BUT LILLIE HAD ANOTHER PLAN . . .
LET ME TAKE CARE OF IT!
NOW, GO AFTER MY MOTHER, PLEASE?
BUT CLEFABLE WASN'T FEELING AS SENTIMENTAL. UNDER THE SPELL OF UB-01 SYMBIONT, IT WAS READY TO FIGHT ITS FRIEND!
IT THREW A TERRIFIC MOONBLAST!
LOOK OUT!

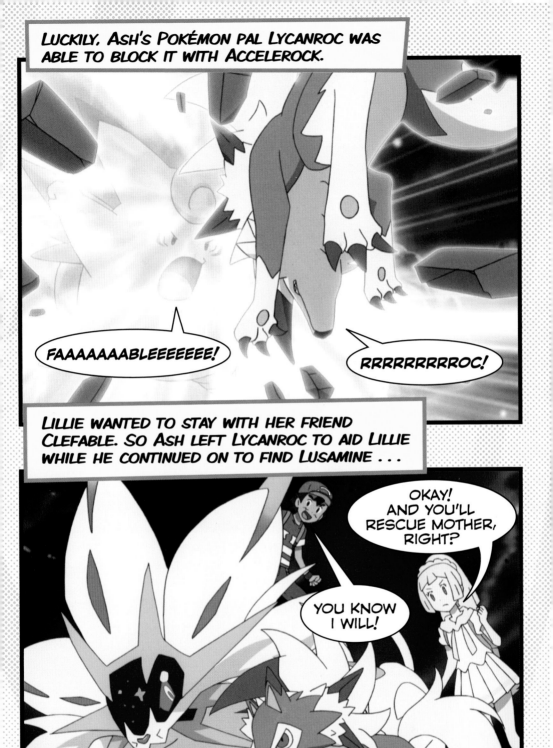

LUCKILY, ASH'S POKÉMON PAL LYCANROC WAS ABLE TO BLOCK IT WITH ACCELEROCK.

FAAAAAAABLEEEEEEE!

RRRRRRRRROC!

LILLIE WANTED TO STAY WITH HER FRIEND CLEFABLE. SO ASH LEFT LYCANROC TO AID LILLIE WHILE HE CONTINUED ON TO FIND LUSAMINE . . .

OKAY! AND YOU'LL RESCUE MOTHER, RIGHT?

YOU KNOW I WILL!

ASH, SOLGALEO, AND PIKACHU TOOK OFF.

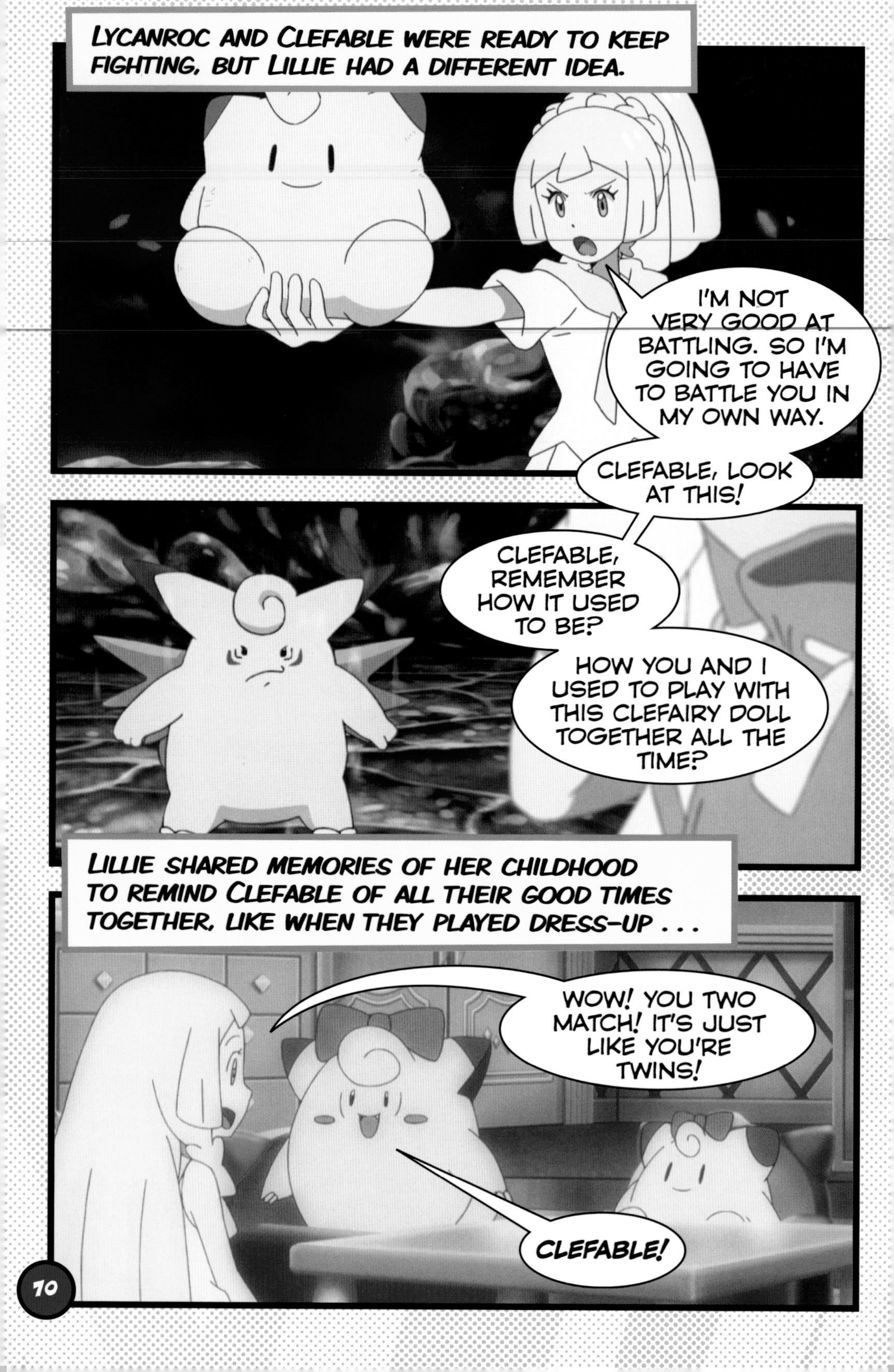

LYCANROC AND CLEFABLE WERE READY TO KEEP FIGHTING, BUT LILLIE HAD A DIFFERENT IDEA.
I'M NOT VERY GOOD AT BATTLING. SO I'M GOING TO HAVE TO BATTLE YOU IN MY OWN WAY.
CLEFABLE, LOOK AT THIS!
CLEFABLE, REMEMBER HOW IT USED TO BE?
HOW YOU AND I USED TO PLAY WITH THIS CLEFAIRY DOLL TOGETHER ALL THE TIME?
LILLIE SHARED MEMORIES OF HER CHILDHOOD TO REMIND CLEFABLE OF ALL THEIR GOOD TIMES TOGETHER, LIKE WHEN THEY PLAYED DRESS-UP . . .
WOW! YOU TWO MATCH! IT'S JUST LIKE YOU'RE TWINS!
CLEFABLE!

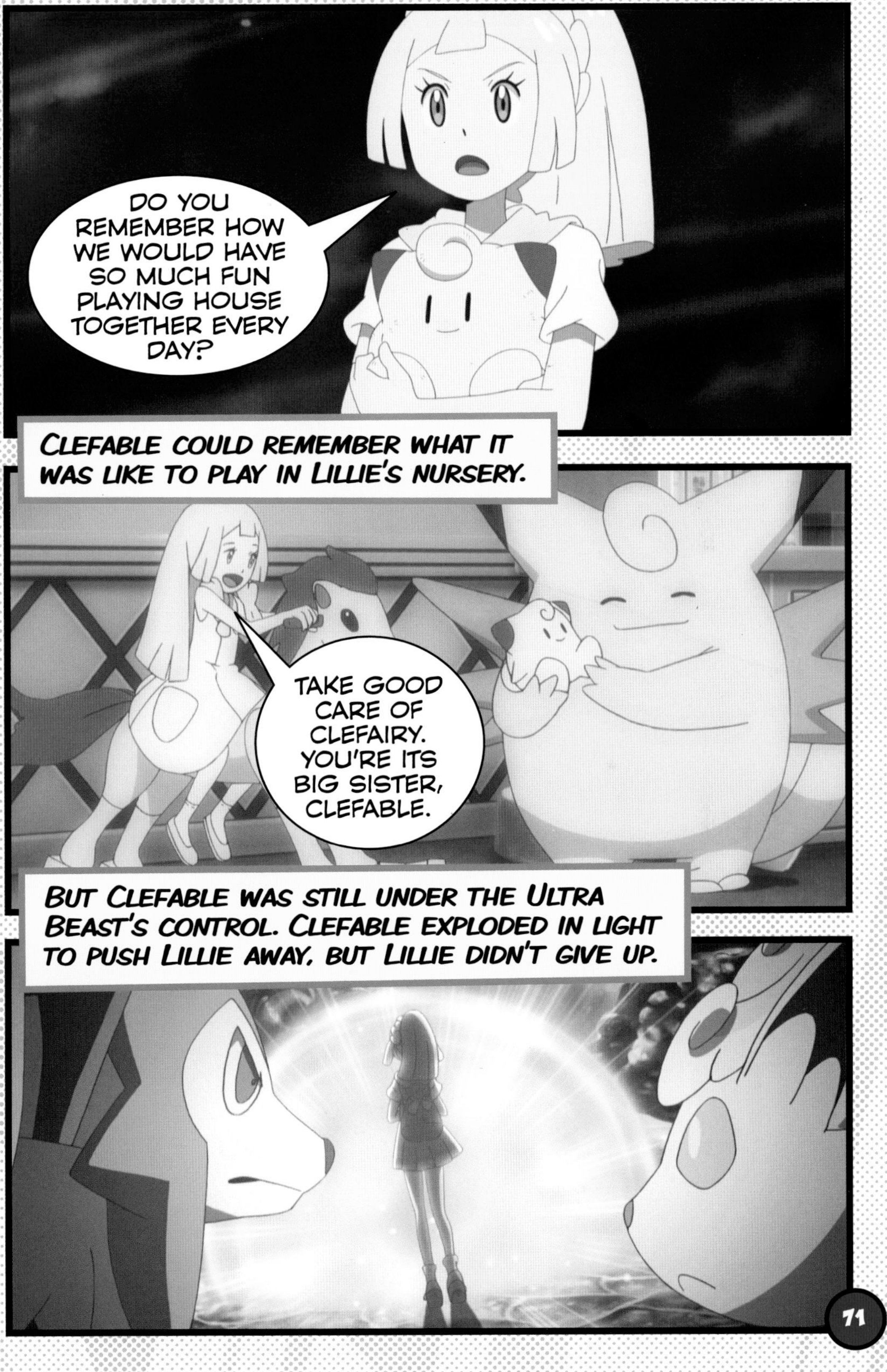
DO YOU REMEMBER HOW WE WOULD HAVE SO MUCH FUN PLAYING HOUSE TOGETHER EVERY DAY?
CLEFABLE COULD REMEMBER WHAT IT WAS LIKE TO PLAY IN LILLIE'S NURSERY.
TAKE GOOD CARE OF CLEFAIRY. YOU'RE ITS BIG SISTER, CLEFABLE.
BUT CLEFABLE WAS STILL UNDER THE ULTRA BEAST'S CONTROL. CLEFABLE EXPLODED IN LIGHT TO PUSH LILLIE AWAY, BUT LILLIE DIDN'T GIVE UP.

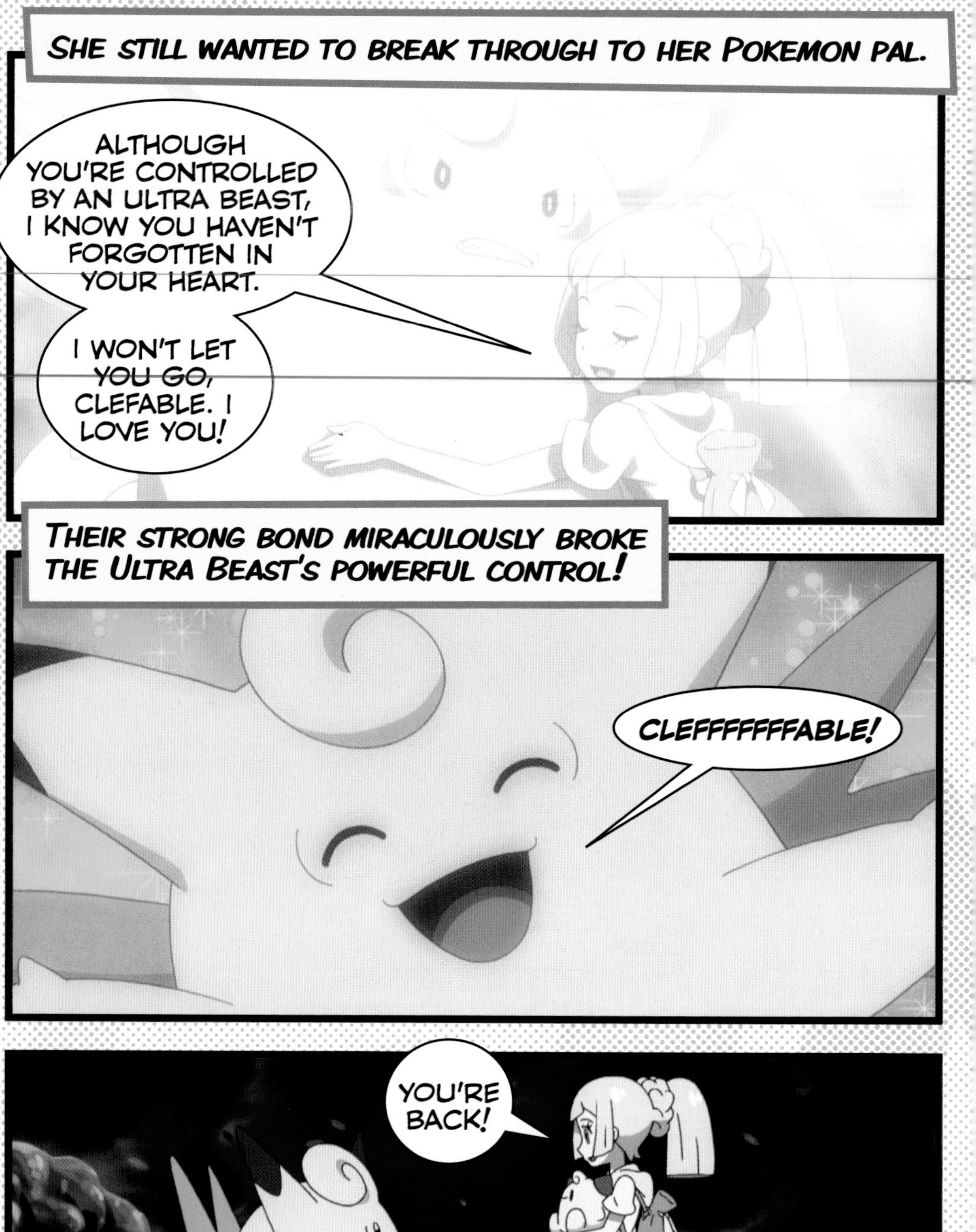
SHE STILL WANTED TO BREAK THROUGH TO HER POKEMON PAL.
ALTHOUGH YOU'RE CONTROLLED BY AN ULTRA BEAST, I KNOW YOU HAVEN'T FORGOTTEN IN YOUR HEART.
I WON'T LET YOU GO, CLEFABLE. I LOVE YOU!
THEIR STRONG BOND MIRACULOUSLY BROKE THE ULTRA BEAST'S POWERFUL CONTROL!
CLEFFFFFFFABLE!
YOU'RE BACK!

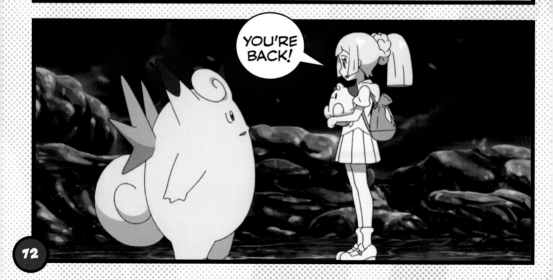

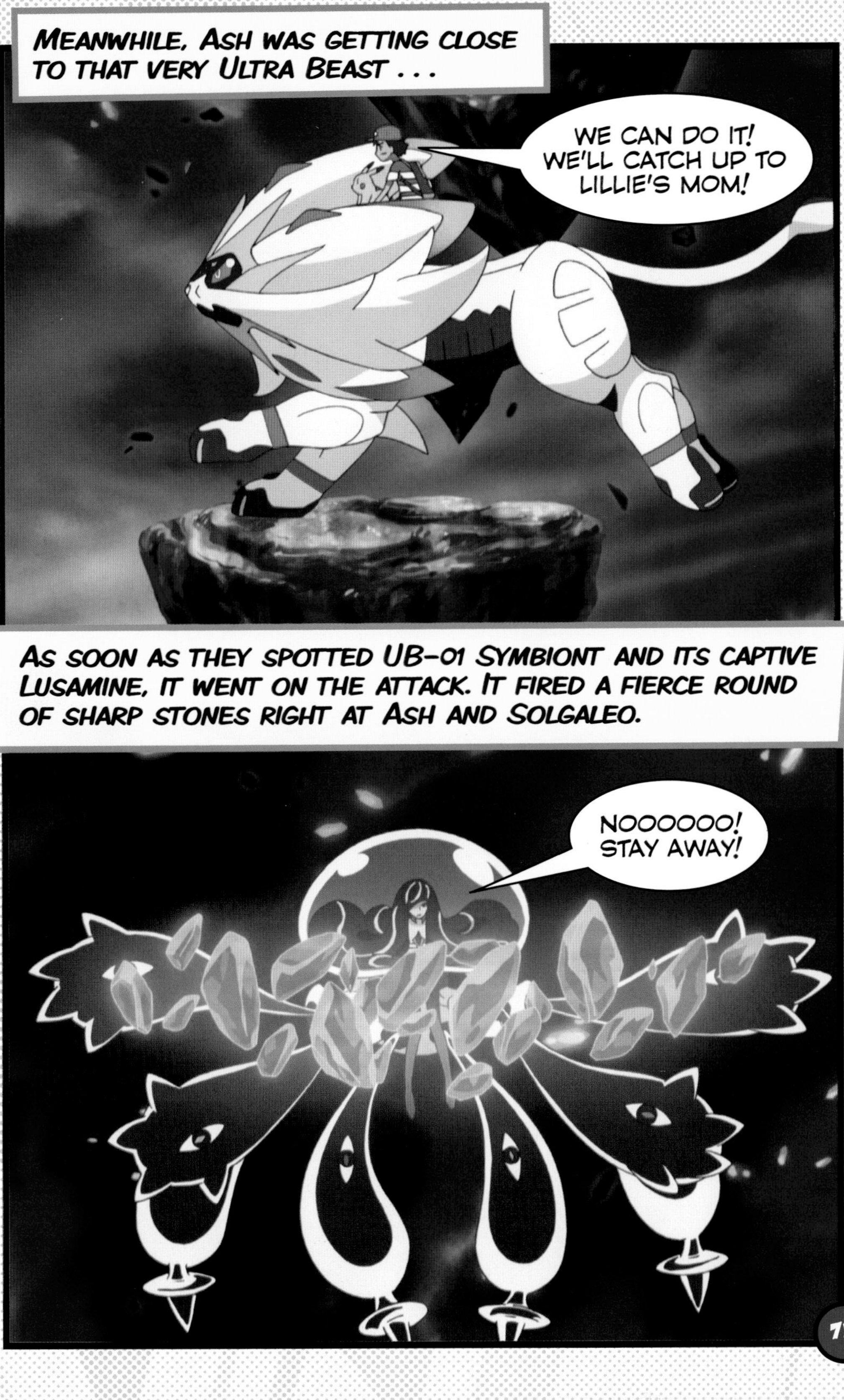
MEANWHILE, ASH WAS GETTING CLOSE TO THAT VERY ULTRA BEAST . . .
WE CAN DO IT! WE'LL CATCH UP TO LILLIE'S MOM!
AS SOON AS THEY SPOTTED UB-01 SYMBIONT AND ITS CAPTIVE LUSAMINE, IT WENT ON THE ATTACK. IT FIRED A FIERCE ROUND OF SHARP STONES RIGHT AT ASH AND SOLGALEO.
NOOOOOO! STAY AWAY!

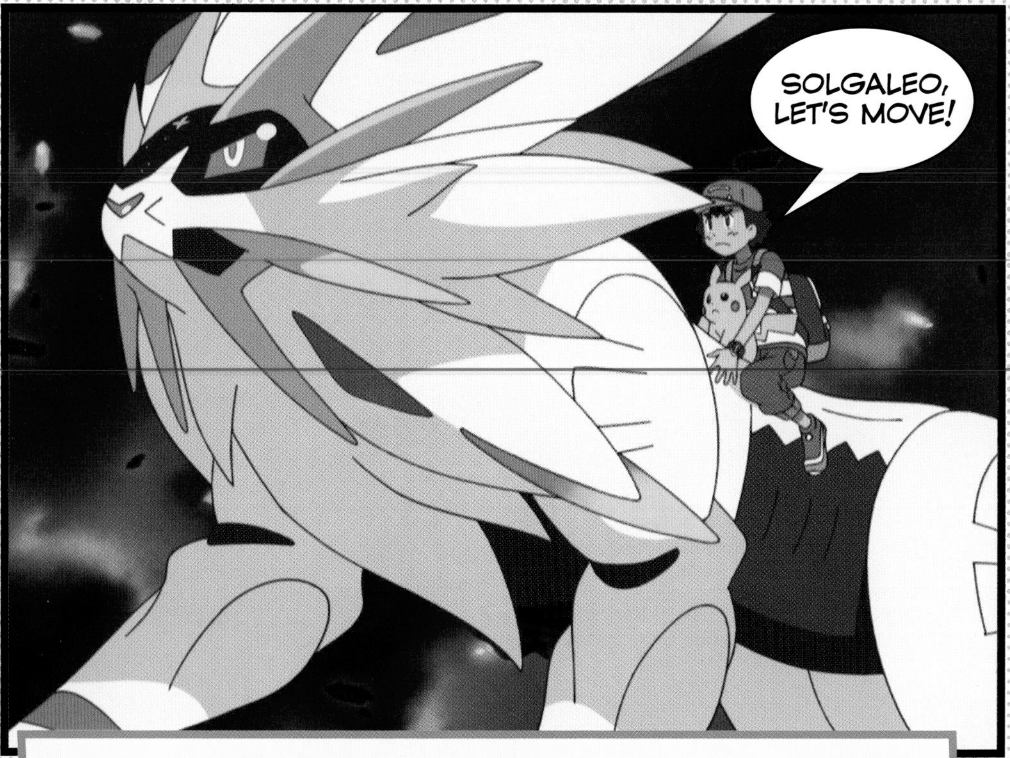
SOLGALEO, LET'S MOVE!

BUT LUSAMINE SURROUNDED THE AREA IN SWIRLS OF GOO.

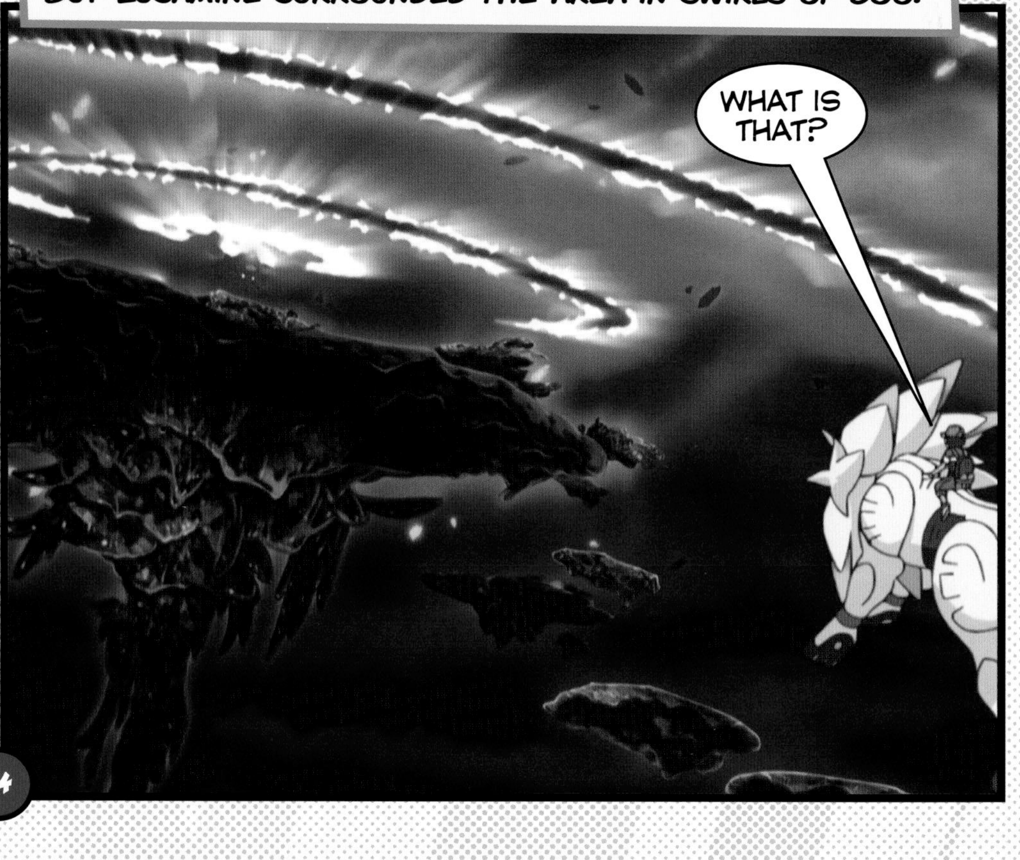
WHAT IS THAT?

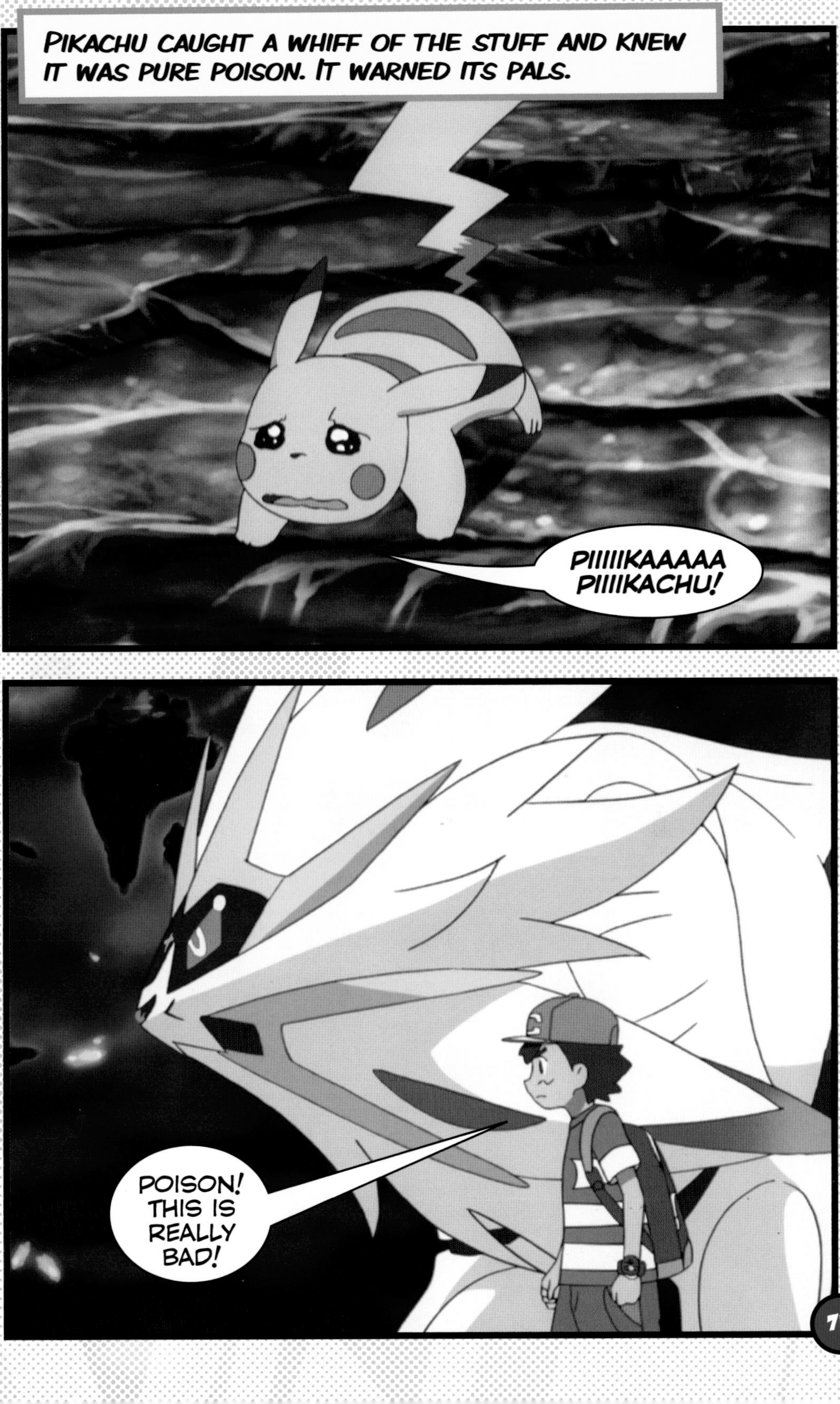
PIKACHU CAUGHT A WHIFF OF THE STUFF AND KNEW IT WAS PURE POISON. IT WARNED ITS PALS.
PIIIIKAAAAA PIIIIKACHU!
POISON! THIS IS REALLY BAD!

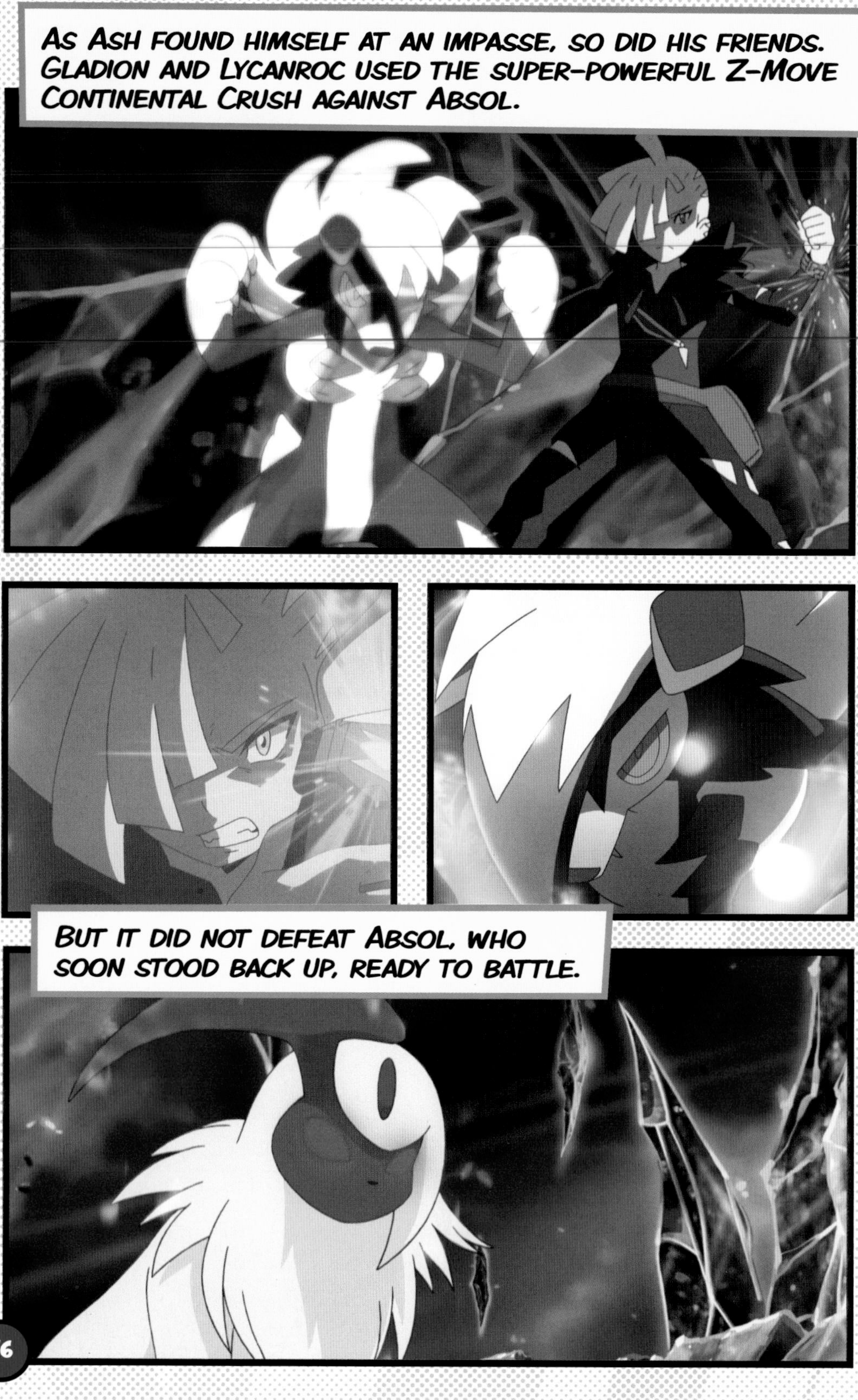
AS ASH FOUND HIMSELF AT AN IMPASSE, SO DID HIS FRIENDS. GLADION AND LYCANROC USED THE SUPER-POWERFUL Z-MOVE CONTINENTAL CRUSH AGAINST ABSOL.
BUT IT DID NOT DEFEAT ABSOL, WHO SOON STOOD BACK UP, READY TO BATTLE.

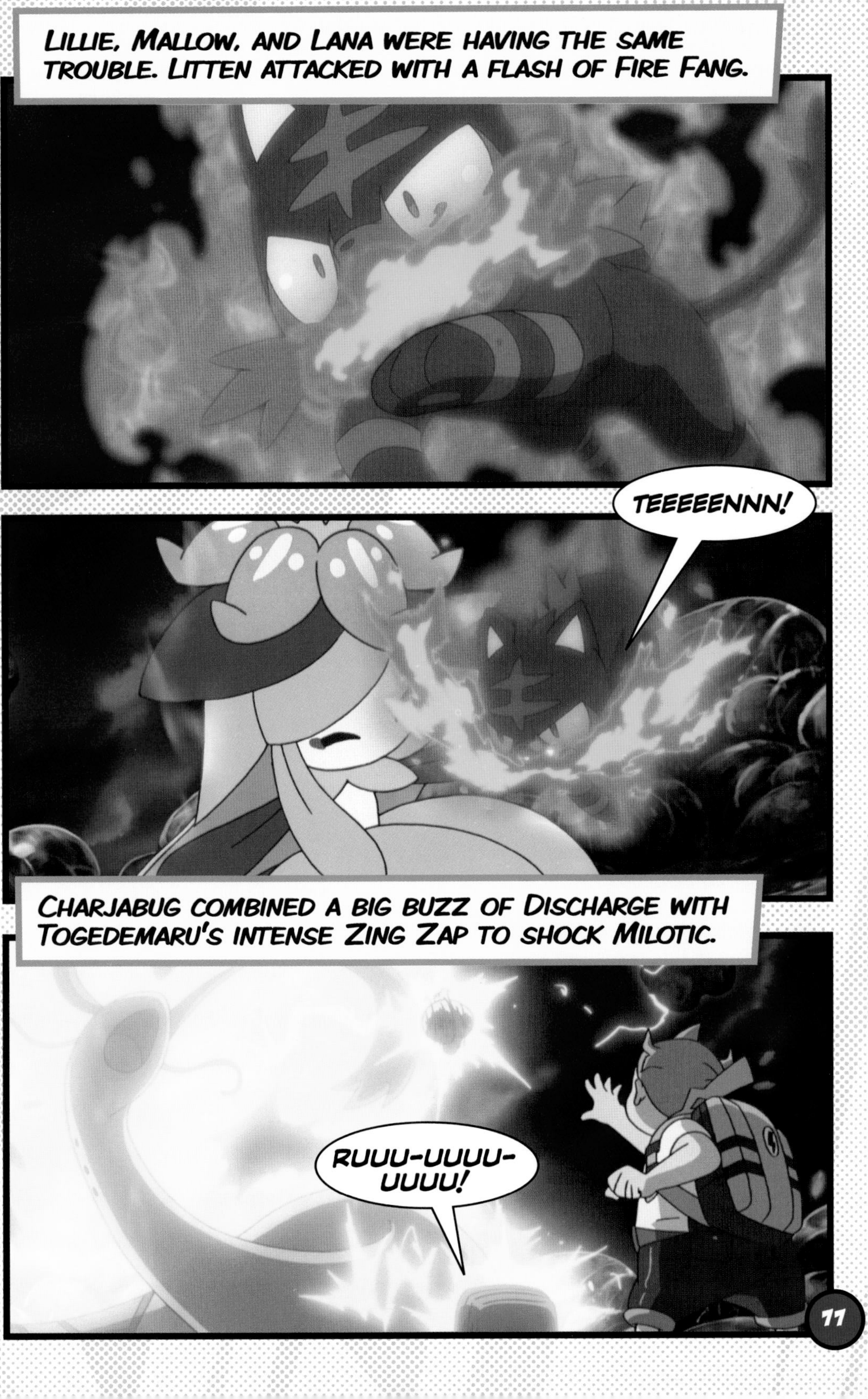
LILLIE, MALLOW, AND LANA WERE HAVING THE SAME TROUBLE. LITTEN ATTACKED WITH A FLASH OF FIRE FANG.
TEEEEENNN!
CHARJABUG COMBINED A BIG BUZZ OF DISCHARGE WITH TOGEDEMARU'S INTENSE ZING ZAP TO SHOCK MILOTIC.
RUUU-UUUU-UUUU!

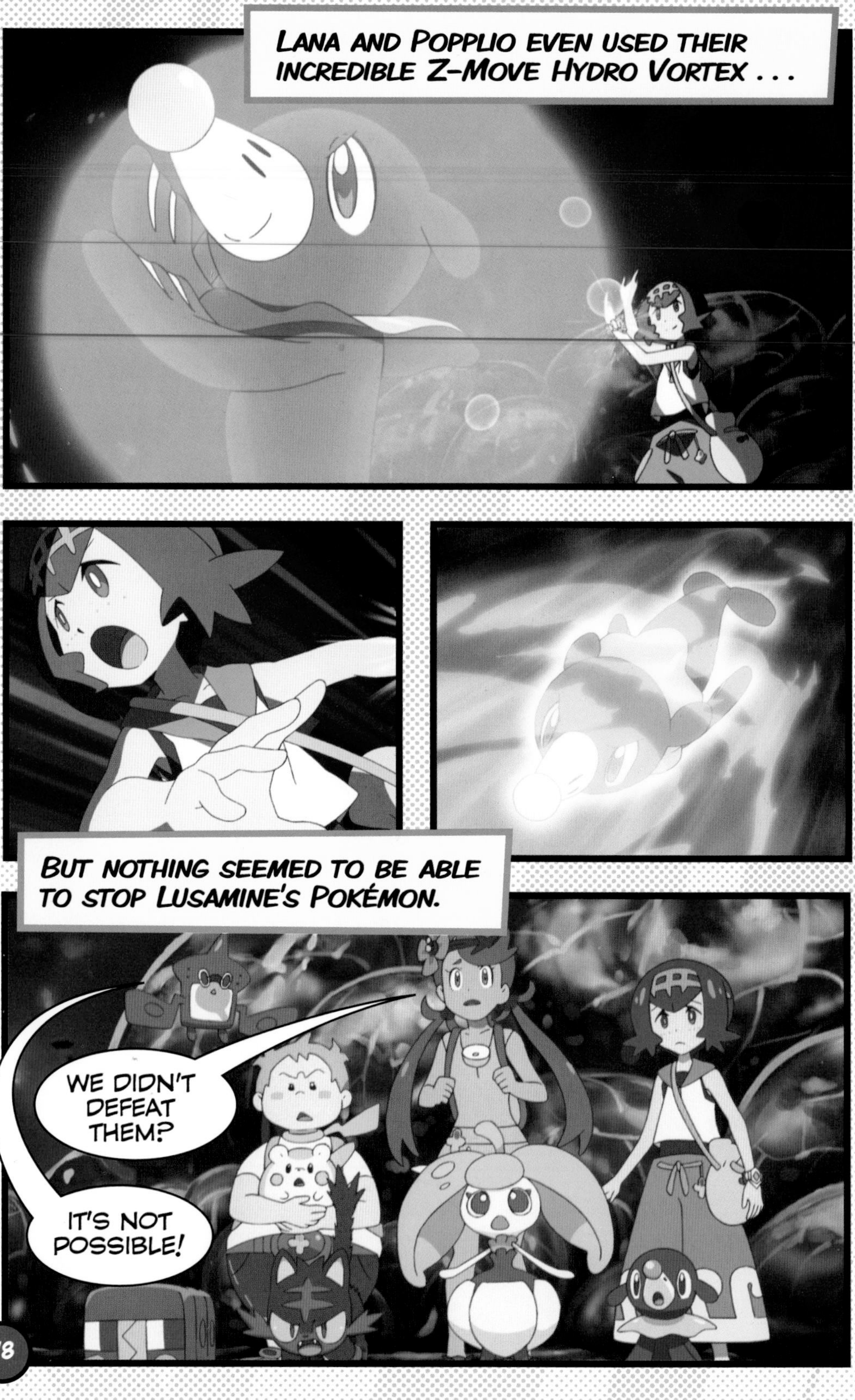
LANA AND POPPLIO EVEN USED THEIR INCREDIBLE Z-MOVE HYDRO VORTEX . . .
BUT NOTHING SEEMED TO BE ABLE TO STOP LUSAMINE'S POKÉMON.
WE DIDN'T DEFEAT THEM?
IT'S NOT POSSIBLE!

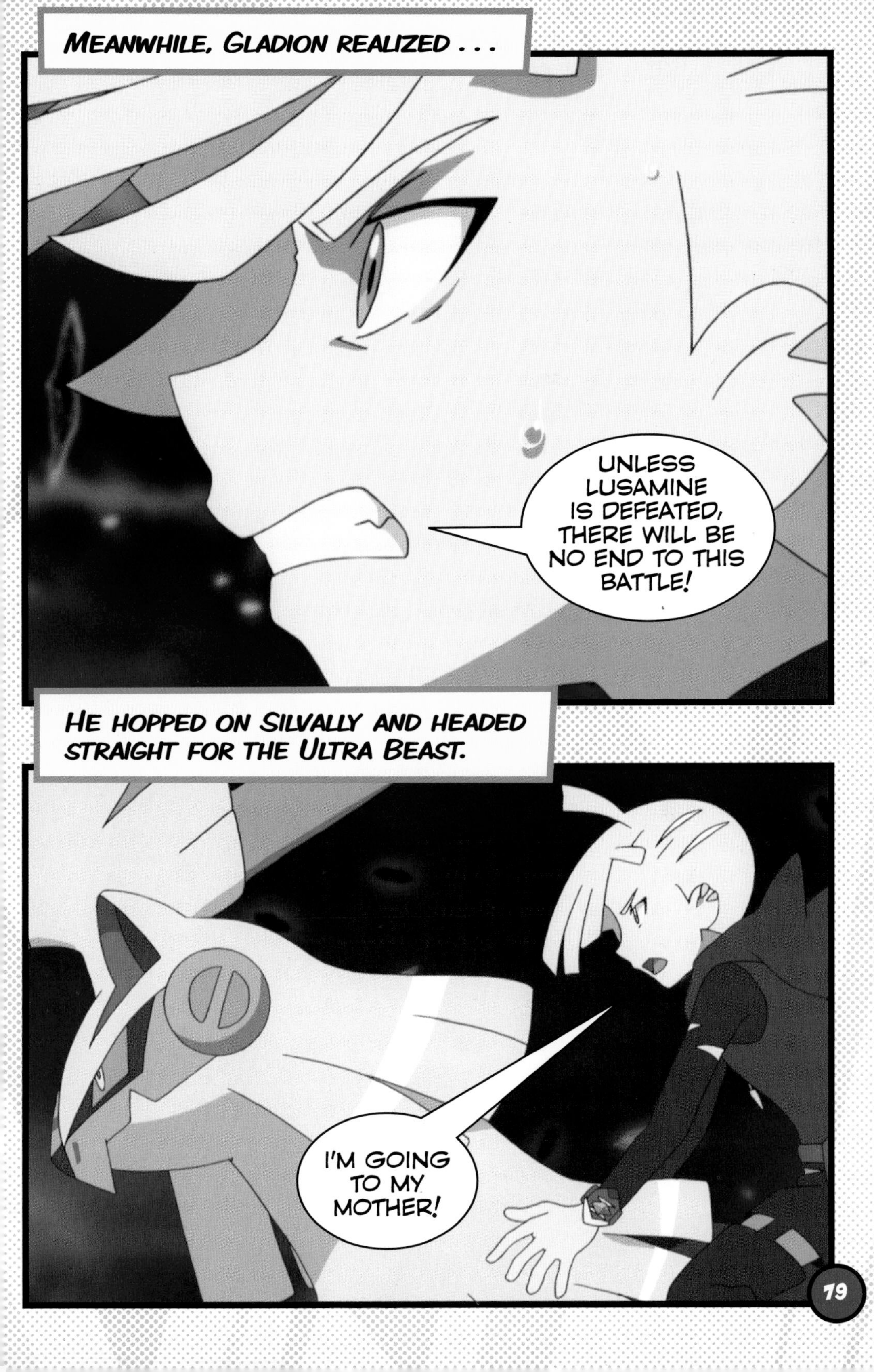
MEANWHILE, GLADION REALIZED . . .
UNLESS LUSAMINE IS DEFEATED, THERE WILL BE NO END TO THIS BATTLE!
HE HOPPED ON SILVALLY AND HEADED STRAIGHT FOR THE ULTRA BEAST.
I'M GOING TO MY MOTHER!

WHILE GLADION WAS ON HIS WAY, SOLGALEO SPRANG INTO ACTION. WITH ASH AND PIKACHU ON ITS BACK, IT TRAMPLED THROUGH THE POISON TO GET TO LUSAMINE.

THANKS, SOLGALEO!

ASH ASKED PIKACHU TO SHOCK THE ULTRA BEAST WITH A THUNDERBOLT BLAST.

PIIIIIIKACHUUUUUUUUU!

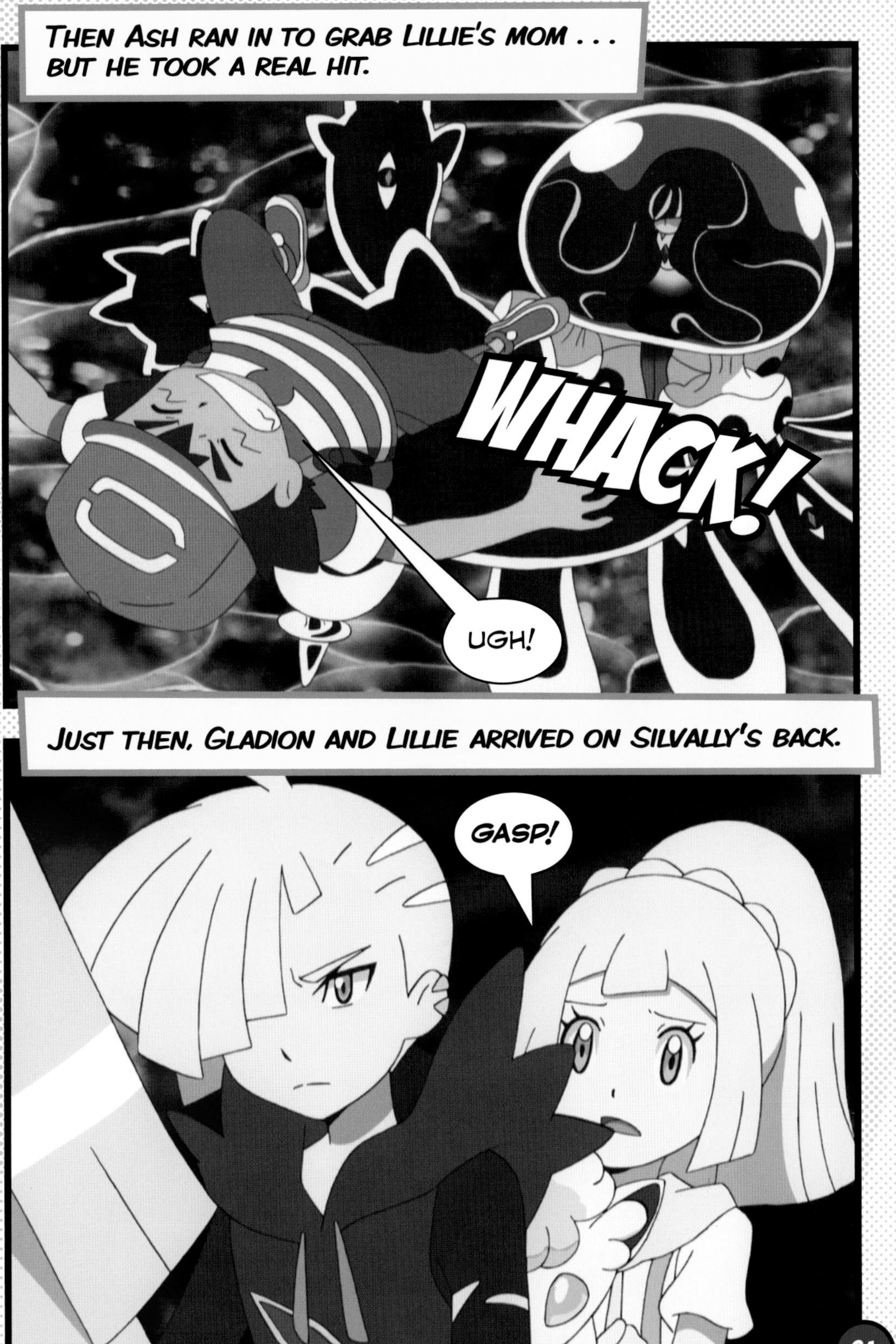
THEN ASH RAN IN TO GRAB LILLIE'S MOM . . . BUT HE TOOK A REAL HIT.
WHACK!
UGH!
JUST THEN, GLADION AND LILLIE ARRIVED ON SILVALLY'S BACK.
GASP!

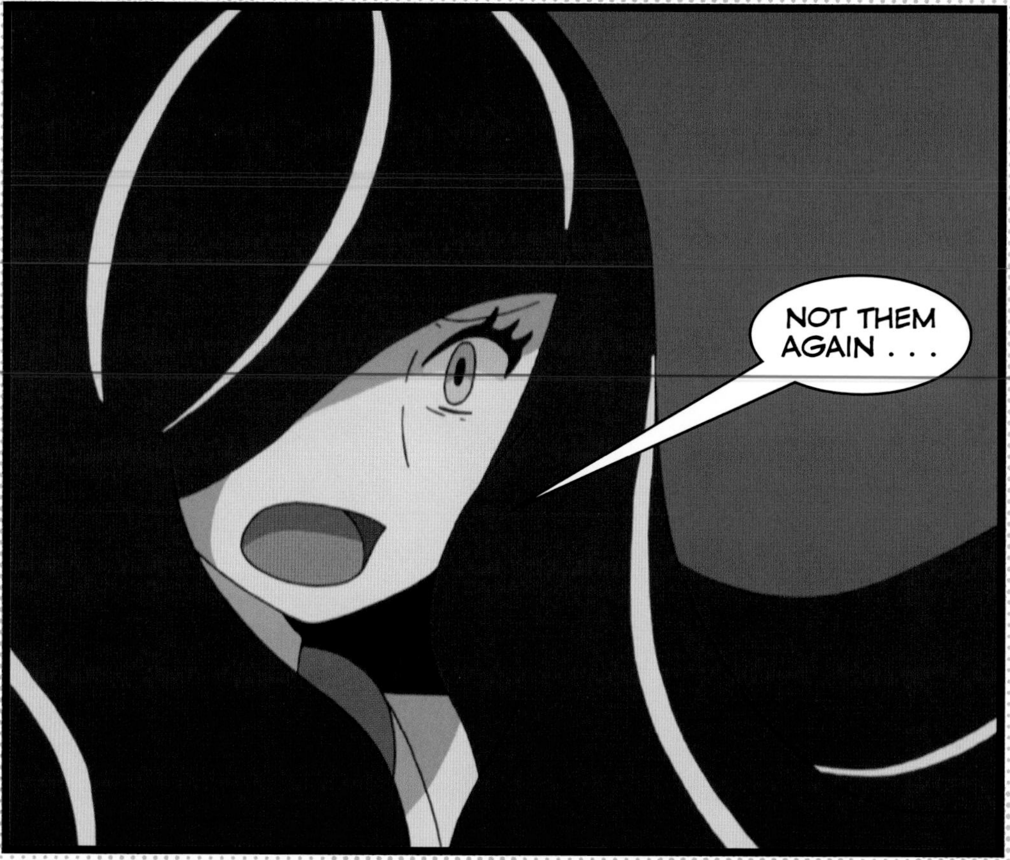
NOT THEM AGAIN . . .

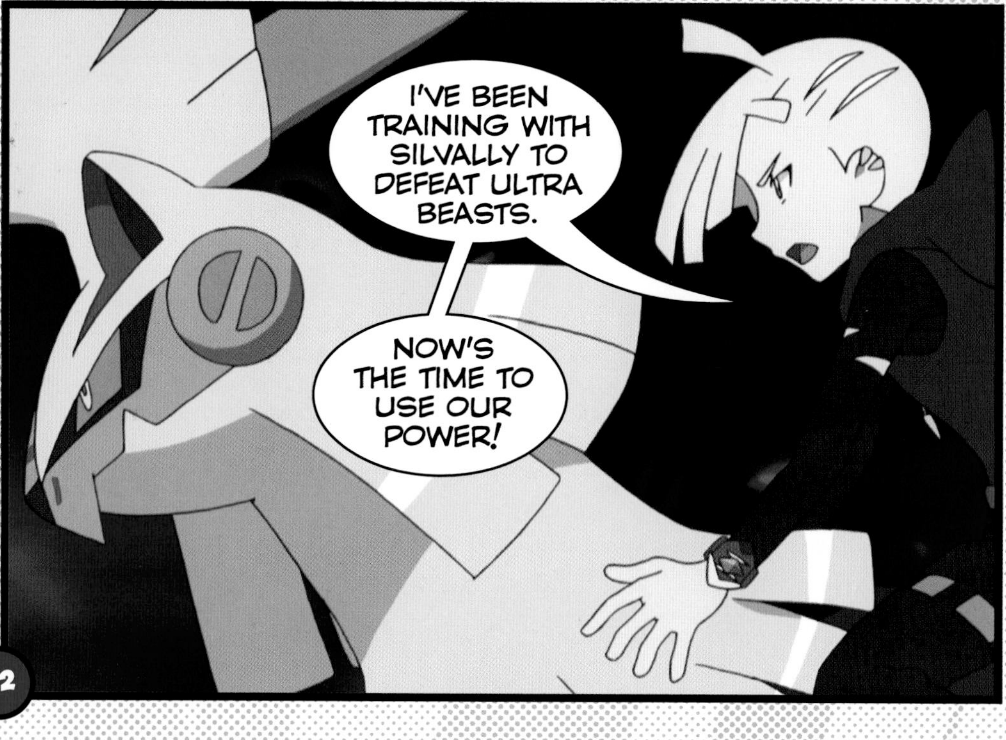
I'VE BEEN TRAINING WITH SILVALLY TO DEFEAT ULTRA BEASTS.
NOW'S THE TIME TO USE OUR POWER!

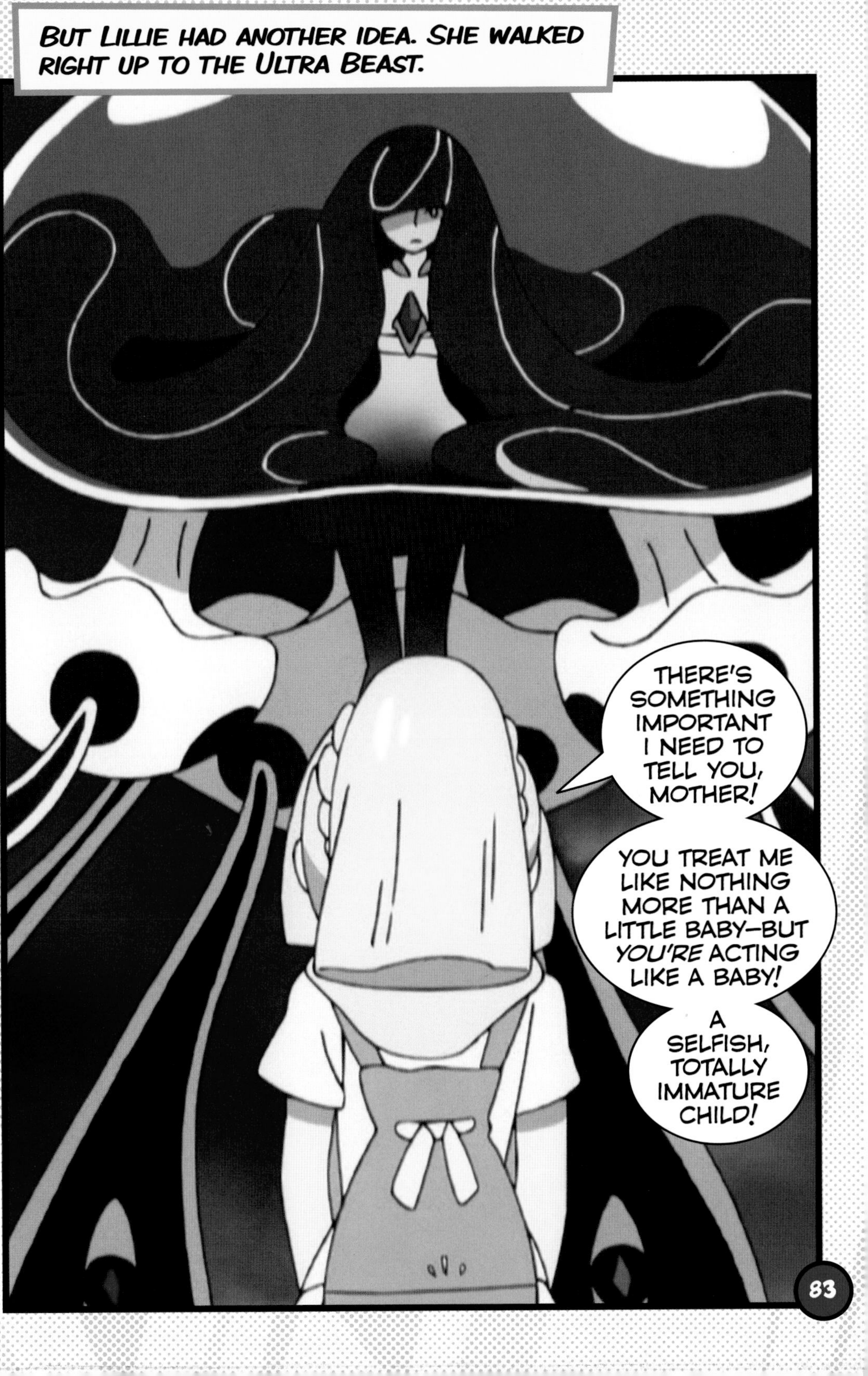
BUT LILLIE HAD ANOTHER IDEA. SHE WALKED RIGHT UP TO THE ULTRA BEAST.
THERE'S SOMETHING IMPORTANT I NEED TO TELL YOU, MOTHER!
YOU TREAT ME LIKE NOTHING MORE THAN A LITTLE BABY—BUT *YOU'RE* ACTING LIKE A BABY!
A SELFISH, TOTALLY IMMATURE CHILD!

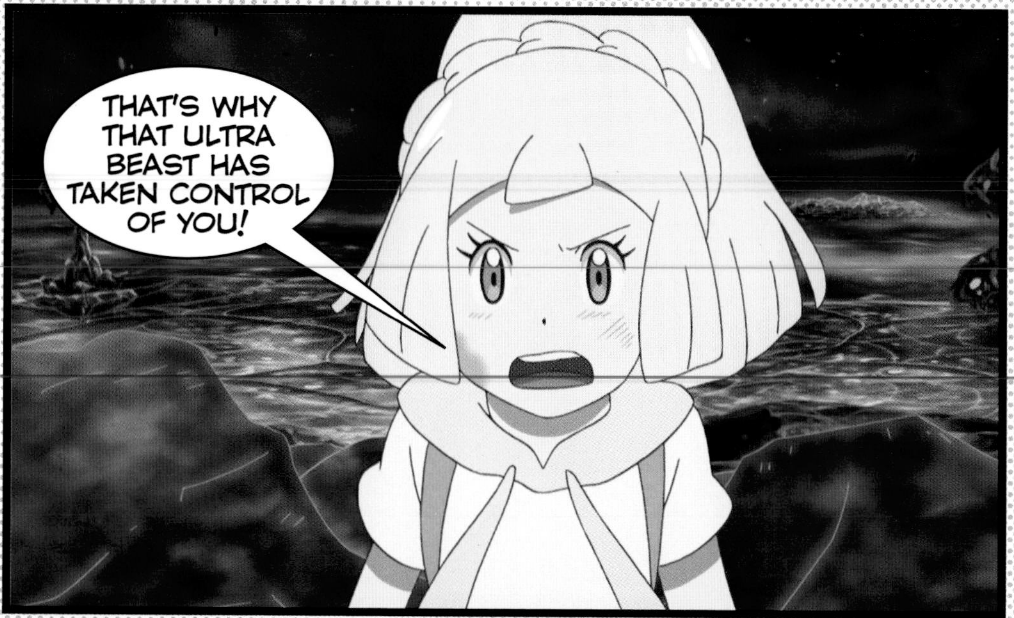
THAT'S WHY THAT ULTRA BEAST HAS TAKEN CONTROL OF YOU!

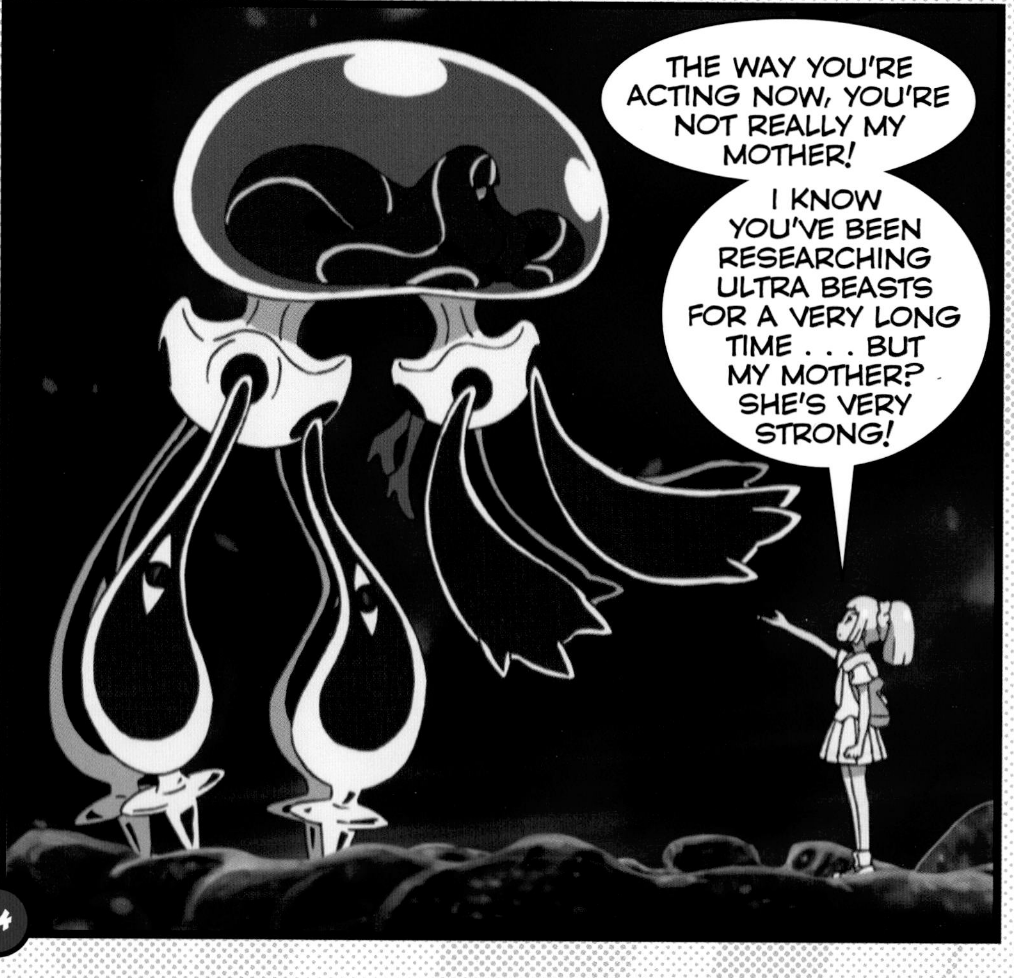
THE WAY YOU'RE ACTING NOW, YOU'RE NOT REALLY MY MOTHER!
I KNOW YOU'VE BEEN RESEARCHING ULTRA BEASTS FOR A VERY LONG TIME . . . BUT MY MOTHER? SHE'S VERY STRONG!

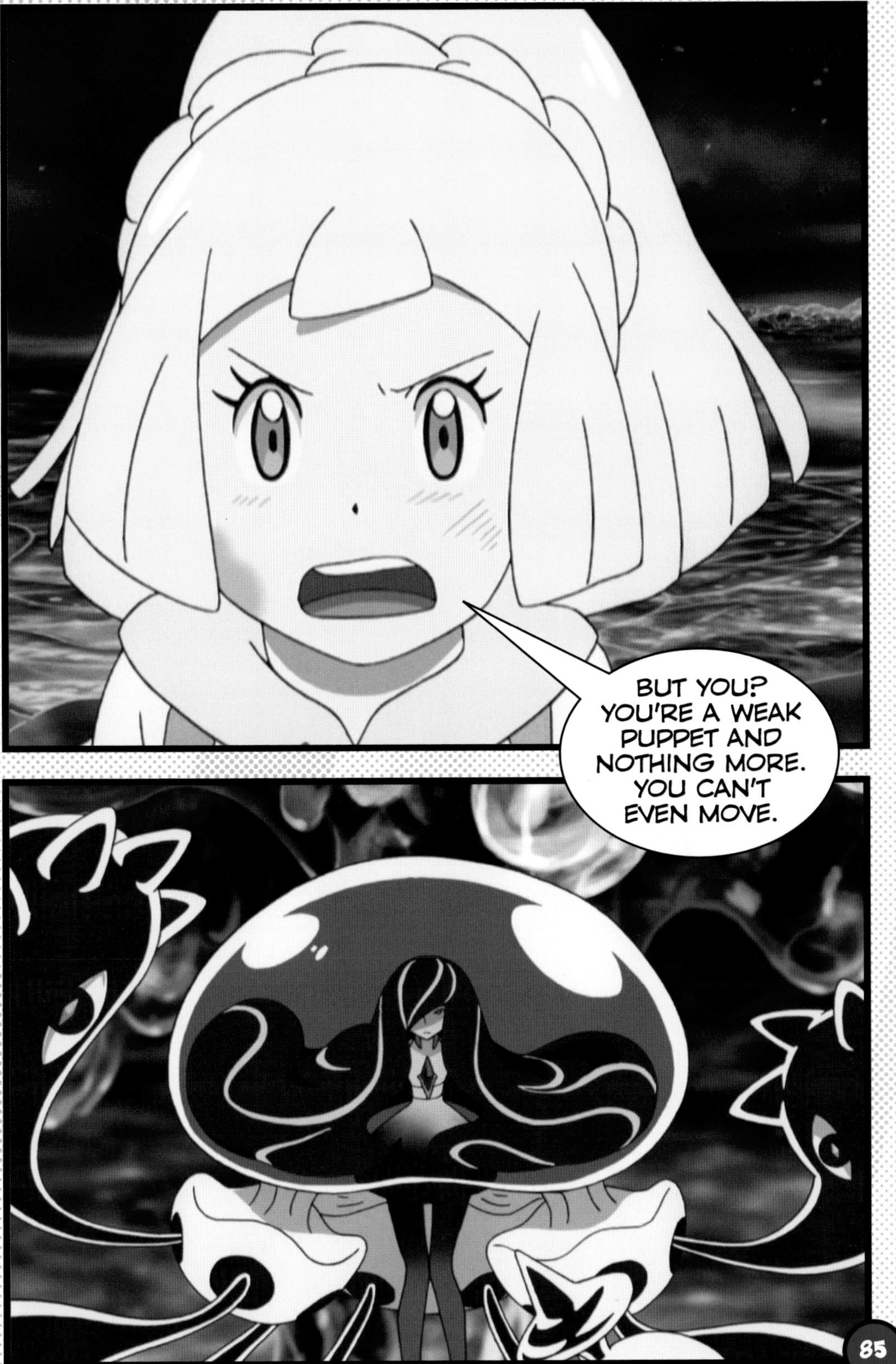
BUT YOU? YOU'RE A WEAK PUPPET AND NOTHING MORE. YOU CAN'T EVEN MOVE.

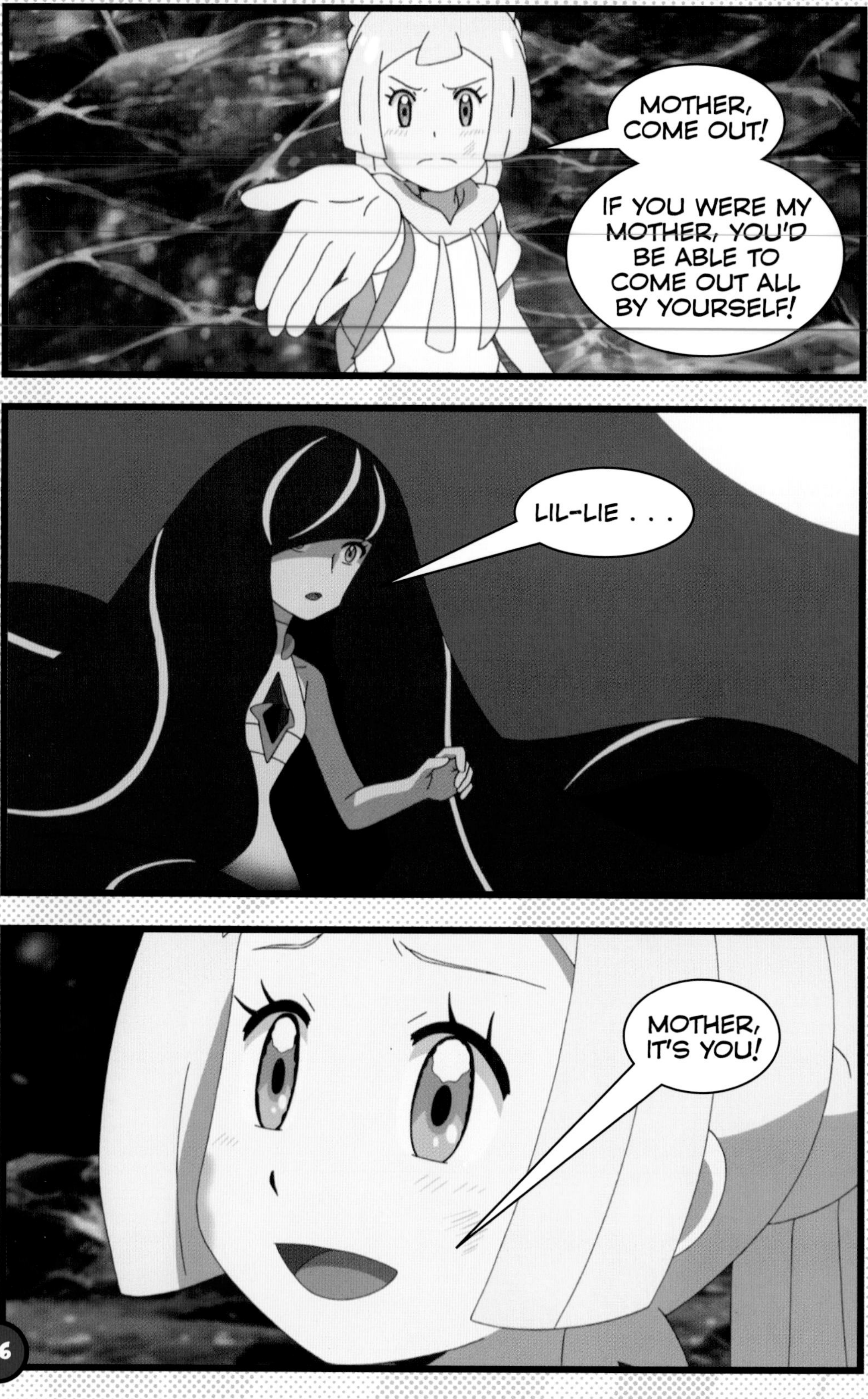
MOTHER, COME OUT!
IF YOU WERE MY MOTHER, YOU'D BE ABLE TO COME OUT ALL BY YOURSELF!
LIL-LIE . . .
MOTHER, IT'S YOU!

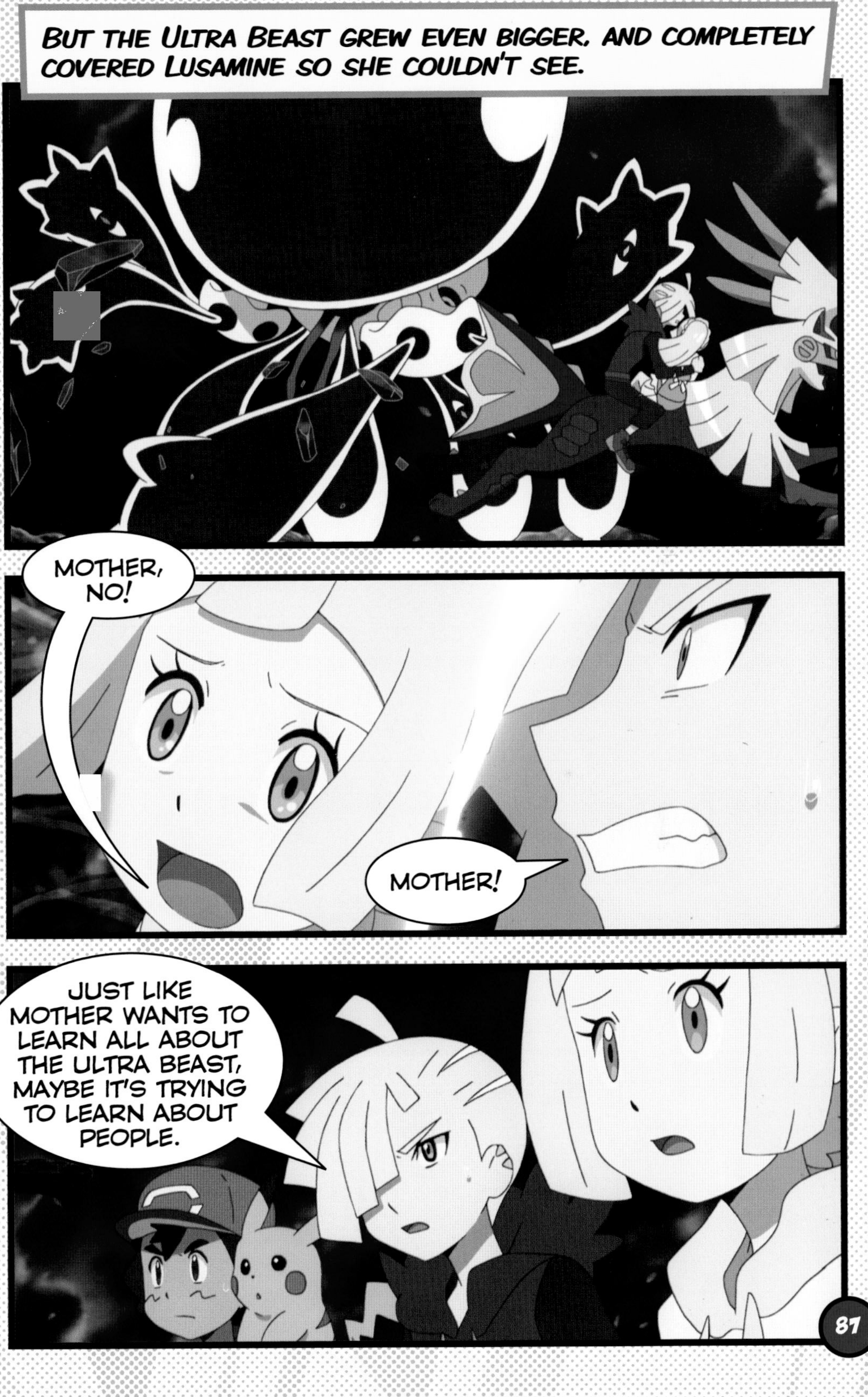
BUT THE ULTRA BEAST GREW EVEN BIGGER, AND COMPLETELY COVERED LUSAMINE SO SHE COULDN'T SEE.
MOTHER, NO!
MOTHER!
JUST LIKE MOTHER WANTS TO LEARN ALL ABOUT THE ULTRA BEAST, MAYBE IT'S TRYING TO LEARN ABOUT PEOPLE.

JUST THEN, THE GROUND BEGAN TO SHAKE, AND STONES SHOT UP OUT OF THE FLOOR. A MOUNTAIN SURROUNDED UB-01 SYMBIONT.

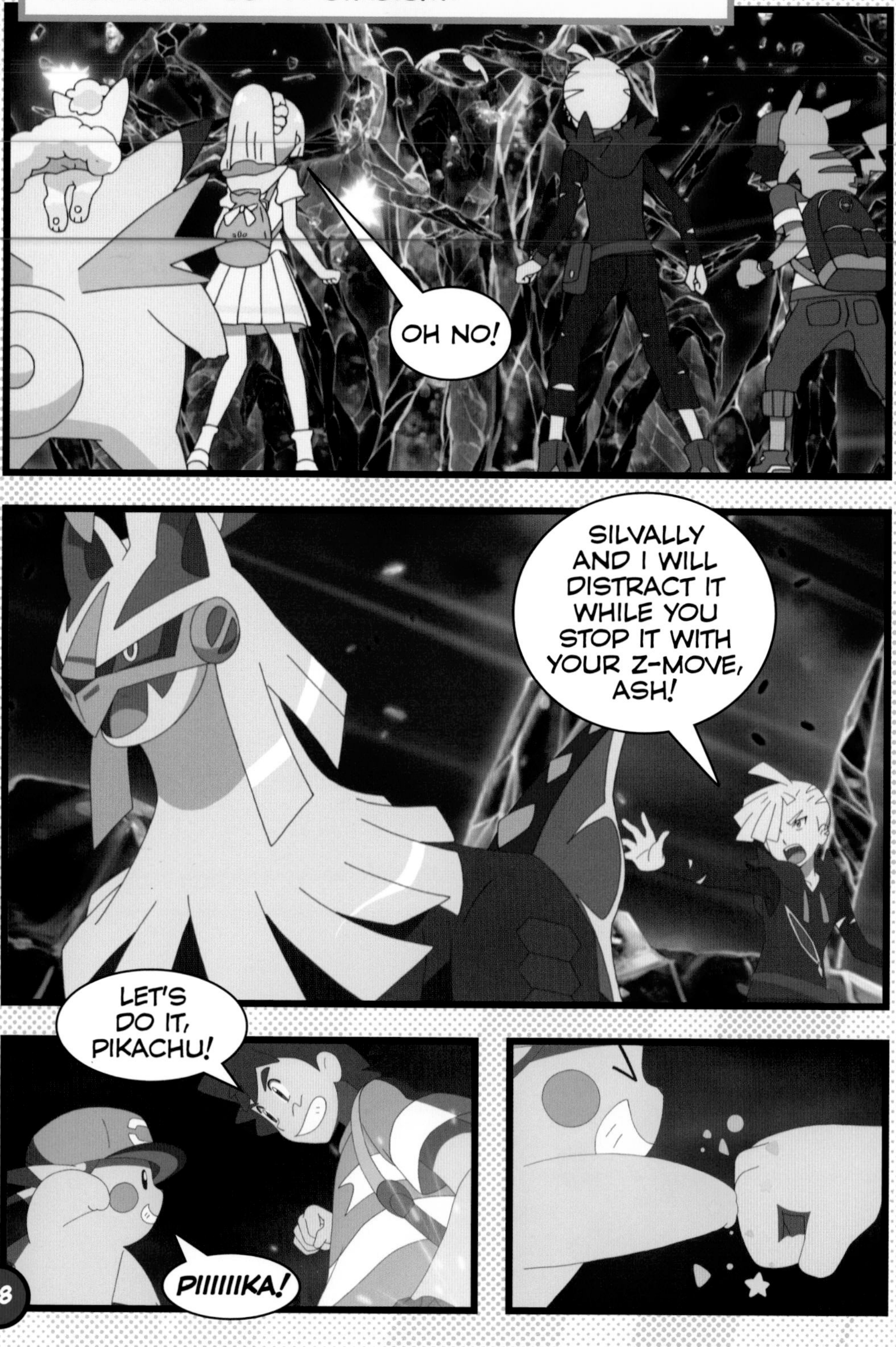
OH NO!
SILVALLY AND I WILL DISTRACT IT WHILE YOU STOP IT WITH YOUR Z-MOVE, ASH!
LET'S DO IT, PIKACHU!
PIIIIIKA!

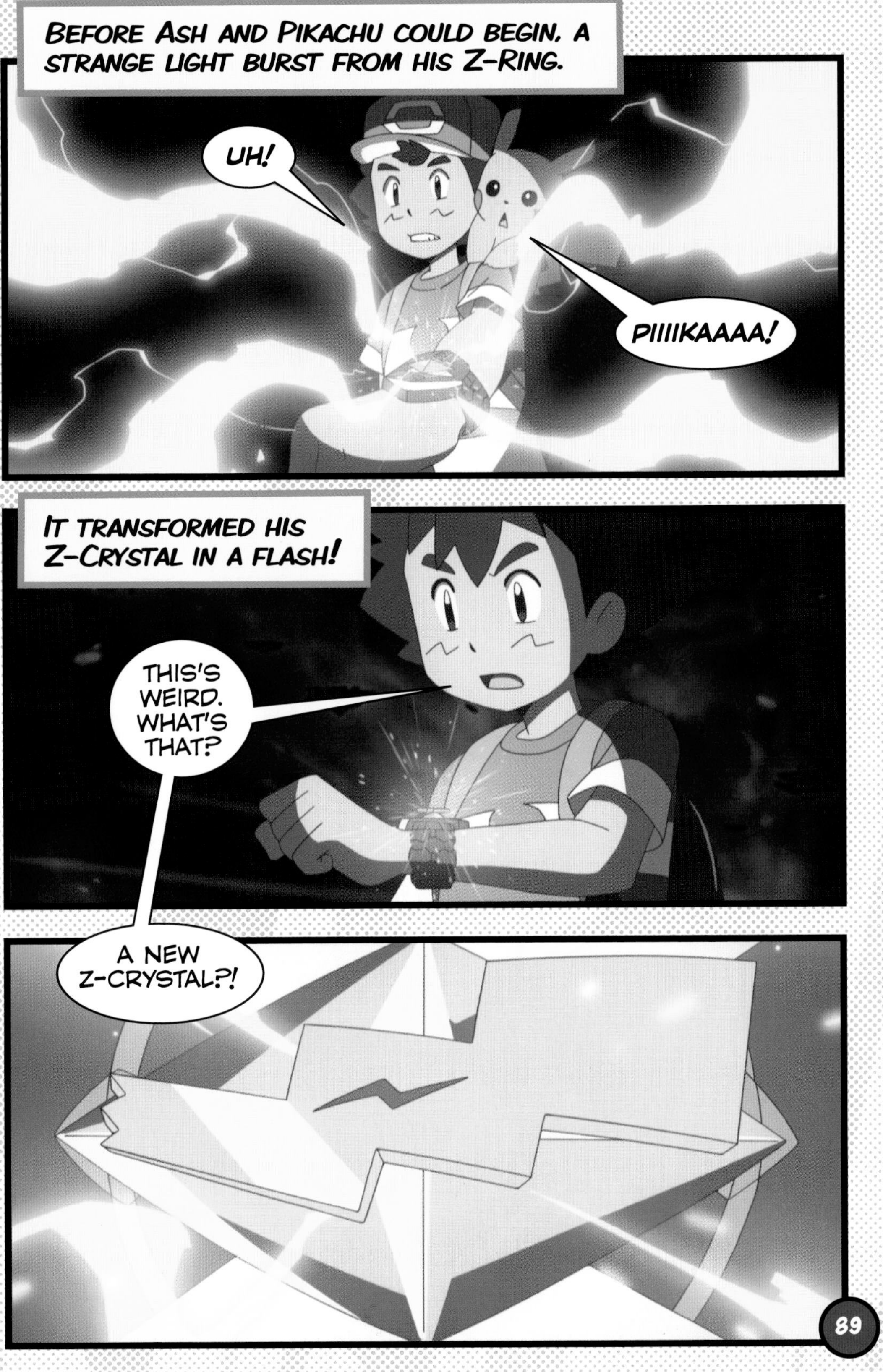
BEFORE ASH AND PIKACHU COULD BEGIN, A STRANGE LIGHT BURST FROM HIS Z-RING.
UH!
PIIIIKAAAA!
IT TRANSFORMED HIS Z-CRYSTAL IN A FLASH!
THIS'S WEIRD. WHAT'S THAT?
A NEW Z-CRYSTAL?!

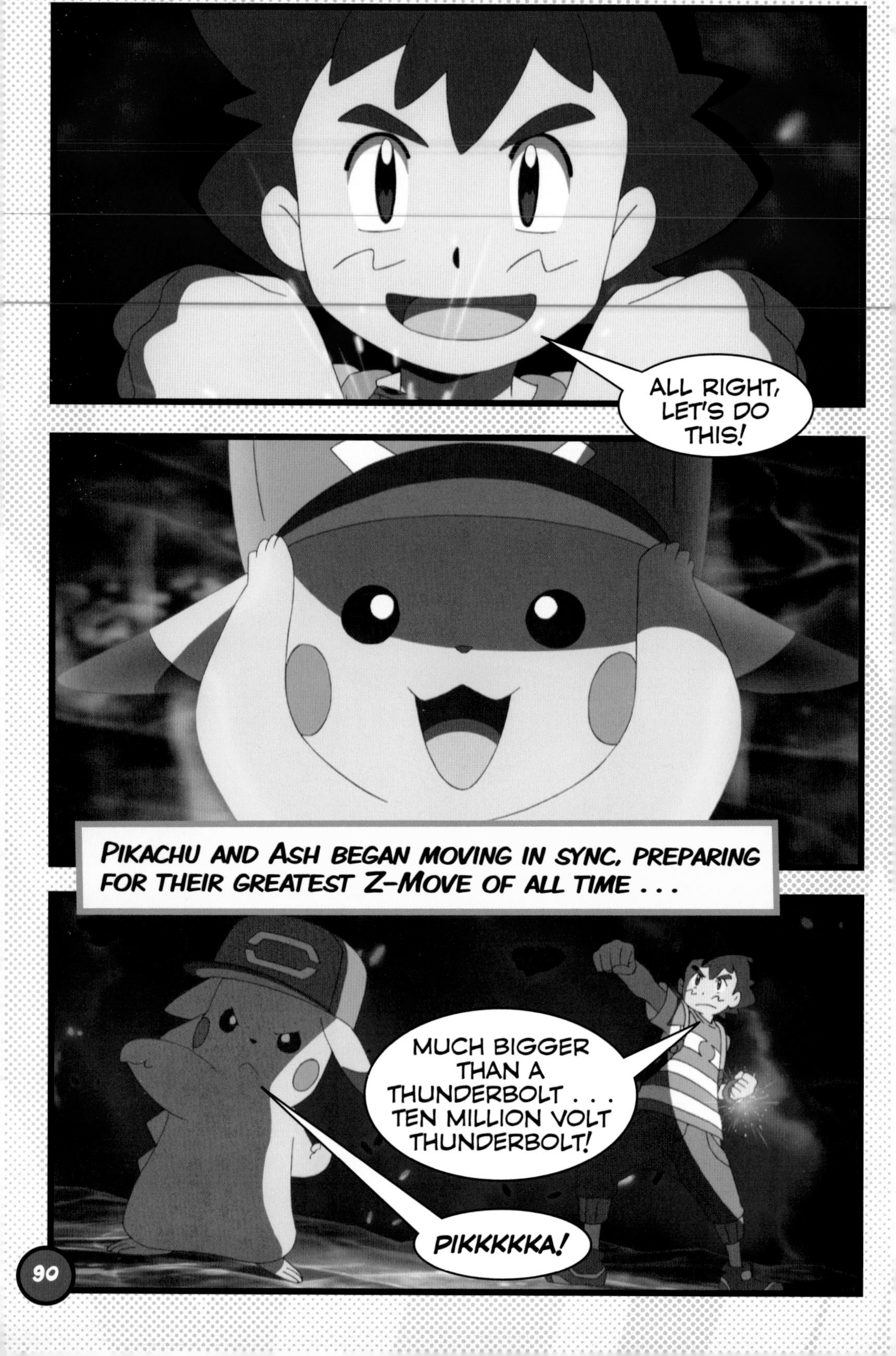
ALL RIGHT, LET'S DO THIS!
PIKACHU AND ASH BEGAN MOVING IN SYNC, PREPARING FOR THEIR GREATEST Z-MOVE OF ALL TIME . . .
MUCH BIGGER THAN A THUNDERBOLT . . . TEN MILLION VOLT THUNDERBOLT!
PIKKKKKA!

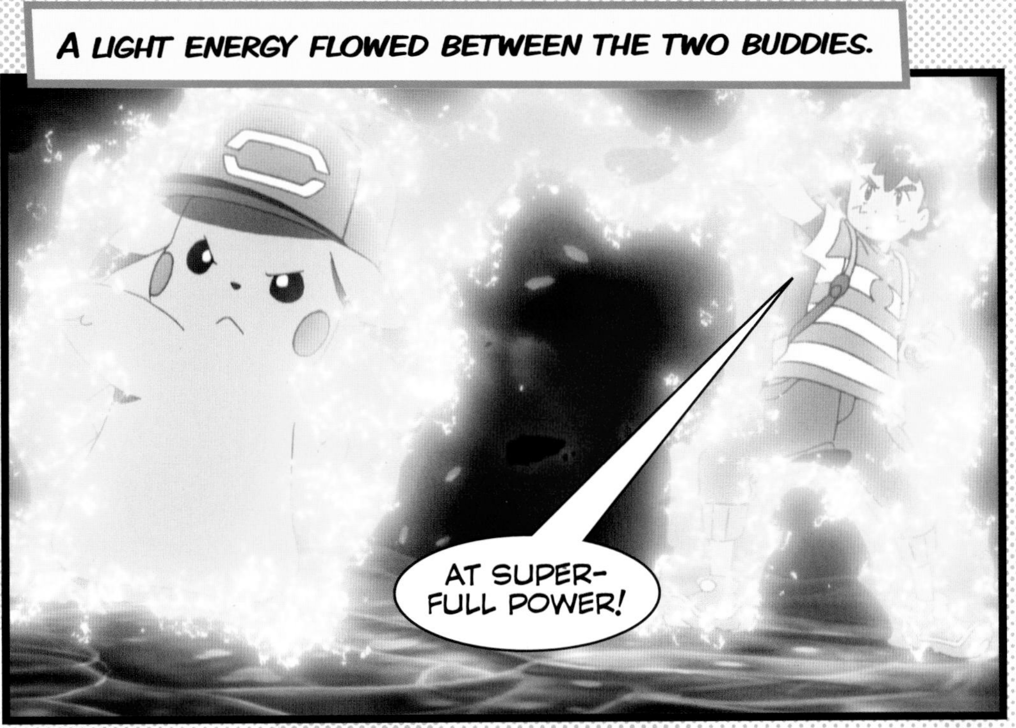
A LIGHT ENERGY FLOWED BETWEEN THE TWO BUDDIES.
AT SUPER-FULL POWER!

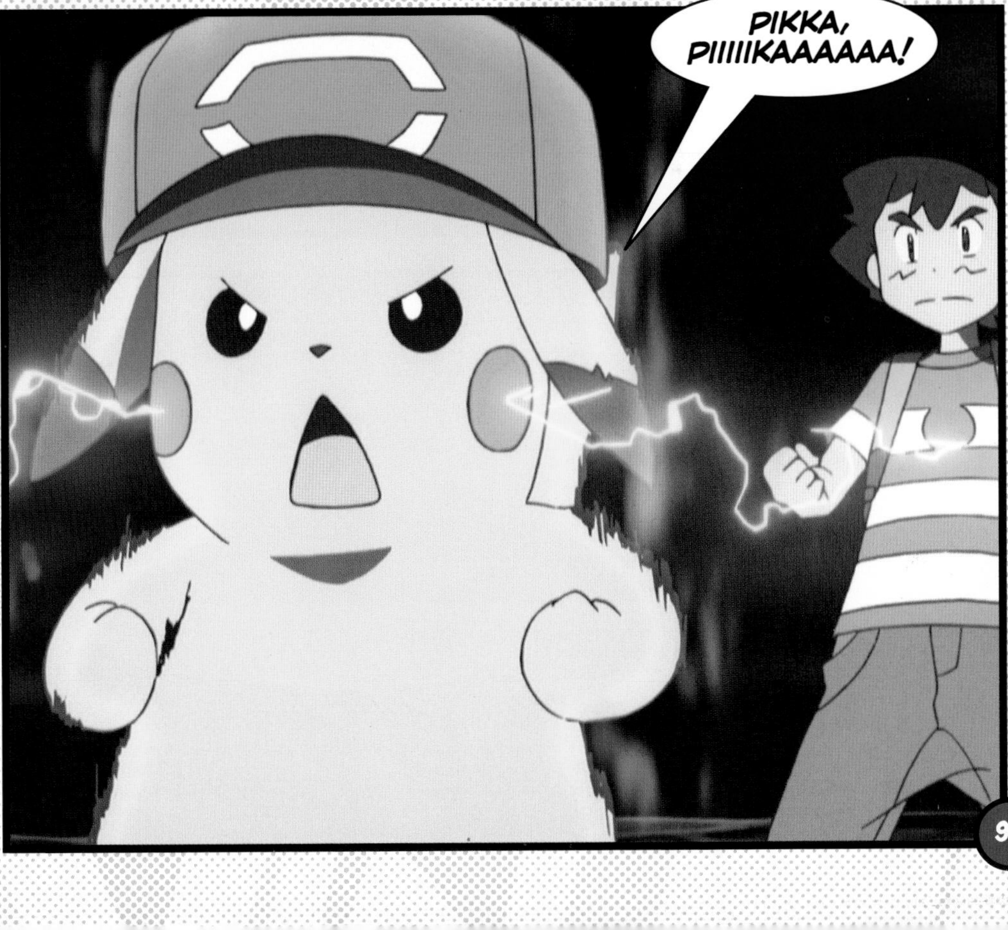
PIKKA, PIIIIIKAAAAAAA!

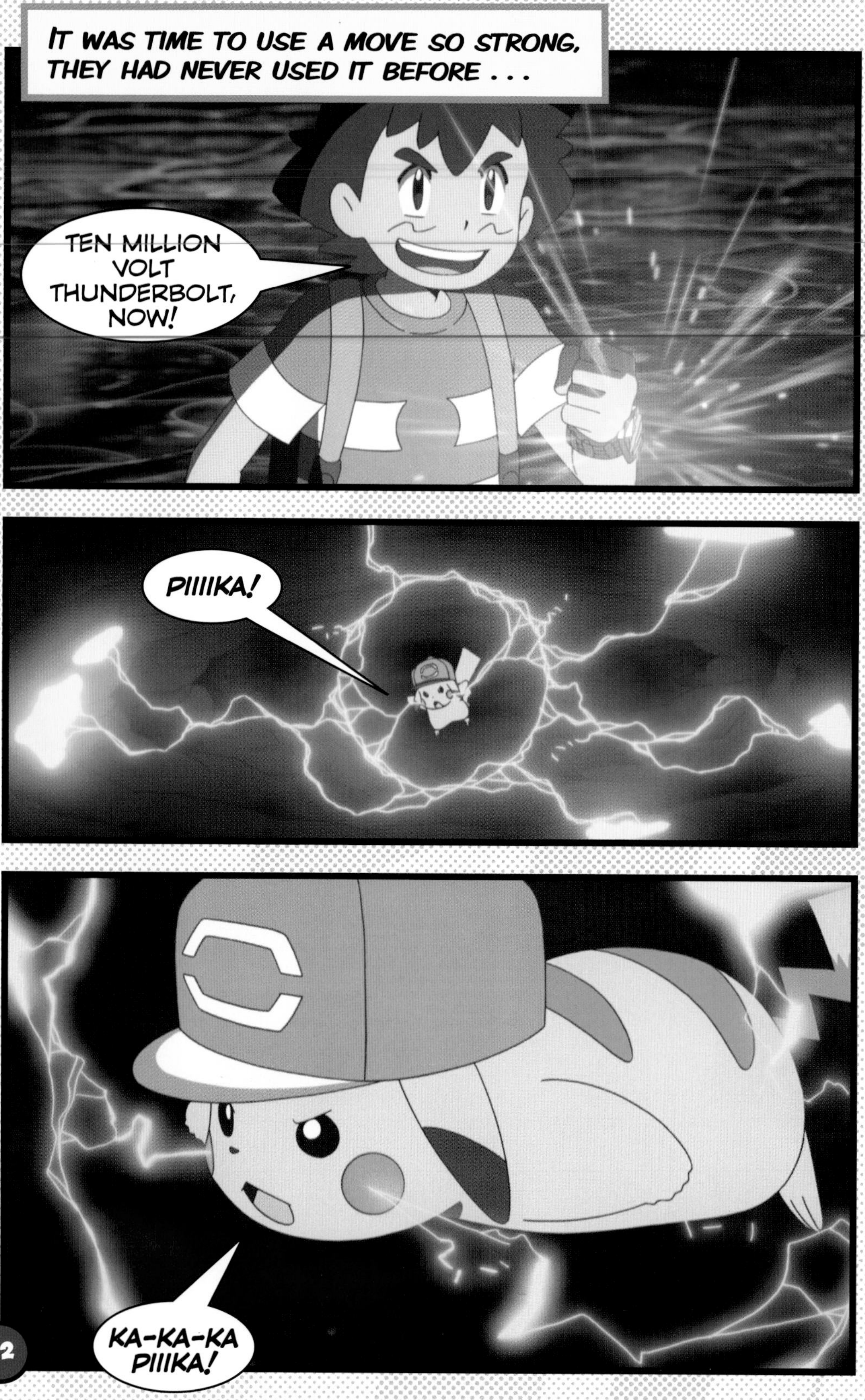
IT WAS TIME TO USE A MOVE SO STRONG, THEY HAD NEVER USED IT BEFORE . . .
TEN MILLION VOLT THUNDERBOLT, NOW!
PIIIIKA!
KA-KA-KA PIIIKA!

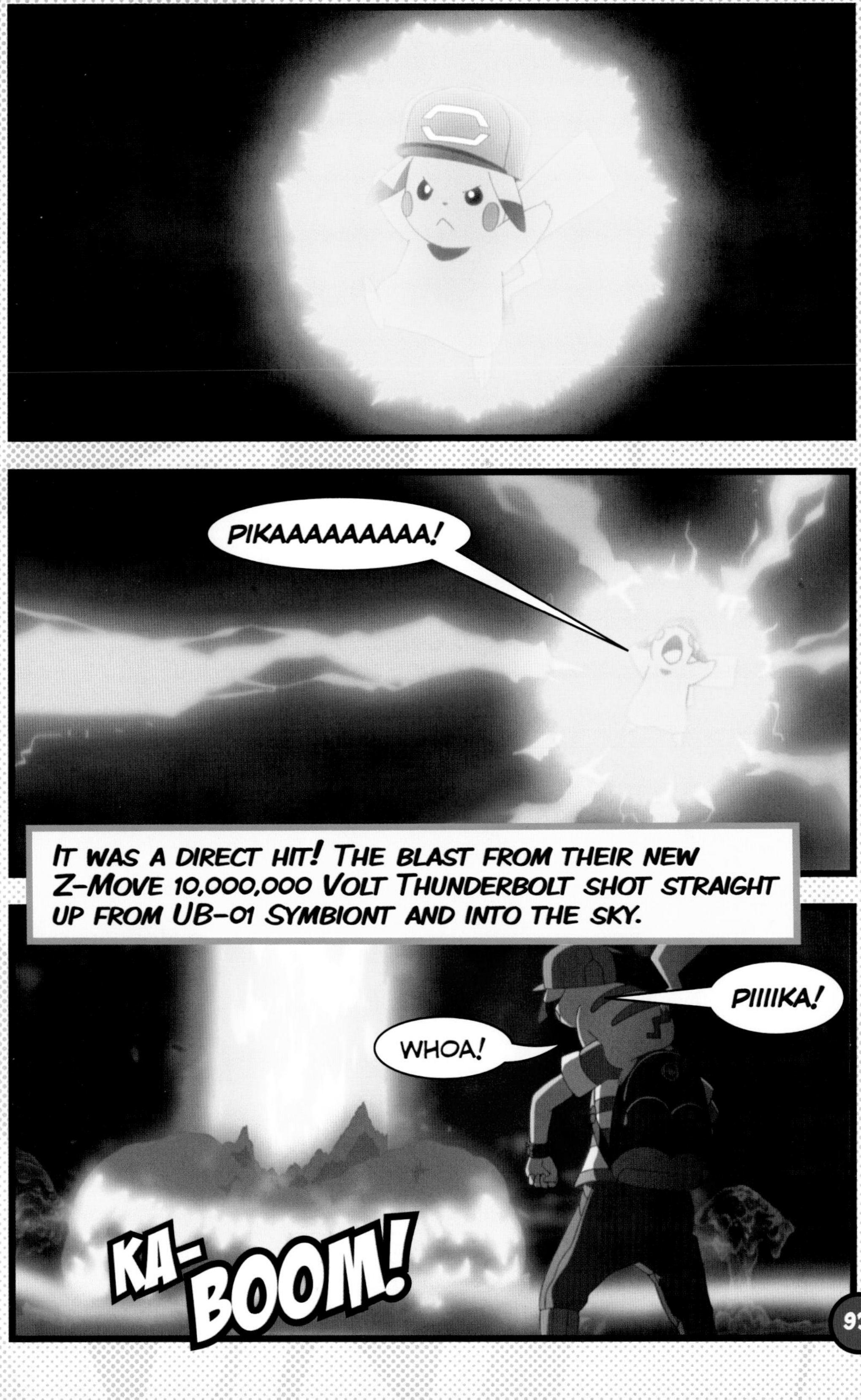
PIKAAAAAAAAA!
IT WAS A DIRECT HIT! THE BLAST FROM THEIR NEW Z-MOVE 10,000,000 VOLT THUNDERBOLT SHOT STRAIGHT UP FROM UB-01 SYMBIONT AND INTO THE SKY.
PIIIIKA!
WHOA!
KA-BOOM!

When the light was gone, UB-01 Symbiont fell to the ground, defeated.

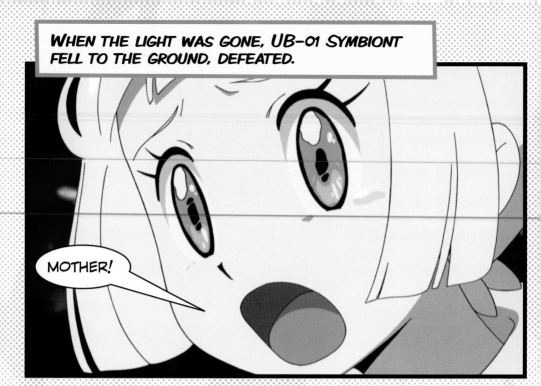

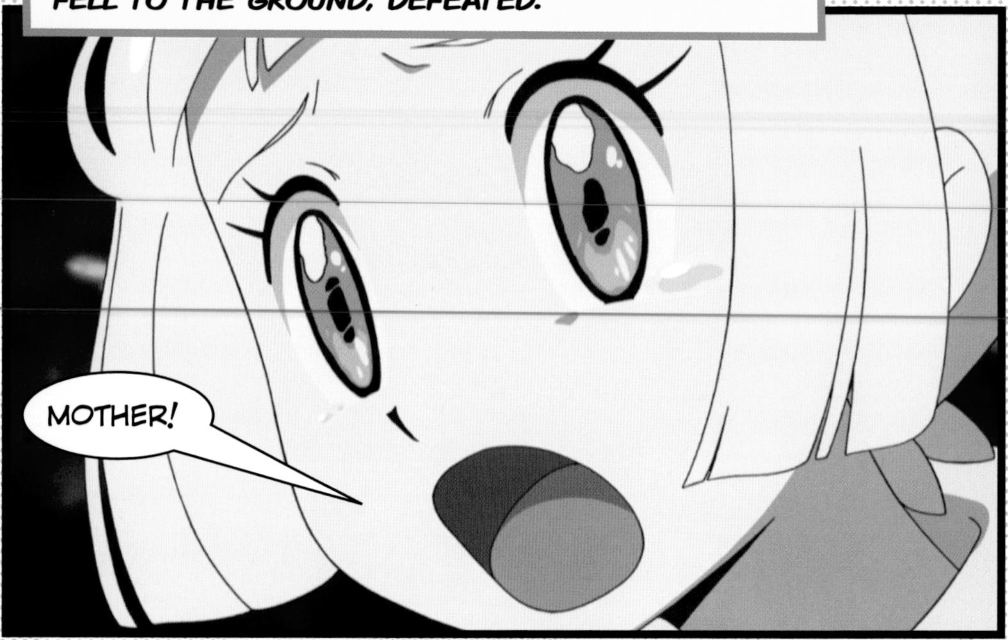
MOTHER!

Lillie and Gladion raced over to rescue Lusamine from the belly of the Ultra Beast. She was tired, but she wasn't hurt.

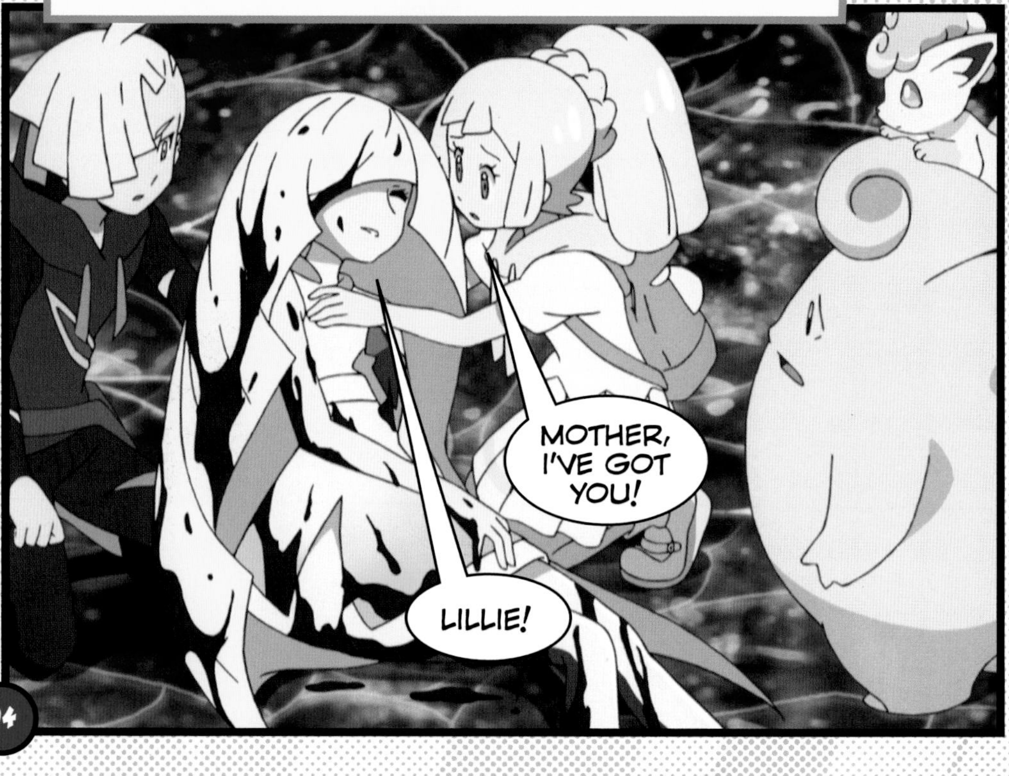
MOTHER, I'VE GOT YOU!
LILLIE!

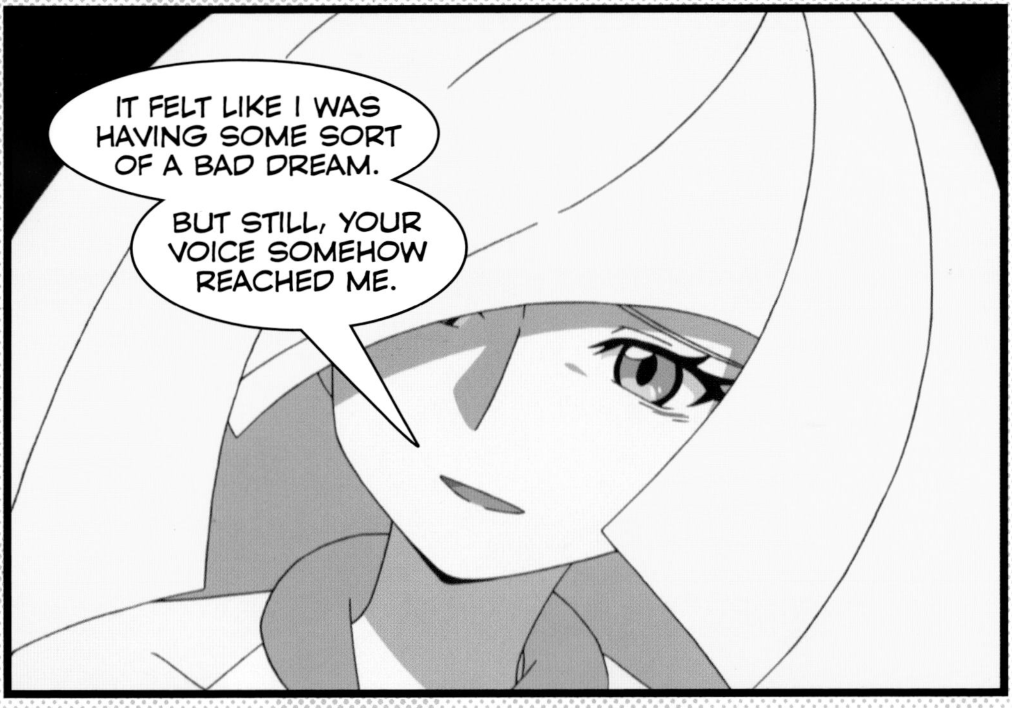
IT FELT LIKE I WAS HAVING SOME SORT OF A BAD DREAM.
BUT STILL, YOUR VOICE SOMEHOW REACHED ME.

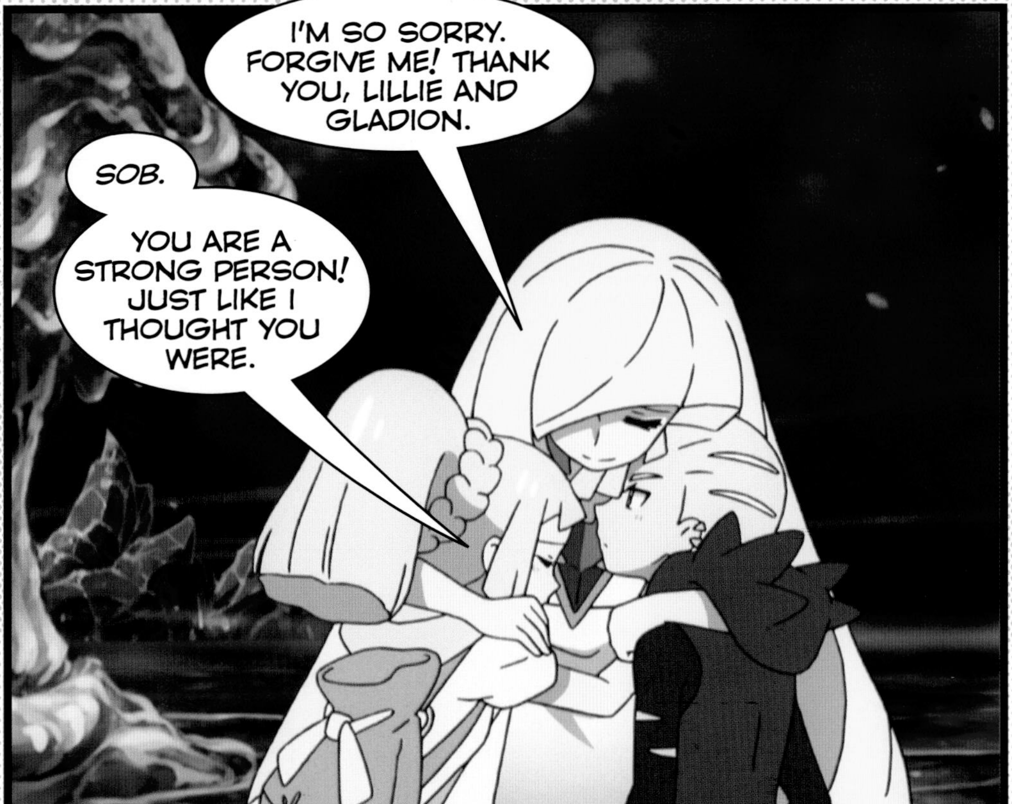
I'M SO SORRY. FORGIVE ME! THANK YOU, LILLIE AND GLADION.
SOB.
YOU ARE A STRONG PERSON! JUST LIKE I THOUGHT YOU WERE.

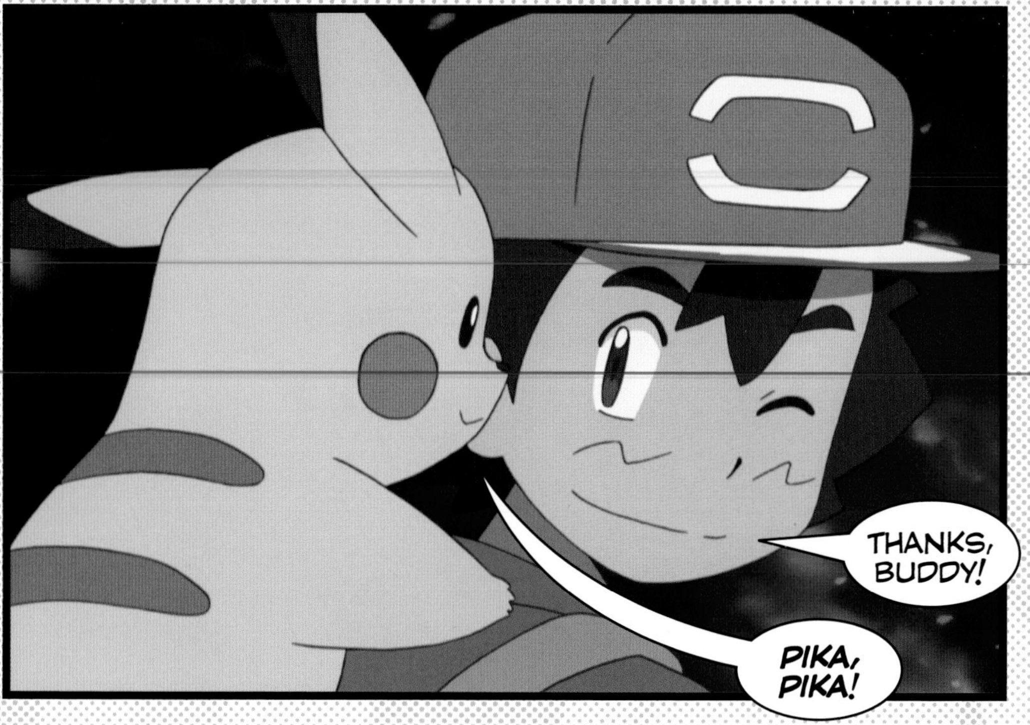
THANKS, BUDDY!
PIKA, PIKA!

THE BATTLE WAS OVER. THE FRIENDS HAD TRIUMPHED TOGETHER!

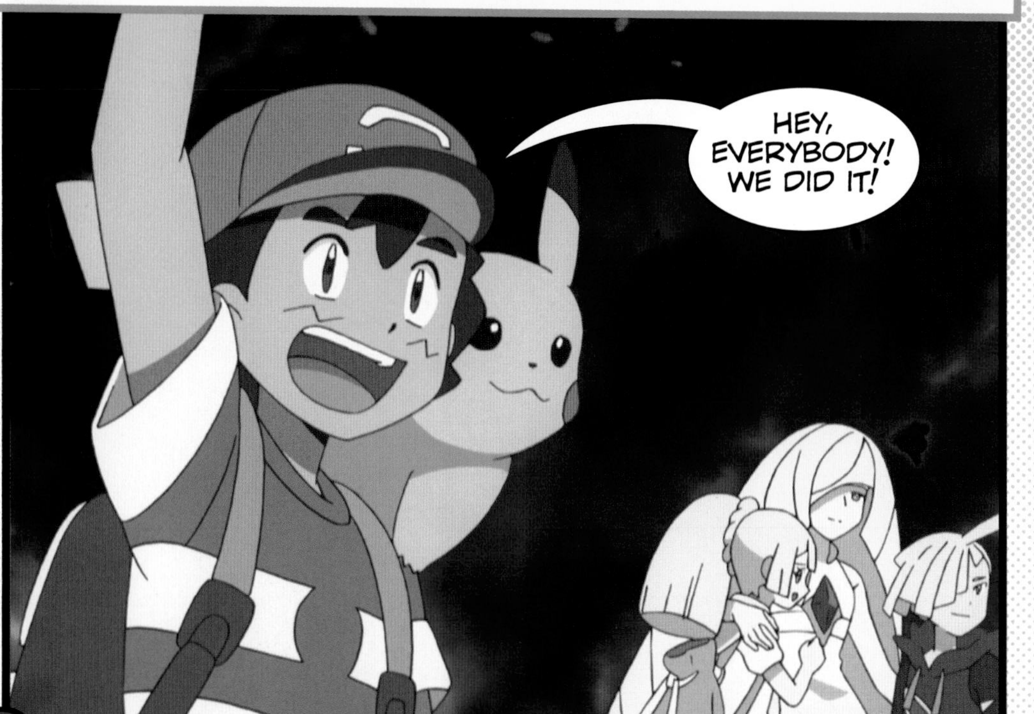
HEY, EVERYBODY! WE DID IT!

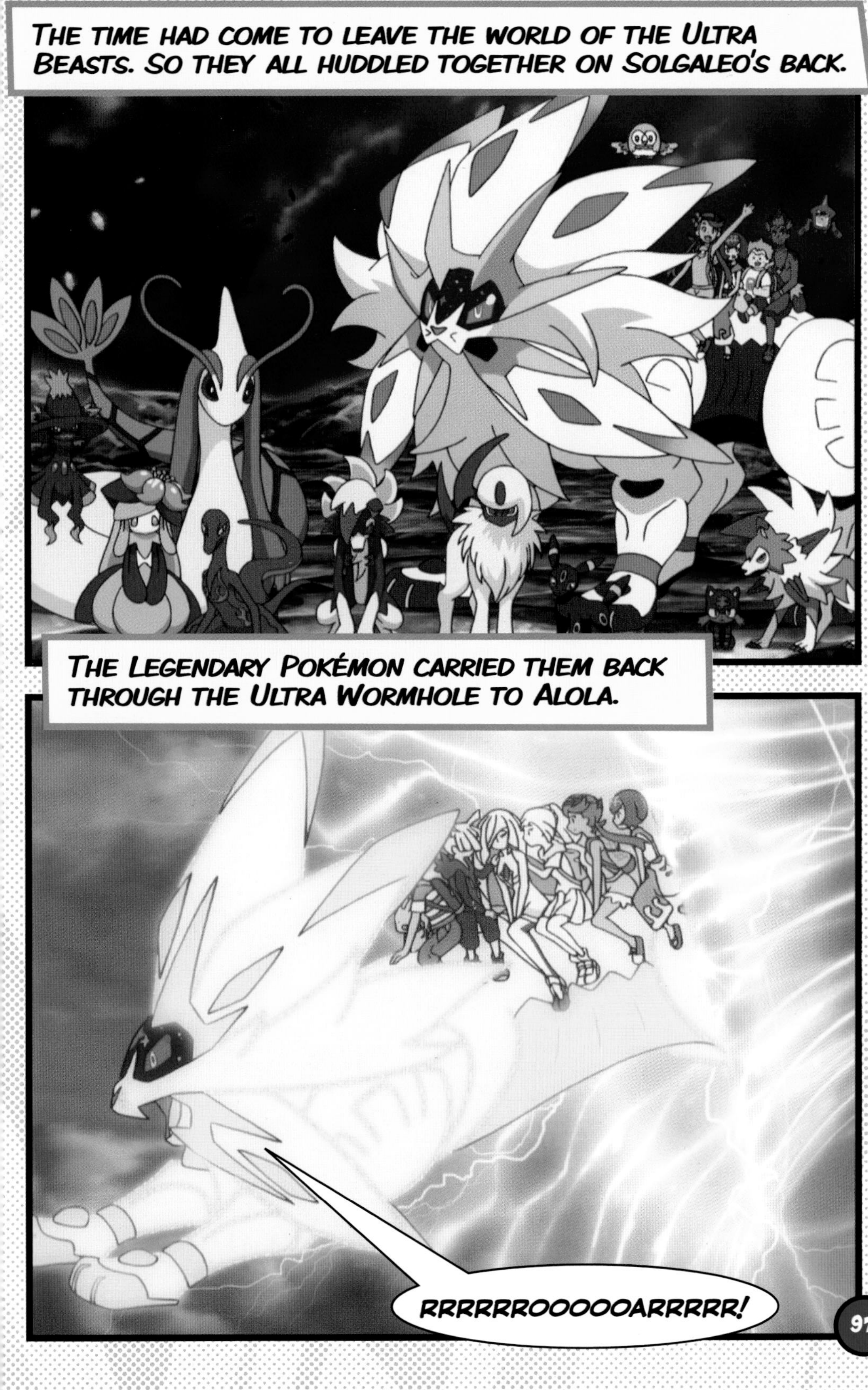
THE TIME HAD COME TO LEAVE THE WORLD OF THE ULTRA BEASTS. SO THEY ALL HUDDLED TOGETHER ON SOLGALEO'S BACK.
THE LEGENDARY POKÉMON CARRIED THEM BACK THROUGH THE ULTRA WORMHOLE TO ALOLA.
RRRRRROOOOOARRRRR!

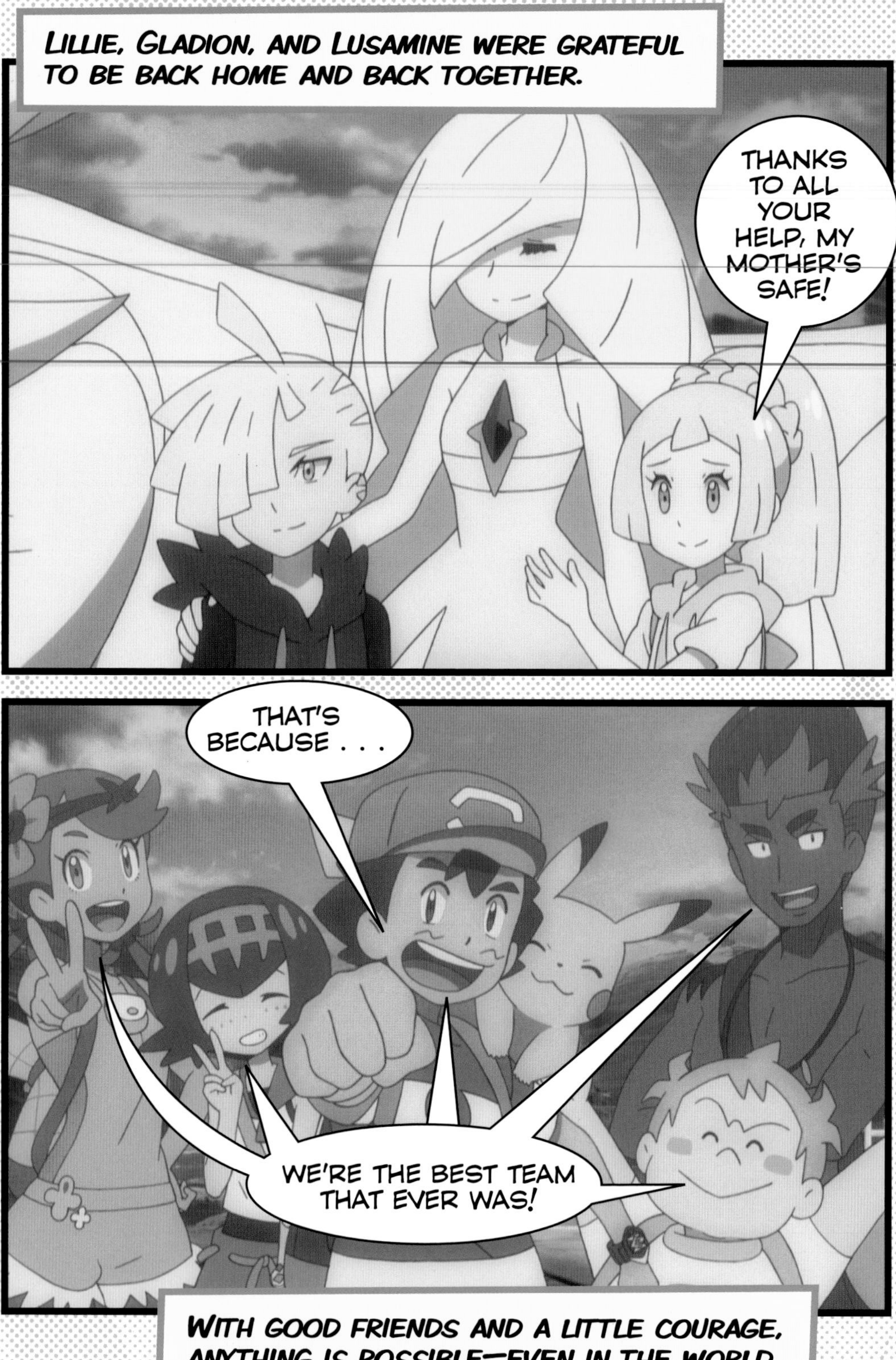
LILLIE, GLADION, AND LUSAMINE WERE GRATEFUL TO BE BACK HOME AND BACK TOGETHER.
THANKS TO ALL YOUR HELP, MY MOTHER'S SAFE!
THAT'S BECAUSE . . .
WE'RE THE BEST TEAM THAT EVER WAS!
WITH GOOD FRIENDS AND A LITTLE COURAGE, ANYTHING IS POSSIBLE—EVEN IN THE WORLD OF THE ULTRA BEASTS!

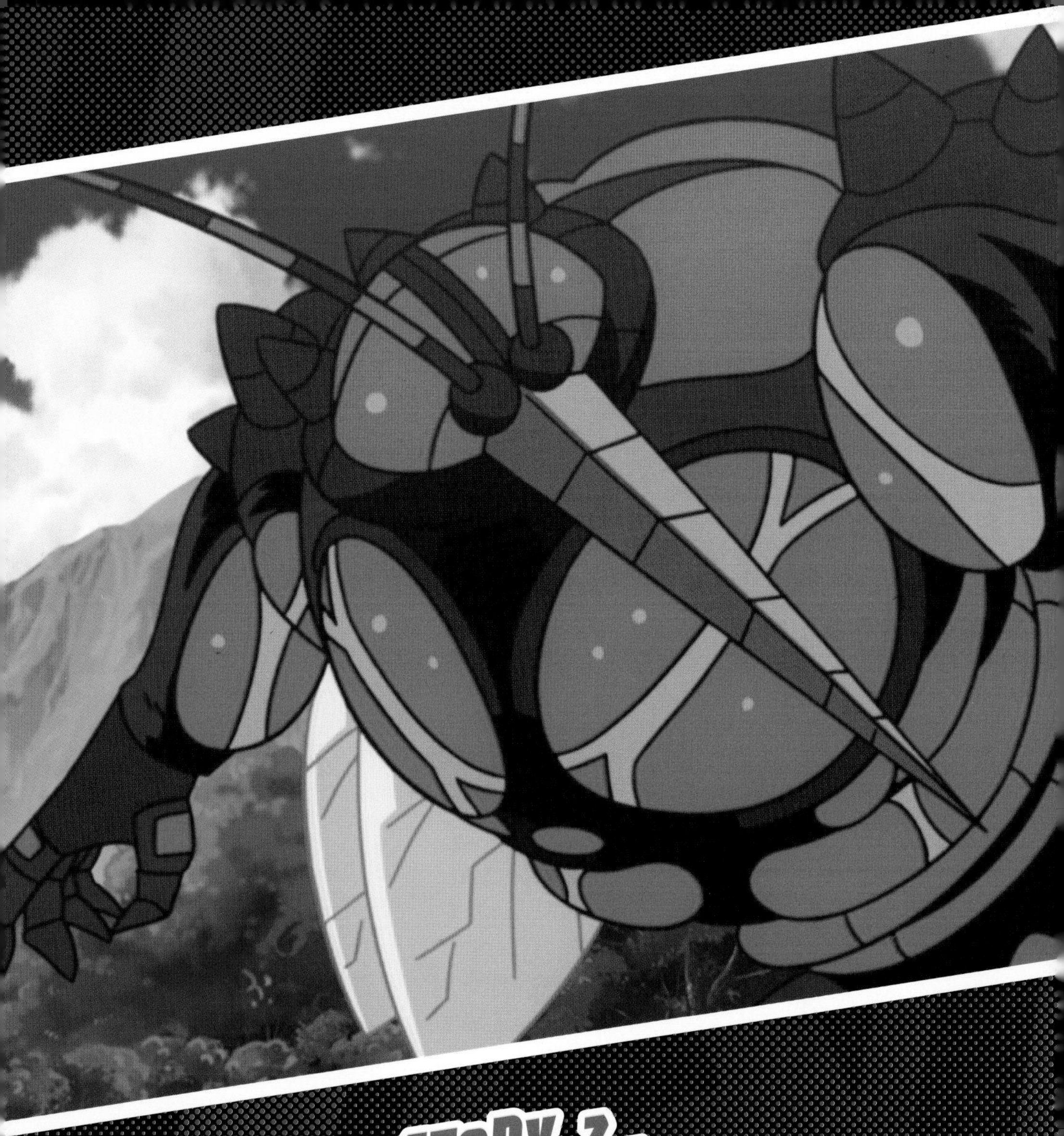

STORY 2: BUZZWOLE BATTLE

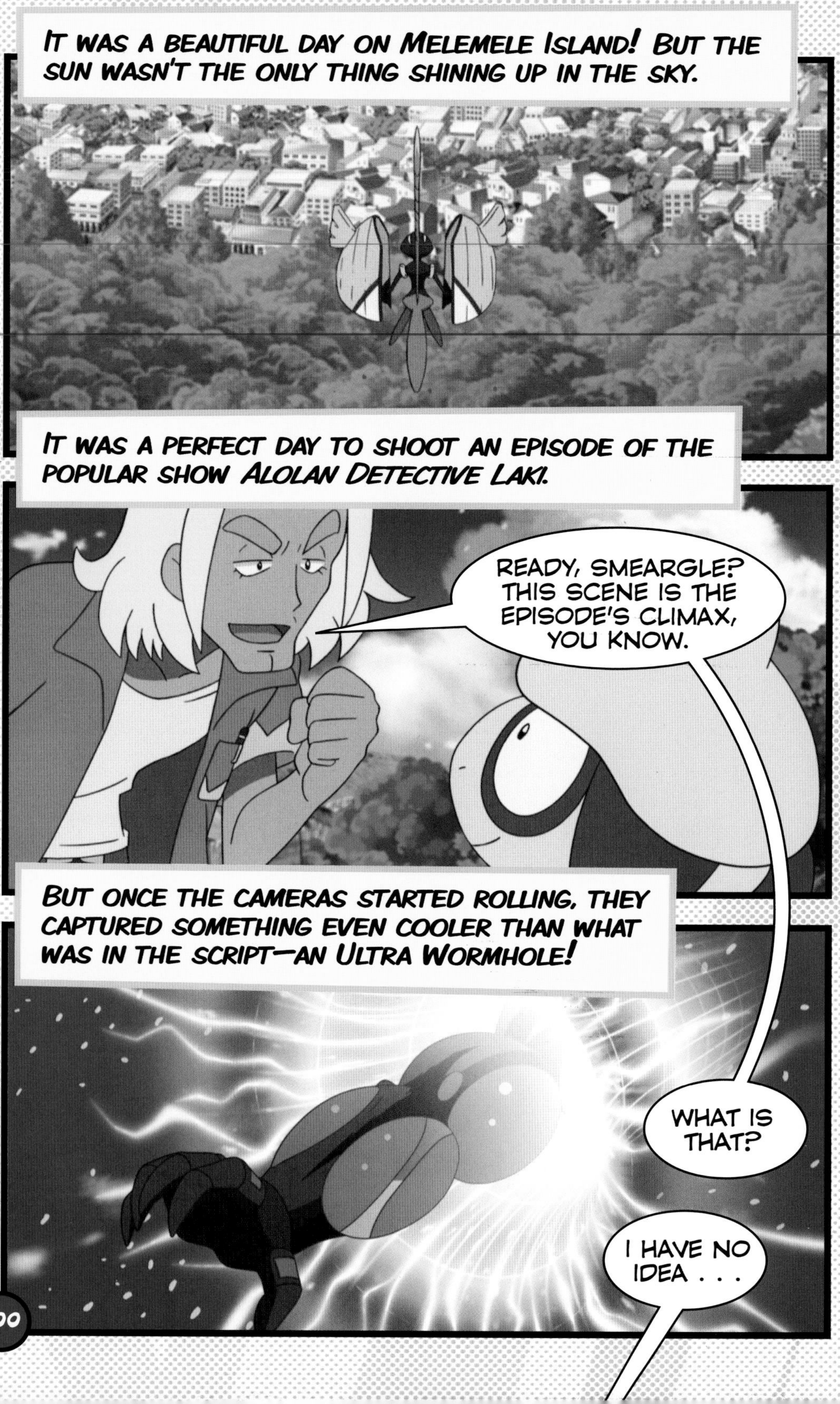
IT WAS A BEAUTIFUL DAY ON MELEMELE ISLAND! BUT THE SUN WASN'T THE ONLY THING SHINING UP IN THE SKY.
IT WAS A PERFECT DAY TO SHOOT AN EPISODE OF THE POPULAR SHOW ALOLAN DETECTIVE LAKI.
READY, SMEARGLE? THIS SCENE IS THE EPISODE'S CLIMAX, YOU KNOW.
BUT ONCE THE CAMERAS STARTED ROLLING, THEY CAPTURED SOMETHING EVEN COOLER THAN WHAT WAS IN THE SCRIPT—AN ULTRA WORMHOLE!
WHAT IS THAT?
I HAVE NO IDEA . . .

SOON, A GIANT ULTRA BEAST LANDED.

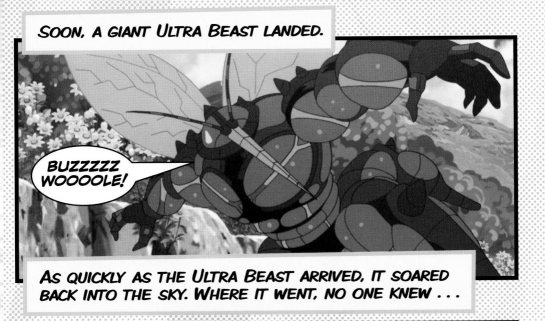

BUZZZZZ WOOOOLE!

AS QUICKLY AS THE ULTRA BEAST ARRIVED, IT SOARED BACK INTO THE SKY. WHERE IT WENT, NO ONE KNEW . . .

MEANWHILE, BACK AT THE POKÉMON SCHOOL, PROFESSOR KUKUI WAS TEACHING THE LESSON HE HAD PLANNED.

YOU SEE, ENVIRONMENTAL DIFFERENCES CAN HAVE A GREAT EFFECT ON THE DEVELOPMENT OF POKÉMON.

OF COURSE, THESE DIFFERENCES APPLY TO ALL LIVING THINGS, INCLUDING HUMANS.

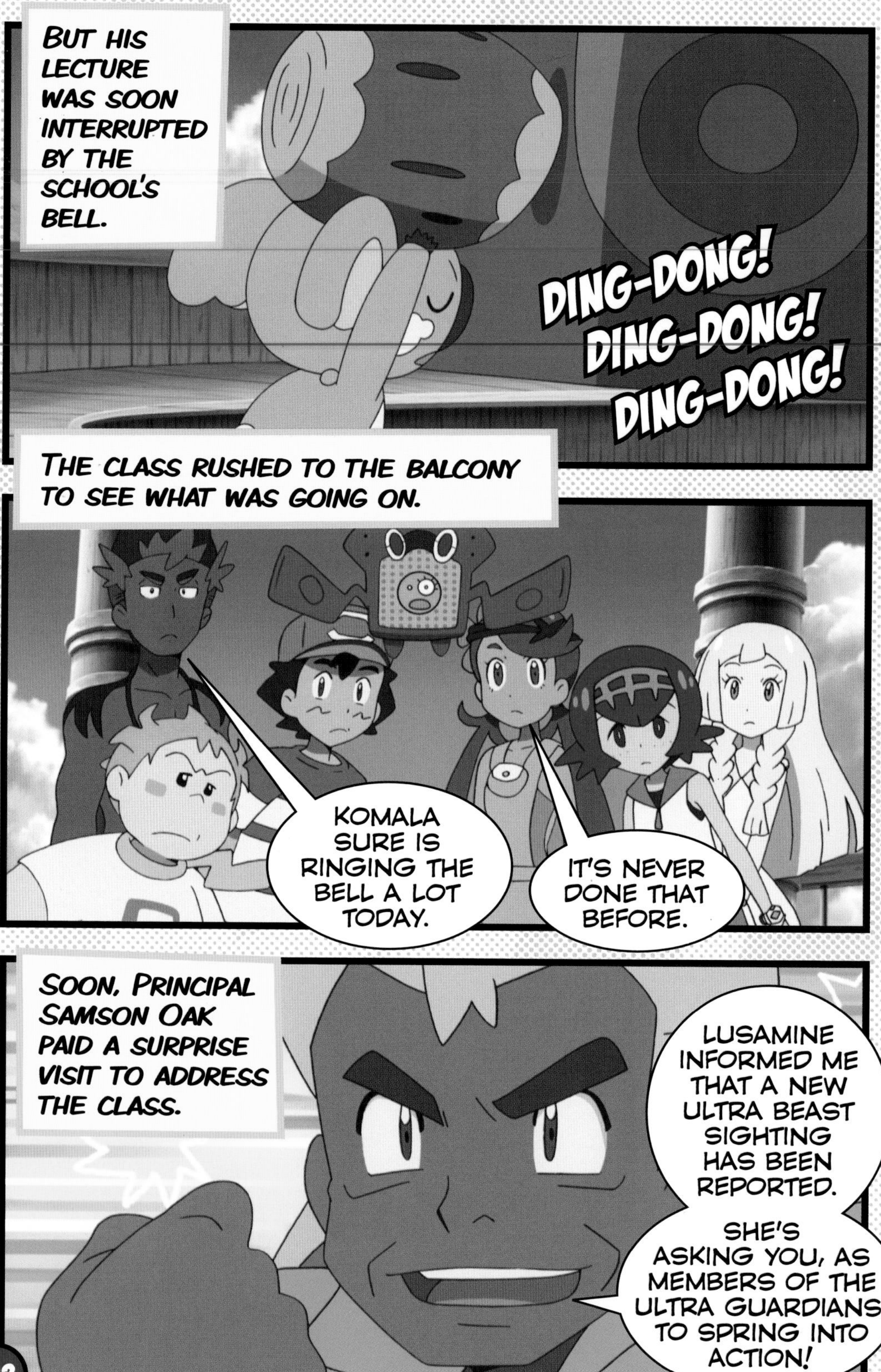

BUT HIS LECTURE WAS SOON INTERRUPTED BY THE SCHOOL'S BELL.
DING-DONG! DING-DONG! DING-DONG!
THE CLASS RUSHED TO THE BALCONY TO SEE WHAT WAS GOING ON.
KOMALA SURE IS RINGING THE BELL A LOT TODAY.
IT'S NEVER DONE THAT BEFORE.
SOON, PRINCIPAL SAMSON OAK PAID A SURPRISE VISIT TO ADDRESS THE CLASS.
LUSAMINE INFORMED ME THAT A NEW ULTRA BEAST SIGHTING HAS BEEN REPORTED.
SHE'S ASKING YOU, AS MEMBERS OF THE ULTRA GUARDIANS, TO SPRING INTO ACTION!

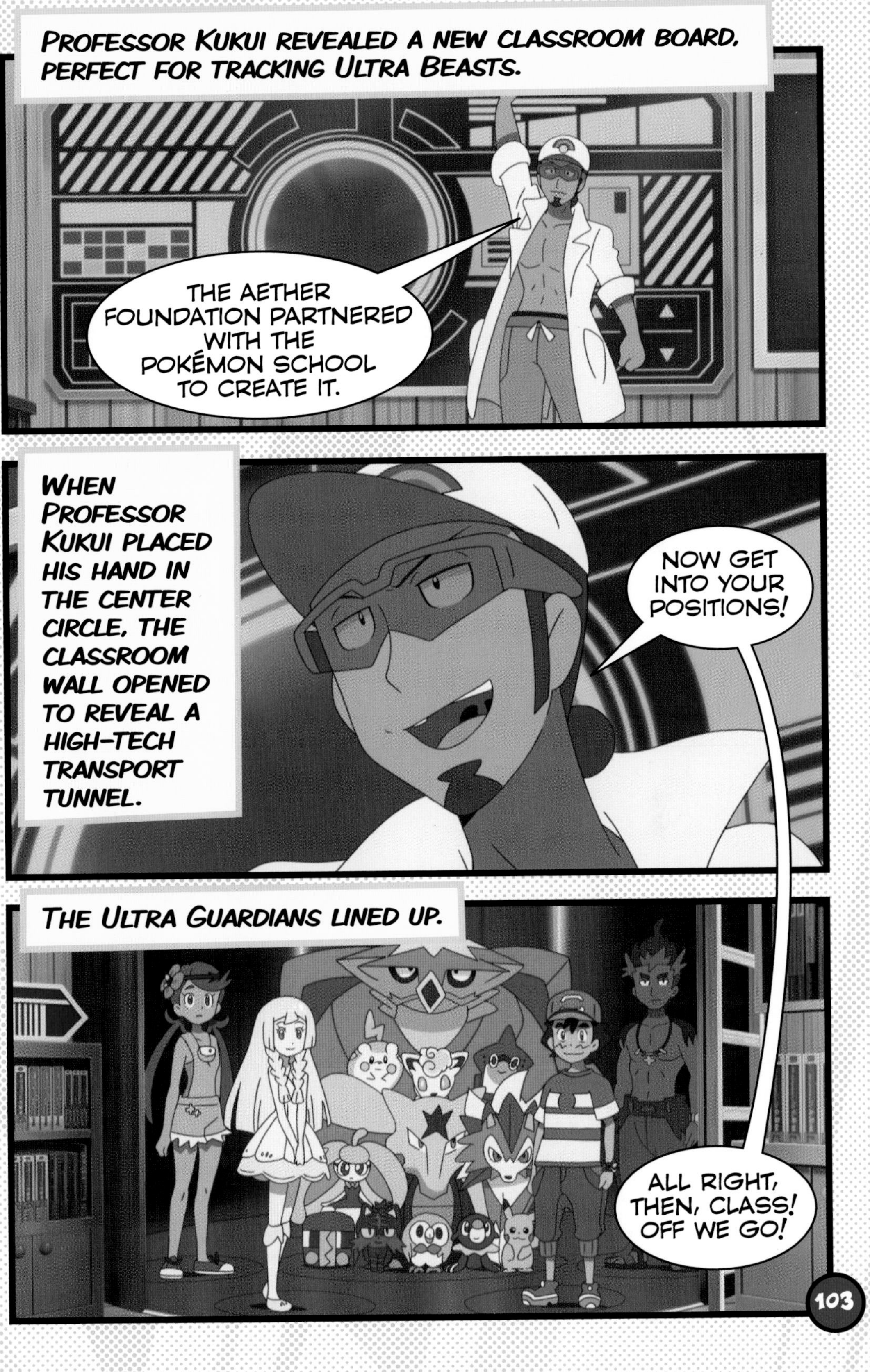

PROFESSOR KUKUI REVEALED A NEW CLASSROOM BOARD, PERFECT FOR TRACKING ULTRA BEASTS.
THE AETHER FOUNDATION PARTNERED WITH THE POKÉMON SCHOOL TO CREATE IT.
WHEN PROFESSOR KUKUI PLACED HIS HAND IN THE CENTER CIRCLE, THE CLASSROOM WALL OPENED TO REVEAL A HIGH-TECH TRANSPORT TUNNEL.
NOW GET INTO YOUR POSITIONS!
THE ULTRA GUARDIANS LINED UP.
ALL RIGHT, THEN, CLASS! OFF WE GO!

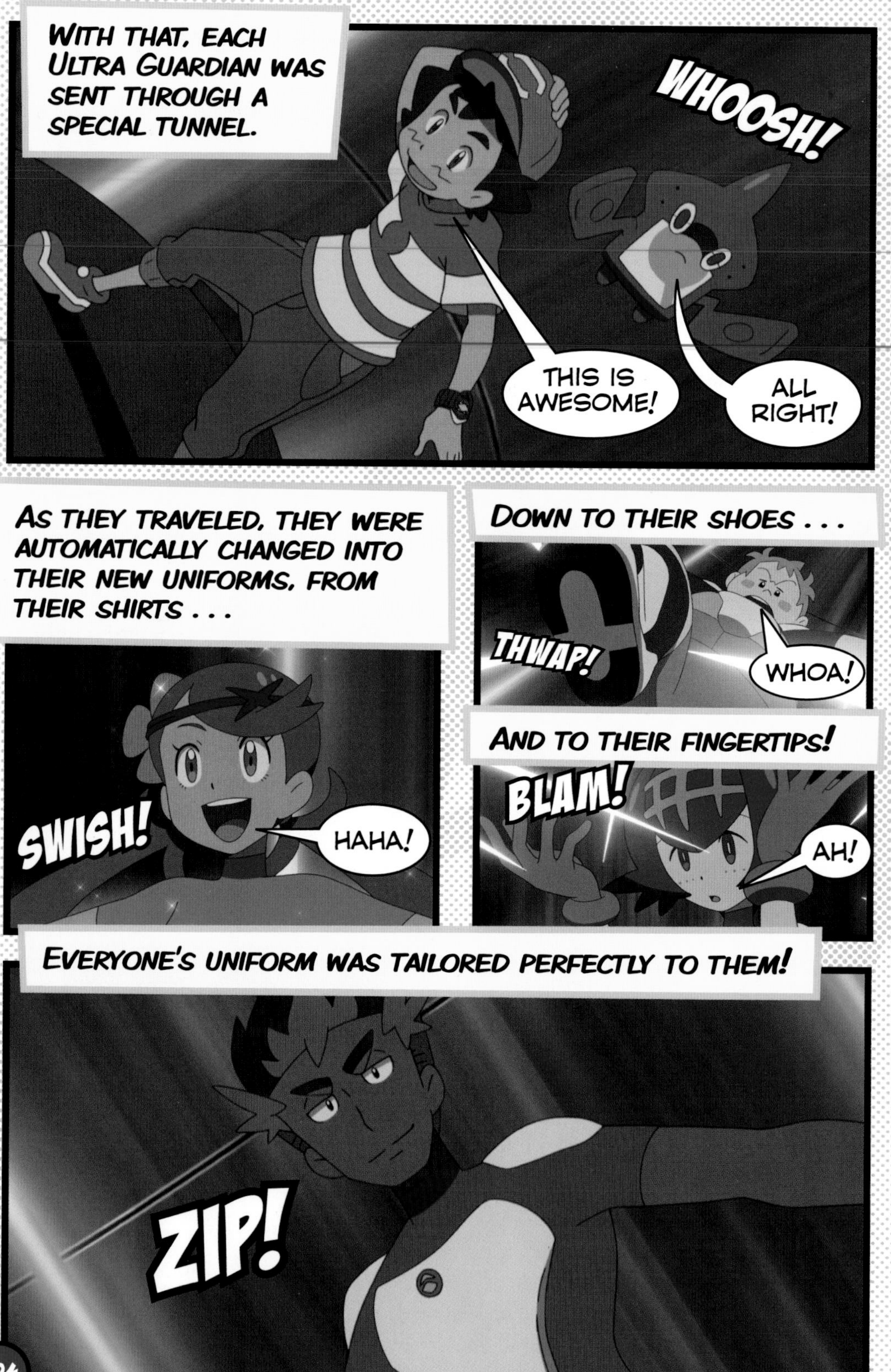
WITH THAT, EACH ULTRA GUARDIAN WAS SENT THROUGH A SPECIAL TUNNEL.
WHOOSH!
THIS IS AWESOME!
ALL RIGHT!
AS THEY TRAVELED, THEY WERE AUTOMATICALLY CHANGED INTO THEIR NEW UNIFORMS, FROM THEIR SHIRTS . . .
SWISH!
HAHA!
DOWN TO THEIR SHOES . . .
THWAP!
WHOA!
AND TO THEIR FINGERTIPS!
BLAM!
AH!
EVERYONE'S UNIFORM WAS TAILORED PERFECTLY TO THEM!
ZIP!

Even the Pokémon each got a special pendant.

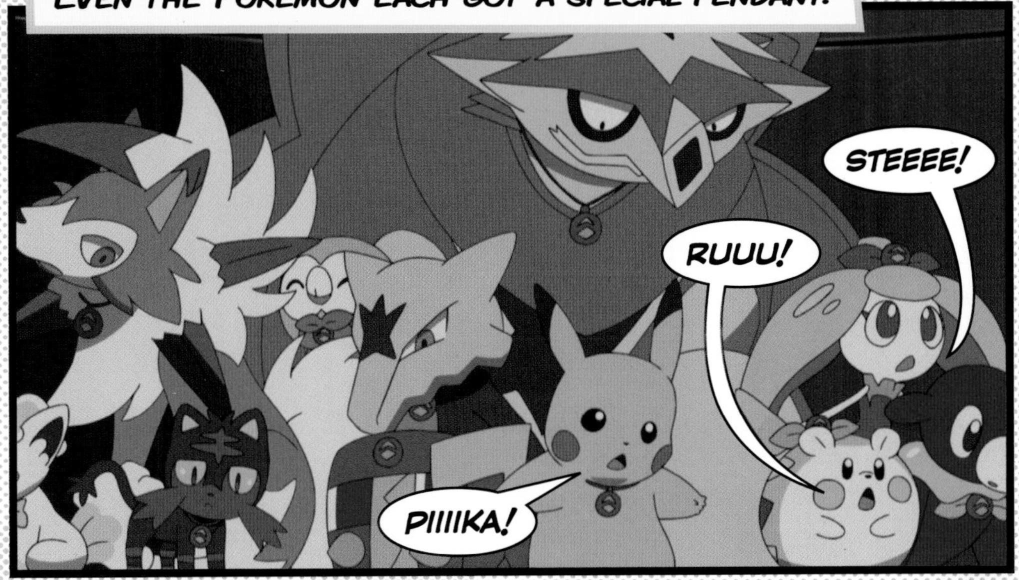
STEEEE!
RUUU!
PIIIIKA!

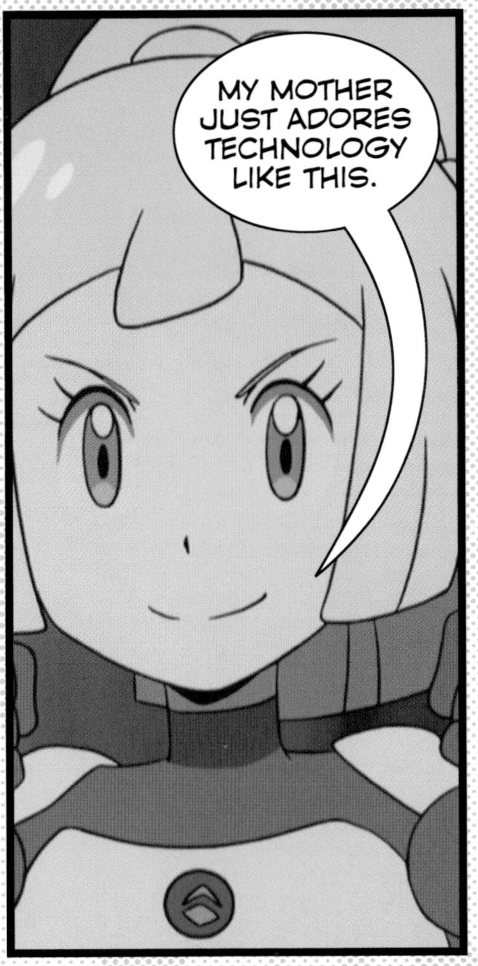
MY MOTHER JUST ADORES TECHNOLOGY LIKE THIS.

Ash was feeling snazzy, and ready to snap into Ultra Guardian action!

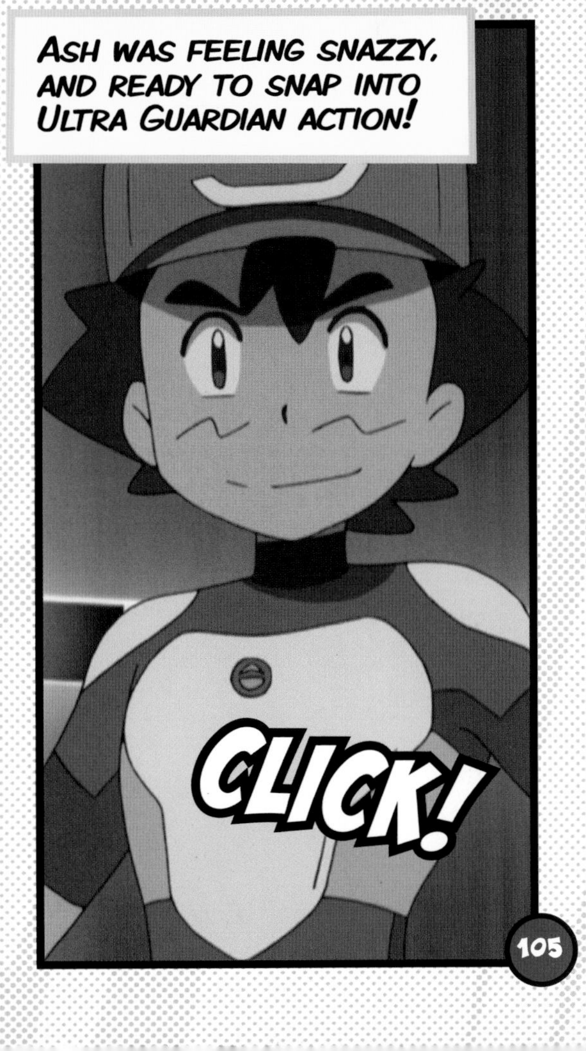
CLICK!

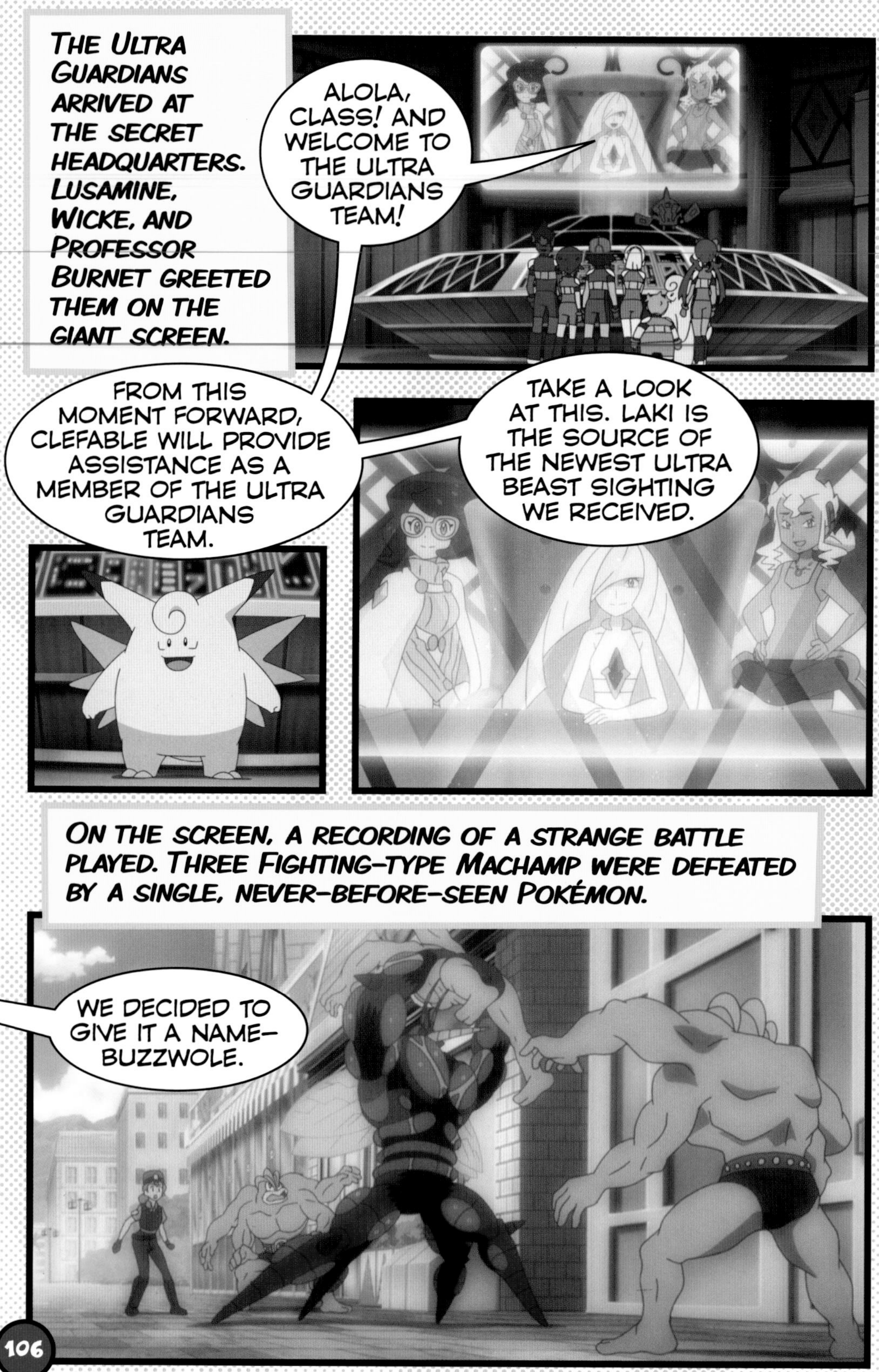
THE ULTRA GUARDIANS ARRIVED AT THE SECRET HEADQUARTERS. LUSAMINE, WICKE, AND PROFESSOR BURNET GREETED THEM ON THE GIANT SCREEN.
ALOLA, CLASS! AND WELCOME TO THE ULTRA GUARDIANS TEAM!
FROM THIS MOMENT FORWARD, CLEFABLE WILL PROVIDE ASSISTANCE AS A MEMBER OF THE ULTRA GUARDIANS TEAM.
TAKE A LOOK AT THIS. LAKI IS THE SOURCE OF THE NEWEST ULTRA BEAST SIGHTING WE RECEIVED.
ON THE SCREEN, A RECORDING OF A STRANGE BATTLE PLAYED. THREE FIGHTING-TYPE MACHAMP WERE DEFEATED BY A SINGLE, NEVER-BEFORE-SEEN POKÉMON.
WE DECIDED TO GIVE IT A NAME—BUZZWOLE.

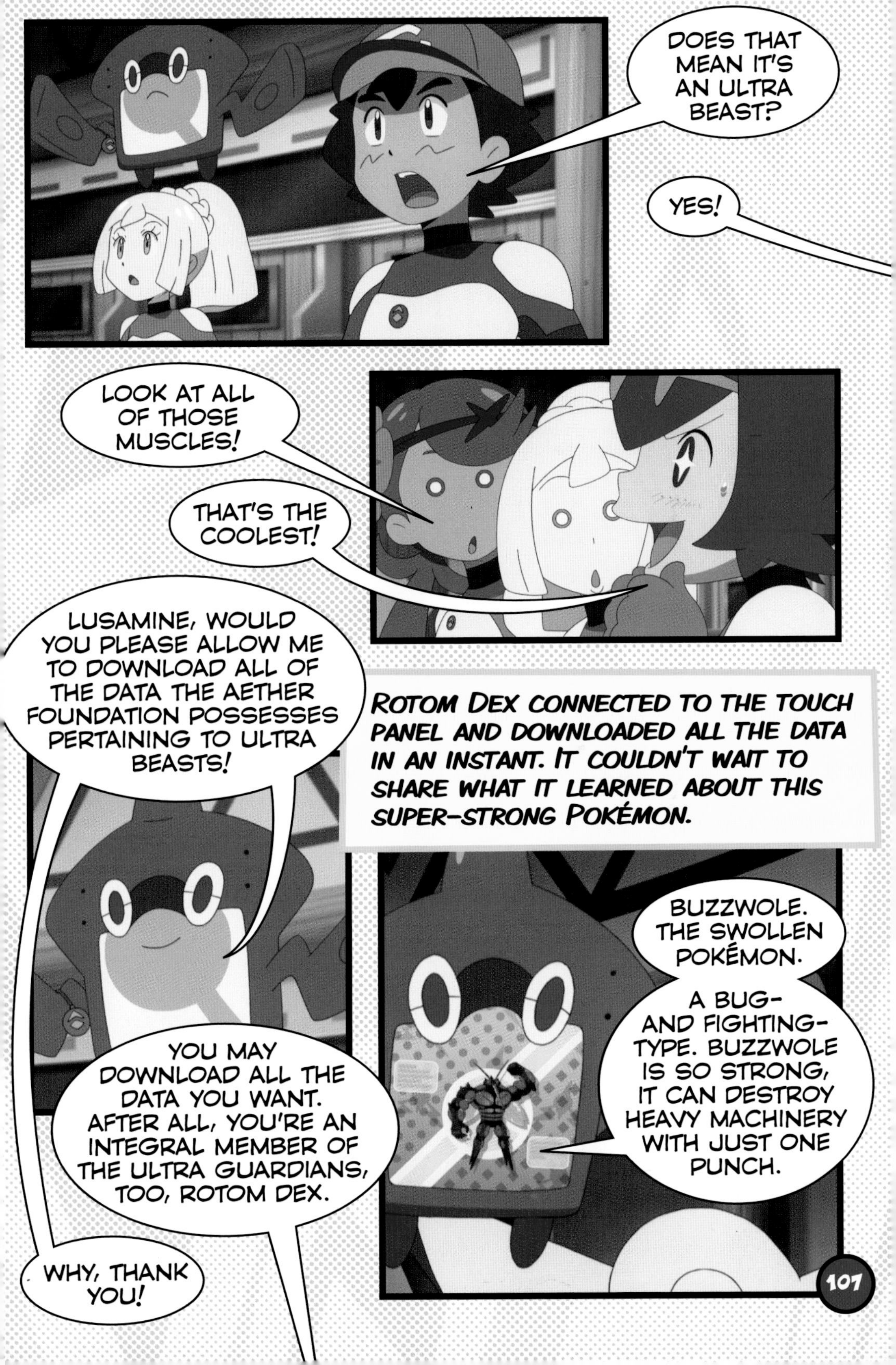
DOES THAT MEAN IT'S AN ULTRA BEAST?
YES!
LOOK AT ALL OF THOSE MUSCLES!
THAT'S THE COOLEST!
LUSAMINE, WOULD YOU PLEASE ALLOW ME TO DOWNLOAD ALL OF THE DATA THE AETHER FOUNDATION POSSESSES PERTAINING TO ULTRA BEASTS!
YOU MAY DOWNLOAD ALL THE DATA YOU WANT. AFTER ALL, YOU'RE AN INTEGRAL MEMBER OF THE ULTRA GUARDIANS, TOO, ROTOM DEX.
WHY, THANK YOU!
ROTOM DEX CONNECTED TO THE TOUCH PANEL AND DOWNLOADED ALL THE DATA IN AN INSTANT. IT COULDN'T WAIT TO SHARE WHAT IT LEARNED ABOUT THIS SUPER-STRONG POKÉMON.
BUZZWOLE. THE SWOLLEN POKÉMON.
A BUG- AND FIGHTING-TYPE. BUZZWOLE IS SO STRONG, IT CAN DESTROY HEAVY MACHINERY WITH JUST ONE PUNCH.

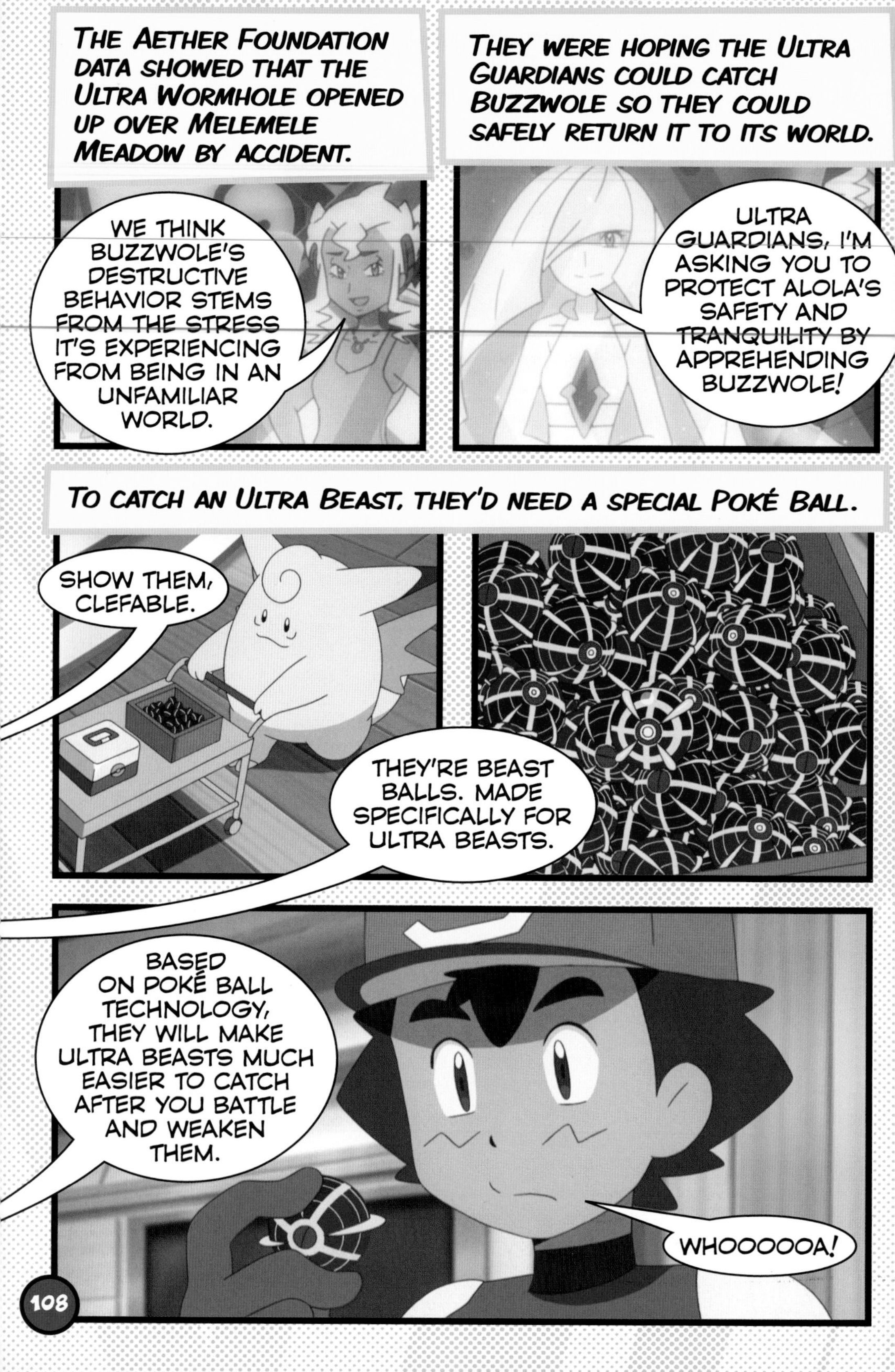
THE AETHER FOUNDATION DATA SHOWED THAT THE ULTRA WORMHOLE OPENED UP OVER MELEMELE MEADOW BY ACCIDENT.
WE THINK BUZZWOLE'S DESTRUCTIVE BEHAVIOR STEMS FROM THE STRESS IT'S EXPERIENCING FROM BEING IN AN UNFAMILIAR WORLD.
THEY WERE HOPING THE ULTRA GUARDIANS COULD CATCH BUZZWOLE SO THEY COULD SAFELY RETURN IT TO ITS WORLD.
ULTRA GUARDIANS, I'M ASKING YOU TO PROTECT ALOLA'S SAFETY AND TRANQUILITY BY APPREHENDING BUZZWOLE!
TO CATCH AN ULTRA BEAST, THEY'D NEED A SPECIAL POKÉ BALL.
SHOW THEM, CLEFABLE.
THEY'RE BEAST BALLS. MADE SPECIFICALLY FOR ULTRA BEASTS.
BASED ON POKÉ BALL TECHNOLOGY, THEY WILL MAKE ULTRA BEASTS MUCH EASIER TO CATCH AFTER YOU BATTLE AND WEAKEN THEM.
WHOOOOOA!

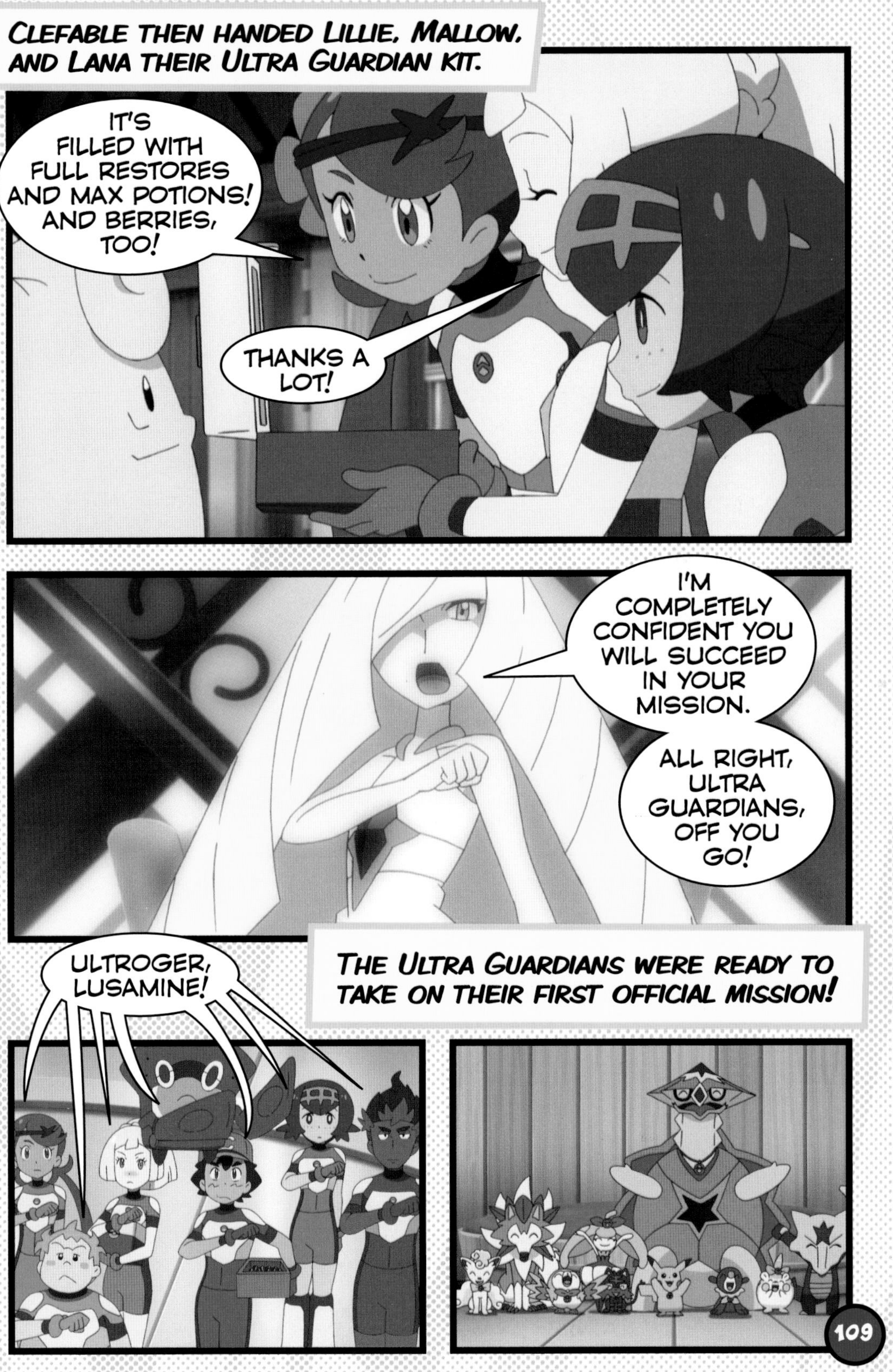
CLEFABLE THEN HANDED LILLIE, MALLOW, AND LANA THEIR ULTRA GUARDIAN KIT.
IT'S FILLED WITH FULL RESTORES AND MAX POTIONS! AND BERRIES, TOO!
THANKS A LOT!
I'M COMPLETELY CONFIDENT YOU WILL SUCCEED IN YOUR MISSION.
ALL RIGHT, ULTRA GUARDIANS, OFF YOU GO!
ULTROGER, LUSAMINE!
THE ULTRA GUARDIANS WERE READY TO TAKE ON THEIR FIRST OFFICIAL MISSION!

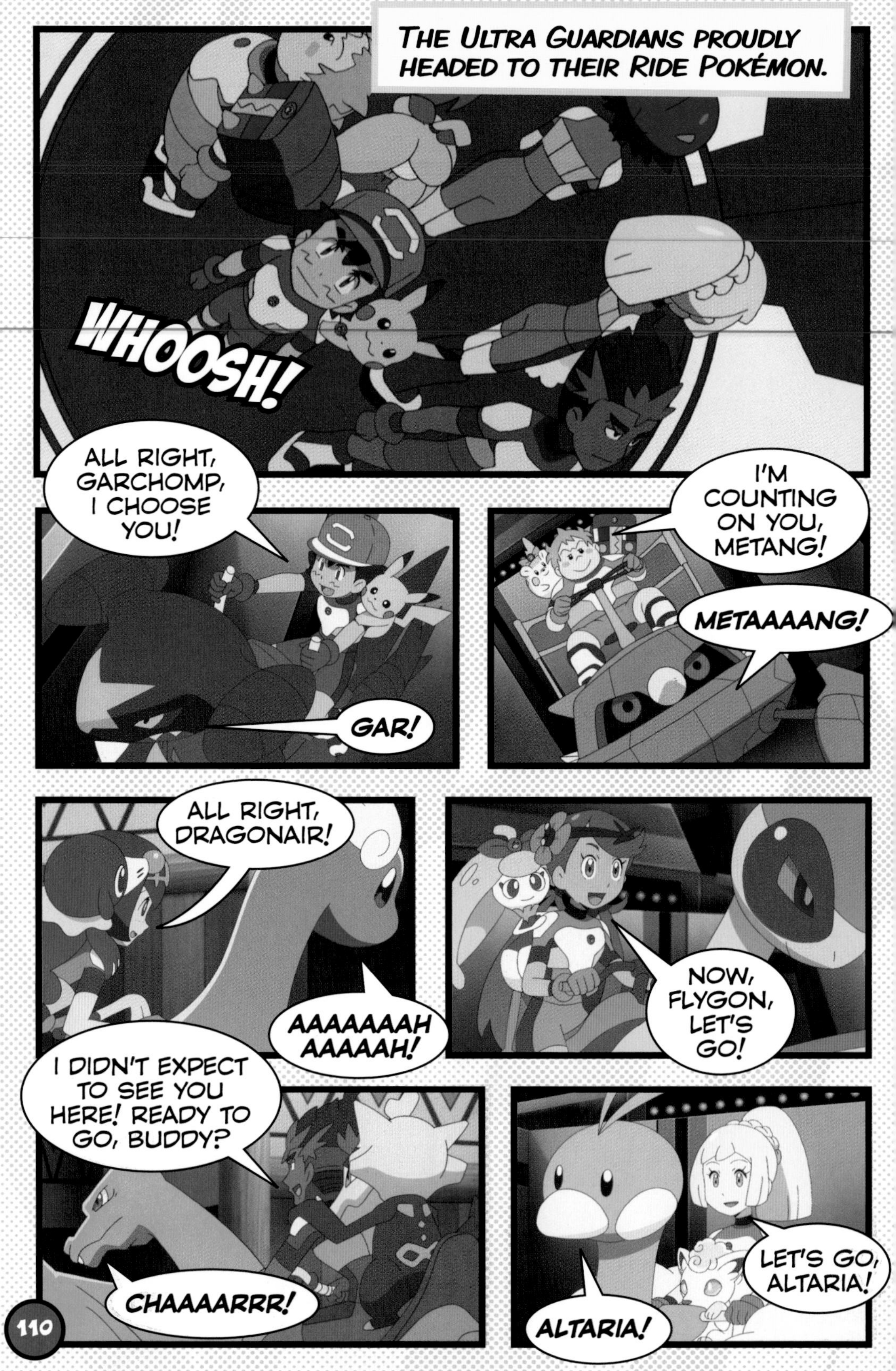

THE ULTRA GUARDIANS PROUDLY HEADED TO THEIR RIDE POKÉMON.
WHOOSH!
ALL RIGHT, GARCHOMP, I CHOOSE YOU!
GAR!
I'M COUNTING ON YOU, METANG!
METAAAANG!
ALL RIGHT, DRAGONAIR!
AAAAAAAH AAAAAH!
NOW, FLYGON, LET'S GO!
I DIDN'T EXPECT TO SEE YOU HERE! READY TO GO, BUDDY?
CHAAAARRR!
LET'S GO, ALTARIA!
ALTARIA!

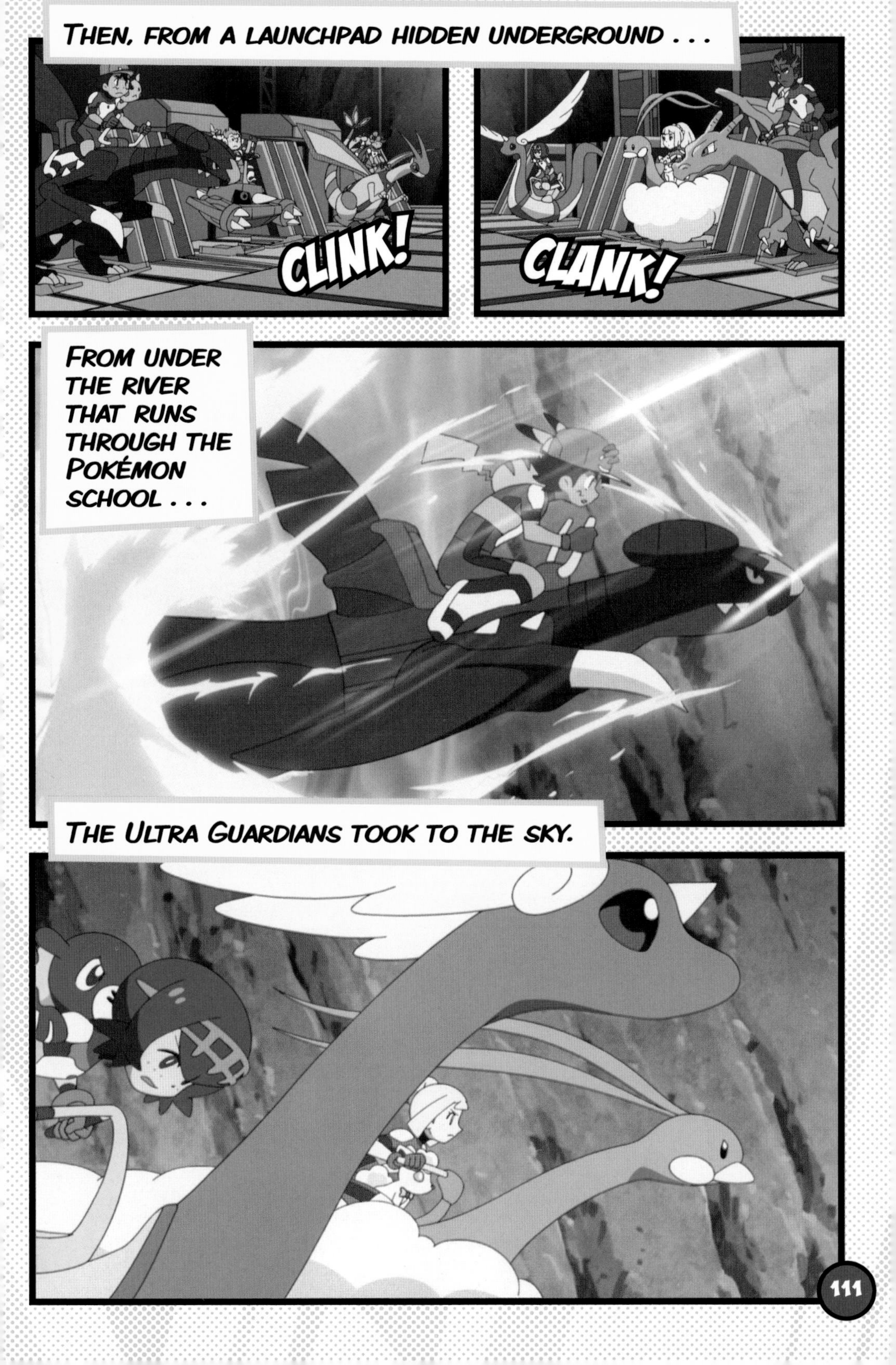

THEN, FROM A LAUNCHPAD HIDDEN UNDERGROUND . . .
CLINK!
CLANK!
FROM UNDER THE RIVER THAT RUNS THROUGH THE POKÉMON SCHOOL . . .
THE ULTRA GUARDIANS TOOK TO THE SKY.

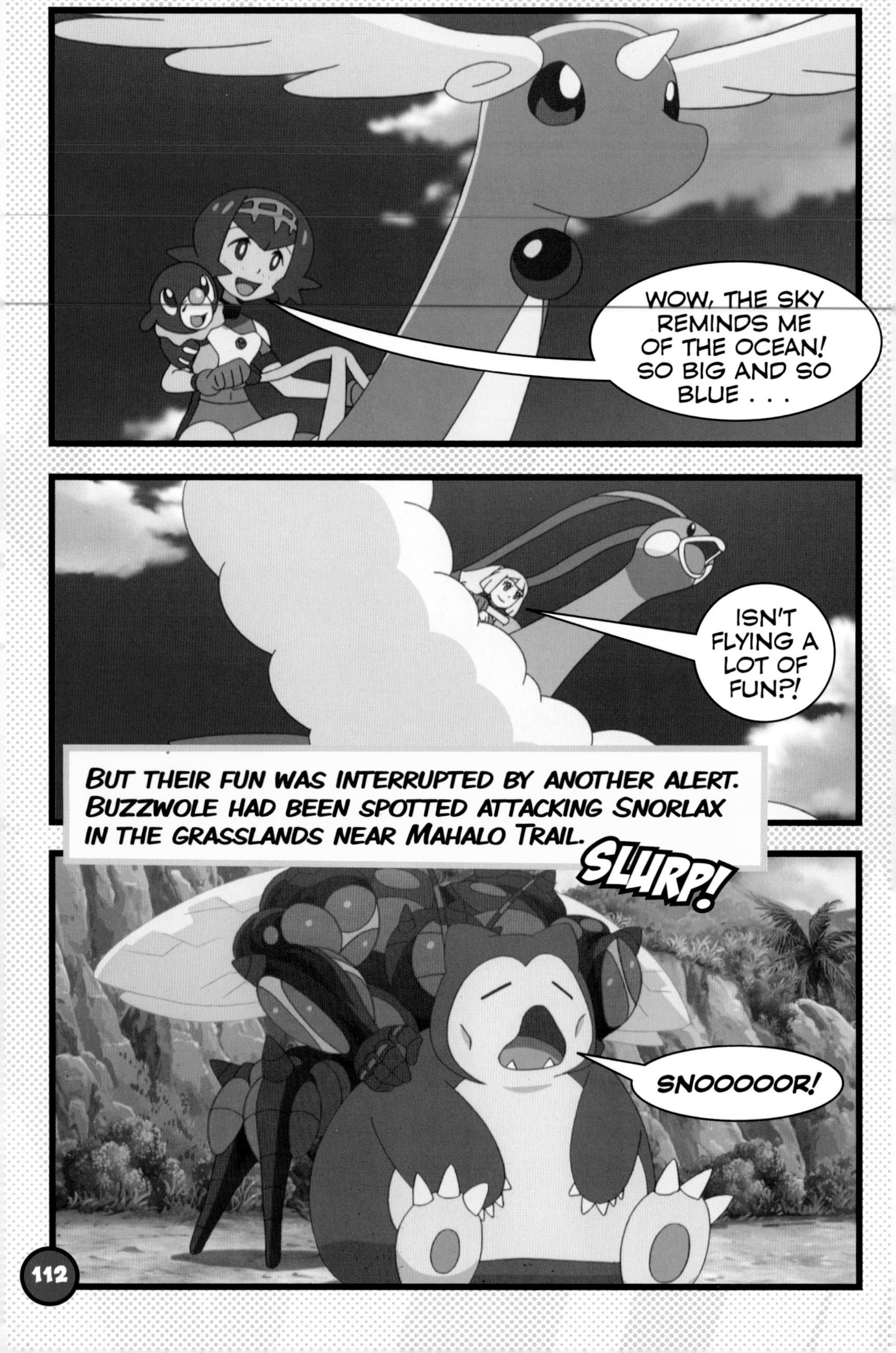
WOW, THE SKY REMINDS ME OF THE OCEAN! SO BIG AND SO BLUE . . .
ISN'T FLYING A LOT OF FUN?!
BUT THEIR FUN WAS INTERRUPTED BY ANOTHER ALERT. BUZZWOLE HAD BEEN SPOTTED ATTACKING SNORLAX IN THE GRASSLANDS NEAR MAHALO TRAIL.
SLURP!
SNOOOOOR!

ROTOM DEX DIRECTED THE ULTRA GUARDIANS TO THE SCENE.

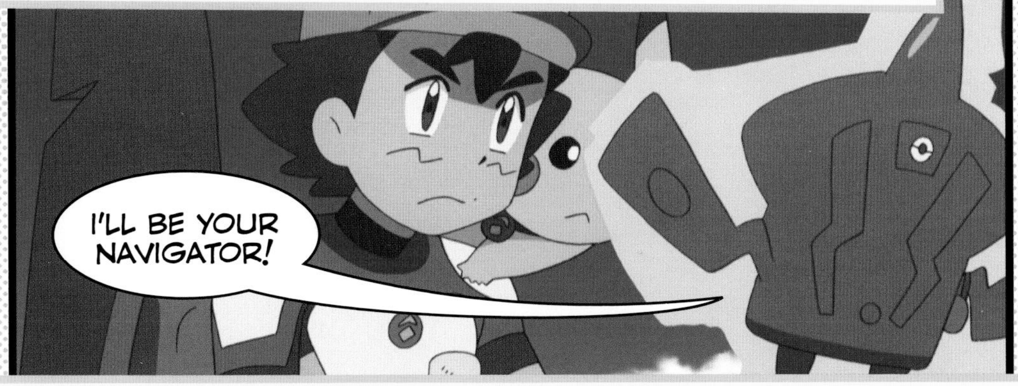
I'LL BE YOUR NAVIGATOR!

THEY ARRIVED SO FAST, THEY FOUND BUZZWOLE STILL IN THE ACT.

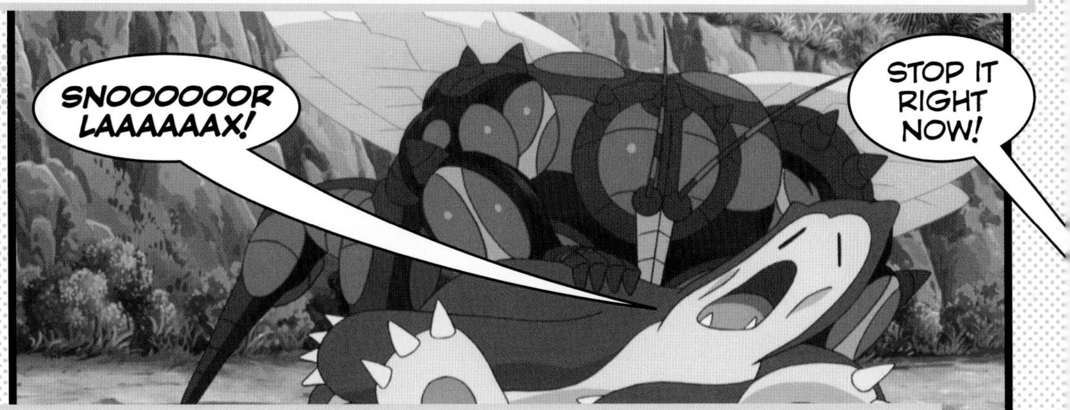
SNOOOOOOR LAAAAAAX!
STOP IT RIGHT NOW!

BUT WHEN BUZZWOLE SAW THE ULTRA GUARDIANS, IT FLED. SOME OF THE TEAM STAYED BACK TO CARE FOR SNORLAX.

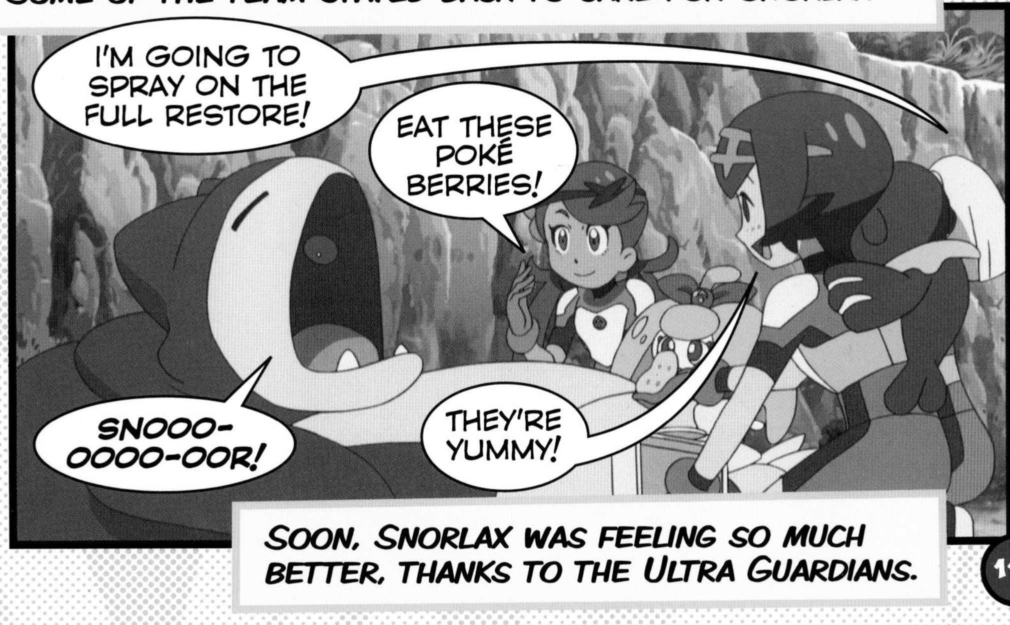
I'M GOING TO SPRAY ON THE FULL RESTORE!
EAT THESE POKÉ BERRIES!
SNOOO-OOOO-OOR!
THEY'RE YUMMY!

SOON, SNORLAX WAS FEELING SO MUCH BETTER, THANKS TO THE ULTRA GUARDIANS.

MEANWHILE, ASH AND PIKACHU CHASED AFTER THE ULTRA BEAST. WHEN THEY CAME FACE-TO-FACE WITH THE SUPER-STRONG POKÉMON, IT DIDN'T YELL, OR EVEN FIGHT. IT BEGAN FLEXING.

ZZWOLE!

ZZWOLE!

HUH?

BUZZWOLE KEPT CHANGING IT POSITION TO SHOW OFF ITS MUSCLES.

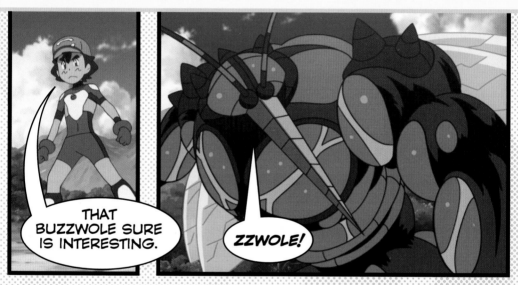

THAT BUZZWOLE SURE IS INTERESTING.

ZZWOLE!

PIIIIKAAA?

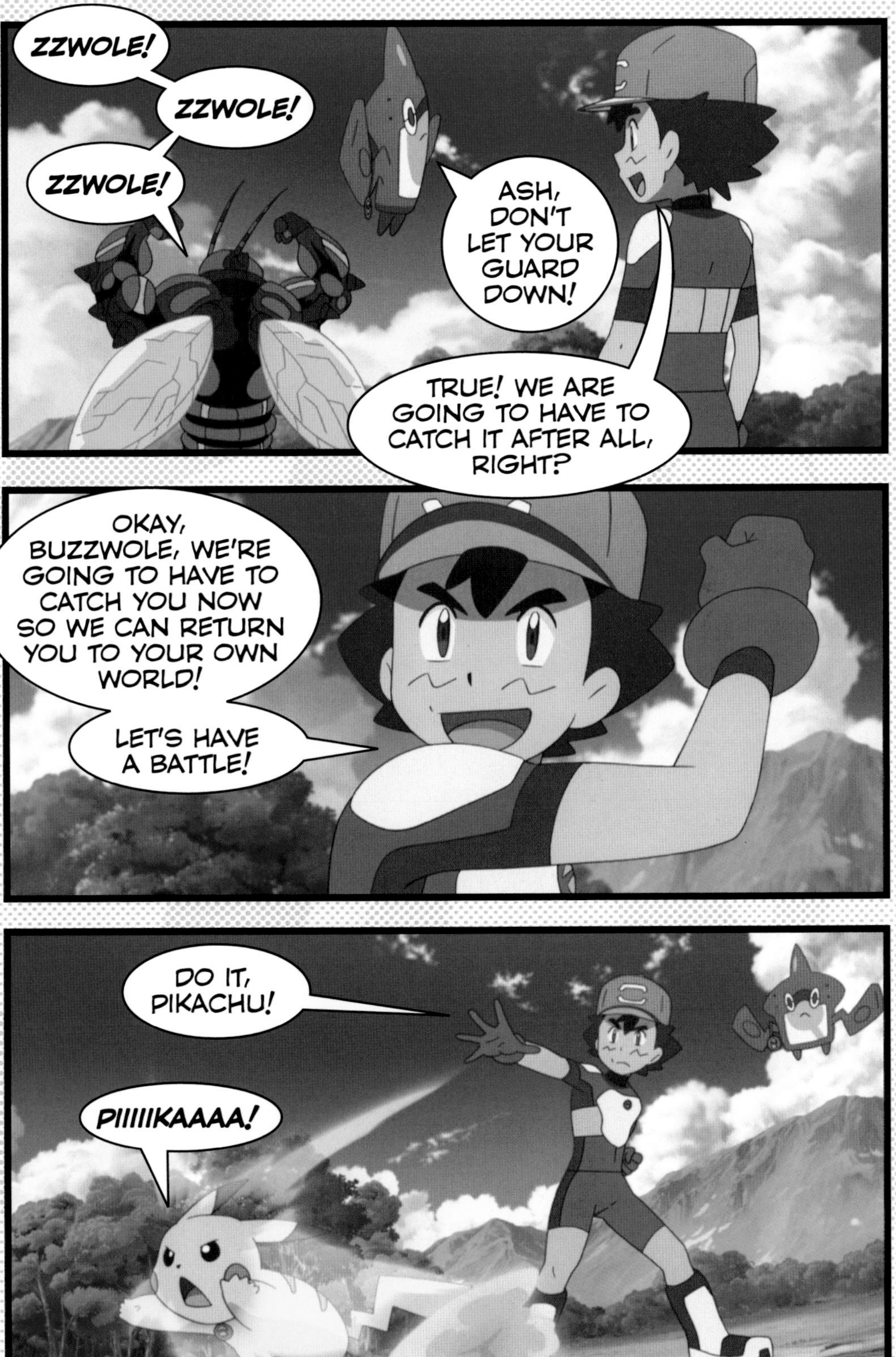
ZZWOLE!
ZZWOLE!
ZZWOLE!
ASH, DON'T LET YOUR GUARD DOWN!
TRUE! WE ARE GOING TO HAVE TO CATCH IT AFTER ALL, RIGHT?
OKAY, BUZZWOLE, WE'RE GOING TO HAVE TO CATCH YOU NOW SO WE CAN RETURN YOU TO YOUR OWN WORLD!
LET'S HAVE A BATTLE!
DO IT, PIKACHU!
PIIIIKAAAA!

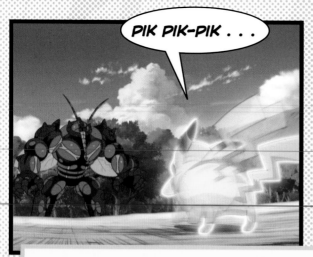

PIK PIK-PIK . . .

PIIIKAAAAAAAAAAA!

BUZZWOLE DIDN'T SEEM THE SLIGHTEST BIT CONCERNED.

WHEN PIKACHU WAS MERE INCHES AWAY . . .

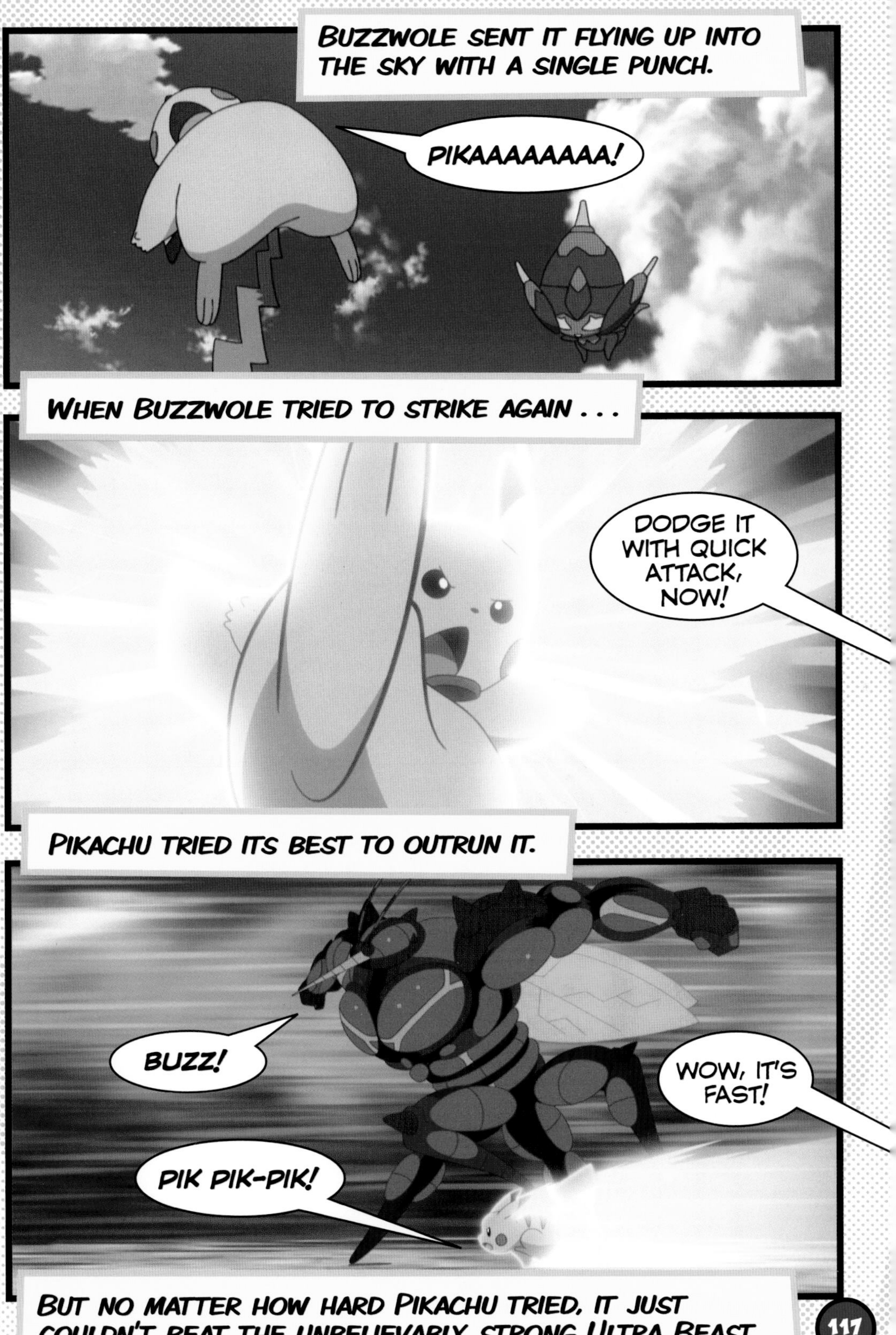
BUZZWOLE SENT IT FLYING UP INTO THE SKY WITH A SINGLE PUNCH.
PIKAAAAAAAA!
WHEN BUZZWOLE TRIED TO STRIKE AGAIN . . .
DODGE IT WITH QUICK ATTACK, NOW!
PIKACHU TRIED ITS BEST TO OUTRUN IT.
BUZZ!
WOW, IT'S FAST!
PIK PIK-PIK!
BUT NO MATTER HOW HARD PIKACHU TRIED, IT JUST COULDN'T BEAT THE UNBELIEVABLY STRONG ULTRA BEAST.

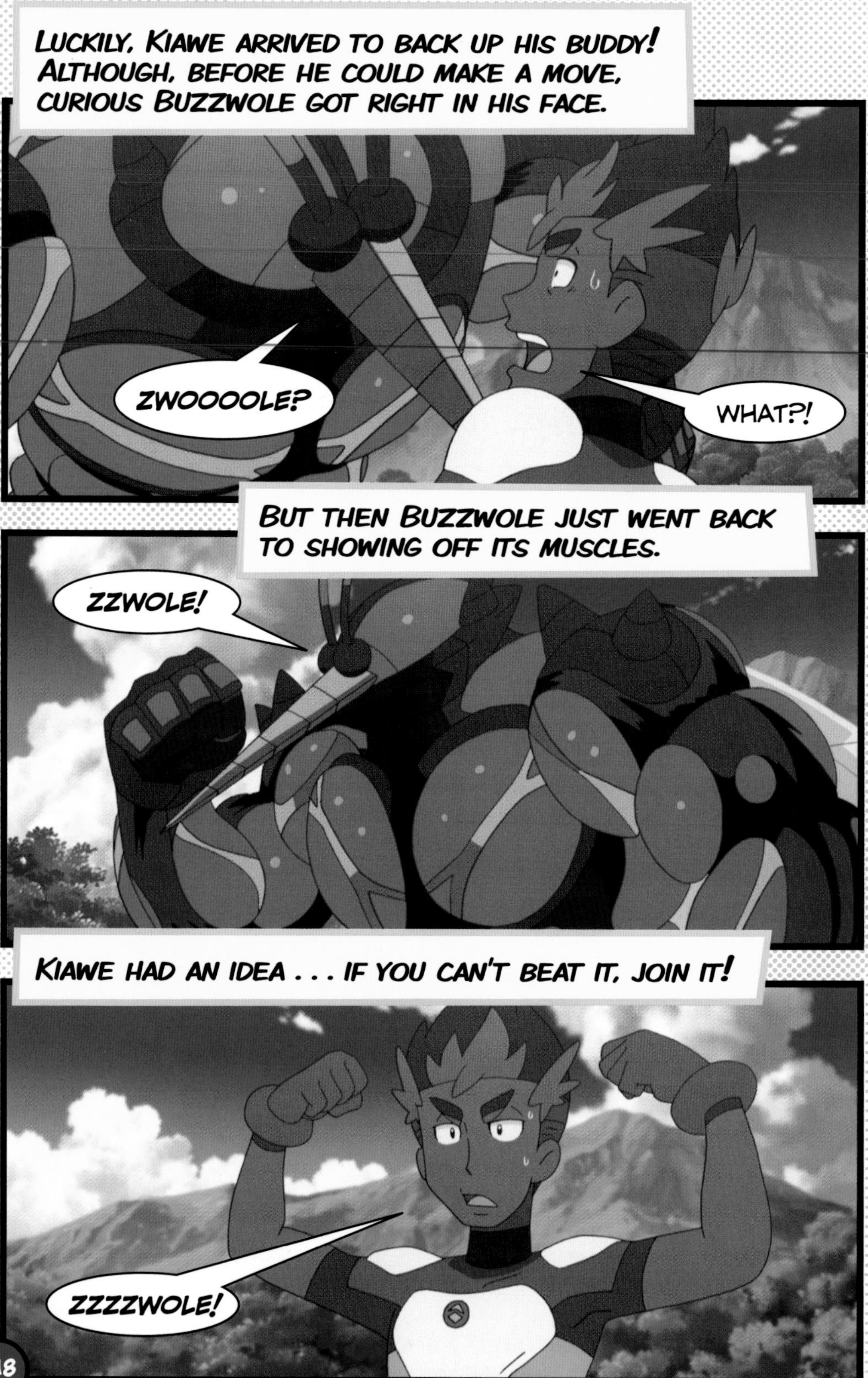
LUCKILY, KIAWE ARRIVED TO BACK UP HIS BUDDY! ALTHOUGH, BEFORE HE COULD MAKE A MOVE, CURIOUS BUZZWOLE GOT RIGHT IN HIS FACE.
ZWOOOOLE?
WHAT?!
BUT THEN BUZZWOLE JUST WENT BACK TO SHOWING OFF ITS MUSCLES.
ZZWOLE!
KIAWE HAD AN IDEA . . . IF YOU CAN'T BEAT IT, JOIN IT!
ZZZZWOLE!

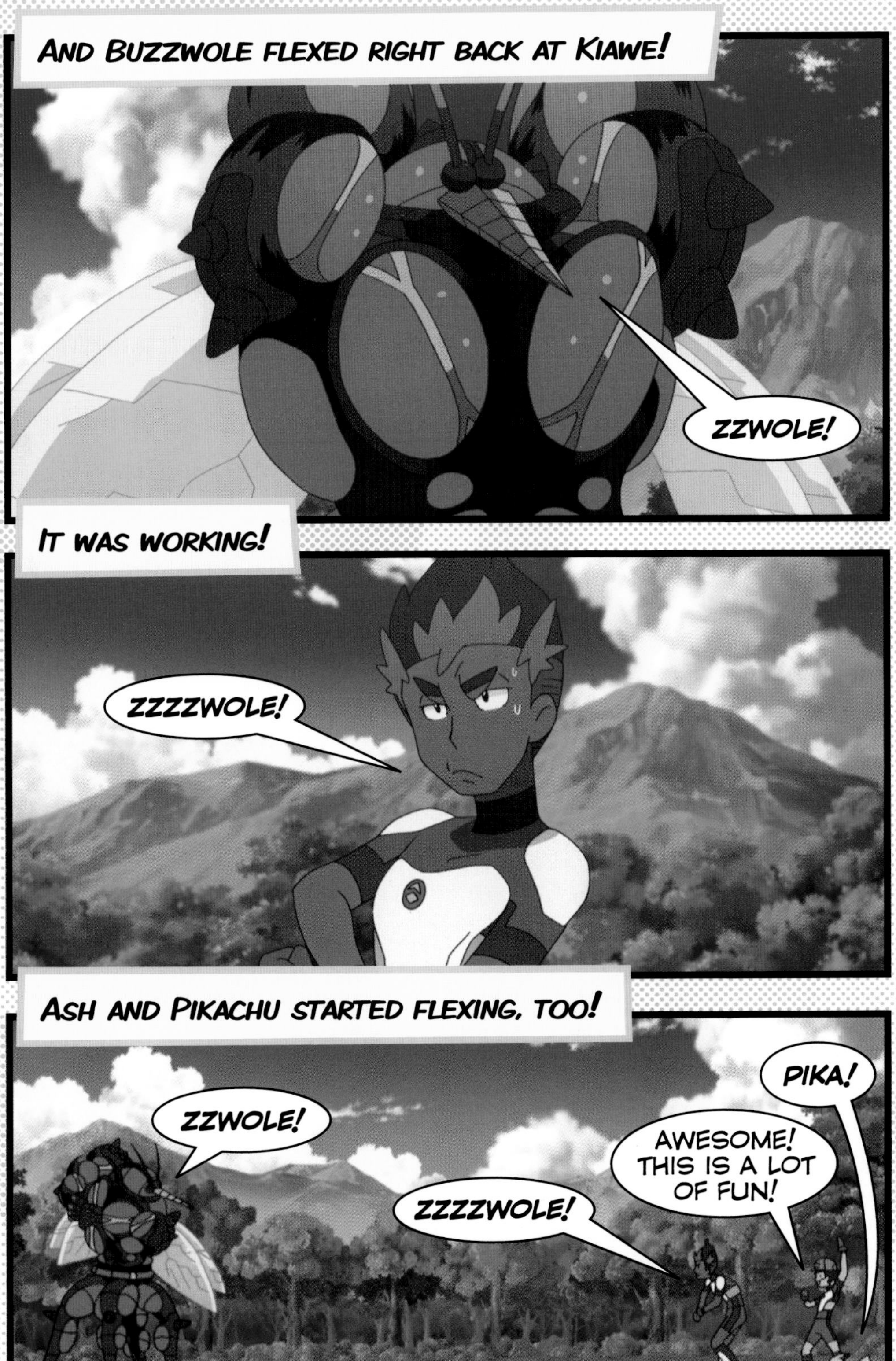
AND BUZZWOLE FLEXED RIGHT BACK AT KIAWE!
ZZWOLE!
IT WAS WORKING!
ZZZZWOLE!
ASH AND PIKACHU STARTED FLEXING, TOO!
ZZWOLE!
PIKA!
AWESOME! THIS IS A LOT OF FUN!
ZZZZWOLE!

Ash was having such a good time with Buzzwole, he almost forgot his mission—to catch it!

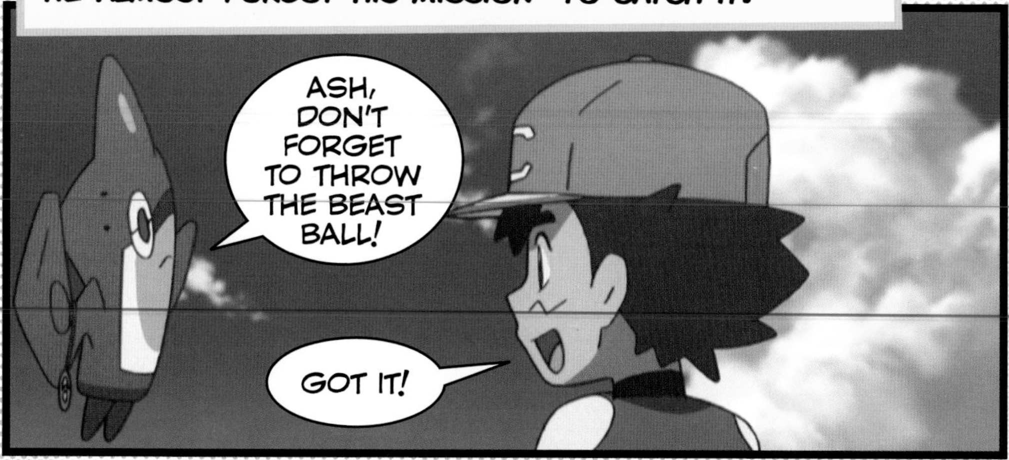
ASH, DON'T FORGET TO THROW THE BEAST BALL!
GOT IT!

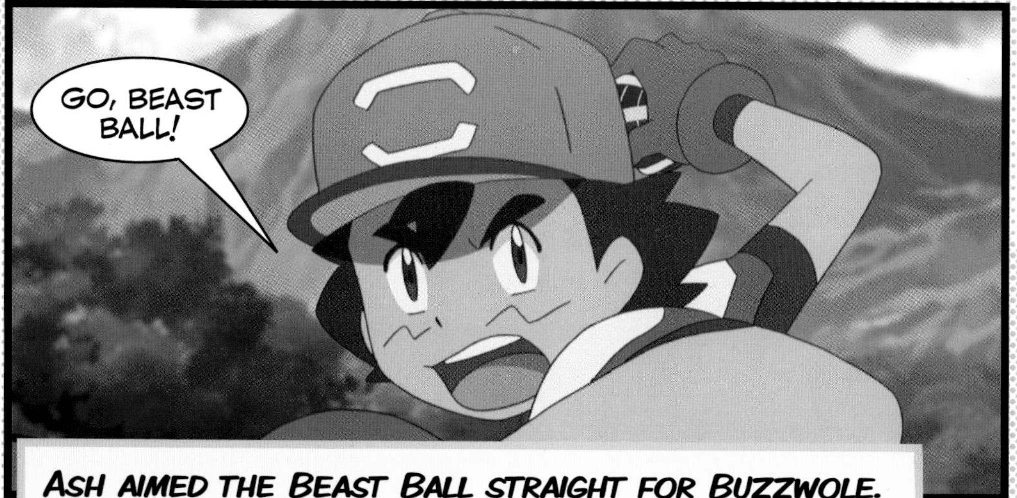
GO, BEAST BALL!

Ash aimed the Beast Ball straight for Buzzwole. The powerful Pokémon slipped right inside, but would it stay put? The Ultra Guardians watched the Beast Ball flash, hoping it worked.

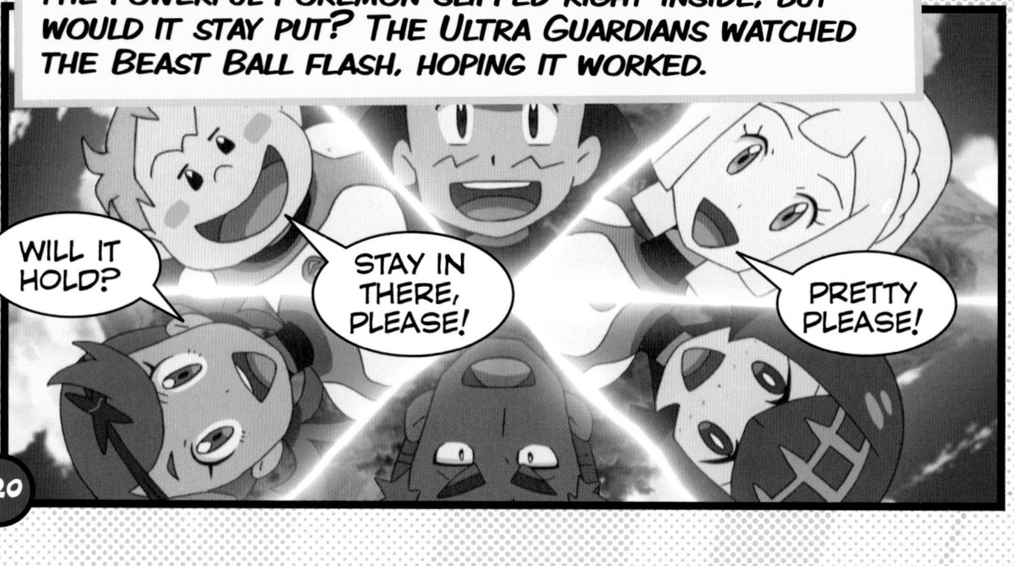
WILL IT HOLD?
STAY IN THERE, PLEASE!
PRETTY PLEASE!

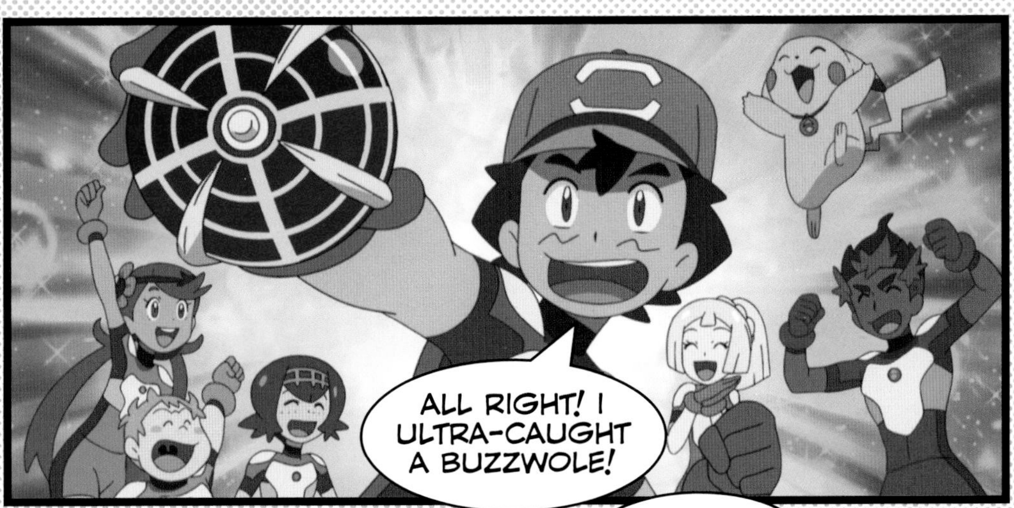
ALL RIGHT! I ULTRA-CAUGHT A BUZZWOLE!

THE ULTRA GUARDIANS ALERTED THE AETHER FOUNDATION THAT THEY HAD CAUGHT BUZZWOLE. LUSAMINE, WICKE, PROFESSOR BURNET, AND PROFESSOR KUKUI HURRIED TO MEET THEM BACK IN MELEMELE MEADOW, WHERE THE ULTRA WORMHOLE HAD OPENED UP.

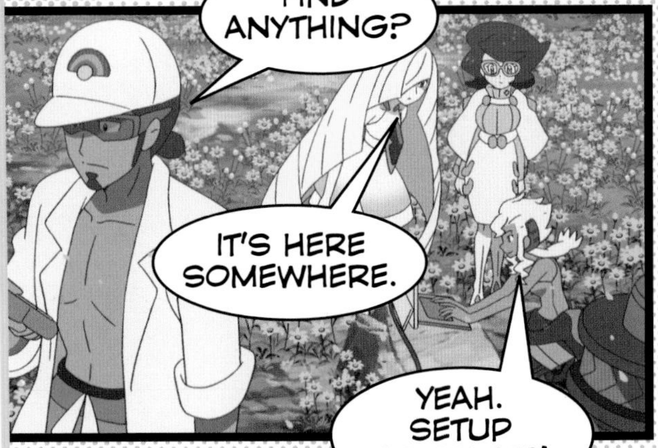
FIND ANYTHING?
IT'S HERE SOMEWHERE.
YEAH. SETUP COMPLETE!

PROFESSOR BURNET USED HER SPECIALIZED MACHINE TO REOPEN THE ULTRA WORMHOLE. THEN ASH CAREFULLY ASKED BUZZWOLE TO COME OUT OF ITS BEAST BALL.

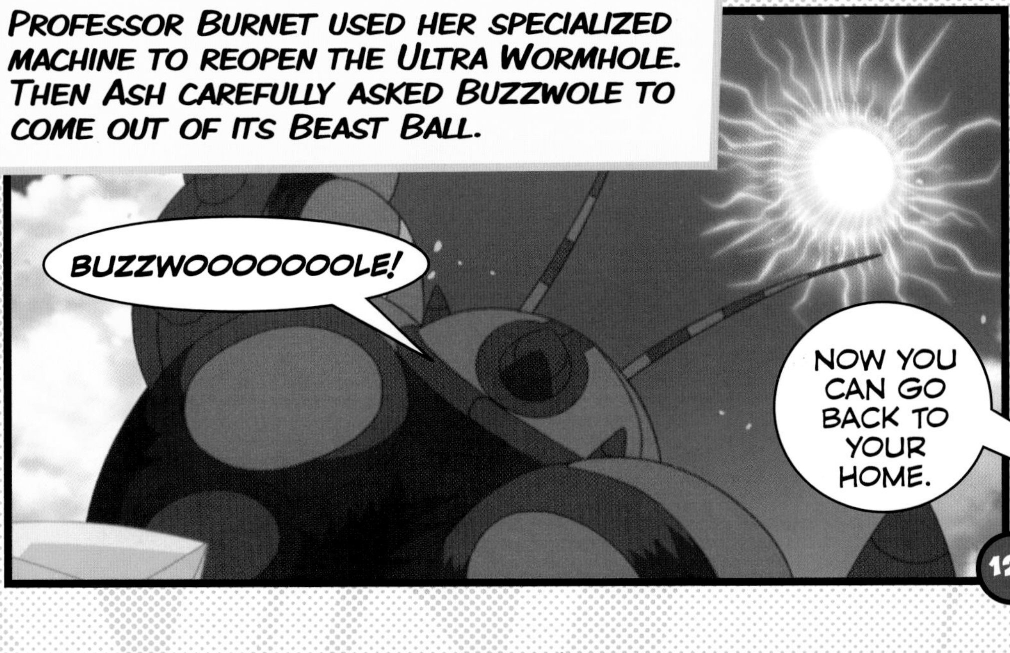
BUZZWOOOOOOOLE!
NOW YOU CAN GO BACK TO YOUR HOME.

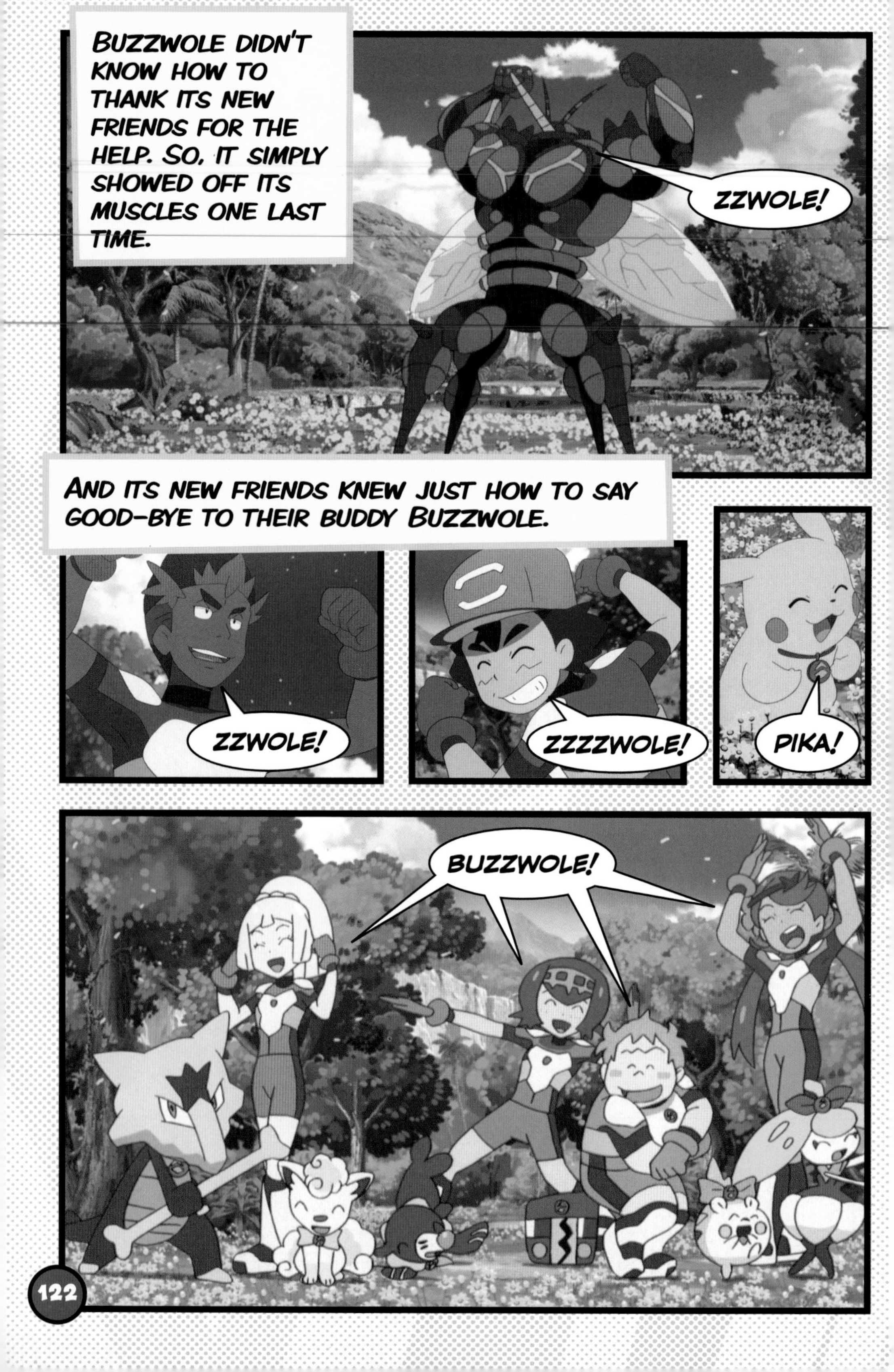
BUZZWOLE DIDN'T KNOW HOW TO THANK ITS NEW FRIENDS FOR THE HELP. SO, IT SIMPLY SHOWED OFF ITS MUSCLES ONE LAST TIME.
ZZWOLE!
AND ITS NEW FRIENDS KNEW JUST HOW TO SAY GOOD-BYE TO THEIR BUDDY BUZZWOLE.
ZZWOLE!
ZZZZWOLE!
PIKA!
BUZZWOLE!

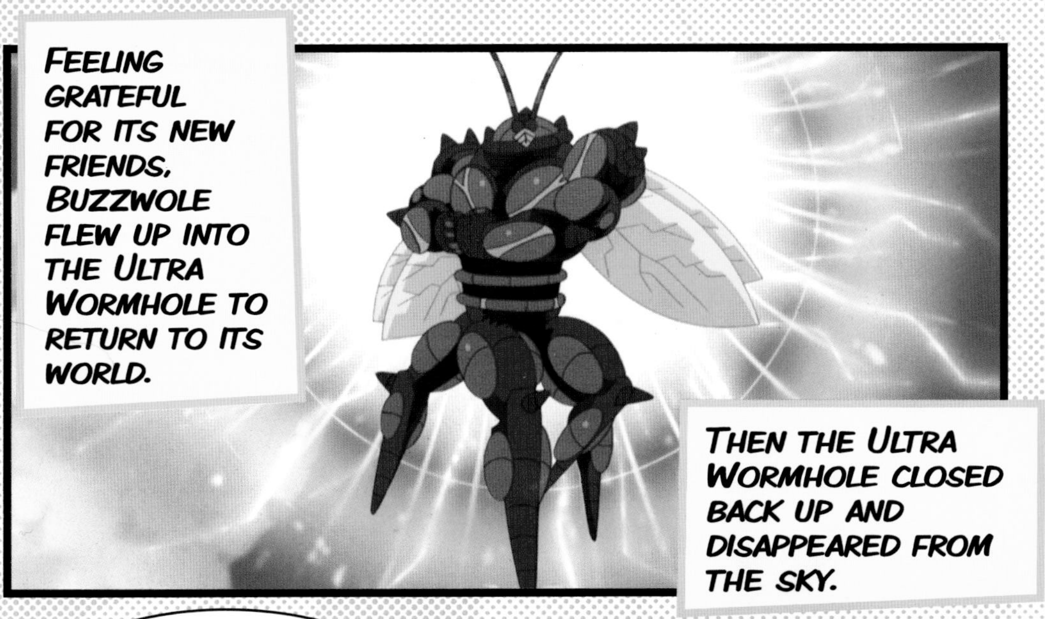
FEELING GRATEFUL FOR ITS NEW FRIENDS, BUZZWOLE FLEW UP INTO THE ULTRA WORMHOLE TO RETURN TO ITS WORLD.
THEN THE ULTRA WORMHOLE CLOSED BACK UP AND DISAPPEARED FROM THE SKY.

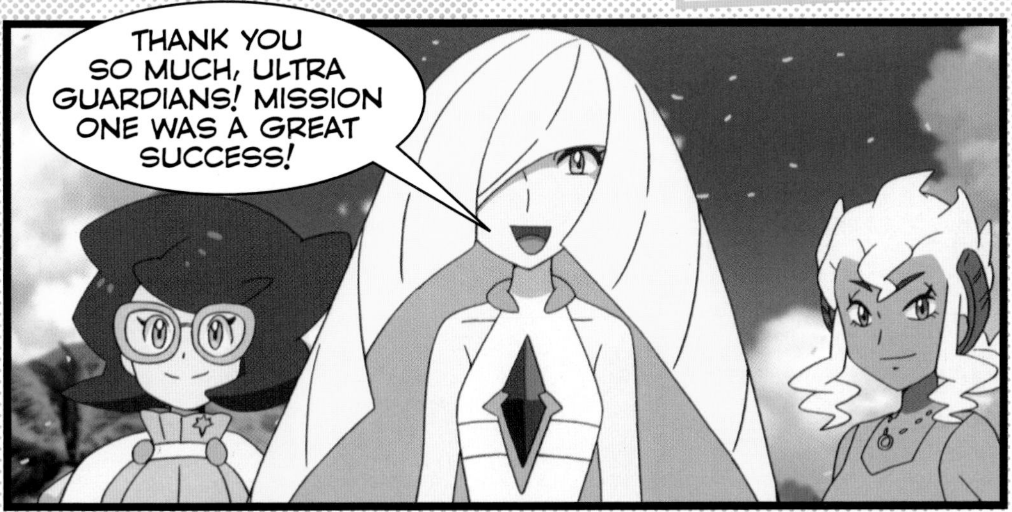
THANK YOU SO MUCH, ULTRA GUARDIANS! MISSION ONE WAS A GREAT SUCCESS!

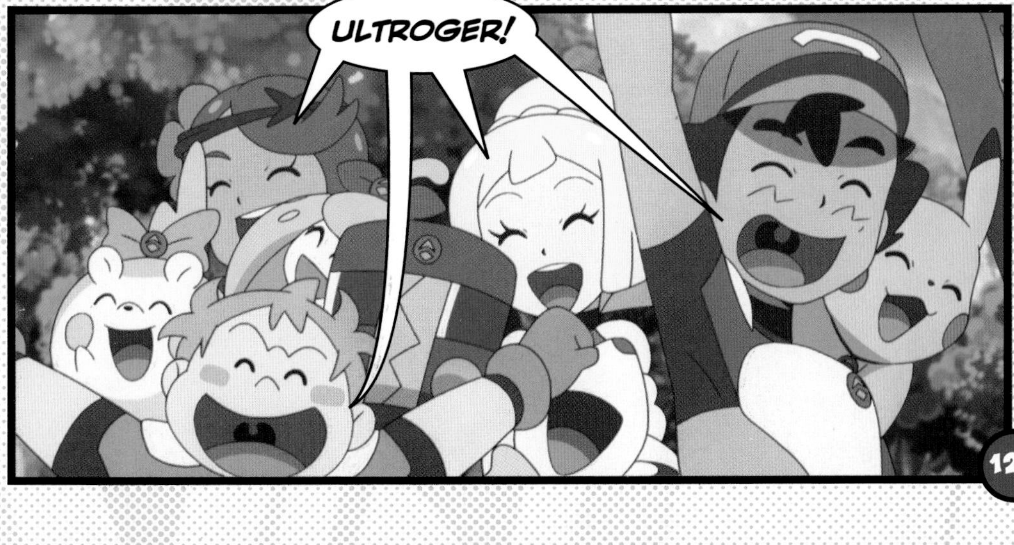
ULTROGER!

DON'T MISS THESE

POKÉMON™

BOOKS AVAILABLE AT STORES EVERYWHERE!